VAULT OF SILENT WHISPERS SERIES

MIDNYTE'S DRAGON KISS

JESSIE D. EAKER

Midnyte's Dragon Kiss / Jessie D. Eaker — First edition

Library of Congress Control Number: 2024906696

ISBN 979-8-9857335-3-2, Trade Paperback

To those who find the strength to overcome.

Contents

Aether
Power comes from the universe.
Can control time, space, and gravity.

	Night-Clan	*Twilight-Clan*	*Dawn-Clan*	*Shadow-Clan*
Source of Power	Obtained from others	Earth and Moon	From within themselves	Generated by action
Influence Emotions	Succubus	Elf	Fairy	Medium
Mental Control	Vampire	Telepath	Pixie	Enchanter
Cast Spells	Sorcerer	Witch	Wizard	Mage
Change Form	Doppel-ganger	Were	Shape-shifter	Alchemist
Mundane	Goblin	Centaur	Human	Troll
Familiar	Chimera	Any animal	Gnome	Gremlin

Chapter 1

I WAS AT MY LIMIT.

Stumbling off the bus, I shoved past the old lady in front of me before running head-on into a bearded man and banging his shin with my suitcase. I wheeled while apologizing but didn't pause in my flight. He cursed to my back as I trotted across the concrete lot toward the nearby street. I had to get away.

I had been trapped on the bus for too long, with too many people, and flooded with too many emotions—especially from the guy behind me. His violent lust had almost made me throw up. He was one sick dude.

And he kept staring at me.

Like all of my kind, my gifts allowed me to sense the feelings of those around me—but not the thoughts behind them. In Sick-Dude's case, his emotions tasted so foul they rolled my stomach, which meant his thoughts were likely just as rotten. And worse, those sick feelings would spike each time he glanced my way. I had to get as far from him as possible and make doubly sure he didn't follow.

I stopped when I reached the curb, trying to decide which way to go. Neither direction looked promising. The dingy puddles in the street were a testament to the mid-June thunderstorms that had passed earlier in the day. They left the late-night air muggy and smelling of damp concrete. The overcast sky gave the darkness an unnerving, spooky feel—only the pools of illumination from periodic streetlamps, or the headlights of the few cars, were able to provide a hint of safety. I suppressed the urge to make shadows into monsters.

Across the street, a brightly lit building identified itself as Main Street Station. It offered no clue as to my direction, but the huge, illuminated dial at its top did announce the time—10:13. I had been on the bus for nearly nine hours, five longer than it was supposed to have been. Which was a problem. With the late hour, all the shelters would either be full or closed. I had nowhere to spend the night. And if that wasn't bad enough, I had to look for an unobserved brick wall, and soon. I needed something to absorb all my excess emotions. I was overfull.

I had been trapped in a sea of people's emotions—anger, joy, hate, love—and in every conceivable combination. I could usually ignore the incessant flood, tuning them out like the chatter of a room's conversation or the drone of an idling engine, and taking only what I needed to nourish my magic. But on the crowded bus and fearing Sick Dude's attention, I frequently sampled the emotions around me. I took only the smallest nibbles, just enough to detect any feelings directed at me. But now I was nearly at my limit. I couldn't use all I had taken during my hours on the bus. So now, I needed to get rid of the excess—somewhere private. That would ensure no one got hurt—and keep me from being discovered.

So a brick wall first, then a place to sleep.

I glanced back at the dissipating crowd of bus passengers and saw Sick Dude staring in my direction. I swallowed. *Why couldn't the guy take a hint?*

Distracted, I stepped into the street. The blast of a car horn and skidding tires made me immediately jerk back—the sedan's bumper stopping mere inches from my leg. To my horror, I realized I had nearly stepped in front of a police car. The officer's angry glare was as bright as his headlights. Fear froze me in place. I doubted he could see through my charm's illusion magic—concealing my horns and tail while leaving my overall appearance intact. To him, I would appear to be nothing more than a skinny, short-haired blonde female. Not the least bit remarkable. But I could not afford police scrutiny. Inside his vehicle, he carried the tools to expose my charm, and if he looked too closely, he might find I wasn't the human I appeared to be.

Not to mention a wanted person.

I hid my panic with a sheepish grin and an apologetic wave. The officer frowned deeper and impatiently motioned me to cross in front of him. When I safely reached the other side, I glanced back to see the police car resume its patrol and prowl purposely down the street. I nearly sagged in relief when it finally passed out of sight without its brake lights coming on.

I didn't think anyone was looking for me yet. There hadn't been enough time. The couple I'd been staying with barely noticed I was around, so they likely wouldn't miss me until family services stopped sending checks. Plus, the police in Philly hadn't *actually* charged me with anything—only told me not to leave town while they completed their investigation. The fact I hadn't done anything was irrelevant. My kind were always assumed guilty.

I shook my head. It was unfair, but Mom and I had managed. Even laughed sometimes. Her loving warmth had shielded me from the cold and uncaring world. But the fates had even shattered that. I now had no home. No money.

And Mom was dead.

I turned right and walked with purpose—my suitcase bumping against my bare leg as I went. With a quick glance over my shoulder, I was glad to see that Sick Dude was no longer there. I sighed in relief. The police car must have encouraged him to move on.

As I walked, I drew near two burly men on the opposite corner, watching me with interest—likely some gang's muscle. I thought them human, but they could as easily be werewolves. There was no full moon tonight, so it was hard to tell.

I hoped they were content to just watch and not decide to shake me down. The only thing of value I had was a few dollars and Mom's silver necklace concealed beneath my shirt. And even that wasn't worth much.

However, sampling their emotions told me it wasn't my belongings that had piqued their interest. No, it was something more basic. When I started out this morning, my shorts, tank top, and sneakers had seemed perfectly suited to a long bus ride in hot muggy weather. But now in the evening, the show of skin could be interpreted differently, especially by males.

Damn. I should have known better.

I kept my head down, doing my best to avoid their interest. It was true that my kind frequently fanned those desires to make them easier to seduce and more eager to part with their money. But that was not me. I would not give up my pride so easily. Contrary to what the police in Philly might think, I was not a thief and certainly not a prostitute.

I hurried on and turned left at the next corner, glad to put their lustful gazes behind me. I resolved to pull on some less revealing clothes when I got some privacy.

After a couple of blocks in my new direction, I was surprised to notice a change in the area—an upscale one. The cars parked along the curb transitioned to Mercedes, Porsches, and even a Bentley. The sidewalk itself improved without a single bit of trash, crack, or imperfection. No doubt magically enhanced—something only the wealthy did.

Pedestrian traffic increased as well. The young men and women strolling along the sidewalk all wore trendy attire that was bright, tight, and revealed a lot of skin. Hair was in every possible shade and each strand styled to perfection. More than once, I caught the scent of someone's expensive cologne.

But while they were beautiful, their eyes held disdain when they glanced my way. The knowing whispers were frequent, and they politely cringed away, almost like I might ruin their pristine appearances. I hid my smile as I wondered what they would do if they knew what I really was.

I slowed, unsure if I should proceed. I didn't want any trouble, but I didn't want to retrace my steps either. I cocked my jaw. *To hades with them.* I would just get through as quickly as I could. I walked faster.

After just another block, I came to the nexus of the increased traffic. A sizable building occupied the corner, outlined in golden yellow lights with a bold sign extending above the street—*Noblelite Dance.* The muffled throb of music emanated from the building, leaping in volume whenever a tuxedoed bouncer opened the door for a group to enter. Judging from the ages of those waiting in line, it must be young adult night.

I wanted no part of this, especially in my overfull condition. I was about to turn around when a stretch limo pulled up in front. All eyes moved to the vehicle, and several whispered conversations broke out. A bouncer immediately jumped forward and opened the car's door. The young woman that got out was about my age and had to be some sort of celebrity or socialite. She wore an elegant black dress that clung to her lithe figure and highlighted her bare legs and high heels. Her long dark hair was loose and reflected the bright lights like polished obsidian. She was talking animatedly to a young man who got out behind her. He ran a hand over his dark hair and tugged down the sleeves of his perfectly tailored tux—his bearing a crown prince surveying his court.

I stopped dead in my tracks. Their manner said they were used to extravagance, used to getting their way, and within Night-clan, they were the top predators.

Vampires.

The young man glanced my way, but it quickly turned into a dark glare, distorting his handsome face into an ugly frown. He motioned a bouncer forward and whispered something. They both looked in my direction.

Damn.

I turned to leave and immediately collided with a young woman, bumping into her hard enough to make both of us stumble. We steadied each other.

"Sorry," I mumbled.

With her freckles and bushy, bright red hair, I had no doubt she was a witch. Her pastel green sundress suited her but was not nearly as elegant as those around us. I couldn't help but think she looked a little frazzled.

She grabbed my arm. "Have you seen a stoic-looking guy with dark brown hair, maybe just a little taller than you? He's probably frowning like he sucks lemons all the time."

Her hand on my bare arm amplified the flow of her emotions. I could feel her concern for someone. A person she held strong affection for.

I shook my head. "Sorry."

"Damn! He must be inside. Thanks anyway." She brushed past me, heading toward the entrance. I, on the other hand, fled back down the street, eager to get away from the venue.

Vampires were bad news for any of the races. I was not particularly afraid of them, but I had to be cautious. Not because they might tap my soul—there was no chance of that—but because they were the upper crust of Night-clan and usually had a connection to the clan elder. I was already on bad terms with the elder in Philly. I couldn't afford to piss off the one here.

But the fact he had looked right at me was unnerving. He couldn't have seen through my disguise, so perhaps he was only reacting to my clothes, or even the girl I had bumped into.

I hurriedly walked several blocks to where the traffic thinned out and the buildings began to look more worn. I took a risk and turned onto an empty street. I sighed in relief when I confirmed no one was following.

Then the Protector smiled down on me for once. Halfway along the block, I found what I needed. I ducked into a dimly lit alley. A lone bulb at the end illuminated the path ahead—its twin at the entrance having been knocked out. The alley was long, running the length of the block and barely wide enough for a truck to enter. It was empty except for a single large dumpster set to one side half-way down. After a few dozen steps, the alley came to an abrupt dead end with high walls, no windows, and no obvious cameras.

I was surprised a homeless person hadn't claimed it. Using the alley for my own shelter crossed my mind, but I quickly abandoned the idea. Either a gang was protecting it, or the area had a strong police presence. Based on my earlier encounter with the patrol car, my money was on the latter. In either case, I wouldn't be long.

In the shadow of the dumpster, I set down my suitcase and rested my hands, fingers extended, against a section of worn red-brick wall. The coarse texture brought a small smile to my lips as I remembered Mom's lessons on getting rid of excess emotions. Red brick was best. The older, the better. It could absorb just about any emotion and safely bury it.

I closed my eyes and allowed my gates to open. A faint blue glow enveloped me as my magic worked. It wouldn't be visible during the day, and only now because I was channeling a lot of feelings.

Gradually, the emotions passed out of me. The ones I had no desire to absorb or change. All the anger, all the frustration, and especially that guy's sick lust, I let it go. The red brick greedily sucked up the feelings, burying them deep inside.

I breathed a sigh of relief as the last of the surplus emotions left me, leaving me more relaxed than I had been since leaving. I turned, placing my back against the wall and propping my foot up on my suitcase. I was glad to get rid of the absorbed emotions. Considering my recent life, I had more than enough of my own.

I gave a sad chuckle. *Welcome to Renweard City.* It had been an enormous gamble coming here, but I really didn't have a choice. My illusion charm was nearly out of magic, and I needed to get it recharged. Sadly, my own magic wouldn't work. It required a powerful witch willing to power up an unregistered charm—both illegal and expensive. My kind frequently had it done, but locating someone required connections. Something I lost when Mom died.

So now, I needed to find my grandfather and hoped he was willing to help. *Assuming he's still alive.*

As I rested, I became more aware of my surroundings. I could smell the well-used dumpster beside me, and in the distance, I could make out traffic noises and a lone train sounding its horn. Overall, it didn't feel too different from Philly.

The thought made me immediately miss Mom. I longed for her hugs and her reassurance. I could almost hear her saying, *"You'll be fine, Lapis, my precious jewel."* She would then go on to say I was going to do great things one day. I smiled. Mom had also told me Santa Claus brought my toys, and the Easter Bunny gave me candy.

My right hand curled into a fist. Why did she have to leave me all alone? It was so unfair. I shook my head, tapping down my anger. No, it actually hadn't been fair to either of us. I was pretty sure she hadn't gone looking for a bullet that day.

I sighed and looked down. I was forever grateful I told Mom goodbye that morning. The prior evening, we had argued over something so trivial I couldn't remember what it was. But that morning, over breakfast, we had made up. I had even hugged her before she left for her assistant manager job at the local GoodQik convenience store.

That day would forever be burned into my mind. I remembered wondering why Mom hadn't answered any of my texts that afternoon. You know, the simple ones like, *Yum, having burgers for lunch,* or *Saw this on social media,* or even *I'm on my way home.* Mom always answered, even if it was with just a smiley face. But that day, she was strangely silent.

When I got home, I remember trudging up the steps to our little apartment. It had been raining, and I had left a trail of drips on the dusty concrete of the stairwell. I was soaked through, having forgotten my coat, so I was looking forward to a hot shower and changing into something dry.

I went to insert my key in the deadbolt but froze—the door was hanging slightly open. I frowned. I knew I had locked it—Mom had scolded me many times to never, ever leave it unlocked.

I pulled out my phone and held my finger over its emergency call button as I cautiously poked the door. It had slowly creaked open. I remembered my shock as I saw that everything in our little apartment had been dumped on the floor or overturned. The room was an absolute disaster. *What the Protector happened?* I remembered asking myself.

Then I heard the scrape of shoes behind me. I jerked around to see two uniformed officers approaching—their coats and hats slick with rain. Their expressions were professionally somber.

"*Afternoon,*" said the closest. His mouth pinched as if he was about to do something unpleasant. "*I'm sorry, miss. Your mother has been—*"

I pulled away from the memory. I slid down the brick wall and squatted at its base, wrapping my arms around me. Like all the races, both magical and mundane, a bullet was the great equalizer. It would kill no matter what you were.

The police said it was a robbery gone bad—a druggie needing money. But strangely, the assailant was never caught. It didn't even make the news. They also said the sacking of our apartment was an 'unrelated coincidence'. That there had been a series of similar break-ins nearby. I didn't buy it. And when I complained to the elder's office, I was brought in for shoplifting only a few days later.

The message was clear. A highly placed individual had wanted something from Mom. Wanted it bad enough to kill. And I would suffer the same fate if I didn't leave it alone.

I hugged my knees tighter to my chest. In the end, it didn't matter. Mom was gone. And sadly, there would be no justice.

Get over it, Lapis, I told myself. *There's nothing you can do. Just accept it.*

But I shook my head in denial, unwilling to let it go. The unfairness of it all made me so *angry*. We were being treated like pieces of useless trash.

And I hated it. Hated my clan. Hated how they treated Mom. Hated hiding my appearance. And most especially, hated what I was—

A succubus.

My kind were the lowest of the low—the bottom of society. Despised and ridiculed for some crime our ancestors committed millennia ago. With our long tails and two horns, we were easy to spot. And easy to hate.

It was so bad most of us—Mom and me included—would hide our true heritage behind an illusion charm. It wasn't a secret that our race existed. It was just ignored. Don't show yourselves, don't use your powers, don't make trouble, and you'll be allowed to survive—if that is what one called it.

If there was any way I could switch my race, I would in a heartbeat. Witch, werewolf, shifter—even a mundane *human* would be better than a succubus. It was a dream I had harbored since watching a news segment a few months before Mom died. It was about some experimental procedure they were testing in California, which took magicals and turned them into humans. The show's commentators had been astonished that people would even consider volunteering for it. They couldn't imagine someone willingly giving up their powers.

I would. If it made me into something people wouldn't hate, I would *pay* to do it.

I laid my forehead down on my knees. Like that was ever going to happen. I was broke.

Mom's funeral expenses had cleaned out our meager savings, making it impossible to live on my own. I was still short of eighteen, so I had to turn to family welfare. They set me up with a foster couple, and we made a plan to get me to my next birthday. I wasn't really happy with them—nor they with me. But they weren't too bad, in a strict, overly religious, money-hungry sort of way. Not that it mattered. I drifted through those dark times with no purpose or direction. I just really didn't care.

But then a voice from the grave woke me up.

I had received the first warning from my illusion charm—it was running out of magic. That wasn't unusual. It would run out every couple of years, and Mom usually handled the whole thing. But this time, I had no idea who to go to.

I was searching through a cardboard box of Mom's old things to see if maybe she'd written down the name of the last witch she used. The box was full, and the book she had been reading before she died fell out. That's when I noticed something in the book—an old picture with a royal blue sticky note attached.

When I was younger, Mom had put up a chore board and would put sticky notes on it for who was supposed to do what. Her tasks were color-coded green, while mine were always dark blue. There was no doubt the note was intended for me, and the task Mom had assigned me was—

"Find him."

The picture was of my grandfather.

I closed my eyes and rested my head against the wall. I was so tired, but I needed to start looking for a place to bed down. I probably had enough money for a room, but I couldn't afford to burn through my little bit of cash that quickly. Since I wasn't sure how long the search for my grandfather would take, I had to conserve and would have to find a bench somewhere. Thank goodness it was a warm night. My tummy rumbled. Maybe I could afford a breakfast sandwich in the morning.

I jumped when I felt something brush against my leg. Looking down, I discovered a solid gray cat rubbing against me. He gazed up in the adoring way cats do, and I couldn't help but smile. I tentatively ran my hand over his silky fur, and he leaned into it, purring loudly. My smile broadened, and I gave him a longer stroke, which he seemed to enjoy.

He was so cute—I had to pick him up. I stood and cradled him in the crook of my arm while the cat gazed up at me expectantly. I thought it strange that his eyes were different colors—one green and one blue.

"You're a pretty one," I said and scratched behind his ears.

"And you're not too bad for a succubus," he purred. "The horns are perfect, but my tail is prettier."

I gasped in surprise and jerked back, dropping him in the process.

Naturally, the cat landed on his feet. He looked over his shoulder in disgust. "You didn't have to drop me." The voice was male—deep and rich—with each word clearly enunciated and with no noticeable accent. It could easily have come from a DJ or an actor.

I took a step back. "How are you talking? You're a *cat*. Even shapeshifters can't talk while they're in animal form."

He looked disgusted. "I am not a shifter, and I am definitely *not* a cat." He sat on his haunches facing me as his tail waved in irritation. "In times past, I was referred to as . . . a god."

I blinked and eyed him skeptically. "No way. You've got to be a shifter trying to prank me."

He sat up erect and wound his long gray tail around his feet, giving him a regal appearance. "I chose this form to be less threatening to your kind." He lifted his front paw and began to lick it. "I can be majestic in whatever form I choose."

I didn't believe him. I stepped to the alley's center and inspected its high walls—there was no trace of a hidden microphone or camera on the walls. What was going on? And more importantly—

How had he known I was a succubus?

I touched the illusion charm tattooed high on my left side and hidden under my arm. I received the reassuring vibration that it was working. This was so odd. It had never once failed to conceal the horns emerging just above my temples and gracefully curving above my short, blonde hair. It even hid my finger-thick pensile tail, which constantly waved behind me.

I shook my head. It had to be some goofball's idea of a joke. Probably using a high-grade illusion detector and magic to make the cat appear to talk.

But I paused as I realized something was odd about the cat—I couldn't feel his emotions. All animals broadcast their feelings, some louder than others, people the most, but the cat's feelings were strangely missing. It was like watching someone play a musical instrument with no sound coming out.

A feeling of dread crept over me. Only powerful magic could shield emotions. This had to be trouble.

I reached for my suitcase. "Fine, Mr. Cat. You just go about your godly ways. I have to leave now."

The cat darted forward to rub against my leg. "You can't go yet, Lapis Midnyte. Don't be in such a hurry."

My eyes went wide in concern. I took a step back. "How did you know my name?"

Ignoring my question, he put a paw on my leg. "Wait just a minute more. I assure you, it won't take much longer."

I looked up, ready to run. "Longer for what?"

"It's time to claim your heritage." There was pride in his voice. "You're the Guardian, and you're going to fix the world."

I snorted. *Now that was an amusing thought.* "Listen, I'm *not* this guardian. I can't even fix my own life, let alone the world."

I took a step, but the cat weaved back and forth before me. I nearly tripped.

He paused in my path and pleaded with me. "Please . . . just a moment more, Guardian."

This was freaking me out. "I told you I'm not this stupid guardian. Now let me *go!*"

He looked up at me with concern. He opened his mouth to protest again, but paused and looked toward the alley's entrance. I could have sworn he smiled. "*It's begun.*"

That's when I heard it. Or rather, felt it—a thud, thud sound that started in my feet and quickly spread up my legs into my chest. I could feel it vibrating my insides. Something heavy was running—

And it was getting closer.

Chapter 2

I WENT TO THE mouth of the alley and peeked up and down the connecting street. It was well-lit but totally deserted. I briefly wondered if I was mistaken and it was simply some late-night road construction.

Then, a block away, a young woman came running around the corner and sprinted flat out in my direction. I recognized the pale green sundress and bushy red hair from the witch I had met earlier. She had been concerned about someone. But now her eyes were as wide as saucers, and even from where I stood, I could feel the fear radiating from her.

A moment later, I understood why.

Out of the darkness behind her came a mass of muscle and

flesh I'd only seen once in a book. Roughly humanoid, naked, and easily as large as an elephant, he had skin a dark grayish-green and arms the size of an oak tree. The biggest damn living thing I had ever seen and a face so ugly, he was hard to look at. His huge mouth was grotesquely stretched around enormous teeth, complete with opposing sets of extended incisors. That mouth would make a shark envious.

An ogre.

And he was pissed.

I couldn't believe what I was seeing. I could more readily accept a lion was walking down the street than an ogre. Not only were they nearly extinct, but they were not native to the continent, and their export was outlawed.

There was no way I wanted to tangle with that monster. I ducked back down the alley and squatted in the dumpster's shadow. There was no place else to hide. Even the cat was gone. I hugged my knees and tried to make myself as small as possible, wishing I had a witch's power to make myself invisible.

My best course of action was to wait until they ran past, grab my suitcase, and head the other way. I had a clear view of the alley's entrance from the gap between the wall and the dumpster, so I would see them go by. I felt bad for the young witch, but there was no sense in adding to the body count.

Unfortunately, a moment later, the young woman caught the corner and swung into the alley. She sped past, not noticing me in the dumpster's shadow, but slowed when she realized it was a dead end. She gave a most unladylike curse before turning to race back out of the alley. She only got two steps before the beast stopped in front of the entrance. She drew back in dread.

The ogre stepped forward slowly, stalking his prey. I could feel waves of anger rolling off him. His eyes were narrowed while his monstrous hands opened and closed as if dying to crush something.

The young woman backed against the wall at the end. "Don't do this, Orion," she called. "Don't let it get you. You can control this."

In reply, the beast slammed a fist into the wall hard enough for the brick to crumble. I stared in horror. Only moments ago, I had been standing in that exact spot.

I squatted in the shadows, wanting to close my eyes and cover my head. Step by step, the beast drew even with the dumpster. I watched anxiously. If he took two more steps, I could slip behind him and run out of the alley. I knew I would be leaving her to her fate with the monster, but this was a matter of self-preservation. There was nothing I could do. Maybe I could get to a phone or something.

To my horror, the beast paused. His face screwed up, and he sniffed the air. He looked one way and then the other. I held my breath as he took one more step forward and leaned around the dumpster to look right at me.

He snarled, his levels of anger reaching new highs. It was so strong it almost made me sick.

He swung a tree trunk-sized arm, and I ducked. It passed just over my head, striking the dumpster with such force it bounced to the alley's entrance.

The young woman noticed me for the first time and gasped. "Orion," she yelled. "Don't hurt her! It's me you want."

But he remained focused on me. He growled and bared his teeth—his hands opening and closing, while his mouth stretched to show those really, really big teeth. I think he was smiling.

At this distance, I could feel a cocktail of emotions pouring off him—anger, hurt, and unexpectedly, deep down inside, an ugly black loneliness. I was surprised a beast could have such a complex mix.

He took a step toward me. I could feel his hot breath.

"Don't do it, Orion," the witch yelled. "Don't make me hurt you."

He looked in her direction and roared, but then turned back to me. He extended a huge hand in my direction. I was convinced I was going to die.

I felt magic gathering. "Girl!" she screamed. "Close your eyes!"

I did as told, and the world lit up. I could see the shadows of blood vessels behind my eyelids.

The beast screamed in agony. He punched the wall over my head, peppering me with a shower of powdered brick. He put a massive hand over his eyes and staggered back. I readied to run, but he stepped beside the dumpster, effectively blocking the entrance.

The young woman squatted beside me. "Did he hurt you? Can you see all right?"

Concern was not only visible on her face, but I could feel it—deep and innocently genuine.

I was shocked. She had a monster chasing her and was concerned about *me*. Had defended me even though I was a stranger to her. Being a witch, she could have easily cast an illusion over herself and used the distraction to escape. Yet she had stayed. I was strangely touched. Recently, no one cared if I lived or died.

The beast roared. Shoving the dumpster aside, he charged. The witch stepped away and started putting up a magical shield, but before it was entirely in place, he hit her with a crushing blow right in the center. While not fully formed, the shield absorbed the bulk of the impact.

But not all.

She was flung back against the wall, smacking hard against it. Dazed, she slumped to the ground.

He roared in satisfaction, radiating smug feelings of triumph.

The mind works in strange ways under pressure. Unbidden, a grade school memory came to mind. It was my first week at my new school. I was quiet, scrawny, and dressed in second-hand clothes. I was beneath the notice of the bullies, much less the rest of the class. One day during recess, one of the bullies-in-training pushed a girl into a mud puddle. She had been innocently looking at the violets growing beside it. We weren't friends or anything, but she was one of the few people that had been nice to the new kid. She broke into sobs while sitting covered in mud. Then the bully broke into laughter at her misery. The bully's smugness—his pleasure at someone's pain—infuriated me.

Inside that quiet, scrawny girl I was at the time, whose eyes didn't even come up to the bully's chest—something just snapped. No one should be treated like that.

No one.

I had launched myself at him with such fury it took three

teachers to pull me off. Mom had to come get me, and I was forced to find another school.

As the ogre sneered at the fallen young woman, I was instantly reminded of the girl that had been pushed into the mud puddle. The delight that emanated from that bully perfectly matched the feelings coming from the ogre. My hands slowly curled into fists, and I clenched them so tight I could feel my nails piercing my own skin. Mom's death, the police's accusation, the guy on the bus, and now an ogre attacking an innocent girl. I'd had enough. I was probably going to die, but I just didn't care.

He was going down.

I stood and moved to the middle of the alley—my face a mask of determination. The collision with the shield had staggered him back, and he stood nearly at the alley entrance. My mind screamed that this was crazy. I didn't have some fantastic superpower. I was good at running and could manipulate emotions, but that was it. And to make it even tougher, I had to touch him to make full use of my magic, preferably with my horns. Which meant I was going to have to be creative. If I only had walls around me, then I was going to use them.

He grinned and stepped in my direction. Projecting defiance, I continued to glare at him. His eyes narrowed, and his pace quickened. I glared back at him and didn't budge, which only fed his anger. Closer and closer, he came. His arms came up to reach for me.

Now!

I spun and ran away from him. He gave a howl of delight and gave chase. I sprinted straight toward the brick wall in front of me. I hadn't won the hundred-meter by luck.

I briefly noticed that the young woman was awake and crawling out of harm's way, but I remained focused on my steps. I had to get the timing just right. I could feel the ground shaking as the ogre charged after me.

Suddenly I was at the wall. I used my momentum to take three giant steps straight up the red brick and then leaped backward in a tight roll. My feet sailed up, my tail provided balance, and in a perfect flip, I landed with legs outstretched around the back of his thick neck. I grabbed his ears for balance and placed my horns against his head. Even if they were invisible, they still worked, functioning like emotional antennas. The closer, the better.

The contact was like turning up the volume. His emotions were coming to me unfiltered. The fear, the anger, and the loneliness were so strong it hurt.

And I took them, channeling their energy into myself.

Then I changed them and fed them back.

Calm. Peace.

He yelled as if I had stabbed him with a knife. He ran into the wall full tilt, nearly knocking me off and his head making a crater in the brick. But I held on. I took his emotional energy, altered it, and fed it back to him.

Calm.

He laid a huge hand on my leg to pull me off. I turned up the emotional volume to full blast. He staggered and punched the brick wall, shattering it while roaring in frustration. But I held on, tapping into every ounce of anger in his being and making it something else.

Calm. Peace.

He slammed his head into the wall again, but it didn't have

as much force. It was followed by another, but it barely made contact. He grew still and slumped to his knees. Then, like a giant tree in the forest, he toppled over. I barely had time to jump clear.

Surprisingly, he began to transform. His features started to melt and run, while he diminished in size, and his skin changed texture and softened. It was like watching one of those animations where someone's face warps into another. In only moments, an unconscious young man lay in front of me. His short, dark hair framed a handsome face that spoke of intelligence and strength. His eyes were closed, and his mouth slack as he slumbered. He was naked, of course, and built sort of—*nice*. Not that I had that much experience. I blushed and averted my eyes.

The witch hurried to the unconscious young man and knelt beside him. I could feel her concern as she laid a gentle hand on his chest. I felt a brief spike of magic. She breathed a sigh of relief, and then she sat back. "Just unconscious," she muttered. "You really gave me a scare, you idiot." She was emitting a complex mix of emotions—relief, concern—but the last one surprised me. *Affection?*

I figured with all the noise, we had surely attracted the police, so I went to pick up my suitcase. Best be far away when they arrived.

But before I knew it, the young girl wrapped her arms around me in a tight hug. I could feel her relief and gratitude. "You rock, girl! To squeeze his neck like that, you must have legs of steel. And running up that wall? Wow."

"It was nothing," I said, while trying to extract myself. "Just a trick I learned in track."

While I appreciated her thanking me, I doubted she would be quite so thankful if she knew I was a succubus—not to mention using my powers on him. If word got back to a clan elder, I could be punished.

She jerked me into another tight hug, ignoring my attempts to pull away. I had never been much of a hugger.

She released me, holding me at arm's length. "I don't know what I would have done without you. I owe you big time. My name's Rore, and thank you for saving my brother."

Brother?

A police car pulled across the alley entrance, filling it with a flashing blue light. Two car doors opened, and a bright light illuminated the area.

"Police!" an officer shouted. "Both of you, get your hands up! NOW!"

I squinted into the light and could barely distinguish two shadows holding guns. I groaned and raised my hands. I knew I should have run when I had the chance.

As the officers approached, one of them blocked the harsh glare from their spotlight. It allowed a clear view of the alley's entrance. Sitting there, with his tail curled around his feet, sat the gray talking cat. He was watching me.

The cat nodded once, then stood and quickly trotted around the corner out of sight.

A chill went down my spine. He knew what was coming. I got an uneasy feeling separate from the approaching police.

Why had he set me up?

Chapter 3

AS THE POLICE approached with guns drawn, I sighed in disbelief. I was so screwed. They had the entrance blocked, so running wasn't an option. Evidence of destroyed property lay all around—crumbled brick spread across the ground and walls decorated with ogre-fist-sized craters. They would surely do a background check on me, and once they found out what I was, I would likely be arrested. At best, I would be sent back. This trip would have been for nothing.

Surprising me, Rore took a step forward. She looked stricken. "Officer, my friend and I . . . we . . . were attacked." Her face crumpled, tears starting down her cheeks. "I thought we were going to die." She turned to me, laid her head on my shoulder, and wept loudly.

I was caught off guard and wasn't sure what to do. But the real surprise was that her feelings didn't match her tears. She was faking. *What was she up to?*

I glanced over at the unconscious young man and then did a double-take. He wasn't there, yet I could still feel the subtle emotions of his presence. It could only be an illusion—Rore must be hiding him. But it wasn't going to work. They would instantly know if we lied. The officers likely had truth detection charms—at least the ones in Philly did. Although it hadn't made a difference when I claimed I was innocent.

With really no choice, I played along and patted Rore's back. I just hoped she knew what she was doing.

The two officers holstered their guns and stepped forward.

"We had a complaint that someone was fighting. What happened?" asked the older of the two—his eyes flicking across the damage.

Rore answered before I could. With tears leaking down her face, she turned her head toward them. "A big green monster attacked us. It hit the walls and . . . and . . ." She gave a mighty sniff and wiped at her tears. "Can I call my grandmother?" Her lower lip trembled.

I was impressed with her acting skills.

The two officers looked at each other. Not surprisingly, I could only vaguely sense their emotions. They were likely wearing magic neutralization charms, which provided broad-spectrum protection against offensive magic. If I dared try to push through to influence their feelings, it would likely set off an alarm.

The older officer nodded. "Miss, go ahead and call. We'll just ask you a few questions until she arrives."

Rore immediately took out her phone and hurriedly typed a text. She looked back up. "Grandmother was going to pick us up, so she should be just around the corner."

I had to force the grin off my face—her act was so convincing. While she was nervous, she was having fun.

The phone dinged a reply, and she glanced down. "Grandmother's coming."

One officer began to inspect the damage to the walls while the other pulled out a crumpled writing pad and the nub of a pencil. "What's your name, miss."

She wiped a tear from her eye. "Aurorah Constance Strewert." She gave a weak smile. "But my friends call me Rore. I live in the west end."

"Witch?" he asked, but it sounded like he already knew.

She nodded.

"Twilight-Clan," he said to himself. He made a note on his pad. He looked back up. "You haven't been practicing any illegal magic or using any contraband charms, have you?"

My eyes flicked over to where her brother lay. Concealing him from the police wasn't exactly legal.

Rore reacted with indignation. "If I could, would there be all this damage?" She gave a dramatic sniff. "We were just here for the dance."

"Sorry, miss," said the officer. He dug in his pocket and pulled out a tissue. He held it out for her.

She took it and blew her nose. Loudly. She was doing it deliberately, but I couldn't help but cringe at the ick factor.

He turned his focus on me. "What about you, miss?"

Before I could open my mouth, Rore buried her face in my shoulder and resumed weeping. I patted her back and looked at the officer. "I'm Lapis Midnyte." I didn't say my clan. It would be a dead giveaway.

As I was hoping, he filled it in for me. "Human." He wrote on his pad. "Dawn-clan."

I wasn't about to correct him.

"Do either of you have ID?" he asked.

Rore whipped out her phone. Her license was tucked into an attached pocket.

He looked to me.

"Mine's in my suitcase," I said. I immediately kicked myself. That was proof I was traveling. Our little ruse might be coming to an end.

The officer turned around and pointed. "Is that it?"

I nodded.

Rore gave a loud wail. "Her . . . her visit has been ruined." She returned to crying on my shoulder.

At the entrance, another vehicle joined the police car—both officers glanced in that direction. A moment later, the silhouette of a woman appeared. Rore broke away and ran toward her. "Grandmother! It was horrible. He was a great big angry beast, and he was chasing me." She wrapped her arms around the woman's neck and hugged her close.

The grandmother's emotions were subdued—*controlled* is the word I would have used. But from their slight flicker, I was pretty sure a whispered conversation was happening. After only a few moments, they broke apart.

With Rore clinging to her arm, they both came closer. The older lady didn't look like a stereotypical grandmother. She had elegant silver hair, cut in a classic bob, and wore glasses that matched her tailored white business suit. The clothes screamed a professional of some kind. *Lawyer maybe?* I imagined she once had red hair like her granddaughter. Just looking at the pair, you could tell they were related. Their facial features were identical.

The elder examined me with cool interest. Her intelligent eyes missed nothing as she gave me a once-over. From the confidence she projected, this woman was used to wielding power, and I was pretty sure you didn't want to get on her bad side.

When she stepped closer, I thought the younger officer's eyes were going to bug out. "Clan Elder Strewert! I had no idea . . ." His emotions were a combination of nervous admiration and excitement. I wondered if he was going to ask her for an autograph.

His partner nudged him, and the younger man blushed in embarrassment. As officers, they weren't supposed to show deference to any leader or any race. But when your own elder surprised you, it was easy to forget. Which, from his reaction, meant he was one of the races in Twilight-clan. I had my money on a witch. If he were a werewolf, he might have trouble doing his job on moonlit evenings.

She cut him off. "Are you done with my granddaughter?" she asked flatly. "I would like to take her and her friend and have them checked out."

The older officer must be human. Since humans were Dawn-Clan, he was less impressed with her station. "Evening, elder. We still have some information we need. It should only be a few more minutes."

She was unmoved. "I appreciate that you're just performing

your job, officer, but my granddaughter has been clearly traumatized. She needs to go. Now."

"I understand, elder, but—"

"Officer." Her gaze grew frosty. "Do I have to call the commissioner? You can get all the information you need from my office tomorrow."

He glanced at his partner, seeking support, but the man was occupied looking at his shoes. The officer frowned, clearly not pleased. I felt sorry for him—arguing with an elder from any of the four clans would not end well.

"As you wish, elder," he finally said. "But I will be speaking with my sergeant."

She gave a tight smile. "I would expect no less. Now step with me to my car so I can give you my card."

They turned toward the alley's entrance, but I wasn't sure if I was included, so I didn't move. The elder glanced back, and when she saw my hesitation, she beckoned to me. "Come along child. We need to see to you, too."

I felt concern coming from her, although more subdued than her granddaughter.

"I don't want to be a bother. I'll walk," I offered while picking up my suitcase. I wasn't sure I wanted to stay mixed up with these people. They were witches, and if they looked too closely, they might see through my illusion. Plus, the grandmother was an elder. Even at the city level, clan elders were powerful. Not just with magic, but also from the people she governed. She could have me crushed without using a single spell.

"Nonsense," she replied. "You're coming with us."

She stared at me a moment more, and I could see the coolness in her gaze. Like the officer, arguing would not be wise. She likely wanted to remove any temptation the police might have to pursue this further.

What had I gotten myself into?

As we walked to the car, I wondered what they intended with the unconscious young man. Neither Rore nor her grandmother seemed worried he might be discovered. I was puzzled since the illusion magic would likely fade once the witches got a block or two away. It seemed odd. Maybe there was a charm involved, and they were going to come back for him. But wouldn't that risk the police stumbling over him?

I schooled myself. It wasn't my concern. I hoped that once we were away from the police, I could convince them to drop me off. The less I had to do with these people, the better.

The elder's car was a white limousine with an open rear door and a spacious interior. A man in a chauffeur uniform stood beside the car with his hands crossed in front of him. He was a large fellow, not only tall but also with a broad chest. I thought he was a werewolf—he certainly had the build for one. It would also make sense since they, along with witches, were a race within Twilight-clan.

His expression was completely neutral, but his eyes were bright and alert. I sensed no strange emotions from him—just professional alertness. From how he carried himself, I thought he might be more bodyguard than chauffeur.

The elder entered the limo, completely ignoring the officer, and took the forward-facing seat closest to the door. With a slight bow, the chauffeur presented a business card to each officer.

I wasn't sure what to do, but Rore grabbed my hand and pulled me into the vehicle after her. I marveled at the interior—

rich white leather with four padded seats—two of them facing each other. It even smelled expensive. I expected Rore to take the remaining forward-facing seat beside her grandmother, but she took the farthest rearward-facing one—like she wanted to be as far from the woman as she could get.

I didn't want to sit with the elder staring at me, so I started toward the one across from Rore, but she jerked hard on my hand and redirected me to plop down exactly where I didn't want to go. Her grandmother, already deep into her phone, glanced up at me coolly.

Rore gave me an innocent smile and patted my hand. The contact heightened my awareness of her feelings—she had grown apprehensive, more nervous than when acting for the police.

I leaned over to whisper, but she glanced my way and gave a tight shake of her head. I sat back instead. I guess we weren't supposed to talk.

The police finished with the chauffeur, and he shut the door with a solid thud. I couldn't help but feel the door to my cell had just been closed.

The chauffeur got in the driver's seat and looked over his shoulder while pulling on his seatbelt. "Where to, Ms. Strewert?" he asked. He had just a plain vanilla American accent. I was expecting something British.

"To my daughter's house." The elder paused a moment. She glanced at me. "But take the long way. I need to speak with these ladies for a moment."

"Very good, mam." He started the car and backed out of the side street.

The elder watched the passing scenery as we drove. I could feel a simmering displeasure inside of her.

Rore shifted uncomfortably. "Grandmother, is it safe?"

The elder nodded. "Go ahead."

Rore breathed a sigh of relief, and I felt the brush of magic. Suddenly, her unconscious brother appeared in the seat across from Rore, next to her grandmother. I now knew why Rore had jerked me to the other seat—I was about to sit on him. Thankfully, he was covered with a blanket.

I couldn't help but gasp. "How?"

Rore shrugged. "I kept them both hidden while Mac carried him to the car."

"I'm impressed," I said. And I was. I had heard of witches doing some amazing things with illusions—my own charm a testament—but Rore had taken it to a whole new level. She had managed to keep two people hidden while putting on her little act for the police. She was one talented little witch.

Rore smiled. I could feel her gentle pride behind the smile. But the feeling crashed as her grandmother spoke.

"What the hades happened?" the elder spat. "I thought he had it under control. And *you* were going to watch him."

The fear Rore projected matched the panic in her expression. It was real this time.

"I don't know, Grandmother. Everything had been going so well. He hasn't lost control in over a year. But something was different this time." She looked over at her brother and sighed sadly. "He's never used that form before, and it took him completely. He didn't even know who I was." Her voice dropped to a whisper. "I thought he might really try to hurt me."

The elder softened a little. "Are you all right?"

Rore nodded. "I'm fine. A few bruises, but nothing permanent." She smiled in my direction. "Thanks to Lapis."

I almost wished she hadn't mentioned my role. The elder's eyes slid to me.

She gave me a calculating appraisal. "I'm sorry, miss. Where are my manners? I'm Elder Terra Strewert. I guess I need to thank you for saving my grandchildren." Her glance hardened as it moved to Rore and then Orion. "They have been getting into trouble recently."

I gave a deep nod in respect for one of her station. "Thank you, Elder. I'm Lapis Midnyte." I glanced out the window at the passing lights. We were rolling through some city neighborhoods in no particular hurry. But moving we were—easing further and further away from the area I had so carefully mapped out before leaving home. "I don't want to be any trouble. You can let me out anywhere."

"So you're not one of Aurorah's friends?" She glanced at my suitcase sitting at my feet. The elder's eyes turned back to me.

Rore jumped to my defense. "Grandmother, don't . . ."

Terra's eyes narrowed. "I was talking to Miss Midnyte," she said with a bite to her voice. "Please don't interrupt."

Rore leaned back and remained quiet, but I could feel the fear and resentment boiling inside her.

I hesitated. I dared not avoid the elder's question. If she suspected I was not what I appeared to be, then there could be trouble. Her granddaughter was a witch, so the elder was likely one too. While the different races could interbreed, the child always inherited the race of the mother. If the mother was a witch, so was the child. This begged the question of how Orion could be her grandchild. Shapeshifters, like humans, were part of Dawn-clan.

Terra smiled politely, waiting for her answer.

"No, I was a bystander," I finally said. "I just arrived from Philly."

"Your accent doesn't sound like it. I would have guessed midwest or possibly California."

"We moved around a lot. I spent my first years in Kansas."

She considered me for a moment. "Lapis is an unusual name. If I remember right, it's a bright blue gemstone that goes back to Egyptian times."

I nodded. "I'm not sure why Mom chose that name. No one else in the family has it. She must have liked the sound of it."

Terra nodded, seeming to file the information away. "And your last name is Midnyte. A good Dawn-clan name, though I can't say I've heard of many humans using it." Terra paused her interrogation. She glanced at Rore and then back to me.

She gave a sly smile. "I guess I should be grateful. Humans rarely get involved with those outside their clan."

She was baiting me. Humans were one of the races with no magic, and the magicked looked down on them. Not that I cared since I was a succubus—ranked even below the level of the powerless humans.

Terra watched me intently as a lion would its prey. I think she was hoping I would react. Unfortunately, her attitude reminded me of a bully, and I didn't like it.

"I'm not exactly sure why I helped," I replied calmly, returning her cool gaze. "It just seemed like the right thing to do. I didn't have time to think about who she was or to what clan she belonged. So, I guess you're right. I'm not as concerned about family ties." I leaned toward her with an unkind smile. "Unlike her own *Grandmother.*"

Terra's eyes narrowed, and I felt a flash of anger. She considered me, her expression guarded. For a moment, I thought I had pushed too far.

Her phone rang. She immediately answered it, irritation in her eyes as she held the phone to her ear and looked away. I breathed a sigh of relief and turned to Rore.

"Are you okay?" I leaned toward Rore and whispered. "You got hit pretty hard."

My asking lit up her emotions. She was so pleased I had asked. I realized this poor girl was starved for acceptance. Considering her family's position, I had to wonder how that was even possible.

"It wasn't that bad," she smiled weakly. "I'm not good at healing magic, but I was able to do a little on myself. Mother will look me over when we get home. Orion too." Then she added, "She's a veterinarian." It seemed important to her.

I glanced at Orion. "He's been out a long time. Is he okay?"

She nodded. "He's fine. He sometimes passes out when he's been in another form. The magic drain is pretty high. Thankfully, the shift back to his true form heals any injuries."

I had read something about that—one perk of being a shapeshifter.

Rore glanced at the elder to ensure she was occupied, then leaned closer to me. "I'm sorry for getting you involved with Grandmother," she whispered. "She can be a bit gruff, but I had no choice. They would have arrested Orion, and we can't afford any more trouble. She's the only one that could have prevented them from doing anything."

I squeezed her hand. "I understand. If I had a brother, I would have done the same."

I glanced at him. I wanted so badly to ask how he could be her brother and also be a shifter. But I thought it might be impolite.

Rore must have sensed my question. "Orion's adopted."

"Oh," I said awkwardly. It was unusual to adopt outside of one's clan. Shapeshifters were in Dawn-clan and witches Twilight-clan.

Rore continued. "Don't say anything, though. He's a little sensitive about it." She thought for a moment. "He's sensitive about a lot of other stuff, too." She paused a moment more. "He's still a nice guy. For a brother."

Just then, Rore's phone chirped. She pulled it out with practiced ease, glanced at the screen, and grimaced. She typed a quick message. "It's Mom. She's going to be upset."

Her response got an immediate reply. Rore sighed heavily. "Yeah. She's *totally* pissed."

The limo rolled to a stop at a T-intersection. The headlights illuminated a tall iron fence on the opposite side with a sign that proclaimed Edgemont Victory Park. The car turned left, and we began to travel along the perimeter of a rather large open area.

Succubi could see better than most in darkness, so I could easily tell the park was well maintained and extended quite a way into the distance. The land gradually rose, so we had a good view of the darkened grounds. I had no trouble picking out the asphalt paths, weaving through the park and dotted with patches of security lights. But what grabbed my attention was a strange building in the distance that resided atop a hill. The park seemed to have been built around it. Strangely, the building had no lights, yet was faintly visible from its own dim internal blue glow. I couldn't make out the details, but I thought it had majestic stone columns, like some grand government building or maybe even a monument.

It seemed an odd place to have a building like that. I wondered what its purpose was.

Vault. The thought came unbidden. *An ancient sentinel, sitting silent and alone in the shadows of the night, faithfully discharging its mission, while hoping and waiting for its long watch to be over.*

I blinked in confusion, unnerved at the sudden thought. *Where had that come from?*

Terra looked up from her phone and glanced out the window at the building. I felt an overwhelming sadness come from her. She was likely replaying a bad memory connected with it.

I tried to hold my tongue, but my curiosity got the better of me. "What is that?" I nodded toward the structure.

The elder jerked as I pulled her out of her memory, but she kept her eyes on the building. "Edgemont Park," she said distractedly.

I shook my head. "Not the park, the building. Is it some kind of memorial?"

Her head slowly turned in my direction, and she blinked in confusion. "You can see it?"

I gave her a puzzled expression and pointed in the building's direction. "It's right there."

Rore leaned around me and glanced out the window. "Edgemont Park? It's nice. That's where the solstice festival will be held this year." She resumed looking at something on her phone.

The car came to another intersection and turned away from the park. The building was quickly out of sight.

Terra shifted uncomfortably in her seat—her emotions all over the place. Her eyes slid to my hands, wrists, and then to my neck, where her gaze froze on the silver chain exposed above my shirt.

"Miss Midnyte, what do you have in your shirt?"

My hand went up to cover the exposed chain. "It's just a necklace my mother gave me."

Terra shifted in her seat. "Could I see it?"

Rore said nothing, but her eyes flicked between the two of us. Like me, she sensed something had changed in Terra's attitude.

"Why?" I asked.

Terra shrugged. "I'm always looking for unique jewelry."

"It's not for sale."

"Didn't expect it would be. But I am curious." She leaned forward. "Please."

I considered not bringing it out, but I dared not push her too far. Plus, she had said please.

I shrugged and pulled out the necklace. It was beautiful in its own way—a silver chain with an amulet that wove silver strands around a dark blue gem. And peeking from the stone's center was a tiny speck of gold.

Her gaze immediately hardened, and I felt her emotions suddenly shift, moving toward alarm. Then like a switch, they suddenly cut off.

With a sinking feeling, I realized she had just raised her defensive barrier—likely because she now considered me a threat.

I am so screwed.

Chapter 4

WITHOUT TAKING her eyes off me, Terra spoke. "Aurorah, I bet you're getting tired."

Rore looked over at us and stifled a yawn. "It has been a tiring day." She suddenly stiffened. "Grandmother, noooo . . ." Her eyes suddenly drooped shut, and she relaxed into her seat. A moment later, she gave a soft snore. People didn't fall asleep that fast—not unless magic was involved.

I fought my rising panic. *Offensive magic*—that spell was illegal. If she would do that to her own granddaughter, what would she do to me?

My fear must have shown on my face.

"Don't worry," said Terra. One corner of her mouth curled

up. "Aurorah's only sleeping. I've been using that spell on her since she was born. She's quite energetic and has always been a pain to put to bed." Terra took a deep breath and pulled herself back to the present. Her eyes narrowed. "You and I need to talk privately."

I glanced at the door handle, wondering if I could jump out of the moving car. My hand inched toward it.

"That's not a good idea, Miss Midnyte. You could get hurt that way. Just relax. I won't harm you."

I glared at her. "Then stop the car."

"I can't do that just yet. I need to determine if you are a threat to my family. Despite how it may appear, I hold them quite dear." She smiled, but it never reached her eyes. That chilled me.

She leaned forward. "I sense a powerful charm on you. Much more powerful than I would have expected for a human. And it's extremely well hidden. I hadn't even noticed it until I went looking."

I held up the necklace. "You mean this?"

"No. I mean the one under your arm."

I quickly spoke the practiced lie. "It's just a cosmetic. I have a congenital condition, and it helps hide it." It was true, sort of.

Terra's eyebrows went up in mock surprise. "Really? I didn't realize that cosmetic charms were now military-grade camouflage spells."

I blinked at her. That couldn't be right. I'd had the charm most of my life and knew it was powerful, but nothing that high class. Mom could never have afforded it. I pushed the thought aside.

"It's a really bad condition," I blurted out.

She smiled with dark amusement. "Must be." She leaned back and considered me for a moment. "Turn it off."

Her smug smile pissed me off. "No," I said flatly.

She was genuinely shocked at my defiance.

"Don't test me."

"Then quit trying to push me around," I spat. "I'm nothing compared to you. Just stop the car and let me out. I won't bother you or your family ever again. But if you keep pushing, I *will* push back."

We stared at each other.

She suddenly smiled and relaxed into her seat. "So that's how it is?" She looked thoughtful. "Well, let me tell you what I surmise. I already know you're not really human, which means you're not Dawn-clan. You're also not a witch or part of my own Twilight-clan. I'd sense it. That means you're either Shadow-clan or, more likely . . ." She leaned forward. "*Night-clan.*"

My heart rate jumped, and I fought to keep my face neutral.

"Yes, Night-clan." She nodded. "But not the usual characters. A vampire would be too arrogant to hide her nature, while a doppelganger would just take the form of what she wanted, and a sorcerer would never stoop to using a plain old charm." She leaned toward me and smiled. "I'd bet you're a *succubus.*"

I tried not to show a reaction.

She leaned back in her seat. "How close am I?"

Just then, her phone dinged. She picked it up and scrolled through the message while I sat contemplating my limited options. She nodded to herself and put her phone back down. "Your story checks out. You have been living in Philly for the past two years. Your mother recently passed away, and the police there would really like to know where you've run off to."

She leaned forward. "So, Miss Midnyte, succubus of the Night-clan. Would you like to tell me what brings you to my city?" She leaned closer. "And turning off your illusion would be a wonderful show of trust. Don't worry. No one can see us."

We stared at each other.

I almost told her to take a hike but realized I was screwed either way. A witch of her powers could probably burn it out if she wanted.

I sighed, glancing at the sleeping Rore and Orion. I reached into my shirt and turned off my charm. I couldn't hide my blush. I felt naked sitting in front of her with my horns and tail visible for the world to see.

Her eyes traced my horns, and she nodded appreciatively. "A pity you hide them. They are quite pretty. You're much more beautiful as a succubus than a human. It's sad most of your kind hide themselves."

Her comment infuriated me. "It's because all the other races treat us like dirt," I spat. "You'd hide, too!"

She considered me. "That might be true. But as long as you hide, society will never change. You should be proud of what you are."

I glared at her. She didn't understand how bad it was. I defiantly reached inside my shirt and turned my charm back on, glad to once more be clothed in its glamor.

Her eyes returned to my silver chain but slid away. She sat back in her seat. "Thank you for indulging me, Miss Midnyte. I had to be sure you weren't concealing any weapons." She thought for a moment. "You seem very comfortable playing the human. You've done this for some time, haven't you?"

"I've worn this disguise most of my life. Mom thought it best if people didn't know what we really were."

"And your trip to this city?"

I took a deep breath and let it out slowly. "I'm here to look for my grandfather. I don't know where he lives or if he's even still alive. I've never met him. He and Mom had some big fight and never spoke again."

"And helping my grandchildren?"

I shrugged. "Like I said, it was chance mostly. He was bullying her." I decided not to mention the cat. I doubted she would believe that anyway. I sighed deeply. "I don't like bullies."

She leaned back and chuckled. "I bet you're not liking me very much right now."

I just glared at her.

She softened. "Thank you for telling me. Contrary to what you might think, I like you. You're brave, quick, and don't back down. I admire that. I also feel for you. You're alone in a strange town with no money and no friends." She considered me a moment longer. I noticed her eyes flick to my necklace again. I wondered what was so interesting about it. It wasn't charmed and definitely not a weapon.

Terra seemed to come to a decision. She leaned forward, putting her elbows on her knees. "Miss Midnyte, I'd like to make you an offer." She smiled. "This could work out for all of us."

I grew angry. *I should have known.* I crossed my arms, my expression hard. "Let me out," I commanded. "I may be a succubus, but I will not be your plaything or prostitute myself out for your benefit. I would die first."

She blinked at me in surprise. "No, no, no. You misunderstand. I would never ask that. Of you or anyone." She shook her head. "No, I was thinking of something completely different . . . And completely legal."

My stare was icy, but she blazed on.

"You see, my grandson has many fine attributes, but a shifter with an anger management problem does have its challenges. Aurorah has been doing a fair job of keeping him in check, but recently things have changed. A girl has taken an interest in him. Like you, she's Night-clan." Terra paused. "A vampire."

I frowned. I didn't particularly care for vampires, but I felt the need to defend my clan. "Those of Night-clan are always made to be the villains. Just because she's a vampire doesn't mean she will drain his life force. He's a magic user, so she can't tap him—or at least not easily. And why would she even want to? I'm sure he's under your protection. The risk of retribution is too high." I shrugged. "It's more likely she just really likes him."

"While that is possible, I've heard rumblings of something different. I think she's trying to manipulate him. She's from a powerful family, and my grandson is . . . well, let's just say he's inexperienced and far below her station. My sources tell me she was the trigger for tonight's debacle."

I shrugged. "So? She pissed him off."

"My granddaughter was supposed to be with him but was conveniently distracted by another from that same family." She leaned back. "There's more. For Orion to shapeshift to an animal, he must have come in contact with it before." She waved her arm. "This city has many animals, but the closest ogre is in the San Francisco Zoo."

"Maybe he touched a display or encountered one in a museum."

She shook her head. "There are too many coincidences. That girl just happened to be where he was tonight, and Rore gets distracted just before this girl makes him angry enough to turn into a beast he's never touched." She shook her head. "I don't believe in three coincidences. Somebody's planning something, and it involves my family. I have to get to the bottom of this."

I shrugged. "So, what do you want me to do? I'm just a succubus."

"True." She smiled. "But you're Night-clan. You understand how they work and can easily spot them. Plus, your abilities give you insight into the intentions of those around you. You'll be able to tell at a glance if that girl truly has feelings for him." She leaned forward. "I need someone on the inside. I want you to befriend my grandson and watch him. Find out who has evil intentions toward him. You're the right age to blend in, and you've already proven you can handle yourself. You even already come disguised. Who would think a mundane human could be a threat to vampires?" She shook her head. "No, if they are plotting something, you have the best chance of exposing it."

I looked out the window. The houses had moved to more upscale suburbs. We must be coming to the end of our car ride.

I considered the offer. Not for the first time, I wished my powers allowed me to read someone's thoughts instead of just their emotions. While what she said made sense, I couldn't shake the feeling that she wasn't telling me everything. But then again, I didn't actually expect her to. A queen never told her pawn she was sending him to his death.

"What's in it for me?" I asked flatly.

A confident smile gradually spread across her face. "In exchange, I'll set you up in my daughter's house so you'll have somewhere to live. You can use it as a base of operations to look for your grandfather. My daughter, Andromeda, will protest, but she won't turn you out." She glanced at the sleeping Rore before returning her eyes to mine. "My granddaughter has her own social problems, so I'm sure she will be thrilled to help with your search. It will give you something to bond over. It's the perfect excuse for you to stay close."

"What would I need to do?"

"Keep track of Orion. Report to me if something unusual happens. But most importantly, determine who means harm to my grandson."

I took a deep breath and let it out slowly as I considered my response. Terra was going to be disappointed. "What you offer is nice and all, but it risks pissing off my own clan and exposing myself. Doesn't seem to be worth it."

Her eyes narrowed as she considered me. She nodded thoughtfully and then leaned forward, her eyes sparkling. "*You'll gain my favor.*"

My eyes went wide in shock. I tried to control my expression, but I was too late. Terra saw it. And smiled.

A favor. A request owed that I could call in at a future time. Some would kill to have a favor owed by the Twilight-clan elder. She could open doors I could only dream about.

And I couldn't help but think about my dream—to become human. It couldn't be that easy.

"You realize," I said, "I'm only a succubus that's won a few track awards. I'm not an ex-marine or some kung-fu master. I will lose if there is a confrontation. Someone could get hurt."

She looked smug, knowing she had me. "I'm not asking you to fight. Only to watch. Besides, I think you underestimate yourself. You took down an ogre. I think you'll do just fine."

I nodded toward the young man. "I don't know if he will accept me. I'm not good at making friends. Just because I'm a succubus doesn't mean I can make him fall in love with me. If I were to try and influence him too hard or too often, he'd notice." I looked down. "Not that I would anyway. I swore never to use my powers like that." I looked back up. "What about Rore? Would I need to watch her too?"

Terra raised a finger in Rore's direction. "I'm not concerned about my granddaughter. Her powers are sufficient to deter vampire manipulation. She'd have to willingly drop her protections or somehow have her magic nullified. Either is highly unlikely." The elder smiled. "Besides, Aurorah is well on her way to liking you. I'm sure she will gladly help you search for your grandfather." Her gaze shifted to Orion, and her face grew concerned. "However, that one will be a harder sell. He keeps to himself mostly and has little experience with the fairer sex. He might need a little coaxing." Her eyes shifted back to mine. "But I think you can handle it."

I wasn't sure what to say. *A favor.* A door opened. The chance of a lifetime. My mind boggled at the possibility.

Terra looked up as the car rolled to a stop in front of a typical suburban house. "Ah," she said. "Perfect timing. We're at my daughter's home."

"I don't know . . ." I said weakly. The possibilities paralyzed me.

"Shh, child. Don't tell me your answer now." She patted my hand. "Stay here tonight. I'll speak with my daughter about you sleeping over. I'm sure Aurorah would love to have you. We'll talk tomorrow. Consider the offer carefully. It could be very advantageous." She nodded. "For all of us."

She quickly got out.

What was it about offers that were just too good to be true?

Why did I feel this was one of them?

Chapter 5

I WAS DREAMING of Mom and my birthday from a few months ago. It was the last one we had spent together.

I came in from school expecting the apartment to be empty, as Mom often worked late. But I arrived to the wonderful smell of homemade pizza—my favorite. As I wandered into our tiny kitchen, I saw Mom's masterpiece of cheese and pepperoni on the stove, fresh from the oven, and on the small table to the side sat a chocolate cake with seventeen candles. Mom was grinning broadly with one of those stupid party hats on her head and her bright pink ribbons—*ribownna*—adorning her horns. She only wore her elegant ribbons for special occasions.

"Happy Birthday!" she announced.

My mouth fell open. Mom worked long hours most days, but she must have taken the afternoon off for my birthday. She stubbornly refused to let me get a part-time job, saying I needed to focus on school and I was going to become an adult before I knew it.

"Mom, you shouldn't have."

She held out a tiny box wrapped in a festive deep purple paper. "Here dear. This is for you. I just couldn't wait."

I didn't know the exact state of our finances, but I knew we had little to spare. "Mom, you shouldn't have. You work so hard."

She just held it out closer to me—her smile wide and her eyes bright.

I gently took the package and slowly opened it. Presents were rare and to be cherished. When I lifted the lid, my eyes went wide. Inside, neatly folded on a white piece of cotton, lay two bright yellow silk ribbons with a complex pattern woven into them. But calling them just ribbons was like calling a diamond just another stone. These were *ribownna*—crafted by hand and magic—and very expensive. In the succubus world, these had special meaning—

They were given when someone came of age.

"Mom . . . I . . ." I didn't know what to say. I was afraid to touch them. "They're beautiful."

She smiled, grabbed my hand, and led me to the bathroom, where I watched in the mirror as she carefully fitted them to my horns. I couldn't believe how beautiful they were.

She nodded in satisfaction and patted my arms. "Oh!" she said, remembering. "I have one more thing."

"Mom," I protested. "This is more than enough."

She produced yet another box with the same festive paper. I opened it, wondering what in the world it could be. Inside, I found a beautiful silver necklace with an amulet that wove silver strands around a dark blue gem. And peeking from the stone's center was a tiny speck of gold. Over the years, I had seen it many times and admired its beauty from where it usually hung—

Around my mother's neck.

I glanced up in shock. "Mom, I can't take this. It's yours. Father—"

She put a finger to my lips and shook her head. She reverently lifted it from the box and placed it around my neck. "Not anymore," she said, her voice deep with emotion. "I've been waiting for you to be old enough to have it. I'm sure he would have wanted it this way. He said it would protect me. And now I give it to you to keep you safe."

She touched my cheek gently, joy in her eyes. "*Never forget that I love you, my precious jewel. You make me so proud.*"

Abruptly, the scene changed. I stared about in confusion. We were in my mom's store, and people were screaming around us. The hazy air stank of gunpowder. Behind me, I found an overturned candy display, and beside it, Mom lay on the floor. I tried to fight my way to her, but no matter how hard I fought, I couldn't reach her. I stretched out my arm and called frantically, "Mom!" But she remained still on the tiles, and there was blood—

I jerked awake, gasping for breath, and fought the covers to sit up. For three panicked heartbeats, I looked around with no idea where I was.

The strange room was a sharp contrast to my dream. It was

filled with bright sunshine, coming playfully through a window framed with delicate shamrock green curtains and a white lace fringe. A small stained-glass rainbow dangled from the curtain rod, throwing bits of color across the overly busy flowers-on-cream wallpaper. The decorations were stylish and feminine, although a bit loud—clearly a young woman's room.

On the fourth pounding heartbeat, my overloaded brain finally engaged, and I remembered. I was in Rore's room. I had been asked to stay the night.

Relief flooded me, and I took a shaky breath. Then another, and finally another, until my heart rate settled into something akin to normal. It was that dream again.

I heard a gentle snore from the bed beside me. Rore sprawled face down across her twin bed with one arm hanging off the edge. The previous night, she had danced excitedly at having me sleep in her room. To her, it was like a slumber party. She did apologize for having to put me on a pallet on the floor since she only had the one small bed. But she assured me her mother had put a special softness spell on my blankets so it would be just as comfortable. It must have worked because I was out as soon as my head hit the pillow. I had no complaints. It was far superior to the park bench I had planned.

With the room's door closed and Rore asleep, I reached inside the sleeve of the borrowed sleep shirt and touched my illusion charm. It gave a reassuring vibration, and I breathed a sigh of relief. But a moment later, as it had for the last couple of weeks, it gave a short vibration, pause, and another vibration. *A warning*—its magic was running low.

Seeking further confirmation, I looked down the sleeve of

my oversized shirt and saw only the unblemished skin under my arm. I sighed. As it should, the charm was concealing itself. If it wasn't, I would see a blue, coin-sized symbol resembling an intricate tattoo.

Before Mom died, I didn't give it a thought. I'd had it since I was three, so I took it for granted. It was just *there*. But now, I checked it every morning, hoping it would keep me hidden for just one more day.

I sighed. Mom had started nagging me to let her get it recharged a few weeks after my last birthday. But I had put it off. I knew it was expensive, so I thought I was doing my part to stretch our money. But then Mom died, and suddenly there *was* no money at all.

When I got the first warning, I thought it would be easy since Mom had always managed it. Why couldn't I? All I needed to do was find out who to go to. Surely, I could work a deal to do chores to pay for it. But I quickly got a crash course in how the real world worked.

Any halfway powerful witch could have recharged it. That was how some made a little extra cash during the holidays. But my charm came with a big problem—it was unregistered and not exactly legal. I couldn't just walk into a magic replenishment shop and ask to have it done. I'd be in jail within the hour.

So to get it done, I needed a shady witch—one that could ensure the recharge couldn't be traced to them. As I learned, those were not only expensive—but impossible to find. All of Mom's contacts had died with her.

Terra's offer was a possible solution. For my favor, I could ask her to have it recharged. But why go that route when I could fix the underlying problem? Make it so the illusion charm wasn't even needed—

Because I'd be genuinely human.

"Is everything all right?" Rore asked behind me.

Startled, I wheeled to find her regarding me groggily. I blushed at having been caught. "No," I blurted. "I was just checking on a bruise I got last night."

She sat up, concerned. "Want me to look at it for you? I can do a little healing magic."

I shook my head. "No, it's nothing. But thanks for offering."

Rore gave a mighty stretch. "Don't hesitate to ask if you need something." She froze and sniffed the air.

I hoped it wasn't me she was smelling. It had been hot yesterday, and I did work up a sweat knocking out the ogre. The day's events, the late hour, and all the exertion had caught up with me. I had crashed.

"Bacon," Rore announced. "Mom's fixing bacon. We've got to get there before Orion wakes up."

I thought about her being bullied. "Does he steal your food?"

She looked puzzled at my comment and shook her head. "He wouldn't dream of it." She grinned evilly. "But me? I do it every chance I get." Still in her pajamas, she sprang for the door and was out in a flash.

Maybe I had misjudged who was really the bully.

I didn't want to show up looking like the moocher I actually was. So I rooted around in my suitcase and pulled out a clean top, a pair of shorts, and of course, my toothbrush. As I was putting my stuff back to close the lid, one of my *ribownna* fell out. It made me pause as I remembered my dream. I hadn't worn them since my birthday—there wasn't much point. The illusion charm would hide them as well as my horns. I stuffed it back in my suitcase.

As I went about my shower and eradicating my morning breath, I couldn't help but think about Terra's offer. Having her owe me a favor would be a huge win.

Could I do it? The potential for getting physical worried me a little. I could throw a punch—I did know a little karate from a free after-school program. Plus, being a succubus made me naturally agile and quick. In a fight, I could likely hold my own.

But my bigger concern was potentially going against my clan. If I actively opposed one of them, especially a well-connected vampire, I could earn the disfavor of the local Night-clan elder. I was already in trouble with the one back in Philly. And I'm sure my exit without his permission would not endear me to him.

When we moved to Philly, Mom had kept us under the radar. She never registered us, so the city elder had no idea we were there. But when she died, the coroner had found her illusion charm, and as the law required, notified the elder. Needless to say, he was pissed at the breach of clan law. He understood it wasn't completely my fault, since I was a minor, but he couldn't let the infraction slide either. He decided that since I hid as a human—the humans would have to deal with me. This basically cut off any clan support I might have gotten.

As I stepped out of the shower, I wiped the fog off the mirror and looked at my reflection. A normal human girl stared back—my horns and tail safely hidden. I leaned my head forward and touched my horns to the mirror. The illusion made it appear like my head was hovering a few inches from its surface. They might be invisible, but they were still there. I always had to be careful not to hit something.

I wondered what life would be like not to have them—to be truly human. Putting on T-shirts would be a breeze, and I wouldn't have to worry about my hairstyle, not to mention I could wear a baseball cap without it looking weird. And what about my tail? It was an absolute pain to keep out of the way. I had to either buy pants that were low on my hips or cut a hole for it to fit through. Although, I did wonder if losing it would make it harder to balance myself.

I would also give up my ability to sense and influence emotions. But I didn't think it would be a great loss. I could get in serious trouble if I even slightly abused my powers. Why have them if I can't use them? Then I thought about the *ribownna* Mom had given me. I could never wear them again. Surprisingly, that bothered me more than anything. I looked into my mirrored eyes. But it would not stop me. It seemed a small price to be human.

Did I dare?

I wasn't sure. I had to ask Terra if her favor would extend that far. I prayed it did.

I dressed and headed for the kitchen. I hoped Rore hadn't eaten all the bacon.

As I rounded the corner, I was struck by the emotions I felt emanating from the room. *Happiness. Joy. Love.* Places or things would, over time, absorb the feelings of those living there. They weren't strong, but I could sense them.

Stone and metal mostly just absorbed feelings and returned nothing. But natural things, like wood, would absorb them and gently reflect them back over time. The floors and cupboards, even the studs in the walls, hummed softly with latent emotions. But the antique wooden table sitting in their kitchen practically glowed with happiness. This was a room that the family frequented and constantly filled with laughter. The kitchen of my old home had similar feelings but not nearly as strong. I knew I would like this family immensely.

Rore and her mother, Andromeda Strewert, were leaning in close and talking softly. The conversation abruptly halted when I entered. I didn't detect any hint of malice or guilt, so likely Rore was filling in her mother about me. It was expected. I was the interloper, after all. It's not like I had any secrets. Well, maybe just one big one.

Rore was seated on the long side of the table, her plate having only crumbs and streaks of leftover syrup. She was chewing on her last piece of bacon. Her mother sat to her left at the table's head, sipping from a rather large mug of black coffee. She smiled as I entered and set her coffee down.

I greeted them. "Good morning Rore and Mrs. Strewert," I said, unsure if I was included in breakfast or expected to immediately leave. Last night, Terra had said I was staying here, but not for how long.

Rore's mother held up a hand. "Please call me Andromeda. Mrs. Strewert makes me feel like an old lady."

Rore grinned and took a breath to speak, but her mother cut her off. "Don't say it. I know what you're thinking."

Rore looked at her in mock surprise. "Mother, I would never call you old. Ancient maybe, but never old."

Andromeda rolled her eyes and then turned back to me. With a smile of genuine warmth, she indicated a chair beside her. "Have a seat, dear. I've got your plate in the microwave so a certain ravenous beast wouldn't eat it." She rolled her eyes in Rore's direction.

"Hey," protested Rore. "I am not a beast."

The mother's eyes twinkled. "Oh yes, you are. If I say the magic words, you transform into a hideous monster."

Rore stopped in mid-chew. "I do not."

Andromeda grinned. "But you do. All I have to say is . . ." she raised her hands in imitation of a spell caster and spoke deeply, "Clean your room!"

Rore just blinked at her as she realized she'd been outmaneuvered. The mother smiled in my direction. I couldn't help but chuckle and felt myself relax.

Leaving her stunned daughter, Andromeda went to the microwave, where she pulled out a plate of pancakes with two slices of bacon. She set them in front of me, adding a quick pat on my shoulder. "Here you go, dear."

I stared down at the plate and was suddenly filled with emotion. Mom used to do that same thing. *Said* the exact same. Had done it my whole life. Suddenly my eyes moistened. I blinked furiously, refusing to give in to the emotion. I couldn't let them see my weakness.

I took a deep breath and let it out slowly. "This looks really good. It's been a long time since I've had a good home-cooked breakfast."

I looked up to find Andromeda watching me with motherly concern. She nodded and patted my shoulder again.

Rore grinned. "Mother's an excellent cook. You're going to love her bacon."

It was hard to remain melancholy around Rore. I grinned back. "Well, with that build-up, I had best get to it."

Both mother and daughter watched me with extreme interest as I picked up a piece and took a hefty bite. But I froze in mid-chew.

You know when you take a bite of something expecting a certain taste, only it's completely different from what you were expecting—like taking a sip of what you think is soft drink but discovering it to be orange juice. Or in this case, chomping down on what I thought was a piece of perfectly cooked bacon but found it actually tasted closer to—

Cardboard.

Rore grinned, obviously pleased with herself. "Not bad for vegetarian bacon. Mom does something that makes it taste really good. I think it's made from tofu."

With no way to keep from offending my hosts, I kept my face neutral and resumed chewing. "Hmmm," I said, trying to decide if I would be able to swallow it.

Those of my clan tend toward being meat-eaters and have highly developed tastes in that regard. It's just in our nature. That doesn't mean we eat slabs of raw flesh, but we do enjoy a good steak or hamburger—well done for me and with a side of fries.

But this? I swallowed and wondered how I was going to get out of eating the rest.

I felt someone approaching and looked toward the door. The young man from the previous night, Orion, rounded the corner into the kitchen. I froze, the faux bacon momentarily forgotten.

He was bare-chested, barefoot, and wearing only a pair of

jeans. He was yawning and scratching his dark, sleep-mussed hair, which only added to the appeal of his handsome face.

He was an excellent specimen of maleness without the thick arms and chest of some athletes. Instead, he had well-defined muscles that spoke of practice and discipline, giving his movements a smooth grace. My first thought was dancer, but that didn't fit. It had to be martial arts.

He froze when he saw me. His face remained expressionless, but inside, his emotions swirled. In quick succession, he went through surprise, uncertainty, pleasure—but for some strange reason, settled on angry annoyance.

"What's she doing here?" he demanded. His voice was deep and rich—a dark chocolate cappuccino with extra cream.

I blurted out an answer without thinking. "Your grandmother told me to ask—"

I felt his anger flare brightly. "It's bad enough that my sister watches my every move. Now I've got one of grandmother's lackeys running interference."

I was taken aback by the venom in his voice. "I'm not—"

He cut me off. "I don't believe you! Odd coincidence that you happened to be right there when I went rogue."

With my own anger rising, I slowly stood and locked eyes with him. "Listen, butthead. I was not spying on you."

Giving me one last glare, he turned on his heel and went back the way he had come.

Frowning, Andromeda set her cup down. "Orion Drake Strewert, do not be rude to our guest," she said firmly. "Especially since she helped you last night."

There was no reply.

"Orion!" Andromeda called after him. A moment later, the front door opened and then slammed hard enough to rattle the windows.

She sighed, radiating motherly concern. I got the impression this was a common occurrence.

"What's wrong with his majesty this morning?" asked Rore, chewing on a piece of bacon. I looked at her curiously. I had thought she had eaten all of hers.

I sat back down and sighed. "I'm sorry I made him angry. I was just trying to explain."

Andromeda shook her head sadly. "It's not your fault. He's probably just embarrassed that he lost control."

Rore jumped to his defense. "That bitch Chaleta set him up last night."

Andromeda glanced at her daughter. "No B-word at the table." She took a sip of her coffee. "I thought they weren't dating anymore."

"They're not. She broke it off. Unfortunately, Orion's heart hasn't figured that out yet. He saw her last night, and she was making out with some new guy."

I reached for the syrup and then noticed my bacon was gone. *Oh.* That's where Rore got it from. I glanced her way.

She leaned toward me, grinning. "Snooze, you lose," she said brightly, popping the last of the piece into her mouth.

I thanked the Protector. Now I didn't have to eat it.

"Aurorah Constance Strewert," Andromeda scolded in that voice only mothers possess. "*Do not* steal your guest's food."

Rore made a face. "There's more in the oven."

"That's Orion's."

"Why? He's gone to Skiff's. Besides, he doesn't even like it."

Andromeda gave her daughter a confused look. "But I buy it for him. He's the one that's a vegetarian."

"It's fine," I interjected. "The pancakes are all I need."

I took a bite of them, and they practically melted in my mouth, vanquishing the remaining fake bacon taste.

Andromeda leaned forward on her elbows with her cup cradled in her hands. I didn't need my powers to know it was motherly-concern time. "So, Lapis. Have you called your relatives to let them know you're here? I didn't see you with a phone, but I'm sure Rore would let you use hers for a quick call or text. They must be worried about you."

I figured this was coming. She's probing to see if I'm a runaway. And in a sense, I guess I was.

I set my fork down, trying to figure out how much I should reveal. Terra had been unfazed by my situation, but I wasn't sure about Andromeda. What worried me was the concern she was radiating. She might contact the police for my own good. That was the last thing I needed.

I gave my head a gentle shake, deciding the truth was best. Or at least most of it.

"I have no one to call," I said. "Father died before I was born, and Mom was killed a few months ago."

Andromeda's hand shot out to cover mine. "I'm so sorry," she said. "I didn't mean any disrespect." She gave my hand a squeeze. "So there's no one?"

"Not that I know of." I sighed. "But I just learned my maternal grandfather might live in this city. It's why I'm here."

Her shoulders sagged. "You've never met him?"

I shook my head. "He and Mom had a falling out before I was

born. But I found an address in Mom's things." I didn't mention that her note had been rather cryptic.

She sipped her coffee, giving herself time to think. After a moment, she seemed to come to a decision. "You're welcome to stay with us until you get on your feet. You helped both of my children." Her smile faded, and I felt her irritation flare—but it was an old, well-practiced feeling. I didn't think it was directed at me. She took a slow sip of her coffee. "For some reason, my mother has taken an interest in you and asked to let you stay. She refused to tell me why, only that you were in a difficult spot." She set her coffee down. "I certainly want to help, so I've agreed."

I felt a hardness grow inside of her. She looked at me levelly, and her eyes locked with mine. "Mother warned me not to probe into your current situation. It makes me a little uncomfortable to be caught up in her affairs. So I have to ask that you do not bring any danger to my family." I could swear her eyes flashed with power. "Because there is *nothing* more important to me."

Like mother, like daughter. I had heard that before.

Andromeda smiled, suddenly back to a sweet mother persona. She took another sip from her cup. "You will be our guest. Nothing else and no favors owed. Is that all right?" Andromeda stood and leaned across to give me a hug.

I nodded. Her maternal feelings were strong, but there was no malice. She had simply stated her feelings. And I could respect that. It reminded me of Mom. She would have taken on a bear to protect me, and I had no doubt that Andromeda would do the same.

"Thank you for letting me stay," I said. "I am honored."

She sat back down. "Good. Now, what's your grandfather's address? We might be able to take you there this afternoon."

I winced. "I don't have an exact address. All I have is an old picture."

Andromeda's expression grew pained. "Oh, Lapis. How long ago was it?"

"Mom was just a baby."

She tried to hide her grimace. "Do you have it with you?" I could feel her concern and disappointment. I knew finding him would be hard, but I didn't think it would be impossible. She was making me think otherwise.

I went to my suitcase and brought back the picture that had started my journey. It was one of those instant snaps that were popular about forty years ago. It wasn't even all that great of a photo—faded, grainy, and slightly off-color. It showed a man of about thirty, holding a one-year-old in a pink dress and white tights. Beside him stood a woman in a yellow sundress with shoulder-length blonde hair. She had her arm around his waist and her head on his shoulder. A small, white cape cod-style home was behind them. It couldn't have been more than two bedrooms. All were human in appearance, but I suspected they were merely in disguise, similar to what I was now.

"Look on the back," I said.

Andromeda flipped it over and read it. Rore leaned over to look with her. I knew exactly what it said. *Jasper holding his daughter Eiheth at our new Byan Street house in Renweard City.*

I leaned forward. "My mother's name was Eiheth, so those had to be my grandparents."

"But Lapis," she protested, "that had to be over forty years ago. Do you have any other clues?"

I shook my head. "I had asked several times about our extended family, but Mom didn't tell me much. Grandmother died in a car accident when Mom was ten. After that, it was only Grandfather. She thought he still lived in her childhood home." I looked down at my plate. "When I asked why we didn't visit or talk, she only said he had disowned her. They had a heated argument and had parted ways." I shrugged. "She wouldn't tell me anything more."

Rore had been watching the exchange with large eyes. She suddenly snatched the picture from her mother and looked at it closely. "In the back is part of the house number."

I nodded. "Yeah, but they're just shadows. You can't read them."

Rore grinned. "I know someone who can enhance the picture." She grabbed my hand. "Skiff can do it. The guy's a freaking genius."

Just then, Andromeda's phone chimed. She reached behind her and pulled it from her back pocket. She sighed. "I'd hoped we'd have a little more time."

"What?" Rore asked.

Andromeda looked at me. "Lapis, my mother's limo is outside." She set her phone down. "She wants to talk with you again."

And I knew exactly what she wanted.

Chapter 6

MAC DIDN'T SEEM surprised when I asked to sit up front with him in the limo. He quickly responded with a "No problem, miss" and opened the door for me. I secretly hoped to ask a few questions about Terra before our meeting. But my attempts at conversation fizzled with his practiced "Yes, miss" and "No, miss" answers. I only got a different response when I asked if he was a werewolf. "Privileged information, miss," was all he said—although one corner of his mouth curled up.

Being a Saturday, I had expected Mac to drive to Terra's home in some lush suburban neighborhood. But to my surprise, he took us downtown and turned into the parking garage of a tall office building. It was completely empty, with not a car in sight. Mac pulled into a reserved space near the elevators and jumped to open my door.

"Is the elder working today?" I asked as I got out.

Mac didn't answer at first. He shut the limo's door behind me with a solid thud that echoed loudly through the empty garage. "Elder Strewert's office is part of her apartment." I detected a flash of concern, but he quickly controlled it. "She's always working."

He offered no more and turned away, leaving me to follow.

Mac stepped to an elevator separate from the rest and placed his hand on a small glass plate. It wasn't until it glowed a soft green that I recognized it as a magi-sig reader. I had only seen those on crime shows. They were supposedly more accurate than a retinal scan and worked off a person's magic signature. Even a doppelganger couldn't get past them.

The elevator took us directly to the top floor, and we stepped out into a lushly decorated entrance with a receptionist desk to one side. It was unattended today.

With a "This way, miss", Mac led me into a huge corner office complete with a conference table, sofa, sink, and a coffee maker that looked like it came off a spaceship. The wall to the right of the entrance was painted with a huge embellished version of the Twilight-clan's logo—the setting sun and evening star. Under it was a long display case holding oddly shaped rocks on black velvet. Its placement seemed a little odd, like it was an afterthought or a recent addition.

But what drew my eye was the floor-to-ceiling windows across the corner walls. They gave a sweeping view of the city and the river that cut through it. I'm sure the office was designed to intimidate those meeting with the elder. And in my case, it was damn well working.

Terra sat in a white leather chair behind a dark mahogany desk. With reading glasses perched on the end of her nose and a finger across her lips, she scowled at the paper she was reading. Today, she wore a plain lavender blouse and a dark purple business suit, which contrasted nicely with the white leather. Even at rest, she exuded confidence and authority.

When I entered, she smiled brightly and took off her glasses. "Good morning, Miss Midnyte. Please have a seat. I hope you slept well at my daughter's house."

She still had her defensive shield up, so I couldn't read her emotions. Cautious woman. I nervously took a seat on the plush sofa across from her. Unlike hers, mine was solid black. I wondered if she was trying to make a statement.

"Good morning, Elder Strewert." I nodded in greeting. "I did sleep well. Your family was very welcoming."

Behind me, I heard the door click softly closed, and glancing over my shoulder, I saw that Mac had stepped outside. Terra and I were completely alone.

Terra smiled. She touched the single earring in her ear—the same stud piece she had worn the night before. Its bright green emerald seemed to oddly clash with her outfit. Maybe it had some significance to her position.

"So, Miss Midnyte. Have you considered my offer?"

Under her steady gaze, I fidgeted. "I . . . I'd be a fool to say it wasn't intriguing."

She folded her hands and rested them on the desk. I noticed her eyes flick to the silver chain around my neck. The amulet was safely tucked into my shirt, but its chain was again plainly visible. I wondered what she found so interesting about it.

She gave me a knowing smile. "Do you have any concerns?"

I shifted nervously in my seat. "I'm not sure I'll be able to do what you want. Orion took one look at me this morning and stormed out of the house."

She chuckled. "That's my grandson, all right. He will come around."

I shook my head. "I don't think so. He basically blew me off as your spy."

She nodded thoughtfully. "Smart lad. But that doesn't change what I would like you to do. And I'm sure a girl of your talents can fix that."

My eyes narrowed. "I refuse to use my powers that way."

She shrugged. "Then don't. I'm not asking you to do something immoral. All I'm asking is for you to stay close and keep Orion out of trouble. Especially from those in Night-clan."

I stared at her for a moment—I had one last question and I was afraid to ask it. Yet, I was more afraid if I didn't.

I licked my lips. "Can I ask something about the favor without it offending you? I've had limited experience with Twilight-clan, and I don't want to make the wrong assumption. The last thing I want is to anger another elder."

She raised an eyebrow, a corner of her mouth curling up. "I agree. Having one elder pissed off, even if it is in another state, is quite enough."

I glanced out the window behind her. This was it. The million-dollar question. I took a deep breath. "I've heard that for my favor, I can choose anything within reason."

She nodded and made air quotes. "*Within reason* is the key phrase. It has to be within my powers or a favor I can call in."

I sat there motionless, unsure of what to do. I needed to ask the question, but I was afraid of what the answer might be. After several heartbeats, I wet my dry lips and just asked. "There is an experimental procedure being done in California. It takes a magical and turns them into a human." I licked my lips. "Can the favor open the door to get me on that trial list?"

She frowned. "I've heard of those experiments." She shifted in her seat. "But a human?"

I nodded. "It's not so bad living as one. At least, it's not the bottom of the barrel like me."

Terra's expression softened to sadness. "You don't want to be a succubus?"

I shook my head. "I've been disguised as a human most of my life. I've seen what it's like on the other side." I looked away. "And how the rest of the world views my kind."

Terra frowned and crossed her arms. For the first time since I met her, she was at a loss for words. "I . . . I don't know what to say. I can't imagine wanting to cut out a part of oneself just because you don't like it." She sighed. "I've also heard the procedure is painful and carries some risks."

I leaned forward. "I don't care. I'd give anything to be something other than a succubus. It's my life's dream."

Terra considered me. She sighed sadly in resignation. "I know the elders of that state. Most of them owe me, so I should be able to get you in front of the right people. But, while I have heard they are having trouble getting volunteers, I can't guarantee you'll be accepted."

I smiled. "That's all I would ask. I'm sure I could convince them I'm an excellent candidate."

She sat back and regarded me with disappointment. "If that is what you want, I can grant it."

This was it. The opening I'd been praying for.

"I'll do it. I'll watch Orion for you."

Terra stood and came around to my side of the desk. She wore a troubled expression. She sat on the sofa next to me and took my hands in hers. I was surprised at their warmth and her gentle touch. "I do want you to watch over my grandson, and I will keep my end of the bargain, but I hope you reconsider what you asked for. I was hoping you would want to attend the local university. We have a close relationship with them. Your grades were good, and your teachers spoke well of you. So getting you in would just be a phone call." She gave a weak smile. "We even have a couple of succubi enrolled."

I shook my head. "I'm sure this is what I want. Having the procedure will set me up for life. I won't have to hide anymore."

She glanced at the chain of my necklace and nodded sadly. "I understand."

I couldn't help but blurt out one more question. "Are you going to tell them . . .?" My voice caught. "What I am?"

Terra gave a slight shake of her head. "Don't worry, Miss Midnyte. Telling them defeats my purpose. Your secret is safe with me." She smiled sadly. "I'm good at keeping secrets."

I sagged in relief. I certainly didn't plan on telling them.

Terra stood and moved toward the door. "I need to get the paperwork. This will finalize our agreement. You're not yet in your majority, so you can't legally commit to anything, but this will help make sure there is no misunderstanding later."

I nodded. She stepped out of the room, leaving the door open. I heard her softly speaking with Mac.

I glanced behind me to ensure they couldn't see me through the door and then leaped up in excitement, pumping my fists into the air. *I was going to be human!* I couldn't believe it. This was like all the holidays rolled into one. I paced the floor, too excited to sit. I wandered over to the display case by the wall and peeked in at its contents.

The objects inside were a strange collection. What I had taken for rocks were actually fossils and pieces of old bones. Under each was a card written in Latin, which I assumed gave the species name. But what was really unusual was a bracelet of what looked like black and silver metal. It seemed out of place and had no identifying card.

I jumped when Terra spoke right behind me. "They're dragon bones."

Startled, I wheeled to find her smiling at me.

"Dragon?" I asked. I thought she was referring to the jewelry but quickly realized she was talking about the fossils.

She nodded. "They're extremely rare."

I looked back at them. "In school, they taught us they died out with the rest of the dinosaurs."

She shook her head. "While according to the fossil record, most of them did die at that time, a few survived. They're the basis for all our myths and legends."

I smiled, thinking she was teasing me. "Did they run out of maidens or something?"

But Terra frowned, dead serious. "No," she said. "They were *hunted* to extinction."

I frowned in puzzlement. "That's not what they told us in

school. They died out millions of years ago because of an aster-oid's impact. People might not be around if it wasn't for that."

She sighed. "Until recently, that's what they believed. But new magical isotope analysis of those bones proves a few were alive as recently as a thousand years ago."

I frowned skeptically. "A discovery like that would have been in the news."

She glanced at me. "It's coming. The academic paper was just submitted for publication." She grinned and winked. "Thanks to a generous grant from the Twilight-clan." Her expression turned serious, and she looked back at the case. "From the analysis, we know they were extremely long-lived with skin and scales immune to magic and too tough for weapons." She leaned close, as if sharing a secret. "We were even able to confirm the legends." She paused dramatically. "They really did breathe fire. Of course, it was due to their extremely high body temperature."

I shook my head. "Then how could they have been hunted to extinction? Especially a thousand years ago."

She sighed sadly. "Poison."

"Why?" I asked in disbelief. "Why kill them all?"

She looked at me levelly. "For their bones and hides. Since they were impervious to magic, they were extremely valuable. For a shield of dragon hide, a king would give half his lands." She smiled. "Or his maiden daughter."

I digested the information. "So if the hides were so valuable, why aren't any left? Seems like they would have done something to preserve them."

Terra sighed. "They did try, but the dragon parts were fragile and easily degraded. Plus, their magic immunity made preservation spells out of the question. Eventually, the dragon parts just succumbed to natural decay. The fossils in this case are all that are left of those once powerful creatures."

I couldn't help but stare at them in awe.

Terra leaned closer. "You know, there was an ancient legend about the dragons."

I snorted. Everyone knew that legend. "You mean the one where only those with a pure heart could ride one?"

She nodded. "But there is more." She leaned closer as if she was about to share a juicy secret. "It also says that if you can kiss a dragon," she whispered, "you are a *true* hero."

"A hero?" I asked in confusion. "Surely, no one was foolish enough to try it. I thought those things were hot enough to melt steel?"

Terra shrugged. "There's no record of anyone trying." One side of her mouth curled up. "But if they did, it must have been one hot kiss."

There was laughter in her eyes. Then it hit me—she was messing with me. I felt almost honored that she would try to relieve my tension by teasing me. I turned back to the case to hide my smile. Maybe she didn't hate me after all.

I pointed to the remaining object in the case. "And what about the bracelet? Is it made from dragon bone, too?"

Her smile faded. She reached up to touch her emerald earring. "That question, Miss Midnyte, is for another day."

Mac chose that moment to enter with the contract. Terra went over it with me, and I found nothing wrong. So I signed it. I was so excited that my hand shook. *I was going to be human.*

"Oh," Terra said as she handed the paper to Mac. "One last

instruction. You are only to observe and report. If there is any trouble, call or come by immediately, no matter what the hour." Her eyes narrowed. "*Do not* try to handle it yourself. Am I clear on this?"

"Yes, mam." I nodded. I couldn't agree more. I didn't want to get killed.

"Good. If you ever need refuge, come here." She nodded toward the door. "I live on the other side of this floor and don't go out much anymore. I will usually be here."

She returned to her chair and picked up her mobile phone. "What's your number?"

I grimaced. "I—I don't have one. When Mom died, our plan was canceled, and I had to turn in my phone."

Terra set hers down. "This will not do. I'll need you to report in at least twice a day. Besides . . ." She sat back and grinned. "We can't have a teenager without a phone."

So Mac drove us to the phone store. The store clerks recognized Terra and fell over themselves helping us. She bought me my dream phone with more features than I could ever use. When I saw the amount, I tried to put it back, but Terra insisted.

While we were looking, Mac disappeared for a few minutes but quickly returned and met us back at the car. Before opening the door, he handed me an envelope.

At Terra's urging, I opened it to find a gift card to a large upscale retailer. It was more than I had ever seen.

"Tell Rore to take you shopping." She looked down at my worn sneakers. "I suggest new shoes, at least."

I was overwhelmed. "I can't take all this. I can never pay you back."

She smiled. "Then consider it an advance on your allowance. Since I'm sponsoring you now, I'll give you a small monthly stipend, at least until you find your grandfather. After that, we'll see what happens."

I bowed formally to her. "Thank you Elder. Your kindness is truly appreciated."

Terra touched my shoulder, indicating I should rise. "Just keep my grandson safe, as well as yourself. That's all I ask. I just worry it will be more difficult than either of us thinks."

But I didn't think so. I was on top of the world.

How hard could this be?

Chapter 7

"WAIT! SHOULDN'T we call first?" I protested.

Rore was practically dragging me down the street toward her friend Skiff's house. She claimed it was only a few blocks away, but we had been walking for at least fifteen minutes. I think her definition of a block was a little different from mine.

Mac had returned me to the Strewert house in a daze, so it was easy for Rore to grab me at the door and immediately pull me down the street. She thought Skiff could help us enhance the picture of my grandfather. And Rore, being Rore, wanted to get it done *now*.

"Are you sure it will be all right?" I asked. I actually wasn't that concerned about her friend, but she had mentioned that

Orion was still there. The last thing I needed was to make him even angrier and have him run off again. I needed to approach this delicately and, at least for now, watch him from a distance. Although, it would be much easier to keep an eye on him if he could tolerate being in the same room as me.

Rore stayed focused on her destination. "Skiff won't care. He likes challenges."

Through her hand's grasp of mine, I could feel her determination and concern. She was going to help me whether I wanted her to or not.

"But isn't that where your brother is? He might not like—"

She cut me off and jerked me to face her. "He's the one with the problem. You saved both his butt and mine last night. So Mister Hardass can get over himself." We resumed walking. "He's really not a bad guy. He just doesn't know how to react when a cute girl kicks his butt."

I stared at her in confusion. "Who did that?"

She rolled her eyes. "Lapis, really?"

It took a moment for the implication to sink in. "Me?" I shook my head. "No way."

She nodded. "It's you." She grinned. "And you *did* kick his butt."

After another block, she pulled me up the walkway of a house a little larger than the others. Lively piano music drifted from inside. It sounded like a classical piece, but I wasn't sure.

Rore ignored the doorbell and knocked with a special two knocks, a pause, and two more knocks. The music immediately halted.

She turned to me. "At least he's not still playing the sad ones."

I couldn't help but ask. "Has he been feeling down?"

She nodded, but her expression turned troubled. "We were going together until last month." She turned back toward the door. "But I broke it off." She sighed heavily. "It's for his own good."

I wanted to ask more, but the door opened. A tall, lanky young man, wearing a black T-shirt with a picture of Ludwig van Beethoven, stood in the doorway. His brown hair looked like he hadn't combed it since awakening. He had deep green eyes which immediately locked on Rore. He smiled cautiously, radiating the feeling of subdued delight.

"Hi," he said. "You didn't have to knock."

"I thought I should since we're not . . ." She looked down. "You know."

He huffed in irritation. "You said we would still be friends." I could feel his disappointment.

"We are," she blurted out. "It's just . . . I have a friend with me, and his Grumpiness is mad at her."

Skiff nodded knowingly and glanced at me in sympathy. "I've heard all about it." His eyes flicked nervously back to Rore. "He's in the back doing his meditation thing while I practice. I don't think you should approach him just yet."

"Actually, we're here to see you." She hit him with a kilowatt smile. "We need your help."

"Me?" He shifted nervously. While his face was neutral, his emotions lit up. I think he still liked her—a lot.

She pointed with her thumb over her shoulder. "I was hoping you could help my friend enhance a picture. She's trying to find her grandfather."

His smile faltered, and his eyes slid to me.

I smiled politely and raised my hand. "Hi, I'm Lapis."

His eyes snapped back to Rore, suspicion creeping into his expression. "So you're going to use me now?" There was a hint of anger and disappointment in his voice. He turned and strode away but left the door open.

Rore sighed. She stepped inside, pulling me along behind.

The room was large and open, with a baby grand piano to one side. With his back to us, Skiff slid onto the instrument's bench and started playing another classical melody—a slower and more somber one. *Was that Moonlight Sonata?*

She stepped up behind him and put her hands on his shoulders. "Please don't be angry," she said. "I'm not using you. It's just that this is going to be difficult, and you're an absolute genius when it comes to things like this."

I couldn't see his face, but I felt his emotions spike. I think he was blushing. As he played, I could feel his anger slipping away, her touch making it impossible to maintain.

"I'm not sure I should," he said without interrupting his playing.

She gently squeezed his shoulders. "Please. She really helped us last night. I sort of owe her."

He stopped playing with his fingers hovering above the keyboard. I could feel his longing and sadness. But then there was a sudden spike in his emotions. Feelings of hope.

He turned toward her with an evil grin. "If I'm going to do you a favor, you have to do me one."

A slow grin spread across her face. "What would you want?"

"Lunch."

She considered for a moment. "You buying?"

His grin broadened. "Gentlemen always do."

"You're a gentleman now?"

"Only around a pretty lady."

"You're the only one that thinks so."

"I'm the only one that matters."

"Pizza. I get to pick toppings."

"Deal." He looked very pleased with himself.

I was amazed at their exchange. They acted more like an old married couple than two exes.

She gazed into his eyes a moment longer and then patted him on the shoulder. She turned to me and headed for the stairs. "Come on, Lapis," she called over her shoulder. "Let's watch a master at work." I could feel pride rolling off her. She wasn't flattering him—she believed every single word.

As I followed her, Skiff pounced on the piano and played a few bars of a bright tune before following us. I couldn't help but wonder what was up with this couple. They seemed to care for each other, yet there was an invisible elephant in the room. I wondered what it was.

At the end of the hall, we entered a bedroom that was something out of a science fiction movie. It was reasonably clean with a bed, desk, and gaming chair, but the semblance ended there. Tools and bits of partially assembled gadgets lay on every horizontal surface except his bed. And on that one, the covers were rolled into a ball in its center.

Rore didn't even blink but went right in and plopped down on the edge of the bed. Skiff bounded in a moment later, and she held out the picture to him. "We need to see the numbers on the house."

He sat beside her and took the picture. She leaned close and pointed out the house. "See."

He blushed and swallowed. His pleasure at having her

invade his personal space was rolling off him. I thought even a mundane could feel it.

"I don't know," he said after a moment. "It's awfully blurry."

She smiled up at him. "If anyone can do it, I know you can."

I felt his determination rise. He went to his desk and cleared away some equipment to get to a scanner. While he was occupied, she grinned back at me. "*I.. told... you...*" she mouthed.

All I could do was nod. She turned back to him to offer further encouragement.

I felt bad about her using him, especially since it was for my benefit. But as I watched them interact, it was easy to tell they enjoyed working together.

I glanced at the open laptop on his desk. What I assumed was a screen saver came up—a simple pair of cartoon eyes with a mouth under it. It seemed to be looking at me.

Skiff positioned his picture on the scanner. "Datiel," he called. "Please, scan this picture."

The eyes moved in Skiff's direction. "All righty," came a bright response from the speakers. "What resolution should I use?"

"Maximum," Skiff responded.

"On it," he replied. I heard the scanner start, but the laptop's eyes flicked back to me.

I stepped closer to the couple to see what was going on. To my surprise, the eyes followed me. I knew it was just a cartoon, but it was a little unnerving.

"How is that screen saver following me?" I asked.

Skiff glanced my way. "That's not a program." He went back to adjusting settings and acting like his explanation should be sufficient.

"Is it like one of those personal assistant things?"

Skiff didn't look up. "Nope. Better."

"Scan complete!" came Datiel's chipper reply. The picture frowned and looked in Skiff's direction. "The quality of the photo sucks. I suggest you scan it again and use your special filter. Then I can compare the two."

"Give me a minute." Skiff rearranged the picture and closed the lid. Then he put his hand on the cover and began to rub it in a slow circle. To my utter surprise, I felt magic gathering. He must be a mage from Shadow-clan—the ones who make magic by action and are masters of all things made.

It suddenly clicked. Mages frequently had familiars, or creatures that helped with their magic. In return for the help, the little beings got to feast on the mage's excess. And the favorite familiar of a mage was—

"He's a gremlin," I exclaimed.

Skiff nodded distractedly.

The mouth on the screen spread into a wide smile.

Gremlins were strange creatures. They had no physical form but instead lived in made things—the more complex, the better. Computers were ideal, with airplanes a close second. Technically, they were Night-clan since they got their magic from others, but they typically hung out with mages because they liked machines.

Skiff's magic reached its peak. "Now, Datiel."

"Working!" came the chipper reply, then a few seconds later. "Got it!"

The face left the screen and was replaced by two copies of the picture. Skiff sat down at the keyboard and began to type. Rore watched over him with pride.

With nothing to do, I stepped over to the window and nudged the sheer curtain aside. It overlooked the backyard with a small patio directly below. The surrounding yard was meticulously landscaped with various plants around it. They looked well cared for, and I imagined they had been quite the sight when they flowered earlier in the year.

In a corner sat Orion with eyes closed, legs crossed, and hands palm-up on his knees. Once again, I couldn't help but notice how handsome he was. Likely because I had interacted with him the previous evening, I could faintly feel his emotions. Usually, I had to be much closer to distinguish someone from the din of people around me. But his were easy to pick out—confusion, disappointment, anger. They were fighting within him so strongly it felt off balance. I wondered what had made him that way.

My hand reached toward the window. I ached to take his frustration and turn it into calm. It would be so easy. But instead, I curled my hand into a fist, clenching it tightly. To do so might reveal what I was. Mom had cautioned me since coming into my powers not to mess with people's emotions—regardless of the intent. The only exception was self-defense.

As I watched, trying to understand my infatuation with him, he suddenly opened his eyes and looked up at the window. For the barest second, our eyes met—and he recognized me.

I immediately dropped the curtain.

"Ah ha!" exclaimed Rore behind me. She gave a clap in delight. "I told you, you're an absolute genius."

I turned to see Skiff blush, most pleased with the praise. "You got the first three numbers, and we can tell there are one or possibly two more digits. That should at least get her in the right neighborhood."

She reached across him and pressed a few keys on the keyboard, putting her face mere inches from his. Her attention was focused on the keyboard, so she didn't notice his blush. He gazed at her lovingly, like he wanted to memorize every curve of her face. A printer started up on a shelf, and he looked away, the moment broken.

Rore practically danced in front of the printer until it finally shot out the picture. I don't know where this girl got her energy from, but she had enough to light the country.

Smiling proudly, she held it out to me. It was a close-up of the house, and I could barely make out the vertically spaced letters—Nine, nine, two. And the hint of another behind my infant mother's head.

I bowed to Skiff. "Thank you. I will remember this."

His eyes went wide at the formal acknowledgment of a favor owed. "You're welcome. It wasn't anything much. You don't owe me anything."

"Maybe nothing for you. But for me, it is everything."

Behind me, I felt a presence at the room's door, and I knew exactly who it was from the emotions they projected.

"What are you doing here?" demanded Orion. His voice was deep and commanding. I wondered what it sounded like when he wasn't angry.

I turned and locked eyes with him. His fury was deep, dark—and directed at me.

In reply, I felt my own anger rise. I had done nothing to earn this—and I'd had enough of his attitude.

I stared right back at him defiantly. "What am I doing?" I spat. "I'm searching for my grandfather. Skiff was nice enough to help me. You got a problem with that?"

My outburst surprised him, and he was suddenly unsure of himself. "No," he said, glancing at Rore and Skiff but finding no support there.

I glared at him. "Did you think I was following you? That the poor human girl was taking pleasure in your torment. Sorry, but that's not happening. I've got more important things to worry about than to mess with you. So just get over yourself."

A worried Rore reached for me. "Lapis, don't . . ."

But I stepped closer to Orion and realized he was a few inches taller than me. "Why are you so angry at me? I haven't done anything to you. If I have, please let me know, and I'll apologize. But, if it's about keeping you from hurting your sister, bring it on. I'll never let you hurt her." I glared at him. "*Never.*"

He blinked in surprise. "I didn't want to hurt her."

"Good. Because I kind of like her. I hope I can be her friend. She grows on you after a while. And if you get your head out of your butt, we might be friends too." I paused and took a deep breath. "Now, let's try this again." I held out my hand and plastered on a smile. "My name is Lapis Midnyte, and I'm from out of town. Rore is helping me search for my grandfather."

He looked down at my hand, unsure of himself, but gently extended his own and enveloped my small hand in his larger one. As soon as we touched, his emotions flooded me. They were strong—more so than any person I had ever encountered. I thought last night was a fluke, but it wasn't. We seemed to have a resonance, and I could feel everything. Anger. Embarrassment. Admiration—

Admiration? Where was that coming from?

He dropped his hand and looked away, cutting off the rich flow of emotions. I strangely missed the contact.

Rore, satisfied we weren't going to kill each other, turned to Skiff. "Can you bring up a map of the city? Maybe we can figure out the general location of the house."

Skiff turned back to his laptop. "Datel, you heard the lady."

A map of the city leaped to the screen and then zoomed in to focus on Byan Street. Skiff hit a few more keys, and ranges of house numbers appeared. I excitedly read through them. *I was going to meet my grandfather.*

Skiff frowned and shook his head. "Where's the rest of them?" He put a finger on Byan Street and traced along its path. "The numbers don't go high enough. The street ends at Edgemont Park. That range of house numbers doesn't exist." He looked at me sadly. "It's as if the street just ends."

Chapter 8

DEJECTEDLY, RORE and I walked back toward her house. Orion and Skiff trailed a few paces behind, talking about some upcoming baseball game.

I still couldn't believe it. I'd traveled all this way for nothing. No house number on that street matched the one in the picture. Mom's clue didn't work, and I was at a dead end. I didn't know what I was going to do next. And especially about recharging my charm.

Rore put a hand on my arm. I could easily sense her sadness and her strong desire to help. "We'll find him. He's got to be out there somewhere. We'll just have to think of something else."

I nodded distractedly.

Rore grinned mischievously. She turned and started walking backward so that she was facing me. "I know what will cheer you up."

There was something about Rore that lifted my heart. "And what is that?"

"Pizza."

I blinked at her. "Pizza?"

"Yes! It's a natural antidepressant. Not only that, it stimulates creativity." She faced forward again and looked over her shoulder. "Skiff, what say we have our lunch today? But Lapis has to come too."

Skiff perked up, clearly thrilled at the prospect. "You're on."

He turned to Orion. "You want to come?"

Orion's eyes moved cautiously in my direction. He shrugged.

Rore's eyes gleamed. "Great! Since Lapis is feeling down, we can all—"

Skiff interrupted. "Damn. I didn't bring money. We'll have to go back." He grinned. "Then we could take my car."

Orion and Rore grimaced. I wondered if it was because of his driving or the vehicle itself.

It didn't matter though. I had a gift card but no money, so I had better sit this one out.

"If it's all right," I said. "I think I'll pass. I've got to watch my money."

"I'll pay for everyone," Orion interjected. His eyes flicked again in my direction. "I haven't had breakfast anyway." Then he turned to Rore, his expression flat. "Skiff can take you another time. But I pick the toppings. No bacon. Veg all the way."

Rore put her hands on her hips and stuck out her bottom lip, the epitome of a spoiled child. "But Ri-ri," she whined. "I can't stand fungi. Mushrooms are uck! Please, no."

The corner of Orion's mouth curled up ever so slightly. "Not gonna happen."

She looked away dejectedly. "I must be losing my touch."

I couldn't help but smile. Maybe there was something about pizza that lifted one's heart.

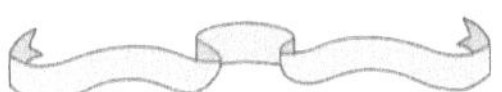

We walked a few blocks to a busy shopping center. In one corner sat a brightly decorated restaurant that left no doubt it served Italian and, more importantly, pizza.

It being just after midday on a Saturday, it was busy. Rore greeted the hostess brightly. "Hello, Tracilyn."

She was a skinny blonde about our age. But the young woman didn't return the warmth and instead gave us a cool, perfunctory welcome. I easily sensed that her feelings were a swirl of disgust, anxiety, and something else which didn't feel exactly right. Her emotional balance seemed off. I couldn't put my finger on what it was. Rore tried to hide her disappointment as Tracilyn grabbed a couple of menus and led us to a table in the back corner.

Rore took the seat against the wall, while I sat beside her. Skiff grabbed the chair across from Rore before Orion could, leaving one remaining seat across from me. Orion hesitated just the barest second before sitting.

Our server rushed over, a smiling middle-aged woman with a pad ready. I thought she was human. "Which one's ordering today?"

Orion didn't miss a beat. "Me," he stated flatly, glancing at his sister while daring her to say otherwise.

The waitress nodded. "The usual? Extra cheese, onions, and mushrooms?"

Rore leaned over, putting on her puppy dog face. "Please, big brother. No mushrooms. The fungi freak me out."

Orion got the most deliciously wicked grin. I liked it when he smiled. "Well, if you insist." He looked at our server. "Extra mushrooms today."

Rore groaned and dropped her head. Our server made a few scribbles on the pad.

Orion leaned forward. "As you tell me, just pick them off."

"Yeah, but pepperoni is so much easier to pick off than tiny pieces of fungi."

"What would you like to drink, honey?" our server asked.

It took a moment to realize she was talking to me. I would have loved to have a soda, but I wasn't paying. So I thought I should play it safe. "Just water."

She made another scribble on the pad. "Same as mushroom kid," she noted dryly.

She gave one last nod and then was off before you could blink an eye.

"You had to do extra mushrooms," Rore complained. "I might start to think you don't like me."

"I like you," Skiff immediately volunteered. He blushed and looked down.

Rore didn't even bat an eye. She quickly took his hand and covered for him.

"Thank you Skiff. I'm glad there is at least one gentleman at this table."

He smiled timidly.

Orion continued to grin until he glanced at me. And then his expression faltered. He turned to Skiff and asked about that ball game again.

When our drinks came, I turned to Rore. I couldn't help but ask. "What's up with the hostess?" I nodded toward the front of the restaurant. There had been a pause in entering customers, and she had stepped to the side, where she was typing rapidly on her phone. She glanced in our direction and typed some more. "She got something against you?"

Rore took a sip of her drink. "We used to be friends. But she's one of Chaleta's gang now."

"Is that the one—"

I broke off as Rore kicked me under the table. I guess I got my answer.

"It's all right, Rore." Orion held up a hand. "I'm under control now. She just got under my skin last night."

Rore gave a heavy sigh. "I talked with Mom. She's worried it's more than just that."

He shrugged. "Shifters sometimes have trouble with their emotions. I just thank the Protector that I'm not a werewolf. I'll take having to control my emotions anytime over being locked to the phases of the moon. At least I have some control." He looked at her levelly. "You witches have it so easy." He looked at me. "And you humans too."

I wondered what he would think if he knew I was something entirely different.

Rore ran a finger around the top of her glass. "Last night was unusual. Mom thinks there might have been a trigger other than Chaleta."

Orion leaned back. "It was just a bad night."

Rore opened her mouth to say something but paused. I followed her gaze to the front of the restaurant, where a young woman about our age had just entered. She was model beautiful, with long dark hair and pale smooth skin, not to mention a feminine shape that was beyond most mortals. Her dark knee-length skirt and scarlet silk blouse enhanced her every curve.

I watched her warily as she smiled at the hostess and said something that was too far away to hear. She was the same young woman I had seen getting out of the limo last night. And accompanying her was the same young man.

He wore no tux today, just a black sports jacket and a white shirt. He whipped off his sunglasses and smiled confidently at the hostess, leaning casually on her podium. I had to admit, the young man was handsome. Beautiful even. And if one wasn't attuned to emotions like I was, they could easily be taken in by his smiles and flattery. However, I could feel his nature. He radiated contempt for those around him, like a shark gliding unconcerned through a school of fish. All were his prey.

Vampire.

"Oh, crap," said Rore under her breath, her eyes going large.

The hostess smiled dreamily at the pair and then pointed in our direction. So that's what all the texting was about.

Rore stiffened. Orion didn't miss the change in his sister. "Please tell me it's not Chaleta?"

She sighed. "All right. I won't tell you."

"Damn," he looked down.

Rore reached across and rested her hand on his. "Think you can hold it together? I don't want to lose our favorite pizza place."

He took a deep breath and nodded.

The couple at the front began walking in our direction, carrying their privileged status like a cloak—the heads of the other patrons tracked their stately progress down the aisle. Chaleta's emotions broadcast a smug confidence without an ounce of affection. It didn't feel like she was meeting a boyfriend—more like she was collecting a wayward possession.

I began to understand why Terra was concerned about this young lady. *She was just playing with him.* Under the table, my right hand curled into a fist. No one deserved to be treated that way.

The young woman stopped at our table and gave a dazzling smile that didn't quite reach her eyes. Her teeth were perfect, with her canines fashionably shortened to add a hint of mystique, yet long enough so there was no mistaking what she was. Vampires no longer drank blood, but they wanted to remind us they were still top predators.

As typical for her kind, her irises were a dark crimson, and these locked onto her intended target. "Hello, Orion," she said sweetly, completely ignoring the rest of us. "I saw you at the club last night. It's been weeks since we talked, and I was hoping to catch you so we could clear up our little misunderstanding." She gave a disappointed sigh. "But you ran off."

Orion's anger began to grow. "You were already with someone. What I don't understand is why you texted me to join you."

She placed a hand on his shoulder. "Maybe I flirted a little, but I was just waiting for you. The guy meant nothing."

"I don't call mashing your lips to his just passing the time!"

If she was deliberately trying to embarrass him, it was working. His anger was rising fast. I guess it was time to do my job.

I stood suddenly, startling Chaleta, and pushed her hand off Orion's shoulder. Then, glaring at her defiantly, I promptly sat in his lap, grabbed his arms, and wrapped them around my waist. "I don't appreciate you talking to my *boyfriend* like that. He did not run away. He was waiting for me last night, and when I joined him, we left. He knew you would be jealous, and we didn't want to make a scene." I smiled sweetly and narrowed my eyes. "Unless you *enjoy* creating scenes."

She gasped in surprise. The human I appeared to be would never dare talk to a vampire that way. It was too dangerous. One didn't tease a shark.

A heartbeat later, Chaleta's frown turned into a smirk. "No matter how angry Orion is at me, there is no way, absolutely none, that he would stoop to dating a magic-blind *human*." Her voice was dripping with contempt.

I stared right back. "At least I don't treat people like dirt and prey on mundanes for a sip of their soul."

Chaleta's eyes narrowed, and she fixed me with an icy stare. To my surprise, I felt her vampire powers touch me, flowing over my skin like dirty water and probing for a way into my soul. Vampires could subtly influence a person, gradually weakening their will, and over time, tapping into their very soul. For the tapped, there was no way back. The vampire owned them. It was why mundanes feared them and frequently wore protection charms. There were harsh laws against it, and most vampires didn't abuse their powers—the risks were too great. But like now, it was still done. You just had to be rich and well-connected to get away with it. And Chaleta certainly qualified.

I could feel her seeking my soul. Only, she would never guess

I wasn't a human. Succubi may be of inferior status, but I was still a magical, and our inherent magic protected us. She might be able to influence me if I was weak or naïve. But I was neither.

I slowly stood to face her. Her eyes grew large in surprise, and she increased her mental onslaught—but it washed off me like yesterday's dirt.

I was sorely tempted to retaliate—succubi didn't have the same limitations as vampires. But Mom had cautioned me many times to only use my powers for self-defense. Chaleta likely thought I had a protective charm, so as long as I didn't show my powers, my disguise would hold. But if I did push back, she, or someone around us, might figure out what I was. Logically, I should do nothing and let her walk away.

But her probing infuriated me. It was like someone touching your behind on a crowded train. It was demeaning. And at that moment, I was on the edge of doing something really stupid—

Orion jerked me back down onto his lap, breaking Chaleta's concentration and causing me to yelp in surprise. He wrapped his strong arms around me, ensuring I stayed put. I was so taken off guard that I just sat there, encircled by his reassuring warmth. But what shocked me the most was the concern and admiration I felt flowing from him.

Orion glared up at her. "Chaleta, you are sadly mistaken. She is perfect no matter what her race." He pulled me tighter to emphasize the point. "You and I have nothing to talk about. I suggest you leave before I let her go . . ." He smiled. "And she rather publicly kicks your butt."

I didn't need my powers to sense Chaleta's anger and embarrassment. A blush spread across her face, and her lips pursed tightly. Vampires always got what they wanted. Yet, Orion had announced he'd chosen a mundane over her. *A human even!*

Her eyes narrowed. "How dare you."

I was afraid she would attack me, but a heavy hand landed on her shoulder. "Now Chaleta," said the handsome young man with her. "Perhaps we should go." He leaned closer and whispered loud enough that we all could hear. "People are watching."

Chaleta glanced around the room and realized that everyone in the restaurant had gone silent, all eyes on us. Several people had their phones out, and I would bet the video was up on social media within the next two minutes.

Chaleta took a step back. "You're right." She gave Orion a contemptuous smile. "I was going to take you back, but I guess I'll have to wait until you tire of your little pet." She looked down her nose at us. "Be sure to keep her on a short leash. She might get bit."

She smiled once more and then strolled back toward the front.

Her companion bowed to us—he emitted cool confidence. "I'm sorry we crashed your lunch. I'll let the hostess know I'm picking up your check. My cousin has been out of sorts lately. Please don't hold it against her." He smiled once more, then glanced at Rore and winked.

The young witch blushed, and against her pale skin, it looked like a sunburn. Skiff noticed and frowned.

The young man promptly turned and followed Chaleta out.

Conversation in the room gradually returned, and I breathed a sigh of relief. I suddenly became conscious of Orion's strong arms around me. They felt good. Too good.

I stood—Orion's arms seemed reluctant to fall away. "Are you all right?" I asked him.

He nodded, his emotions an odd mix of relief, concern, and confusion. He looked away. "Yes, but you shouldn't have gotten involved. I can handle my own battles."

I blinked at him in disappointment. Not even a thank you.

I sank back down in my seat. "I didn't mean to embarrass you by saying you were my boyfriend. I know you don't like me. I was just afraid you might get really angry."

He opened his mouth to say something but promptly shut it and looked down at the table.

Rore grabbed my arm and glared at her brother. "Unlike the ass across from you, I *appreciate* you jumping in. You were so cool." She softened. "But Orion's right—you should be more careful. Chaleta's from a powerful family. Zeek was the guy with her, and his father is someone you don't want to mess with."

I suddenly had a bad feeling.

Skiff nodded in total agreement. "That's for sure. Zeek's father is the Night-clan elder."

Damn.

Chapter 9

"I'M STUFFED," sighed Rore with a hand over her stomach. "That was good pizza. I shouldn't have eaten that last piece."

We were walking back to their house after finishing our meal. As before, we were two by two, with Orion and Skiff walking behind.

She looked back over her shoulder. "Good choice, Ri. Even if it did have mushrooms."

"I think so too." I gave Orion a subdued smile over my shoulder.

Orion looked down. He was broadcasting embarrassment and regret. I wasn't sure how to interpret that mix.

Rore frowned and stopped on the sidewalk, turning to face

her brother. "Ri, a thought just occurred to me. The Solstice Festival is this week."

Orion gave her a puzzled frown. "So?"

"Who are you going to take? You know you'll be fair game if you don't have someone."

"I'm not going," he stated flatly. "I don't see why the guy has to spend the evening with whichever girl asks. It's a stupid tradition."

Skiff joined in. "Yeah. It's not fair. Isn't that sexist or something?"

Rore rolled her eyes. "You know that will not fly with Mom. She's very much into tradition. If you go stag, the first unaccompanied girl there can snag you. You know *she-who-won't-be-named* will be waiting, and once you're in her arms . . ." She frowned. "You may relapse."

Orion's eyes narrowed. "No way in hell. Not after what she did. Besides, I don't dance to her standards." The side of his mouth curled up into an evil grin. "And who, pray tell, are you going with? You haven't dated anyone since you broke up."

Rore got a disgusted look on her face. "I have you know I'm going with Skiff."

The young man, who had seemed depressed by the entire conversation, suddenly perked up. "I am? You never said anything."

"We always go together," she countered.

Skiff grinned evilly. "I might have accepted someone else's invitation."

Rore's eyes grew round. She stepped closer and stabbed a finger into his chest. "You better not have. Is it Darla again? I told her to bug off."

Skiff glanced upward playfully. "You made it clear we weren't a couple after prom. *Remember?* Something about giving ourselves a chance to grow." He looked away in playful seriousness. "One of us might have moved on."

Rore's mouth drew tight. "It *was* her, wasn't it?"

Skiff broke into a grin. "Calm now. Ro-ro. I wouldn't dare go with anyone else. We've been going to the festival together since we were in diapers. I'm not going to stop now."

Rore visibly relaxed. She glanced my way and saw my puzzled expression. "It's just a tradition," she explained. "Our Moms used to take us together, and we just kept it up."

I somehow felt that wasn't the whole story, but I wasn't going to press.

I heard a phone beep, and Skiff pulled his out. I felt his emotions suddenly change—shifting from amused to concerned.

He put his phone away and stepped between Rore and me, wearing a smile that didn't match his feelings. He casually draped his arms over our shoulders and motioned for Orion to join us.

We leaned in, and he whispered to us. "Don't look, but there's a black van behind us. Datiel says it's been following us."

"Chaleta again?" Rore asked.

He shook his head. "She left with Zeek in his sports car."

I stared at him in confusion. "How does your laptop know all that? Has he hacked into someone's cameras?"

Skiff shrugged. "Satellite imaging. Datiel knows some other gremlins in military intelligence. They trade information sometimes."

"Trade?" I asked. "What do they get?"

He grimaced. "Reassurance that I haven't hacked their systems again."

I blinked at him. "Uh-huh." It sounded like there was a much bigger story there, but now was not the time. I pulled out my new phone. "I'm going to get a picture. Pose for me."

They all nodded.

I stepped in front of the group, holding up my phone while they pulled into a crazy pose. Behind them, about a block down the street, was a nondescript black van with darkly tinted windows. It looked like a delivery van but had no marking.

I managed to take a couple of pictures but doubted they would do much good. It suspiciously had no license plate.

I rejoined the group and held out my phone to them. They nodded as they saw my pictures. I leaned in close. "I need a better one of the license. I'm going to get closer."

Orion put a hand on my arm. I could feel his concern through the contact. "They could be dangerous. Let me do it."

But we never got to finish that discussion. The van started its engine and slowly pulled away from the curb. I strained my powers to feel anything from the vehicle, but it was strangely blank. Even at that distance, I should be able to feel *something*—

Unless they were shielding themselves.

I got my phone ready. The others followed my lead, and we began walking leisurely in our original direction.

Behind me, I heard a vehicle approach. I held my breath. My mobile phone seemed a feeble weapon against whatever might attack us. If Night-clan was involved, it could be any of several nasty races. I had no desire to meet any of them.

Orion must have picked up on my distress. He inched closer

to me and took my hand. I felt his courage through the touch and found it strangely reassuring.

A moment later, the dark van rode past, and I got a few more pictures. It had a temporary license taped to the back window but was otherwise unmarked. We watched as it drove down the street, turned at the next intersection, and left the neighborhood.

I let out a breath I didn't realize I was holding.

"That was creepy." Rore stood transfixed in the direction the van had disappeared. "Do you think they were watching us?"

Skiff shook his head. "Datiel said they followed us from the pizza place, making stops in front of houses as if they were making deliveries. What made him suspicious was that no one got out."

Rore hugged herself. "Still, we should be careful." Rore smiled at Skiff. "It's a good thing you had Datiel watching." Then she frowned. Her eyes narrowed. "Wait a minute. Why *was* Datiel watching? He doesn't do things like that by himself. Someone had to tell him."

Skiff paled.

She put her hands on her hips. "Stancliff Albert Daemynson, were you checking up on me?"

Skiff held up his hands and took a step back. "Now Ro-ro . . ."

Rore glared at him. I felt the tingle of angry magic crackling around her. "That is creepy!" she yelled at him. "Have you turned into a stalker?"

"Ro-ro, it's not like that. I was worried about you. I saw you talking with Zeek last week, and I didn't like the way he looked at you."

Rore scoffed. "You know he wouldn't dare touch me—Grandmother would fry him. Besides, his powers won't work on me." She blinked at him in surprise. "You're jealous?"

He dropped his eyes and shook his head. "No . . . well, maybe." He shrugged. "Anyway, I checked him out. While Zeek's clean, Datiel made an unusual correlation. Since he came to town a few months ago, four young women have disappeared. They were all witches."

Rore considered him for a moment, and then the magic died down. She wrapped her arms around him in a tight hug. "You don't have to be jealous." She leaned back and hit him with her kilowatt smile. I thought Skiff was going to melt. "And thank you for caring." She stepped back. "Just don't do it again."

Skiff nodded.

Orion and I exchanged a glance. Crisis averted. The couple that was not a couple was still a couple. Figure that one out. But, as I watched them smile at each other, I couldn't help but wonder—

Why had Zeek winked at her?

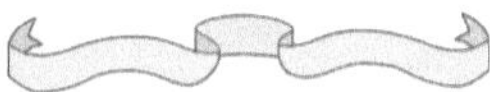

I watched Rore enter search terms into her laptop's browser. She was researching my grandfather's address, looking for some reference to it. She had been pounding the keyboard for nearly an hour but was coming up empty.

We had seen a chastised Skiff off to his house and then returned to the Strewerts. Orion went into his room and shut the door while I followed Rore to hers. She immediately jumped on her laptop. Her ability to multi-task took it to a new level. In one of the screen's windows, she was running searches on my grandfather's address, while in the other she scanned for a new dress, and at the same time, flipped through a sales flyer and texted with her mother. Not to mention talking to me while doing all that. Her energy level was something else.

Rore didn't seem bothered by the black van incident and had insisted on doing the online searches herself. I was glad because the van had unnerved me. I kept stepping to the window and checking the street while my thoughts circled. Was it Terra checking up on us, the police making sure Orion stayed out of trouble, or even someone Chaleta had hired to keep an eye on us? There were just too many possibilities.

I had sent the pictures of the van to Terra. I wasn't sure what she could do with them, but at least I was earning my keep. She had simply texted back, *Good job.*

I jumped when Rore sat back in her chair, grabbed handfuls of her hair, and yelled at the ceiling. "I don't get this! Where is your grandfather's street?"

"You don't have to keep searching, Rore." I sat down on the bed. "I do appreciate all you're doing, but the note on the back of the picture must be wrong."

Rore swiveled in her seat and took my hands. Through the contact, I could feel the warmth of her strength and determination. "I'm going to find your grandfather if it kills me."

Orion poked his head in the door. He had changed into a loose T-shirt, shorts, and running shoes. "I'm going for a run. After that pizza, I need one."

A run. I hadn't gone for a run since Mom's funeral. I missed it. Then I had a more sinister thought. Orion would be alone, and that van was still out there.

I shot up. "Can I come with you?"

Orion frowned. I could tell he wasn't crazy about the idea. "I run pretty fast."

I pulled out my suitcase and started taking out my running clothes. "Good, then maybe I won't leave you too far behind."

Rore burst into laughter. "If what I saw last night was any indication, you're going to be a dot in her rearview mirror."

Orion blushed and looked insulted. I made shooing motions while grabbing the bottom of my shirt. He finally sighed and backed out, closing the door.

As I changed, being careful of my horns in Rore's presence, she plopped cross-legged on her bed. "Don't hold back on him."

Puzzled, I glanced her way.

She leaned forward and whispered, "He can't stand being coddled. Just be yourself and kick his butt." She grinned.

I blinked at her. *Please tell me she wasn't trying to be a matchmaker.* There was no way I would get involved with any-one right now. Least of all, someone I was supposed to be protecting. Besides, he hated me.

A minute later, I joined Orion outside doing stretches.

When we were ready, he pointed down the street. "There's a park a few miles from here. I typically run to the park, along its trails, and back. The overall distance is almost seven miles." He frowned. "Don't worry if you can't keep up."

I straightened and grinned as I looked into his face. He had no idea.

"I won't worry. But you should." I took off. I didn't mention that while in school, I had placed first or second every year since I was a freshman. "Hey!" he called from behind me.

I set an aggressive pace—probably a little too aggressive— but hey, he'd challenged me. And I never walked away from a challenge. It helped that my kind were naturally quick and nimble—not superhero level, but just a tad above a human's.

Or a shifter, for that matter. As long as they didn't cheat and transform into a horse or something. To his credit, Orion didn't cheat and still managed to keep up.

He directed us into the park and to the trail. It was nice to feel the combined motions of my heart pumping, my lungs filling, and my legs all moving. The steady thud, thud of my feet on the trail helped me relax.

The trail had bushes and ancient oaks on both sides. It was nice to be out and feel their majestic shade. Plants emitted emotions too, but differently from people—softer and gentler than animals. The oaks and surrounding scrubs were emitting contentment as they soaked up the sun and sipped at the moisture deep in the ground. The serenity of the park soothed me.

The trail passed close to a public restroom with drinking fountains out front.

"Hold up," called Orion.

I slowed to a halt in front of the restrooms.

Orion was right behind me. He put his hands on his hips and breathed heavily. "I usually stop for some water. Want some?"

Also breathing heavily, I nodded and checked my watch. We'd been running for about forty minutes. Not bad, but I was capable of better. I hadn't been keeping up with my training. That was something I intended to fix.

We took a moment to drink. I eyed the restroom. In my haste to leave, I had missed an important step in my running preparations. Unfortunately, my bladder was reminding me.

I headed for the women's side. "I'll only be a minute."

Orion nodded. "When you come out, we're going to race back."

I grinned evilly. "You're on."

I trotted inside. Like a lot of public restrooms, there was no door, just a long privacy corridor that turned into an area with sinks and stalls. Surprisingly, it was empty and eerily silent. I thought it odd since the park was fairly crowded but shrugged it off and did my business in the further stall.

Feeling much relieved, I opened the stall door but froze—a chill running down my spine. It just couldn't be.

A gray cat, with each eye a different color, sat in front of the door. He seemed to be smiling.

Chapter 10

"HELLO, LAPIS." The cat sounded happy to see me. "You're doing well after your little adventure."

I blinked at him. It was that shapeshifting prankster I'd met in the alley. "What are you doing here?" I spat. "You set me up. I nearly got killed."

"Me?" The cat cocked his head to one side. "How could I have possibly arranged it? You had just gotten into town."

I glared at him. "How do you know that?"

He rolled his eyes. "You were carrying a suitcase and came from the bus station. Anyone could figure that one out."

I didn't have time for any more pranks. I stepped around him to wash my hands.

Turning on the water, I glanced at my reflection in the mirror. My eyes went wide in horror.

My horns were visible!

I glanced behind me. And so was my tail.

I quickly felt under my arm for the illusion charm. Its tingle was still there, so it should still be working. Which could only mean—

I wheeled on the cat. He still sat there, gazing up at me. "Do I have your attention now?"

"What . . .? How . . .?" I sputtered. "*Put it back!*"

"I can't understand why you want to hide your heritage. There was a time when your race was highly regarded and sat beside kings."

"That was a thousand years ago and has nothing to do with today. Now put it back!"

He cocked his head to one side. "Only if you give me a few minutes of your time. I have something important I need to tell you."

I glanced at the door in panic. If someone were to come in, they would see me. My secret would be out. Rore would kick me out of her house, and Orion—

I scrunched my eyes shut and clenched my fists, trying to get my panic under control. "Please," I begged. "Don't let them see me."

The cat gave an almost human sigh. "All right. I didn't mean to upset you, but I need you to heed my words."

I cracked open an eye and looked in the mirror. The illusion was back, and I appeared to be a plain human girl again. I breathed a sigh of relief.

He stood and paced in front of me. "You really need to get your charm recharged. You don't have much time left."

I swallowed and considered the cat, trying to reason through what he was. A shifter seemed most logical, but how could he talk to me? Even the most potent shifter was bound to the form they chose. But, like all of Dawn-clan, their magic came from themselves, so he wouldn't be able to use a spell to speak. It also didn't fit with the other clans. A werewolf could only transform at night and a doppelganger into another person. And what about my charm? He hadn't turned it off—he had negated it, like covering a lightbulb without turning it off. How was that even possible? Regular magic just didn't work that way. The only explanation was that whoever this cat was, he was skilled and extremely powerful.

I remembered back to when he first introduced himself. He had called himself a god. He seemed to have the ego of one. Then a realization slammed into my brain. *Surely not.* There was one race. *Oh, Protector.*

While the other races used Night-clan to frighten their children, it was different for us. We were told horror stories about the most powerful of all the races. They were said to be able to speak to the Protector himself.

The Aether.

I knew of only one person who had been involved with that race. According to Mom, it was my father.

And he'd been killed because of it.

My heart leaped into my throat. I carefully faced the cat, my voice shaking. "W-who are you?"

"You may call me Bast."

"You're not really a shifter, are you?" I began to inch away from him, sliding slowly along the counter.

I could swear his lips pulled back slightly in the semblance of a smile. "What do you think?"

"I think you're an Aether," I blurted out. The counter ended, and I started easing along the wall.

He nodded. "You might be right."

"Are you going to kill me?" I was ashamed of the tremor in my voice. This was a childhood horror come to life.

He snorted. "Why in heavens would I do that? First off, you're the Guardian. And second, I don't like the taste of succubi."

I gasped.

He frowned. "I was joking. Don't be so serious. I don't eat people."

"But you're an Aether, and I'm Night-clan."

"What has that got to do with anything?"

"You hate my kind."

"I do *not!*" He growled in agitation. "I don't know where you people pick up these strange ideas. I do not dislike any of the races, and especially not your kind."

We considered each other for a moment.

"Mom said one of your race killed my father."

"I did not!" he spat. "Not only did I mourn his passing, but it was a great loss to all the races."

I was taken aback by his anger. But I was even more surprised that he seemed to know my father personally.

With a visible effort, he calmed himself. "Now *please*, can we get on with this? I have some important information to pass on." He started licking his paw.

I eyed the door and made a break for it—

Only to suddenly find myself standing back against the counter. I hadn't felt any magic or movement. He had just . . . put me there. Instantly. If I hadn't been sure before of what he was, I definitely was now.

"Are you done?" he asked in irritation. "I will not hurt you, and you really need to listen to me. So quit playing around."

I cautiously nodded.

He took a deep breath. "Now, listen closely." He sat up and wrapped his tail around his legs. He said formally, "To find what you seek, you must look in this city's recent *his-tor-y*." He pronounced each syllable succinctly.

I gave him a puzzled look. "History?"

He stood and arched his back in a very cat-like stretch. "*Recent* history, thank the Protector. Only one generation back should do."

He turned and strolled leisurely toward the exit.

I watched him as I digested the information.

Before reaching the exit, he looked over his shoulder. "Also, watch your back. Someone is plotting to steal the things you hold dear."

Things I hold dear? I don't have anything! Mom's dead. And our valuables were either stolen or smashed. I have nothing left that's dear to me.

"Who is it?" I called after him.

But he ignored my question. "Make your alliances *now*, Guardian. While you still have time. You're going to need them."

"*Who is it!*" I yelled after him.

He continued around the dividing wall and I ran after him. But when I looked on the other side—

He had vanished.

Orion was surprised when I stepped outside. "That didn't take long. Did you find a mess in there?"

I scanned the area, even looking behind him. *Where did that cat go?* He couldn't be *that* fast.

"You . . ." I hesitated. "Haven't seen a cat, have you?"

He looked puzzled and shook his head. "No, is that why you came back out so fast? You were inside only a few seconds."

I stared at him in disbelief. I had to have been in there for at least fifteen minutes. I hadn't been in a hurry to do my business, and then I talked with Bast. But Orion was acting like no time at all had passed. In fact, he was still breathing hard. I checked my watch, and my eyes grew in surprise. Only a minute had passed.

Legends said that the Aether were masters of physical space—distance didn't apply to them. Some said they could even stop time.

Oh, crap. Why was an Aether interested in me? *Why?*

Orion touched my shoulder. "Are you all right?" He bent closer. "You look like you've seen a ghost."

I could have handled a ghost easier than an Aether. He had ripped away my disguise like it was nothing. He could have exposed me with a thought.

"I'm fine," I lied, trying to keep the tremor out of my voice. I wasn't even close to being all right.

He grinned. "Ready to race me back? No cheating this time."

I hated to lie to him, but I needed a moment to think about what had just happened. "Why don't you go ahead. I'll catch up in a couple of minutes."

He looked concerned. "I can wait."

"No," I insisted. "You go ahead." I draped an arm across my stomach. "I just need a moment. Female stuff . . . you know."

He blushed. "Are you sure? Mom won't like me leaving you."

"It's all right. I only need a moment more."

He sighed. "All right then." He turned and started down the path. He glanced back at me one last time, and I waved.

When he disappeared around a bend, I glanced over my shoulder at the restroom. That cat was an Aether. Bast, he had called himself, and he had known my father. I mentally kicked myself for not finding out more, despite my panic. The things he talked about confused me. Guardian? Choose my allies? Someone after me? What was he talking about?

And what about his denial of being involved with my father's death. Mom had gotten upset every time I asked how he died, so I learned to avoid the topic. All I was able to find out was that he had died while performing some secret Aether task and that they had been responsible for his death.

There were just too many questions.

I sighed and started jogging back down the trail out of the park. I set a leisurely pace and put my body on automatic while my brain tossed around the problem. Unfortunately, I didn't come up with anything new. I wondered if I dared to mention it to Terra.

I left the park and jogged up the sidewalk toward the

Strewert's house. I just let my feet carry me. Traffic was light on the street, so it was easy to pick out the approach of a vehicle behind me. I wasn't paying attention to it other than to make sure I didn't cross in front of it.

So I was taken by surprise when a black van jumped the curb right in front of me and pulled forward enough to block my path. I immediately swerved to run around when the side door popped open, and two men jumped out. One of them was a nondescript man of average build with close-cropped hair and wearing a suit. If he'd had an earpiece in his ear, he could easily have passed for a secret service agent. His emotions were cool, with no excitement or anger. I had picked up more feelings from someone being in the library.

But the other man, I recognized in an instant. He radiated a sick combination of lust and desire that turned my stomach. He was dressed all in black with round wireframed sunglasses. His greasy hair hung long, and he wore a black narrow-brimmed hat that looked more like something out of the last century. Even though I couldn't see his eyes behind his dark glasses, I knew they were dissecting me, piece by piece.

It was the man that had been on the bus.

He grinned at me. "Hello, Lapis," his voice was deep silk, and I couldn't help but shiver. "You need to come with us. You gave us a bit of a fright, running from Philly like you did."

I tried to flee, but Mr. Secret Service grabbed me, pinning my arms to my sides and lifting me off the ground. I struggled and kicked, but it was like beating against a mountain.

"Let me go!" I yelled. "HELP!"

He tried to stuff me into the van, but I caught the side of the door with my foot and shoved back. The man staggered but quickly recovered. He shifted so I could no longer reach it.

I was determined not to go in that van. I knew that if they got me behind that closed door, I would never emerge the same.

I gathered my magic and hit him with all the emotion I had stored inside me, changing it to absolute terror.

But it washed off him like a warm shower. It had no effect.

To my horror, I realized he was wearing some type of protection charm. One specifically designed to protect against a succubus attack.

They know what I am.

I struggled harder.

The man in dark glasses pulled out a stun gun and pressed it against the flesh of my arm just below my sleeve. "Now Lapis, you must calm down."

A pain like I had never known shot through me. My body spasmed, and I jerked repeatedly. I went limp and nearly passed out.

Mr. Secret Service threw me into the van. I landed on my back, desperately trying to get my body to work. But all I could see was glasses-man smirking at me.

I was going to die.

Out of nowhere, a bundle of teeth, claws, and brown fur landed on top of him. Glasses man fell backward and landed hard, banging his head against the curb and knocking his hat off. On his chest stood a very pissed-off German Shepherd.

Orion!

The dog didn't pause but immediately leaped for Mr. Secret Service. The man was ready for him and reared back to punch.

But suddenly, the dog became a blur, and a half second later, changed into a gray squirrel which sailed past the man's fist and landed on his face. The squirrel bit down on his nose, causing the man to scream. He reached to grab the animal, but the squirrel had already moved to the other side of his head and chomped down on his ear. The man howled and tried to shake him off.

I managed to get my legs working enough to roll out of the van. Groaning, I rose to all fours and made a glacially slow effort to crawl away. Glasses man sat up and shook his head to clear it. He stood and stepped toward me.

My body wasn't entirely mine to command, but I decided I had to use my last weapon. While my illusion charm made the horns on my head invisible, they were still there—very real and very hard.

As he approached, reaching to touch me again with the stun gun, I lunged forward with all my remaining strength and jabbed my head right into his crotch. He let out an oof sound and bent over before finally toppling onto his side.

Now *that* felt good. Or at least it had for me.

The action sapped the last of my strength, and I collapsed exhausted while my head spun. Whatever that man had done to me, it had messed me up. I struggled to get back on all fours and tried to crawl away.

In the distance, I heard sirens. *Not the police.* Someone must have seen the struggle and called 911. Terra said she would handle the Philly police, but it would be best not to tempt the local ones.

Mr. Secret Service finally got Orion off him and ran to the man with glasses. He bodily lifted him and threw him into the van, climbing in after him and slamming the door. The van immediately took off.

"Lapis!"

Somehow, I managed to flip over onto my back. A concerned Orion leaned over me—his phone in one hand and the other holding mine.

I tried to return to my crawl. "No police," I gasped. "I can't . . . no police."

Orion yelled into his phone. "Rore! We need cover. NOW! I'll explain later."

There were words from the other end, but I couldn't make them out.

Orion scanned the area. Seeing what he wanted, he grabbed up something I couldn't see and then scooped me up into his strong arms. He ran to a small tree and then set me down in the grass of someone's yard. He sat beside me, then set his phone down and pressed speaker. Immediately I heard singing. It took a moment to realize it was Rore's voice. It was so beautiful—

And chocked full of earth magic. The light dimmed as a concealment spell formed around us.

Just then, a police car pulled up to the curb where we had been, and two uniformed officers got out. They seemed puzzled as they looked around.

"Is this the spot?" asked one.

The other took his hat off and scratched his head. "Yeah. I guess it's another prank."

After looking around a bit more, they drove off.

Exhausted, my head fell back. I could feel consciousness leaving me. Some part of my brain noted that Orion did not have any clothes on.

He had carried me while he was naked.

Interesting.

On that thought, I passed out.

Chapter 11

I GRADUALLY BECAME aware of keyboard clicks, followed by a pause and someone whispering softly, "Not that one." Then it would repeat. After about three or four cycles, they would groan and mutter a very unladylike curse. "Where *are* you?"

For the second time that day, I had no idea where I was. My eyes shot open, but I calmed at the sight of the delicate shamrock green curtains, the stained-glass rainbow, and the flowers-on-cream wallpaper.

Rore's room. Her bed. I judged from the dimly lit window it was early evening. I must have been out for a couple of hours.

How did I get here? Last I remembered, Orion was hovering over me while I lay on the grass. Although, I seemed to have bits of memory where he was carrying me. He had saved me from the attack—

The van!

I had to get away.

I sat up, throwing off the thin blanket and putting my feet on the floor. My head started to throb, and the world spun. I grasped the bed for support but missed and fell back on it. I lay there a moment as the world gradually began to settle.

Rore came into view, leaning over me. She was smiling gently. "I was going to warn you not to make any sudden moves, but I think you've figured that out for yourself."

It wasn't easy, but I focused on her. "Is Orion all right?"

She nodded. "You've been out for the last hour. His majesty has been coming in to check on you about every five minutes. I think he has a reminder set on his phone." She touched my shoulder. "You need to take it easy for a bit. You had a nasty shock."

"Did they hit me with a paralysis spell?"

She shook her head. "Nope. Just a good old fashion stun gun. At least that's what Mom said. She checked you over and said your vitals were fine. She gave you a little healing magic but said you would likely wake up dizzy and have a headache."

I held up my hand and flexed it. It responded sluggishly, but at least it was working. I certainly didn't want to do that again. They almost got me.

And that was the most horrifying thing. I thought they were after Rore or Orion, but they weren't.

It was me.

Which completely flipped the dynamic. I needed to talk to

Terra. Instead of protecting her grandchildren, I had put them in danger. While I had enjoyed my stay, it was likely over.

There went my chance of becoming human.

I put a hand to my head. The throbbing was settling down to a more decent pounding. "Did the police—"

She cut me off. "They didn't see you. I was sort of working blind, but I got the illusion up in time."

"How did you cast an illusion through the phone?" My brain hurt thinking about it. Rore's magic came from the earth and moon. All of Twilight-clan were that way. But earth-magic and machines didn't mix well. Casting through a phone shouldn't be possible. It would be like growing vines out of a laptop.

Rore smiled. I could sense the pride behind it. "Skiff figured it out. I told you he's a genius. I don't understand it myself, but it's why I have to sing. The sound is the medium. I just put the magic into it."

"That's amazing," I said.

Skiff was a mage, so machines were his specialty. But to step out of his own magic to work with another spoke volumes. The guy was very talented. I could understand why Rore felt she might hold him back.

I lay looking at the ceiling. Rore gently shifted to sit beside me; she radiated concern. "Orion said people in a van tried to grab you. It was the same one that had been following us. Did they hurt you? Other than stunning you, I mean."

I carefully shook my head.

Rore licked her lips. "He also said something spooked you in the park restroom. Did someone attack you there? They didn't molest you, did they?"

I shook my head again. I couldn't say what I really wanted to—*I had met an Aether, he talked nonsense, and he briefly suspended my illusion charm.* I closed my eyes. "No one attacked me there. Only the van. I must have had my guard down when it came up behind me."

Rore pulled her leg underneath her. "Lapis, we really should call the police . . . ."

I sat up in panic—only to immediately wince and lay back down. My head still wasn't happy with my sudden movements.

"No police. *Please.*" I hated the whiny tone in my voice. The police here might be different. But the ones back home wouldn't help. Terra said she would fix it, but now I wasn't sure she would. I had become a liability.

"Lapis . . ." Rore rubbed her hands on her knees. "It doesn't take a rocket scientist to see you're in some kind of trouble. Please let us help you."

Her emotions matched the concern on her face. I wasn't some magical lie detector, but I was pretty sure she believed what she said. Her earnestness nearly broke my heart.

"Why?" My treacherous mouth gave voice to the question in my heart. "Why do you want to help me? You didn't even know me until yesterday."

She looked down. "Because you kept Orion from hurting me. You didn't have to do that. Most people would have run at the first opportunity. But you didn't."

"Rore. I'm not some hero. I just did what I felt was right, and I was lucky it worked out."

Her gaze held mine. "I'm not so sure. There's something about you Lapis. I don't know what it is, but you have this confidence about you. Even Orion notices it. When you're around, he's in control of himself." She sighed. "Orion is a powerful shifter, but sometimes he has trouble controlling the animal he's transformed into. The further he shifts away from being a person, the more trouble he has overriding its instincts." She looked up at me. "But he stayed in control. It was something to do with you." She took my hand, her expression pleading. "I know my big brother is a big hulking, moody pain in the ass." She locked her gaze with mine. "But he's the only one I've got." Her lips curled into a smile. "And some days, I even like him. So you've got to help him. Help us."

I didn't know what to say.

Rore looked down. "I don't have many friends. And you seem to have good . . . friend potential. Of course, if you don't want to be friends with a ditzy, frizzy-haired, redheaded witch. I can completely understand."

I was touched. I hadn't had friends in many years. Mom moved us so frequently that I just gave up. A good friend would be wonderful, but there was a larger problem.

"Rore, I'm not sure you understand. They knew my *name*. They wanted me." I reached across and touched her hand. "I haven't a clue what they want. I might be putting you, Orion, or your family in danger. I'm afraid of what your grandmother will do when she finds out what's happened."

Rore frowned as she absorbed the information.

"You need help Lapis. If not us, then maybe your grand-father."

I smiled. "We tried. But that was a dead end."

Rore looked over her shoulder at the map on her laptop. "I've gone up and down that street on the map looking for the house in the picture. I even looked at places with similar names. It's like the street vanished."

"Maybe it was a different city."

Rore shook her head. "No, I looked there too." I could feel her frustration. "I think we're looking at this all wrong." She turned and took my one hand, clasping it in both of hers. "Don't give up Lapis. We're going to find him."

I could feel the rush of emotions through the contact. Her earnestness. Her caring. As I looked into her eyes, I couldn't help but wonder if she would feel the same way if she knew what I really was.

There was a knock on Rore's door, and Andromeda stuck her head inside. "Dinner's ready. I hope you feel like joining us, Lapis." She hesitated. "My mother is here and will be eating with us. She wants to speak with you." One side of her mouth curled up wickedly. "But if you need to rest a little more, I'm *sure* I can make her understand." I think she was relishing the prospect of refusing Terra.

I stood and my legs held. I wouldn't be doing any races today, but I could manage. "I better speak with her and get it out of the way."

Andromeda considered me for a moment. I could feel her concern. "Are you all right that we didn't call the police? Mother agreed it was the right thing to do, but I'm not sure."

I stood. "Keeping the police away is what I need right now."

Andromeda opened her mouth, but I held up my hand.

"Please, don't ask me more right now," I said. "I promise I'll tell you everything when the time is right."

Andromeda nodded sadly. "I understand." Then she brightened. "So come on. I'm sure the healing magic increased your appetite." Then, with one last smile, she left.

I knew I needed to be wary of these people, but there was something about them I felt I could trust. What had Bast said—*Make your alliances now.* I guess, in a way, I was. And having Rore for a friend—there were worse fates.

I stopped by the bathroom on the way, so I was the last one to arrive. The family had gathered with Andromeda at her usual spot at the head of the table, while Rore was on her right. Beside Andromeda on the left sat Terra, with Orion sitting beside her. I assumed the empty place beside Rore was for me.

I could feel discomfort radiating from all of them. Thankfully, it wasn't directed at me, but at Terra—their grandmother seemed less than welcome.

This evening, Terra wore a black suit and a pink blouse. It was set off nicely with a string of pearls around her neck. She still wore the single-stud earring with its bright green emerald. Once again, it didn't seem to go with her outfit.

She watched me with interest as I came in and sat beside a slightly stiff Rore. Orion's eyes kept flicking from his plate to the older lady sitting next to him. He wasn't afraid, but wary. I couldn't help but wonder what the deal was.

Terra frowned as I entered the room. I gave her a slight bow. "Hello, Elder. Good to see you again."

Her frown deepened. "You might not say that once we talk."

"Mother." Andromeda laid a hand on Terra's arm. "She just woke up. Take it easy on her."

The emotions Orion and Rore emanated set me on edge. I knew witches had a matriarchal culture, with the oldest female of the family being the leader, which might explain Orion and Rore's discomfort. It also might have to do with her visiting right after the van attack. This was likely not just a friendly dinner. Was she going to insist I leave? Kick me out? I couldn't blame her if she did.

I took my place beside Rore. Andromeda smiled at me. "I hope salad is all right. We're not only trying to watch our weight, but Orion won't eat meat or chicken. I think they call it a pescatarian."

"Salad is fine with me," I said politely. It wasn't, actually. I was more of a meat and potatoes person—as long as the potatoes were fried. But I could choke down some green stuff if I had to. I didn't want to upset my hosts. I was just glad there was no broccoli.

Andromeda took my plate and, from a large bowl, began to heap a healthy portion onto it. Terra watched me coolly.

I decided to strike first. "Elder, were you informed about the van that tried to abduct me?"

Terra nodded. "I was. Did you know them?"

"I recognized one of them. He had been on the bus on my trip down, but that was the first I'd seen him. I didn't know the other."

"What did you do to them?" Terra asked flatly, her expression cold.

"Mother . . ." Andromeda tried to interrupt, but Terra waved her off. "How did you do it?"

My mouth opened in surprise. "I'm not sure I understand.

They attacked me. Orion fought them. I did nothing to them except head-butt the one that used a stun gun on me."

"So, you had nothing to do with their murders."

I stared at her in shock. "*What?* Murders. I didn't . . ." I shook my head. This wasn't making sense. "How . . .?"

"So you're saying you had nothing to do with it?" Her eyes narrowed. "They were both from Philly."

I set my fork down and sat up straight. "I'm not even sure what you're talking about, Elder."

Terra held out her hand to me across the table. It glowed a gentle blue.

The tension in the room went through the roof.

Andromeda frowned. "Mother, not now . . ."

"Hush," Terra spat. "This is important." Her eyes narrowed as she glared at me. "Your hand, Miss Midnyte."

I knew what was coming, and I glared back. A truth spell. She was calling me a liar.

I was surprised at the explosion of anger that came from the other side of the table.

"Grandmother!" Orion jumped up, knocking over his chair. He leaned on the table facing Terra. An ugly, dark ire radiated from him. But that wasn't all. His skin shifted and then slid back. He was fighting his anger and was on the verge of losing control.

I could feel real fear emanating from Rore and Andromeda. They saw it too.

Andromeda gasped. "Mother . . ."

"This is not a courtroom, Grandmother," Orion spat, ignoring his mother. "Don't pick on her. She's done nothing wrong.

In fact, they attacked her! I bet you've already investigated and know who did it."

Terra wheeled on Orion. "I have to make sure she's not a threat to our family. *Now sit down.*"

Fur sprouted on his arms and then faded back to skin. His nose was distorted and was about to extend into a snout. Why couldn't Terra see it? *He can't take any more.*

"Grandmother . . ." he growled. He was at his limit.

I didn't even think. I reached out a hand and covered Orion's with my own. His gaze shot to me, and through our touch, I felt a rage so hot I almost jerked back. Yet, I could feel the struggle inside. While he wanted to let it go—to let the beast rage—he was holding it back by sheer force of will.

I couldn't let it go any further. Through our contact, I breathed in his anger as easily as air. Just a bit. And when I'd taken enough, I changed it and let it back out as coolness, soothing his anger in calm.

"Orion, it's all right," I said to cover my action. "Take a deep breath. I'm okay with this."

I felt the change immediately. The fuzziness of his skin and the distortion of his nose returned to normal. Orion blinked. He took a deep breath, righted his chair, and sat down, seeming to follow my instructions. But his eyes were on me.

I pulled my hand back. The whole exchange had happened in only a few seconds. I hoped I hadn't been too obvious.

But the elder had noticed. Her expression was cold.

I turned my attention back to Terra, returning her icy stare. "You already know all my secrets. I have nothing to hide from you—" I nearly spat the word. "*Elder.*"

I held my hand out to her.

She frowned. "You're a disrespectful little girl."

"And you're being a bully."

The tension in the room was so heavy you could cut it.

"That's irrelevant," Terra stated. Yet, the corner of her mouth curled up slightly. I think she was pleased I was pushing back.

She stared at me a moment more before she took my hand, grasping it firmly. Her grip was stronger than I expected, and her barrier was firmly in place. It felt so odd to touch someone and feel no emotions.

The elder took a deep breath. "Lapis Midnyte," she barked in a tone I'm sure made her underlings quiver. "Did you murder the people in the van that attacked you?"

I couldn't feel the truth spell, but I was sure it was there. I glared back. "No."

Our joined hands gave a gentle pulse of green light. Truth.

The others watched in trepidation, not sure what to do about the contest of wills.

"Did you cause their deaths?" Terra asked.

"No."

Another pulse of green light.

Orion glanced at me nervously. I could feel his frustration rising.

"Do you know or suspect who killed them?" Terra continued.

"No." Truth again.

"Do you mean harm to this family?"

"No," I stated firmly. The green was a little brighter.

"Are you working for anyone other than me?"

Both Rore's and Orion's eyes shot in my direction. I kept mine locked on Terra.

"No." Our hands pulsed green again.

She paused. We stared at each other for three heartbeats. I was afraid she was going to ask if I was human. That would be game over for my cozy living arrangement and a signal that Terra was abandoning our agreement.

Terra's eyes flicked to Andromeda, who was watching with a mix of discomfort and frustration. I think everyone at the table was holding their breath.

"The police in Philly think you stole from a department store. Claimed to have caught you on camera. Are you a thief, Miss Midnyte? Did you steal?"

Andromeda winced. "Mother, that's not . . ."

Terra held up her other hand. "Hush. Let her answer. It's important you hear it." The elder turned her gaze back to me with a slight smile. "Tell them."

Orion reached across to grab our joined hands. "You've embarrassed her enough. Leave her alone!"

I didn't feel the magic, but Orion was pushed back into his chair.

Terra focused back on me. "Tell them, Lapis. Are you a thief?"

I turned my gaze to Orion, who was struggling with the restraint. I could feel his anger rising. I looked right into his eyes as I gave my answer. I couldn't help when the corner of my mouth curled upward. "No. I am not a thief."

Our joined hands glowed green.

Truth.

Terra's eyes twinkled—she knew it all along. The elder just wanted the rest of the family to know for themselves. *She was helping me.*

"One last question, Miss Midnyte." She paused. "Do you . . ." She grinned. ". . . like salad?"

My mouth flew open in surprise. "I—" She jerked her hand back before I could answer.

There was a collective sigh as Terra settled back into her chair. Rore patted my arm.

To my surprise, Terra lowered her defenses, and I could once again sense her emotions. *Perhaps a gesture of goodwill?* But what shocked me more were the feelings she projected—affection and—*pride?* She was proud of me?

"My apologies, Miss Midnyte," said the elder. "I was clearly in error."

"Mother. Really?" Andromeda scolded. "She's our guest. Please be a little nicer."

Terra nodded and picked up her fork to stir the remains of her uneaten meal.

I leaned forward. "Since I passed your test, will you at least tell me what's going on?"

Terra grunted. "I owe you that much." She set her fork back down. "My sources tell me the van and its two occupants were found in the parking lot of an abandoned warehouse down by the river. They were both dead, with no visible wounds. The coroner hasn't ruled on it yet, but some type of magic was used." She looked at me. "They were from your old city, so I can only speculate that someone here objected to their attempt to capture you and wanted to make sure it didn't happen again."

"And it wasn't you?"

She gazed at me levelly. "Miss Midnyte. We don't do things like that in Twilight-clan." She paused. "Unlike some other clans."

I got the unspoken message. *Night-clan would.*

I decided to tackle the elephant in the room. "Do you want

me to leave? I'm not sure why, but I've attracted someone's . . . *interest.*"

Terra considered me. "That is up to my daughter. It's her house. But I would prefer you stay and continue as you were—at least until you find your grandfather. It's not good to be without protection in this city."

I stared at her in shock. I was sure she was going to ask me to leave.

"Really? I can stay?"

I looked at Andromeda. She nodded. "I'd like that."

Rore nudged me. "You'll still have to sleep on the floor."

Orion seemed to find something very interesting on his plate. He nodded. "You're a good runner, but I doubt you could beat me in a fair race."

I smiled. "Thank you. All of you."

Terra pushed her plate away. "So. Speaking of your grandfather, how is the search coming?"

I sighed. "Not so well. Rore's been a tremendous help, but so far no luck."

Terra leaned forward. "I bet you've already searched for his name and address."

Rore spoke up. "We've not only looked at all that but did searches on variations. Nothing. It's like the upper numbers of Byan street ceased to exist."

Terra cocked her head to one side. "Does the street end at Edgemont Park?"

Rore nodded, clearly puzzled. "Yes, it does."

Terra leaned forward. "Well, the reason the upper end of Byan street doesn't exist is that about eighteen years ago, there were a series of explosions in that area. It took out whole blocks. Edgemont Park was built after the wreckage was cleared."

My mouth fell open. What was it Bast had told me? *To find what you seek, you must look in this city's recent history.*

An explosion certainly qualified.

Andromeda frowned, setting her fork down. "Mother, that's not exactly right. I remember because Orion came to us right after that. His parents were killed when the tornado came through. It set off a fire in that area, but there were no explosions."

Terra sighed. "Do you remember what the weather was the night it caught fire?"

Andromeda frowned in puzzlement. "No. How would I remember that? It happened a long time ago."

Terra's face pinched in remembered pain. I could feel the waves of grief coming from her. "I do. It was the night your sister Constellation died. I remember it perfectly. It was a clear night when we received the news."

Andromeda sighed sadly. "Mother, you know you sometimes confuse your facts. We've talked about this before. I've never had a sister. There is no Constellation."

The news floored me. Terra's grief was genuine. It had been dulled over the years, but it was still a wide-open wound. After all, a mother never really gets over the loss of her child.

Terra blinked at Andromeda before looking away. "Of course. I must have been thinking about one of my friends."

"Mother . . ." Andromeda gave a sad shake of her head and resumed eating. She changed the topic by asking about Orion's plans for the Solstice festival. It was an odd shift.

But I wasn't paying attention. The new information was racing through my brain. Explosion or fire, it didn't matter. Either would undoubtedly rewrite the landscape.

But I couldn't help but wonder why Terra recalled the events differently. A faulty memory was a simple explanation. But from my experience, Terra's mental capacity was not the least bit impaired. And her grief had been real. Terra believed she had lost a daughter that night.

Something just wasn't adding up.

Chapter 12

AFTER DINNER, I went back to Rore's room. I was eager to check out the new information on Edgemont Park using the searches already set up on her laptop. But just as we finished, she received a call and stepped away to take it. So I had no choice but to sit on her bed and wait.

I sighed and looked around the room. Typical girl's decor, but the flowered wallpaper was much too busy for my taste. There was a poster on one wall of some handsome pop star whose name escaped me. Framed awards for various academic achievements hung above her desk. I had trouble reconciling them with Rore's description of herself as a dumb redhead. She was obviously pretty smart.

Her closet door was closed, but earlier, I had seen the disordered jumble inside. I wasn't sure how Rore could find anything in it. She was a bit of a pack rat.

Propped up in the corner was a skateboard. It looked like it had been recently ejected from the closet and put there temporarily. There was nothing special about it—pink with glitter embedded in the finish. I could tell from the wheels, and lack of scuff marks, that it hadn't been used much. A shame, really. I was pretty good with a skateboard and would love to ride one again. Mom had given me a second-hand one for Winter Solstice one year. I had run it up and down the streets until I finally wore it out.

I was surprised to feel a gentle presence coming from the skateboard. Something lived within. I grinned. Probably a gremlin. They loved to inhabit made things. Most people were unaware of their presence unless they were a mage. Or a succubus.

The skateboard looked homemade. I couldn't help but wonder if Skiff had put it together. Since he was a mage, he might have induced a gremlin to live inside it.

On Rore's desk, a flash from her laptop caught my eye. The open screen had switched to one of those screen savers that goes through your personal pictures. A bright one had attracted my attention—a summer day with a younger Rore and her mother at a sporting event. It flipped a second later to one of Orion with a comical expression on his face. It looked to be from the same sporting event. I couldn't help it when the corner of my mouth curled up. I liked his smiles.

Rore breezed in with a plate of chocolate chip cookies. "Sorry I took so long. I just needed to finish that conversation."

"Skiff?" I asked.

She plopped into her desk chair and offered me a cookie. "It was Zeek. He wanted to apologize for what happened at the restaurant. After that, we just chatted for a little while. It felt good. I haven't talked to a guy other than Skiff in years."

I couldn't hide my frown. This was not good. I had defended the vampires to Terra, but she was right—they didn't think highly of the other races. If Zeek was being nice, he wanted something.

"He asked you out, didn't he?"

I felt a guilty discomfort coming from her. "He did. He invited me to a party tonight, but I'm not going." She made a face. "*It's Chaleta's.*" She popped the rest of her cookie into her mouth. "But we left it open to do something another time." She offered nothing more, and I could tell the subject was closed.

On the laptop, the picture switched to one with Rore and Skiff standing side by side in formal attire. Rore looked quite cute in a dark jade gown, and Skiff had a dark suit, but I couldn't help but notice that the corsage on her wrist perfectly matched the boutonniere on his jacket. The picture spoke of a closer relationship than they currently had. I wondered what had happened.

"Is that your prom picture?" I asked.

Rore glanced at it. The picture changed to a mountain scene with her and Skiff smiling into the camera. I could feel her emotions drift to sadness. "Yeah, and that one is when we visited the Smoky Mountains." She quickly looked away.

Don't do it. Don't ask. But my mouth had a mind of its own. "Why did you break it off? You two seemed so happy."

Her shoulders slumped. "Because he's an absolute genius."

I gave her a puzzled frown. "I'm not following you."

She smiled wistfully. "When he took the placement tests, they made him retake them because he scored so high. He's already in advanced classes and even chats with some researchers at Berkley. MIT is trying to recruit him."

I shrugged. "So he's got brains. Is that a reason to break up with him?"

She shook her head. "I'm not nearly as smart as he is and will be going to the local university. The fool was going to follow me there." She sighed sadly. "I couldn't allow that. He'll do something great one day, and I won't be the one to hold him back." She shrugged. "So I cut him loose."

Waves of sadness and grief were coming from her. "How did he take it?" I asked gently.

"About as well as you'd expect. We argued, but I wouldn't budge."

"He still cares for you."

She looked down. "I know." She took a deep breath. "But he'll get over it. There's probably some girl out there who's prettier than I am and a match for his brains. Someone who will make him happier than I ever could."

"That seems rather drastic."

She nodded distractedly. "It's hard." She took a deep breath and let it out slowly. "But it had to be done. He'll thank me for it one day." She turned back to the screen, and that prom picture popped back up. Her hands froze over the keyboard, and for several heartbeats, she sat unmoving with her back to me. She radiated waves of sadness and longing. My heart broke for her. She had been enduring the pain of her decision, suffering in silence.

All alone.

I couldn't help myself. I stood and wrapped my arms around her from behind. She turned and buried her face in my shoulder. "It hurts Lapis. I know it's the right thing to do. But it hurts so bad."

I just held her as my shirt soaked up her tears. "I know."

I was tempted to take her sadness and turn it into something more pleasant. But that would be wrong. This was her grief, and she needed to feel it so she could heal.

And so we sat until Rore got her emotions under control. She pulled back and smiled at me sheepishly. "Sorry for the meltdown, but I needed that."

I smiled. "Anytime. I'll help however I can."

Grabbing a tissue from the box on her desk, she wiped her eyes and turned to her laptop. She blew her nose and took a deep breath. I could still feel her sadness, but it wasn't as bad. It shifted to hope. She looked over her shoulder and smiled. "Now, let's look for your grandfather's address. Shall we?"

She held her fist out, and we bumped ours together. "Let's."

She brought up a map of Edgemont Park and the surrounding streets. She pointed. "Here's Byan Street, and this is where it runs into the park. And . . ."

Her fingers flew over the keyboard. It took a few more minutes of searching, but she brought up what she was seeking.

"This map is the same area from about 20 years ago." The map wasn't near the quality of the modern one—just a simple picture of an old map. Rore's finger traced Byan Street on the old map. And indeed, it continued past where the future park would be. The map didn't have the street numbers, but we could guess from the blocks.

"Look!" exclaimed Rore. She flipped back to the present-day map. After a bit of searching, we found a street that followed the old Byan Street path. But it had a different name—Edgemont Victory Street. Rore and I shared a glance. Only a few blocks along that street were the house numbers we needed.

She zoomed in to a street view of the houses and moved quickly through them.

She stopped and took her hands away from the keyboard.

I gasped.

The picture was of my grandfather's house.

I was jerked out of sleep by a breeze on my face and my phone ringing persistently. It must have cycled to voice mail because it paused for a few seconds and then started again.

Bleary-eyed, I fumbled for it and found it was Terra. What could she want this late? My phone said it was just before midnight. I had been asleep for a little over an hour.

But as my groggy brain began to work, I noticed a breeze coming from Rore's window—it was slightly raised. And to my shock, Rore was not in her bed. *Damn.*

After a brief celebration for finding my grandfather's house, we made plans to visit the next morning. When things quieted down, the day's events quickly caught up with me. Exhausted, I called it an early night—at least by Rore's standards—and got in my blankets. I had drifted off while she sat on her bed with her phone. Only now she was gone.

I groggily accepted the call, but before I could say anything, Terra jumped in.

"I just happened to check on my grandchildren before retiring. I see both their phones are not in the house, while yours still is. So, Miss Midnyte, where is my grandson?"

I suddenly didn't feel groggy anymore. "I . . . I'm not sure. I was asleep."

"Aren't you supposed to be watching over him?"

I cocked my jaw in anger. "Don't I get a sleep break or something?" My voice was louder than I meant.

"Not when my family is concerned. Find him. Unless your beauty sleep is more important than my favor. And pray nothing has happened to him while you're getting there." She disconnected.

I stared at the phone for a moment, not believing she had hung up on me. I wanted to call her a couple of choice names but decided against it. She knew Rore had left, so she might have the room bugged.

I got up quietly and crept out to Orion's room. Also empty.

Great.

I returned to Rore's room and started pulling out clothes while I texted Terra. *Both gone. Do you know where they went?*

I only got to pull on my T-shirt when I received a reply. *Orion at this location. Aurorah in transit. Probably chasing him. Looks to be a large party. Dress appropriately, or they won't let you in.*

I was puzzled by the location she sent me. But it activated an app I didn't think was standard on my phone. I could see a blue dot at a house and another pink one not too far away, inching in blue's direction. The house looked to be about twelve miles away.

I turned my head toward the ceiling and gave a silent

scream. How in the Protector's name was I going to get there? And a party? I *hated* parties—too loud and too many overpowering emotions. I looked down at my plain jeans and shirt. I was so screwed. These were definitely not party clothes. I only had one dress that looked hideous, and Rore's clothes were the wrong size. I started to pull stuff out of my suitcase. I didn't have that much to begin with—just a few pairs of jeans and T-shirts. And worse, the one at the bottom had the knees ripped out from a skateboarding tumble. Mom had been so angry at me about that.

My eyes went wide. That was it! I quickly pulled on the ripped jeans and an old T-shirt of my mom's with a rock band's logo on it and tied it high at the waist. My lace-up canvas shoes would have to do. I grabbed my brush and sighed as I gave my hair a quick run-through. I then glanced at Rore's cosmetics on her dresser. *Please don't be mad at me.*

I quickly selected a red, red lip gloss and black, black eyeliner. I hurriedly applied it. I smiled. Not bad for a succubus. I frowned. But I was still missing something.

I glanced over at a series of hooks on the wall. There were several hats and a few coats. A hat would be perfect, but it wouldn't sit right with my horns. A short, black leather jacket caught my eye. It was too big for Rore, so it had to be Orion's. I'd heard him mumble something about her stealing his clothes.

I strode to it and slipped it on. I instantly fell in love with the cool leather. It had to be one of the nicest things I'd worn. The sleeves were too long, and the shoulders a bit wide, but it would work. Plus, it had a faint young man smell, which made me think of Orion. It just felt right.

I glanced at myself in the mirror. The bad girl look was not my usual fashion statement—I was more of a stay-in-the-background kind of person. But for this, it worked, and that's all that mattered.

I stepped to the window. I raised it and looked down. It was just a little over five feet above the ground with a bush in front of it. But someone had been kind enough to put a few blocks behind the bush so that one could easily step out. Rore must use this fairly often.

I looked out into the night. How was I going to get there? Orion had probably just transformed into something four-legged, and Rore had enough funds to hire a ride. Me? I wasn't a shifter, and I was broke. Andromeda had left for her shift at the animal hospital a few hours ago, so that wasn't an option. I grimaced as I thought about calling Terra, but she already wasn't happy with me. I sighed. If I ran, everything would be over before I got there. Maybe I could hitch a ride.

I felt a burst of emotion behind me. Sadness. Longing. Loneliness.

I turned but didn't see anyone. I knew it had been there. My eyes were once again drawn to the skateboard in the corner. That was the source. The little gremlin inside was trying to get my attention.

I hurried to the skateboard propped up in the corner. I squatted and laid a hand on its bright pink surface.

"Are you trying to get my attention?"

I was shocked to feel a burst of happiness. I had sensed gremlins in the past, but they generally ignored me. Mom said they were strange creatures and did as they wanted. Even mages who could imbed them into machines called them fickle.

"You think I should ride you?"

I felt joy coming from him.

I considered it. It might be a little faster than running, but I didn't know about the hills between here and that house. A skateboard could quickly slow me down.

"I appreciate the offer, but I doubt it would help."

The board went sad. Almost depressed. I guess I could understand. If I was a gremlin inside a skateboard, I would have taken residence only so I could sail down streets going as fast as I could. I felt terrible about leaving him.

I sighed. "Can you go fast?"

The burst of joy was so strong it nearly knocked me over.

"Do you know the way to . . ." I rattled off the address.

Again joy.

I grabbed the board and tucked it under my arm. I swear, if the little gremlin could, he would have danced. We eased out the window.

The sidewalks were empty, but there were ample streetlights to see the way. Setting the skateboard down on the sidewalk, I pulled my phone out and got my bearings. I prayed the little gremlin wasn't thinking too highly of his abilities.

I grinned. "All right, Mr. Skateboard, I haven't done this in a while, so take it easy on me."

I got a feeling of confidence mixed with happiness. I guess that was an *I will.*

I took a deep breath. Stepping on it, I shoved off—

And nearly fell on my butt as the thing shot forward and entered the street.

As I fought for balance, the board sped up. He was powering it! I squatted and shifted my balance. We overtook a slow-moving car; I think we had to be breaking the speed limit. My eyes grew large as we approached an intersection, and the light turned red. A sleek sports car was waiting, ready to enter, and to my horror, it started rolling forward.

The skateboard gave a burst of joy and determination, putting on an incredible burst of speed. I was too scared to close my eyes. We sailed through the intersection just ahead of the approaching vehicle, which missed us by mere inches. I felt the glow of happiness and accomplishment from the skateboard.

It angled toward the right into a new street, and I was forced to bank with it. I shouldn't be able to hang on the board as easily as I was. There likely was some magic involved in keeping me on board. The street went up a steep hill, and the damn thing accelerated, powering up the slope. How much magic did this thing have? This was unreal!

When we crested the top, my stomach lurched as we became airborne for a few seconds. I kept my knees loose and absorbed the landing. That had been—

Fun.

I couldn't help but grin. As my confidence grew, I relaxed my posture and began to move with the board. The little gremlin sensed my intent and followed me perfectly. With the wind in my face, whipping my hair, it rode like a dream. This was *way* cool.

Ten minutes later, we entered an expensive neighborhood. The board slowed, and we stopped in front of a house that could easily pass as a mansion. It had a stone-paved driveway with an entrance protected by a granite fence and an open iron gate. Tall shrubs lined the path leading to the stately gray stone house. Every window was lit, and throbbing music came from inside. I had expected Chaleta's family to have money, but this was something from a storybook.

I checked the locator app on my phone, and sure enough, it said Orion was just ahead. Rore, however, was close but still approaching.

I found a suitable bush and hid the skateboard behind it. "I'll be back," I whispered to it. "And thanks."

The little gremlin gave a burst of joy. I was definitely going to ride that board again.

I turned toward the house and took a deep breath, bracing myself for the walk up the driveway. *I hate parties.*

Before I had taken two steps, a beat-up old junk heap of a car pulled up to the curb. From its looks, I was surprised it could even run. Rore jumped out, and when the overhead light came on, I could see Skiff was driving. He didn't look happy, and neither did she. Frustration was their primary emotion, with Skiff's reaching toward anger and concern. They exchanged a couple of terse words, which I couldn't make out. But it was easy to see he did not want her there. He took off as soon as the door closed—I was assuming to park—but from his speed, I wasn't sure.

Rore watched him leave, sadness mixing with her frustration. She sighed and turned toward the house. She was so intent on her destination that she almost walked right past me. She glanced my way and then did a classic double-take.

"What are you doing here?" I could feel her surprise. "I left you dead asleep."

I crossed my arms across my chest. "I know. I'm a little pissed that you left me behind."

"But . . ." she stammered. "This isn't your problem."

"Actually, any problem that affects my friend affects me." The side of my mouth curled up. I hooked a thumb over my shoulder toward the house. "I believe you're going into a lion's den. You could use some backup."

I didn't need my ability to see she was overwhelmed. Her eyes glistened, and her bottom lip quivered. She hugged me. "Thank you. You don't know what this means to me. I thought I was alone."

I couldn't help but wonder why she would react so strongly. There was some trauma there that she hadn't told me about. She had mentioned no other friends besides Skiff and Orion. Was it possible all of hers had abandoned her? It was a horrible thought.

She stepped back. "Skiff's a little angry with me. He's been banned from the property for stealing gremlins. He can't help that they keep following him home."

My eyebrows went up. Could that be how the little gremlin knew where to go? Surely not. He did seem a little overpowered for just a skateboard.

She continued, "I wouldn't have even come if it wasn't for Orion. He's not supposed to be here either. I'm afraid Chaleta will make him relapse."

She pulled back, looking puzzled. "But how did you get here so fast? Skiff had to drive me."

I shrugged. "I borrowed your skateboard."

Her eyes went large. "You're kidding. Skiff wanted to help me ride better and put a gremlin inside it. I haven't been able to get on it since. That thing is scary."

I couldn't tell her I had communicated with the gremlin inside it. I grinned. "Yeah, it's definitely enchanted. Really surprised me, but after I adjusted, I got along just fine. I'm pretty good at skateboarding."

She shook her head in disbelief. "You must be. That thing has a mind of its own. Skiff says he put a gremlin in it named Glitch. The way it acted, I thought the name was appropriate."

I nodded. *Glitch.* I liked it. Next time I would know what to call him.

Rore patted my arm. "We'll talk later. I have a brother to collect."

"Do I look all right?" I asked, suddenly nervous.

Rore snorted. "You're kidding. Most of the guys, and probably some of the girls, are going to have their eyes pop out. You're hot. I almost didn't recognize you." She turned up the drive. "Now come on. We need to hurry."

As we approached, the music got louder. The front door was open, with a short, brute of a man standing just outside of it. He had an elongated nose, tall, pointed ears, and was wearing a tailored black suit. Strangely, he had a set of goggles pushed up high on his forehead. They were an odd fashion statement. I wondered if they served some other purpose.

I leaned toward Rore. "Who is that at the door?"

She whispered back. "That's Herbert, the Nachtman's bodyguard. He's a Goblin. He ensures nothing gets inside that isn't supposed to, like alcohol or drugs." She sighed. "Or uninvited guests."

Goblins were Night-clan, and like humans, were mundane with no magic. But they were exceptionally strong and loyal to a fault. Goblins were prized as servants and would frequently attach themselves to powerful households—especially those of vampires.

As we neared the door, I felt a calm boredom coming from him, and thankfully, no malice. Herbert blocked our entry with an extended arm. I swear it was as thick as an oak tree.

Rore smiled sweetly. "Hello Herbert. We're here for the party."

His eyes narrowed. "Miss Strewert. I don't recall you being on the invite list."

"Zeek invited me."

"He didn't mention it to me."

Rore put on a perfect pouty face. "I wasn't going to come, but I changed my mind when I found out Orion was here."

Herbert rolled his eyes. "Yes, he is here. Another disaster waiting to happen."

Rore gave him her most sincere smile.

He put a hand to his chin. "Miss Strewert, are you sure you want to go in? The young mistress and her friends didn't exactly treat you well last time."

"I didn't do anything."

"True. But *they* did. Master was not pleased when your grandmother phoned saying he had to pay for a new dress. Master doesn't like being told what to do."

She smiled innocently. "I'll be careful. I promise."

He glanced at me and then back to Rore. "She with you?"

Rore put a hand on my arm. "Of course. This is Lapis, my BFF." She grinned brightly at me.

He sighed. "All right. Just don't get me fired. Do you have any contraband?"

Rore made a face. "Of course not."

"Good, then you don't mind if I check."

He pulled down his goggles. I broke out in a cold sweat when

I realized it was a charm detector—likely one that could see through illusions.

He studied Rore for a moment, nodded, and then turned to me. The charm under my arm suddenly heated, ramping up its protections, and increasing the drain on its already low magic. In protest, my charm gave a brief double vibration. I prayed he hurried, and it didn't give out in the middle of the party.

Herbert finally leaned back and raised his goggles. "Okay, you're both clean. Enjoy yourselves." He thought for a moment, then added. "Please don't pick a fight. I'm feeling a little hungry this evening." He gave us a wide smile, one with a lot of sharp teeth.

Goblins didn't really eat people. It was just part of the mystique. But from the way Rore shuddered, I wasn't sure she knew.

"Of course," she smiled back nervously and led us inside.

We entered a large foyer with clumps of people talking or singles playing on their phones. Rore steered us to a set of stairs leading down toward the source of the music. As we descended, the light grew dim, and the air swirled with special effects fog. I felt like I was intruding into a loud and misty dungeon.

We emerged onto a basement dancefloor complete with a DJ, flashing lights, and music so loud I could feel it vibrating in my chest. It was packed with people of all races and sexes, dancing to the throbbing beat or sitting around the edges on chairs and sofas. Everyone was dressed in hip fashions, tightly fitted to their perfect bodies, and revealing a lot of skin. Their eyes tracked our progress—some wearing smirks and others leaning to whisper to their partner. This was the territory of the wealthy and well-connected. Our intrusion was not appreciated.

Rore scanned the crowd, looking for Orion. She took my hand and pushed through the dancers, leading me toward the other side of the room. I followed her in a daze. I was on sensory overload—the music, the people, the pressure of their feelings. Their emotions filled the room with a cacophony of lust, envy, jealousy—too many to take in. I was way out of my comfort zone, and I clearly didn't belong.

I was ready to bolt.

But I couldn't. We had to find Orion. While Orion's own magic should protect him from a vampire's influence, I had seen firsthand that Chaleta did not respect boundaries. My fear was that she would convince him to either lower his barrier, or worse, have some way around it. Then she would tap him. I could not allow that to happen.

Pull it together, Lapis. I took a deep breath and focused my thoughts, drawing on a trick my mother had taught me several years ago.

I had been about twelve and was getting ready to compete in my first track event. I had taken one look at the crowd and fled. Mom had quickly found me huddled in a corner. She could feel my emotions and knew instantly what was wrong.

She squatted in front of me. "Lapis, my jewel, you can do this."

"But the people," I protested. "I can feel them. They're just waiting for me to mess up."

She smiled. "Then prove them wrong. You're the best runner here today. If you don't compete, you've let them win. It's okay to be afraid."

I thought of a quick fix. Mom was a powerful succubus, so maybe she could help. "Will you take my fear?" I begged.

She gave me a loving smile and pulled me forward to kiss my forehead. I expected the fear to drain away, but it didn't. I looked up in surprise.

"I'm sorry," she said, smiling. "But I can't do that. If I did, then you would definitely lose."

I was puzzled. "How's that?"

"Your fear is just misdirected energy. Energy you don't want to waste. Instead, use it to channel their negative emotions and turn them into *confidence*. Confidence that you will win."

Needless to say, I did compete. While I finished fifth, I learned a valuable lesson.

I opened my eyes. These people would not stop me from reaching my goal. I would obtain that favor. *I will protect my friends.* If they were blasting me with negative emotions, then I would just blast back.

I lifted my head and straightened my shoulders. I took some of the negative emotions and transformed them into confidence, radiating it around me. While it didn't stop the whispers and sneers, I could see they sensed the difference.

Rore looked around, frustrated. "I don't see him."

A hand touched her shoulder. She spun to find Zeek standing beside us.

"Hello, Rore," he said, smiling, his crimson eyes pulsing as they reflected the dance floor lighting. "I'm so glad you decided to come." He smoothly took her hand and kissed it. "The evening just got a little bit brighter."

She blushed.

Zeek turned to regard me. The room was too crowded to isolate his emotions completely, but I could tell his smile wasn't reflected in his eyes. "It's good to see you too, Lapis. Maybe later I can introduce you to some of my friends." Our gazes locked. "I'm sure they'll like your *taste*."

My eyes narrowed at the veiled threat. I pulled Rore's hand from his and stepped between them. "Save your games for one of your groupies. Where's Orion?"

His smile faltered, clearly not liking the disrespect. "You certainly enjoy jumping between people, Lapis." He gripped my arm and pulled me out from between him and Rore. I nearly stumbled. His vampire reflexes made it happen so fast.

He whipped me around to face the other side of the room. He leaned close. "I saw him wandering around over there earlier. I'm sure he's found Chaleta by now, but perhaps you better check." He turned back to Rore. "And while you're gone, I'll dance with this beautiful creature."

Rore hesitated for the barest moment. *Was she actually tempted?*

But she shook her head. "I really can't, Zeek. I hope you understand. Orion's a little fragile right now."

He grinned. "I do understand," he said. "But trust me. They are perfectly fine." He reached to touch her bare arm.

I was tired of delaying. I intercepted his hand, grasping it firmly in my own. "Can't you understand the word *no*? She doesn't want to dance." My eyes held challenge.

He matched my glare and turned his dark crimson eyes to stare into my own. Through our contact, I could feel his vampire magic slam against my barrier—no simple probing, but a full-on attack. He likely thought I was magic-blind and would never feel it. Perhaps even hoping that my charm was cheap and he could simply overpower it.

But the only effect it had was to really, really piss me off. I had sworn to Mom I would only use my powers for self-defense. I thought this qualified. Mine worked differently than a vampire's. Theirs only attacked one's will. But with mine, I used their feelings. Only a witch's defensive shield could stop it.

And he was not a witch.

I inhaled some of the emotions around me and changed them into anxiety. I then fed them into Zeek.

I stepped closer into his space. "She *said* she didn't want to dance. Now, where is Orion?"

He tried to pull his hand back, but I wouldn't let go. Fear began to creep into his eyes. "We shouldn't disturb them right now."

I increased the apprehension to fear. "Where . . . is . . . he?" I asked firmly. Two dudes stepped closer to intervene, but I hit them with the same fear I was feeding to Zeek. They hesitated with wide eyes, likely convinced I was the most terrifying girl they had ever seen.

Zeek tried to step away. I grabbed the front of his carefully pressed shirt and pulled his face toward mine.

I added disgust to the mix, gradually ramping it up. "One last time. Where is he?"

His eyes grew wide. "Up . . . Upstairs. Her bedroom." He clamped a hand over his mouth.

I released him with a slight shove, and as I did, the fear drained away. But before I turned, I saw recognition, and he frowned deeply. *He knew what I was.* I, a lowly succubus, had dared to use my powers on a mighty vampire. If he complained to the Night-clan elder, there could be consequences. But I'd have to worry about that later.

"Thank you," I said politely.

I turned to find that the music had died, and everyone in the room was staring with a mix of shock and awe. The DJ seemed to catch himself and hurried to put on another song. Conversation in the room gradually returned.

Rore glanced at me with a strange expression. She knew something had happened between Zeek and me, but she wasn't sure what. I took her hand and led her toward the stairs.

People immediately stepped aside for us, clearing a path. I dragged Rore up the stairs to the foyer and then found another elegant staircase going up.

As we moved further upstairs and away from the throng of people below us, I could sense individual sets of emotions. And there was one particular set I recognized. I had been able to sense Mom's combination of feelings at a distance, but never anyone else's. Yet, I was sure it was Orion. And there was something not quite right. I could feel a growing anger.

Oh, no. I pulled Rore up the stairs. "We have to hurry."

The landing led to a hall with several closed doors that were probably bedrooms. Orion's emotions were coming from the one at the very end. His emotions were swirling. I ran to it and barged inside without knocking.

The bedroom was large with curtains, bedspread, walls, and even the carpet, all various shades of bright pink. But it was what was in the center that drew my eye. Chaleta was wearing a hip party dress, much too short. It clung to her curves, leaving little to the imagination. Orion stood with his arms around her, and I could feel the dark magic swirling around them. She was pressed up against him and was leaning in for a kiss.

My eyes went wide. She must have gotten past his barrier. *She was going to tap him.*

Chapter 13

"NO!" I YELLED.

I didn't even think. Reaching deep inside, I pulled up revulsion—the kind one feels when something is utterly disgusting—and flung it at the vampire.

Orion jerked upright as if someone had hit him. Chaleta slapped a hand over her mouth and fled to the bathroom. Retching sounds came from inside. I winced. I guess I hit her a little harder than I meant, and Orion must have caught the edge.

Rore followed me into the room a second later, but Orion's eyes were all on me. "What are you doing here?" he snarled.

I gazed back at him coolly. "Accompanying your sister. She had this strange notion you might be in trouble." I could sense his churning emotions. Something about the mix felt really odd.

He frowned. "Did I look like I was in trouble?"

I glared back at him. "More than you know." I couldn't tell him what she was doing—a human wouldn't have known.

Rore took his arm and tried to pull him away, but it was like pulling on a mountain. He didn't budge.

"Come on, Orion," Rore pleaded. "Mom will freak if she discovers you snuck out of the house again."

Chaleta came out of the bathroom, wiping her hands on a towel. She had regained her composure, but from her guarded glare, she was sure one of us had done something. I hoped she didn't figure out it was me. I didn't need someone else reporting me to the elder.

Orion's emotions continued to swirl. They were so . . . Then it hit me. *Out of balance.*

All living things have emotions, which come in millions of variations and combinations. Like the colors of the spectrum, there wasn't just one blue, but a multitude of shades and tones. So when I felt Orion's emotions, I could instinctively tell the mix wasn't exactly right. His were shifted toward anger, making his mix off balance. I had noticed this before when he was an ogre. At the time, I had attributed it to what he was, but now I wasn't so sure.

Could it be a charm?

It would certainly explain his swirling emotions. It might even be affecting his soul's barrier, which would give Chaleta an opening to influence him. It would likely be similar to my illusion charm, and the only evidence would be a small mark on his skin. It could even have been placed there without his knowledge.

My heart sank. When a charm was applied to a person against their will, it was called a different name—*a curse*. Night-clan had a class of people that did just that. *Sorcerers.* This was bad.

I decided to think about it later. I had a more immediate problem and went with a temporary fix. I took a deep breath, and like an artist mixing her colors, I adjusted Orion's emotions, making them more normal. At my ministrations, I could see his shoulders and face visibly relax.

Chaleta discarded the towel on the bed and smiled at Orion. "Sorry about that, my love." She took his other arm while fixing Rore with a glare, likely thinking the witch had hit her with a spell. "It must have been a bad shrimp." She frowned. "A very bad one."

Rore tugged again on his arm. "Please, Bro. Let's just go."

Chaleta huffed. "Can't you see he wants to stay. We were fine before you and your little pet burst in."

Orion seemed unsure as his rebalanced emotions allowed him to think clearly. "I . . ."

She put her two fingers over his lips. "Later. Kisses first, then talk." Chaleta nudged Rore aside and then put her arms around his neck, plastering her body to his. She smiled up at him as she teased the hairs on the back of his head.

At that moment, I felt Orion's emotions begin to shift into that odd mix again. There was definitely something going on and Chaleta was in the center of it.

I grabbed her arm and pulled her back. "Orion," I said firmly. "You need to come with us. Can't you see she's just using you?"

That was the wrong thing to say. His anger went through the roof. Orion glared at both Rore and me. "I'm staying," he growled. "You're the ones that need to leave."

His emotions were right back where they were. And it pissed me off. I reached inside Orion and adjusted them once more. I couldn't keep doing this. We had to get him out, and I could see only one way to do it. I was going to have to make Chaleta angry.

Very angry.

I shoved Chaleta out of the way. I stepped right up to Orion until his face was inches from mine. "What if I don't want to go away, you jerk! This soul-sucker doesn't care for you one bit. Not like I do. I'm your girlfriend, remember?"

"Hey!" Chaleta protested.

I shoved her again. Harder. She staggered backward to trip and fall on her bed.

Now comes the dangerous part. I reached out and amplified the vampire's anger.

Chaleta's eyes narrowed. "Get out," she ordered. "Or I'll have Herbert throw you out."

I fed her more frustration, building on what she already had. I gave her a wicked smile. "Then make me. You're too weak to take me on yourself and too stupid to realize he doesn't want you. He's *mine*."

I turned to Orion, leaned up, and jerked his head down.

Then I kissed him.

I meant it just to piss off Chaleta, but as soon as our lips touched—it was like nothing I'd ever felt. I was admittedly not that experienced with kissing, but the few I'd had were *nothing* like this. His lips were soft and firm, and as I melted against him, I felt a tingle going from my head to my toes. I pulled back, and we looked into each other's eyes. I expected anger, but instead, there was surprise.

Chaleta snarled and spun me around. She slapped me hard enough to rattle my teeth. "You and ketchup head find somewhere else to stink up."

I again shoved her back, feeding her even more anger. Her face turned bright red.

"Like I said. Leave my man alone."

She bounded back and, using her lightning-fast reflexes, gripped me around the throat. I knew it was stupid—vampires were strong—but I needed her to be even more angry. So I fed her more.

Snarling in rage, she shook me and threw me against the wall. I landed hard enough to see stars and slumped to the floor.

Chaleta was immediately on top of me, pounding away. I covered my head, and fortunately, my thick jacket padded her blows. Orion grabbed her and bodily lifted her away. She screamed and turned her blows on him.

A moment later, Herbert burst into the room. The bodyguard lifted Chaleta off us, plopped her on the bed, and pointed a finger at her. "Stay." From his deadly tone, there was no arguing.

Displaying lots of sharp teeth, he turned to Orion, Rore, and me. *"Out. Now."* He didn't shout, but there was no denying the command in his voice and the deadly look in his eyes.

The three of us filed out of the room, with Herbert following close behind. The goblin didn't speak again until we were outside the house. "Go home," he said tersely. "And don't come back."

Rore protested. "But she started it. We were just defending ourselves."

Herbert shrugged. "Based upon Chaleta's temperament, I believe you. But I need my job. Now move along."

We turned and walked down the driveway to find Skiff waiting for us. "Done already?" Then he spotted me. "What are you doing here?"

"Being a nuisance," grumbled Orion. "Chaleta and I were making up. But that's not going to happen now."

Maybe it was all the emotions in the air this evening, or perhaps it was Chaleta beating on me, but I lost it. I wheeled on him and stabbed him in the chest with my finger. "No, she wasn't. And you're too much of an idiot to see it. She's using you."

He glared right back. "You're crazy. We did break up, but that was because she was scared of how close we were becoming. She's over that now and wanted to get back together."

"Bull!" I shouted. "She's got something to do with your sudden outbursts of anger. I don't know how she's doing it, but you're going to hurt someone if you're not careful."

Rore jumped to my defense. "She's right Orion. Since she came around, you've started to lose control."

Orion glared at his sister. "You don't know what you're talking about. You're just jealous because I at least have a significant other. You trashed yours."

Rore gasped. Inside, I could feel her emotions crash. Her bottom lip trembled. "That was different," she said weakly.

Skiff jumped in, not liking what was being said. "Orion. That was harsh."

He turned on his friend. "You stay out of this. It was you she trashed."

Then he turned to glare at me. His lovely eyes darkened, and his lips pursed in anger. "And what was that kiss stunt you pulled?"

Our eyes locked. "Are you saying you can't stand to kiss a lowly person like me?" I growled.

That set him back. "No, I mean— We're not— It was just unexpected." His expression hardened. "You know what I mean."

I got right in his face. "No, I don't. You've had it out for me ever since I arrived. So what's your problem?"

"You're a distraction," he spat. "Everything was fine before you came."

Something was still rolling his emotions and putting him out of balance. It had to be a curse—maybe one that increased when Chaleta had been nearby. Whatever it was, I needed to root this out at the source. I was afraid to adjust his emotions much more. Sometimes doing it too much could cause long-term problems. As for me, I had my limits too, and I was pretty much at them. A good brick wall would be good right now.

I got in his face. "You idiot! You've got a curse on you. Take off your shirt. I'll prove it to you."

He pulled back in confusion. "What? *Here?* Are you crazy?"

"Humor me. If I don't find something, I will admit I'm wrong and promise never to bother you and Chaleta again." I glanced at his sister. "Rore won't either."

He smirked. "For that, you got a deal."

He pulled off his T-shirt, revealing his muscular chest. He stood waiting.

I didn't know what I was looking for. Trying not to notice the warmth of his skin, I ran my hands lightly over his chest. I used the light on my phone to see better, looking for anything that was unusual. I moved to his back and found nothing there either. I stepped away in frustration. It had to be there. But where?

He grinned in satisfaction. "Giving up?"

I pursed my lips in thought. My charm was under my arm. Could his be there too?

I raised his left arm and ran my hand along it. To my surprise, I felt my mother's amulet grow warm. I looked closer and held my phone light up to it. There was what looked like a tiny tattoo of a complex design, no bigger than a dime. I ran a finger over it. It emitted a tiny emotional feeling. I extended my power toward it—

Like lightning jumping between clouds, it connected. The terrible, angry thread of emotion wrapped itself around me. I gasped. I could feel the anger rising inside of me—a worm in my soul that wanted to eat me from the inside out. I couldn't move; my lungs were paralyzed. It had been booby-trapped, waiting for a magical detection to spring. I was sure I was going to die.

And then my mother's amulet did something it had never done before. It flashed scorching hot. I could feel it burning against my chest. This was immediately followed by the quick retreat of the coiled anger that bound me, evaporating in a white flash. One minute it was there, and then it was gone. I blinked. *What the hades had just happened?*

Rore looked at me in amazement. "What did you just do? I saw dark magic reach out and grab you, but it vanished a moment later."

I tried to shake off my moment of terror. "I'm not sure. Whatever it was, it must have had a self-destruct." I turned back to Orion and saw that the curse was gone. "How does that feel?"

He blinked at me. I already knew the answer. I could feel his emotions shifting back to their normal state. "It's not there anymore," he said in amazement.

I cocked my head. "Now, who was right?"

He stared at me, unable to find words.

I turned away from them, my own emotions in turmoil. Too much had happened this evening. "I'm going back to bed." I stepped over to the familiar bush and pulled out the skateboard.

Skiff recognized it immediately. "You rode Glitch?" he asked in surprise. "No one's been able to ride him before."

I shrugged. "He does great. You just have to listen to what he's telling you." I glanced at Orion. "Unlike some people."

I stepped on it and shoved off, quickly accelerating away.

"I could give you a ride!" Skiff shouted.

But I didn't stop and soon put them all behind me.

I rode around for a while, trying to calm myself. I did find an old brick wall where I could dump my surplus emotions. At least, that was a relief.

It was late when I arrived back at the Strewert's house. I climbed in the window to find Rore already in bed and snoring softly. Thankfully, she had left it open for me.

I laid down on my pallet, expecting to be out immediately.

But my mind was awash with memories from the evening. Chaleta had been close to tapping Orion. Closer than either he or Rore realized. If we hadn't intervened, she would have owned him. I shuddered at the thought. And that curse was not simple magic. It had not only negated Orion's natural protection, but had been booby-trapped. It had to be from a very powerful, and expensive, sorcerer. Definitely not something a love-sick vampire would do. None of it made sense. And worse, all the perpetrators were Night-clan. If I made too much noise about this, it could be life threatening.

However, there was one thing that troubled me the most. My fingers stole out from under the blanket and touched my lips.

Why in the world did I kiss him?

With the curse making Orion act like a jerk, and Chalita so close to tapping him, I'd just reacted.

But what was even more disturbing—

Why had it felt so . . .right?

The next morning, I jerked awake, but thankfully without the panic of the previous one. The bright sunshine was again coming playfully through the window, using the stained glass rainbow to spray color across the walls. I was tempted to just lay there. But my stomach had other plans. I was seriously hungry.

Rore was still asleep with the covers pulled over her head. I couldn't help but smile. She had her problems, but she was all right. She had volunteered to get me to my grandfather's house later this morning. I prayed it wouldn't be a wasted trip.

After visiting the bathroom and brushing my teeth—I hated morning breath—I padded barefoot into the kitchen. No one was up yet, but the previous evening's activities had left me starving. I wondered if it would be all right to get a bowl of cereal.

I looked up, sensing the emotions of those in the house. Rore was where I had left her, and it seemed Andromeda was also still in bed, which made sense—she had worked the evening shift.

But there was another presence emanating from out back. I went to the kitchen sink and glanced out the window. Orion was sitting, lotus pose, in the center of their patio. He had his eyes closed, meditating. Maybe I could ask him where the cereal was.

Stepping outside through a sliding glass door, I watched him as I approached. He was shirtless, wearing only his pajama bottoms, and clearly not expecting company. I didn't want to bother him, but I was ravenous. I waited a moment, hoping he would notice me.

"What do you want?" he asked neutrally, without opening his eyes.

"I . . . I'm sorry to interrupt, but I was hoping it would be all right to have some cereal."

He opened his eyes and considered me. He then suddenly rose in one smooth motion, and I marveled at the grace of the movement. Without looking at me, he went inside. "I am too."

I followed a moment later.

He pulled two cereal boxes from the cabinet and set out milk, bowls, and spoons on the counter. He raised an eyebrow and nodded toward the boxes.

I went for the sweet, multicolored loopy things. Mom used to buy them when I was younger, but as I got older, she had graduated to the flaky stuff with no sugar.

Orion naturally went for the fruit brand. While his expression was neutral, I could sense a swirling of emotions inside him. Thankfully, they were normal, and anger wasn't one of them.

We leaned against the counter, eating in silence, which was killing me. I tried a neutral topic. "Do you meditate every day?"

He paused mid-chew, but then nodded and offered nothing more. I did notice his brand flakes seemed very interesting.

"Does it help?"

He shrugged. He shoved the last bite into his mouth and then drank what was left in the bowl. A drop of milk remained on his chin.

I couldn't help myself. I reached up and wiped it away with my finger. I kept my expression neutral but winced inwardly. I don't know why I did that.

His eyes bored into mine, and I sensed the storm within swirl even faster. I couldn't break the gaze. All I could see were those lovely, dark eyes.

He opened his mouth to speak—

A yawning Rore shuffled into the kitchen and broke the spell between us. Orion looked away.

Rore was still half asleep, with shoulders slumped and hair looking like a red explosion.

Orion turned away to put his bowl in the dishwasher while I busied myself with finding another loopy thing in my leftover milk.

Rore was oblivious and opened the cabinet, searching for a

bowl. She stared inside, trying to muster her thoughts around what she needed. "Morning," she said sleepily.

I returned the greeting, but Orion paused, looking into my eyes one last time. He turned to leave.

Rore selected a bowl with cartoon characters around the outside. "Not even a good morning, bro," she said.

He paused but did not look her way. "Morning," he said reluctantly.

Rore selected the loopy cereal and poured herself a bowl. "Are you still angry at me?" she asked without looking up.

He looked over his shoulder. "Yes."

Rore pulled the milk out and poured it over her cereal. "I was just worried about you."

He looked away from her. "I know."

"We good then?"

There was a pause. "Yeah." And then he walked away.

Rore continued eating as if this was normal. I was amazed at the interaction between the two siblings.

"You're a good sister," I commented.

She snorted. "When I have a blockhead for a brother, you have to be."

I glanced at the disaster that was her hair. It was the same shade as her mother's. "You have your mother's hair," I commented. But it made me wonder about other things. "Does Orion know his parents?"

Rore shoved a heaping spoonful of loopy things into her mouth. She shrugged. I had to wait for her answer while she chewed. "No. He came to live with us just after I was born. He's only six months older than me. His parents died during that big tornado when he was a baby." She sighed and returned to fishing in her bowl. "Grandmother brought him to my folks but wouldn't say who his parents were. She might not even know. After he lived with us for a year, they adopted him."

Deciding there was nothing left in her bowl, she put it in the dishwasher.

I put my bowl in beside hers. "You two get along so well."

She shrugged. "We've always had a pretty good relationship." She smiled. "Orion, Skiff, and I were the terrors of the neighborhood growing up. We were pretty close." Her smile faltered, and she looked down. "Then Skiff had to fall in love with me. The idiot."

She sighed and pushed off from the counter, heading toward her room. "If I'm going to tame my hair before we leave, then I better get started."

I followed. I was going to see my grandfather. It seemed so unlikely when I started out, but now here we were. I might have someone after all.

But I couldn't shake the feeling that this was not going to go as I wanted.

Chapter 14

"THIS IS THE ADDRESS," Skiff announced as we pulled up in front of a run-down house in a dilapidated neighborhood. Across the street, grimy-faced children stopped playing and gawked with open curiosity. The oldest of them glared with suspicion. Three houses down, throbbing music echoed through an open window, while in the other direction, I could make out angry yelling. At least there was no trash on the street.

At one time, the small house had sported a bright white stucco, but it now had missing patches and peeling paint. Two windows were on the front and framed with faux shutters of what might have been black at one point but had faded to dark gray. A waist-high chain-link fence wrapped around the yard with overgrown bushes around its edges. The closed gate brandished a "Beware of Dog" sign; however, there was no trace of the advertised animal.

Rore sat beside me in the backseat. She frowned. "Not the best of neighborhoods. I think someone was shot not far from here last week."

She had no idea. This was upscale compared to some of the slums Mom and I had lived in, especially at first. It actually wasn't so bad. You had to look at the people and not their possessions. The fact the children were even outside meant this was not that bad of a place.

I took a deep breath and steeled myself. This is why I had come all the way from Philly. He might not even live here anymore. I opened the car door.

"I'll come with you," Rore said, opening hers.

I shook my head. "No, I need to do this alone." While I would have welcomed her company, I couldn't afford to have her with me. I might need to drop my illusion to prove who I was.

She looked concerned. "Are you sure?"

I nodded. "If I go inside, I'll wave to let you know I'm all right."

I stepped out, the gravel crunching loudly under my shoes, and gently shut the car door. The air was faintly scented with someone's cooking roast, and in the distance, I could hear a dog barking—he didn't sound happy.

The gate's rusty hinges resisted as I tried to open it, only to squeak loudly when I pulled harder. I stepped to the door, and from inside, I could hear a TV program playing—loudly. From the laugh track, it had to be a sitcom.

The faded front door had been painted over many times and had deep chip marks in it, showing it had been a shade of teal in times past. I took a deep breath. There was no doorbell, so I knocked.

I waited several minutes, but no one came—likely unable to hear me over their program. I knocked again, louder.

From inside, I heard movement, and then the jangle of the door locks being undone. After what seemed like ages, the door creaked open to reveal an elderly man leaning against the open door. He had a full head of gray hair and a two-day stubble. His frown was so deep it looked like it had been engraved into the lines of his face. He appeared human, but there was more to him than appeared—I couldn't read his emotions. Which meant he was likely blocking them.

But the real tell was his eyes—the same shade of blue as mine.

"What the hell do you want?" he shouted, irritation on his face.

I had practiced this introduction in my head many times, but my words deserted me. "I'm Lapis," I said, as if that explained everything.

He blinked at me. "That's good to hear. Now, get off my property before I call the cops. I don't give to charities." He moved to shut the door.

"Wait!" I shouted. "Are you Jasper Midnyte?"

His frown deepened. "As a matter of fact, I am. But I still don't give to solicitors, and I definitely don't plan to vote in the next election." He moved to shut the door.

"I'm your granddaughter."

He froze, then looked me up and down, his eyes lingering on my hair. Rore wasn't the only one that got hers from her mother.

His eyes narrowed. "I have no granddaughter, or daughter, for that matter." He gave a dismissing flick of his hand. "Now leave."

In panic, I said the first thing that came to mind. "Eiheth was killed."

The door slammed shut, but I didn't hear movement inside for several seconds. Then, it hesitantly reopened. The old man stared at me, his expression one of disbelief and profound sadness.

"Did you say Eiheth . . . was killed?"

I nodded. "Mom was murdered about six months ago. I didn't know how to reach you."

"You're lying," he snarled.

My own ire rose in response. "Why would I lie about something like that? Let me in, and I will prove who I am."

He glared at me. While I couldn't sense his emotions, I could see doubt and irritation playing across his face. He finally pushed the door wider and turned away. I waved to my friends and followed him inside.

Grandfather plopped down in a recliner and muted the blaring sitcom. Then he just looked at me, his eyes flicking up and down as if searching for some defect. I grew uncomfortable, but after several long moments, he locked his gaze with mine. "Lower your *zouvaiyut*."

I gasped. I'm sure my face turned bright red in embarrassment. I couldn't believe he'd asked something so . . . *personal*. Several of the races could raise magical protection barriers to keep out what they didn't want. Succubi included. But ours was limited to emotions.

I had learned early how to use it to protect my emotional core—my soul. Without it, a less-than-scrupulous succubus could forcibly take over my emotions. Then I would love them so much I would do whatever they wanted—a prisoner in a cage I would never want to leave.

Mom had taught me to never let down my *zouvaiyut*, or soul barrier. That was something you only did with someone you trusted completely, like a lifemate or your child. And an old man I didn't know certainly didn't fit that criteria.

"No!" I stated firmly. "It's rude of you to ask."

One corner of his mouth curled up. "Correct. It's something a succubus would never do. So you're at least of our kind and not one of their doppelgangers."

I had heard of that race before. Mom had mentioned them a couple of times. They were Night-clan, same as me, and like a shifter, they could change their bodies. However, doppelgangers could only change into people that had died. From her tone at the time, she hadn't thought very highly of them.

Grandfather reached inside his shirt, no doubt touching his illusion charm. A moment later, it fell away, showing his true appearance.

In most aspects, he looked the same as he had before—with one noticeable difference. From the sides of his head sprouted two magnificent horns. As with most males of our kind, incubi as they were sometimes called, his horns were large and rounded. They were a dull gray color and not nearly as bright, or as I quickly realized, as feminine as my own. I imagined in his day that he would have been considered quite handsome.

I reached inside my sleeve and touched my illusion charm. I

was nervous about doing this but realized I needed to confirm who I was with him. Steeling myself, I gave it the silent command to deactivate.

As it dropped, I saw his eyes go immediately to my horns. They weren't nearly as pretty as Mom's had been. I had even remarked to her about it once, wishing mine were more like hers. She had smiled and explained that a succubi's horns grew for her entire life and changed as one aged. She assured me mine were lovely now and would grow even more beautiful than hers.

As he examined me, he grew sad. "Just like your mother's," he whispered. He started to blink rapidly, his eyes growing moist. "You look just like her when she was that age." His voice grew hard. "Before *he* took her away."

Grandfather diverted his eyes and struggled with his grief.

I knelt beside his chair and took his hand. "I'm sorry I couldn't come sooner. Mom only left me this picture to find you." I pulled it out to show him.

He took it from me and smiled. "I remember this. We had just moved into the house. A neighbor took the picture." He whispered. "My little baby."

He handed the picture back. "What happened to her?" I noticed he didn't say my daughter.

I sighed. "She was killed by a human trying to steal from her store. The police said the man panicked and shot her."

He frowned. "Unlikely. Eiheth would never have allowed him to get in that state. She was a virtuoso of emotions. Better than me even. She would have sensed his fear and taken it from him." He looked at me levelly. "I bet they never found who did it."

I blinked in surprise. "They didn't. The police said he fled the scene."

He looked quite angry. "It was them. No doubt, looking for your mother's necklace. Fat lot of good it would do them." He mumbled softer. "The bastards."

He seemed puzzled by my confusion. I pulled mother's necklace out of my shirt. "You mean this one?"

His eyes got big. "The *Morning Star Brilliance*," he breathed. Understanding flooded his face. "Did they kill her shortly after she gifted it to you?"

"She gave it to me for my birthday, which would make it about three months before she died."

He slapped the chair with his hand. "Damn. Damn! DAMN!" He glared up at me. "She never told you!"

I furrowed my brows in confusion. "Told me what?"

"About your father. About the Morning Star Brilliance."

I shook my head. "She just said Father was accidentally killed before I was born doing something for the Aether. And I have no idea what that star thing is."

He blinked at me as the information sank in. "She was . . . protecting . . ." He sucked in a huge breath. "You need to leave," he stated abruptly. "*Now!*"

"What? Why?" I asked in surprise.

"Get out! You're a danger to both of us," he said, his voice rising. He reached inside his shirt and activated his charm. "Leave now, or I'll call the cops. You're not welcome here." He pulled himself out of his chair.

I was shocked at his sudden change. I stood and activated my own illusion charm, returning myself to human form.

"I don't understand."

"Get . . . out . . . now!" he shouted.

"But . . . but there is so much I need to ask you," I pleaded. "And . . . And I'm all alone." I hated the whine in my voice.

"NOW!"

Tears of frustration sprang to my eyes. "Don't make me leave. I don't have anyone."

His expression softened a little, but his voice was firm. "Leave."

I pulled an index card from my pocket and set it on the television. Rore, in her ultra-preparedness, had insisted I carry it. It had her address and my phone number in case I needed to leave a way for my grandfather to contact me.

Without a word, I went to the door. I opened it and looked back at him.

"Please," I begged. "Can you at least tell me where to get my charm recharged? It's almost out. Mom always handled it, and I don't know who to ask."

He looked sad. "I can't help you," he said softly. "For your own good, don't come back."

With wet eyes, I went out the door. It closed solidly behind me. My vision swam as I went up the walkway and through the gate. As I got in the car, Rore saw my state and immediately pulled me into a hug.

It was only then that I let the floodgates open.

By the time we reached the Strewerts, I had myself back under control. I went to Rore's room and lay on her bed, just staring at the ceiling. She knew I needed to process the rejection and worked nearby on her computer. Still, concern was radiating off her. She badly wanted to ask me what had happened and why he had turned me away. I wish I knew.

It was like my grandfather wanted to connect with me, but something held him back. Something he was afraid of.

I sat up and pulled my necklace out to look at it. It looked back at me like it always had—a silver chain with an amulet attached containing a dark blue gem with a tiny speck of gold. It didn't look to be anything special, but it had horrified him that I had it.

What could it all mean?

I returned the amulet to my shirt and buried my face in my hands. *What was I going to do?* With no help from my grandfather, getting my illusion charm recharged became my number one priority.

I contemplated asking Terra for help. But I couldn't risk losing my one chance to become human. No, for this one, I was on my own. And the best way to find someone to help was to locate another succubus. I glanced over at Rore. And to do that, I couldn't take anyone with me.

So I wasted away the rest of the afternoon considering my options, trying to figure out how to get Rore to leave without arousing her suspicions. My best thought was to sneak out after she went to sleep.

I must have dozed off because a chirp from Rore's phone woke me. She picked it up, read the text, and then glanced in my direction. From her emotions, I could tell she was disappointed.

"What is it?" I asked.

She shook her head. "It's nothing. Skiff's going to a movie and wanted to know if I wanted to tag along." She sighed. "But we'll do it another time."

I had to bite my lips to keep from smiling. My excuse had just arrived. "Why don't you go with him tonight. Spend some time with him."

"No." She shook her head. "I'll just stay in."

"It's because of me, isn't it?"

She had a deer caught in the headlights look. "Ahh . . ."

I smiled. "It's all right. Go with him. I promise I won't do anything stupid." I crossed over my heart.

Or at least not too stupid.

"You're not going to leave us, are you? I want you to stay." I could feel the warmth in her emotions.

"No, not unless you want me to." I lowered my voice. "I don't really have anywhere to go."

She came to sit beside me on the bed. "Lapis, you're welcome to stay as long as you need. Mom doesn't care. She understands you're in a bad spot and wants to help."

"Thanks. I don't know what I would do without your help."

She patted my hand. "We all want to help." She glanced longingly at her phone. "So I'll stay with you tonight."

I shook my head. "No, go with him. I'm sure Skiff will be disappointed. As you will too."

She brightened. "You could come with us."

I kept my expression neutral and sighed. "I don't think so. I'm not feeling it, so I'll just stay in this evening."

She eyed her phone again. "You sure you don't mind?"

I smiled. "I'm sure."

She picked up her phone and began to type furiously. She

paused, and it only took a moment for it to ding again. Her face broke out into a huge grin.

"But I've got to hurry." She threw her phone down and leaped to her closet, going rapidly through her clothes. She selected a dress and quickly changed before running off to the bathroom.

I swiftly grabbed her phone and sat on it, hoping she didn't notice.

She dashed back in and stepped to her dresser. I was amazed as she quickly did her hair and makeup to transform herself into a beautiful young lady, complete with a small leather purse. She turned to me and smiled.

"What do you think?"

"I think he's going to be watching you instead of the movie."

Right on cue, I heard a horn beep out front. "I'll be back before midnight. Mom's here but will be leaving for work after dinner, and Mr. Moody-butt is in his room, probably playing a game." She looked around. "You seen my phone?"

"You put it in your purse," I lied.

She started to look.

"You better hurry," I quickly said. "You don't want to be late."

"Right!" she darted out the door but darted right back. "Call Skiff if you need me."

I nodded. "I will."

And she was gone. A few minutes later, I heard Skiff's old car drive away. But I continued to sit on Rore's phone. It wasn't that big, but it sure was hard.

As I expected, Andromeda poked her head in the door. "We're going to order Chinese. Would you like some? It'll probably be an hour."

"Sounds good to me." I smiled back at her.

"All right, let me know if you need something."

I waited until she left, counted slowly to sixty, and then pulled out Rore's phone. She should be more careful.

I hated to lie, but I had to borrow her phone. Terra had already admitted to tracking both of ours and would likely notice us not being out together. I shook my head. No, for this, I didn't need anyone to know my destination.

I pulled out my phone and looked up where I was going. It only took a few searches for me to develop my plan.

To find another of my race.

After Andromeda left for work, I eased quietly out of Rore's bedroom window and headed out with Glitch. The little gremlin was practically dancing at the prospect of a long trip at high speed. My destination was on the other side of town, but with the skateboard's swiftness, I thought we could do it in about thirty minutes.

I hopped on Glitch, and he basically took over, guiding me toward my destination. This left me with time to think. I was taking a big risk doing this, but I couldn't think of a good alternative. My kind would know the best place for an illegal charm recharge. Not for the first time, I wished I could do it myself—but my magic didn't work that way. Being of Night-clan, I got what I needed from other living things—their emotions.

But the charm needed the magic of a Twilight-clan witch. Finding one to provide a magic boost was actually fairly easy, but in my case, there was more to it. My charm was unregistered and recharging it was illegal. Since all magic carried a signature, special steps had to be taken to hide it so it couldn't be traced back. That was what made it expensive.

I weaved with Glitch as he made a few turns at high speed. I tried not to think about what I was about to do.

Finding another succubus was going to be difficult, at best. Our numbers had been diminishing—not that the other races shed tears over it. But one thing we all had in common was the need for emotions. It was like an essential nutrient we required. Without it, we would gradually lose our ability to absorb others' emotions and then die.

Mom and I discussed this at length several times. Young succubi, like me, required little in the way of emotions. She had joked that there was enough teen angst around to satisfy my needs. But as we grew older, our requirements increased. Things like attending sporting events or concerts could provide a rich mix of what we would need for a month. Unfortunately, some of my kind developed a taste for the more unsavory emotions. A few preferred places of adult entertainment for their perverted fix. It was those that had caused our entire race to have a bad name, when in fact, it was a very few that partook. But there were others that were worse. Some preferred grief and sorrow, seeking out funerals and hospitals. I prayed I never ran into one of those.

I had originally thought to try a stripper bar I had found online but realized they would never let me in. I refused to go to a hospital, and there were no concerts or games this evening, so I chose something in the middle—the airport. The emotions there weren't as strong as in some other places, but there was a steady supply of joyful reunions and tearful goodbyes.

That's where Mom preferred to go when she needed to resupply. She would sit and pretend to watch the arrivals and departures. Someone like her is who I hoped to find.

When we arrived at the airport, I hid Glitch and went inside. After consulting the flight schedule, I took a seat outside the security checkpoint and along the wall of the waiting area. A few others sat around me, passing the time while they waited for their parties to arrive. I carefully checked each person, sampling their emotions. The fact I could feel them confirmed they weren't of my kind. Like my grandfather, they would have shielded themselves, and I would feel nothing from them.

I huddled in my jacket and waited, listening to the announcements and the bits of conversation around me. I saw movement out of the corner of my eye and chuckled to glimpse a small gray mouse dart along the wall and quickly vanish around the corner. Most places had repellant charms, but I guess in a place this big, some would get through. It'd been a fast little bugger, too. I didn't even get a chance to sample its emotions. I smiled, remembering the night Mom and I had spent in a run-down hotel between one of our frequent moves. There had been mice nearby, and I had entertained myself by sampling their simple emotions. When Mom saw what I was doing, she was horrified and sent a burst of fear to make them scurry away. My smile grew sad. Protector, how I missed her.

An arrival announcement crackled over the speakers, startling me out of my memory. A few moments later, clusters of people came from the gates. Several of those waiting jumped up to meet their loved ones, radiating their joy and delight. I paid particular attention to those walking alone but found their emotions were flat—likely frequent business travelers.

Sadly, as I checked through them, there were none of my

race. I huddled deeper into my jacket and sighed. I would have to wait for the next group.

Then I felt eyes on me. I looked around, and no one seemed to even notice I existed, but I was sure someone was watching me. I let my gaze go to the shops surrounding the waiting area. There was a coffee stand, currently closed, and beside it, a tiny convenience store—the kind that sold souvenirs, bottled drinks, and anti-nausea charms. Behind the store's counter stood a plump, middle-aged man, giving me a creepy stare. Reluctantly, I reached out to feel his emotions, but I couldn't find any. My eyes went wide in understanding—*he was one of my kind.* I had to admit, this was the perfect place to work. Get paid and get your nutritional needs met at the same time.

I got up and leisurely strolled to his store, where I leafed through a few magazines. He leered at me, and I took an instant dislike to him. But I had to see if he would give me the information I needed.

I steeled myself and went to the counter. From his smirk, I had no doubt he knew exactly what I was.

"What can I do for you, pretty lady?"

I summoned up all my bravado and looked him square in the eye. "I'm new in town, and I'm looking for someone to recharge my charm. Unfortunately, they're hard to find."

He nodded and glanced around to make sure no one was watching. "I know someone good, and for the right price, will completely seal their lips." He looked around. "But not here. Someone might be listening."

I nodded. "Where?"

He jerked his head toward a door to the side. "Back room. Wait three minutes, then follow me."

I nodded and went back to examining the cheap souvenirs. He waited a few minutes, then pulled out a "Be Right Back" sign and placed it on the counter. He made a swift exit through the backroom door.

I tried to count off the minutes, but it felt like forever. I couldn't help but glance at the closed door and, for a moment, wondered if going in there was wise. The guy was an incubus.

When I was young, Mom had given me "the talk"—the one all moms give their daughters about avoiding dark places and strange men. But for succubi, there was one more. Never allow yourself to be alone with an incubus you don't know. They had the same powers as you—and they could be stronger.

I sighed. But what choice did I have? I had to find a way to recharge my charm.

Thinking I had waited long enough, I strolled to the backroom door and quickly slipped through.

The room was narrow and dimly lit. Metal shelves stacked with merchandise lined both walls, leaving a narrow aisle. At the end of the room sat a small table that must serve as a desk. The man leisurely slumped in an office chair facing me—elbows resting on the chair, hands and fingers intertwined across his middle-aged paunch. He had a wide grin on his face—classic villain pose if I ever saw one. He'd been watching way too many spy thrillers.

"So you want to have your charm recharged?" he asked, dark humor in his voice. "It will cost you, though."

"I don't have any money." I held out my empty hands. "As I said, I'm new in town."

His grin faltered. He stared at me, considering.

"Please, just tell me, and I'll be on my way. I'll pay back the favor."

"Nothing's free, pretty lady. But there is a way to earn it." His grin returned.

"What do you want?" I asked with more confidence than I felt.

"Drop your *zouvaiyut*."

I couldn't help but gasp. "Are you crazy? There's no way I'd do that."

I saw him move, but I realized it too late. He was out of the chair and had his hand around my throat before I could even move. "Lower your soul barrier, and I'll get your charm recharged for you."

"No!" I croaked. I tried to kick him, but he turned to the side, and my blow glanced off.

He pulled me close and squeezed my throat tighter. His breath stank of the garlic from his last meal. "I guarantee to take care of you. I might even make you my wife. You'll never have to worry about anything again." He grinned wickedly. "Now, be a good pretty lady and drop your *zouvaiyut*." He pulled me closer until I felt his hidden horns rub against mine. I shivered at the touch and wanted to throw up. As his face loomed in front of me, all I could see were his perverted eyes.

I was in big, big trouble.

Chapter 15

I SHOVED AGAINST the incubus, but he was too strong. It was the way of our race—succubi were lithe and fast, while incubi were strong and powerful. I didn't stand a chance against him.

On top of that, I felt him probing my emotional barrier, pressing against it, and searching for some weakness. It was like he was groping my private places.

"Stop it!" I yelled at him.

"Drop the barrier," he commanded. "It's only a matter of time before you succumb to me. Make it easy on yourself. With a young body like yours, I'm sure we'll have a *lot* of fun."

I struggled harder, but he held firm.

So what's a girl to do when a predator sticks his ugly face in yours? Well, attack it.

I grabbed him by the shoulders and pulled him tight against me. Then, turning my head slightly to the side, I bit down hard on his nose.

He howled in pain and shoved me away. I staggered backward off balance and unexpectedly collided with something soft and furry. *Funny, I hadn't noticed anything but shelves in the room.*

But at the contact, a new set of emotions filtered into my consciousness. I had been so focused on the incubus I had completely missed another presence in the room. A *big* presence. And strangely familiar. I glanced up to see a grizzly bear standing over me. A big, brown one—its lips pulled back into a snarl. Two huge hairy arms wrapped around me possessively, pulling me tightly against him. The bear roared in rage, causing the metal shelves to rattle and my insides to shake.

For an instant, I panicked in primeval terror and tried to get away. But the bear held firm. Then I noticed it didn't smell like a wild animal, nor did the anger emanating from it feel like one. It instead felt more like—

Orion!

Thankfully, his anger was not directed at me, but at the incubus. I knew I was going to be in trouble with Orion, but at that moment, I didn't care.

The incubus' eyes widened, and he backed to the desk behind him. With surprising speed, he ducked and darted past us. Orion swatted at him but missed as the incubus fled through the room's only door.

Orion released me and then dropped to all fours. He turned

to give chase, but I put a hand on his shoulder. "No, let him go. There might be someone out there that would hurt you."

But he suddenly wheeled and faced me. His growl became more intense as his anger grew. Only this time, it was directed at me.

"Orion, you can calm down now. I'm not in danger."

With teeth bared, he edged closer. I took a step back in uncertainty. Rore had said that larger animals could cause him to lose control, and I could sense his emotions racing inside him.

My encounter with the incubus had been brief but intense. Maintaining my soul barrier had sapped a lot of my ability. I thought it wise to conserve what strength I had left, so I chose a simpler approach to dealing with Orion's anger. I wrapped my arms around his furry neck and hugged him.

"Thanks for saving me," I said softly, luxuriating in the smell of his Orion-scented fur. "I know you're angry with me, and I don't blame you. But can we talk later? That man will probably come back with reinforcements."

Orion froze. After a moment, I gradually felt his emotions settle. He pulled away and sat back on his haunches. The bear nodded. He nosed me on one side, but I couldn't figure out what he wanted.

"Come on. Change back, and then we'll leave."

He nudged me again.

"I don't understand," I said. "We need to hurry. Why don't you change back, and then you can tell me."

He looked at me a moment and then stood on his hind legs. His transformation back to human form was very quick. It was then that I realized what his problem was.

He didn't have any clothes on.

I blushed and slapped my hands over my eyes, turning my back to him. The vision of his nakedness and his wicked smile would forever be burned into my memory. Not that I minded.

"You could have given me some warning," I complained.

Behind me, I heard the pad of barefoot steps and then the sound of a zipper. "I did try to tell you," he snickered.

I huffed. "I don't speak bear."

"True, but you *saw* bare." He chuckled. I heard clothes rustling. "You can turn around."

He had already donned shorts and was just pulling down his T-shirt as I turned. The shirt hugged his chest, highlighting his lean muscle and strong arms. I couldn't decide if he looked better dressed or naked. I blushed again at the wicked thought. I had no time for this.

"How did you find me?"

He grinned. "You have Rore's phone. Skiff did something to ours so we could track each other. When you slipped out after Rore had already left, I knew it had to be you."

He grew serious and stepped closer. "Why are you here? And why were you with that man?"

"Uhhh . . ." I didn't know what to say.

"You're not into drugs, are you? We can get you help."

I shook my head. "I'm not."

"You're not selling . . ." His eyes flicked to my chest.

I blushed. "No, I'm not!" I stated emphatically. I grabbed his hand and pulled him toward the door. "We'll talk later. For now, let's get out of here."

He slung the smallest backpack I'd ever seen over his shoulder, easily no bigger than my hand. I raised an eyebrow in question.

He shrugged. "Skiff made it. It adjusts to my size so I can carry my clothes no matter how small I am." He plucked at his shirt. "But it doesn't hold much."

He grabbed my hand and led me to the door. He slowly eased it open and, seeing no one, led me to the store entrance. But when he peeked into the corridor, he jerked back. "That guy is coming with two guards. One has a gun."

"We'll run for it," I said and tugged on his arm.

He shook his head. "No, we'll never make it. They're wearing comms and will call ahead as soon as we bolt." He thought for a moment. "I can create a distraction so you can get out."

"What about you?" I asked in concern.

"Don't worry." He grinned. "No one notices a mouse."

"All right. But be careful."

Orion nodded. "Don't wait on me. I'll meet you back home." He dropped his arms to his side. "Oh, would you please take my clothes for me? Mom gets mad when I come home without them."

Then he changed. If I hadn't seen it, I wouldn't have believed how fast he transformed. An eagle arose from his clothes and took off out the door. He flew straight toward the approaching group, and with a cry, began to beat the incubus with his wings.

I gathered up Orion's belongings and slipped out into the corridor. With the distraction, no one paid me a second glance. I quickly made my way to the exit.

It only took me a few minutes to retrieve my skateboard and shove off toward the Strewert home. As I wound my way down the streets, my mood sank.

The evening had been a complete and utter bust. And on top of that, I dared not go back to search there again. Plus, Orion now knew that something was up. He was going to demand answers, and I had no clue what I was going to tell him. I sighed sadly.

As if to illustrate the point, my charm vibrated. Only this time, twice. I looked up at the sky and gritted my teeth in frustration.

What in the Protector's name am I going to do?

When I crawled back into the window of Rore's room, I had hoped she would be asleep. But from the way the rest of my evening had gone, I should have known she would be waiting for me.

"You came back," she said, sounding slightly surprised.

She got off the bed where she had been sitting cross-legged with her computer in her lap. She came over to help me inside. "Where did you go?" she asked. She was genuinely interested, with no trace of malice in her voice. I immediately felt guilty.

"Out," was my simple reply.

"Were you with anyone? It's not safe. Not after what happened with the van."

"Of course," I blurted out. "Orion and I met up."

It wasn't *exactly* a lie. We *had* met up. But only because he'd followed me.

She gasped, her face lighting up in wonder. "You had a date?"

"I wouldn't call it a date. Like I said, we just met up." I slipped off the jacket and hung it on its peg, the weight of the phone in the jacket reminding me I still had Rore's.

I took it out and turned to see her smiling as wide as a crescent moon. "Where did you meet?" she asked excitedly.

I grimaced and handed her the phone. I ignored the question, hoping a distraction would work. "You left this. I took it with me because I planned to return it if I saw you. I hope you didn't mind."

"Oh, I wondered what happened to it. I'm losing it all the time."

Wanting to make a quick exit, I hurriedly grabbed my nightshirt from my suitcase, accidentally pulling out my ribownna with it. The ribbons fluttered to the floor. I huffed and absentmindedly stuffed them back in my suitcase.

"So, where did you and Orion meet?" she repeated. I could tell she was not going to drop it, so I had to give her something. I couldn't tell her where we had actually gone. I grinned. *Or could I?*

"The airport. I like to watch the planes land."

It wasn't exactly another lie. I did like to watch the planes. I just liked other stuff a whole bunch more.

She beamed. "And Orion went with you?" She giggled. "Other than Chaleta, no other girl has caught his attention." She leaned forward. "Did you have a good time?"

I inched toward the door. "Well, we would have, but some guy started getting a little grabby, and Orion had to step in."

I thought her eyes were going to bug out. "He rescued you?" She put both hands over her mouth. "Oh . . . my . . . Protector. This is serious."

I couldn't believe she thought we had something going. Orion obviously didn't like me. Besides, I had much bigger problems. I shook my head. "He was just being polite." I finally made it to the door. "I've got to get a shower." I fled to the bathroom.

Locking the door, I turned on the water and hopped in before it had even warmed up. I scrubbed where that incubus had grabbed me, trying to remove even the thought of his sick touch. When my skin began to turn pink, I realized I was as clean as I was going to get. I leaned against the side and just let the water run over me. My insides were still trembling from the encounter. It was humbling to realize I wasn't as independent as I thought. And just how much Mom had shielded me.

I was surprised when the hot water started cooling, realizing I had been in there a very long time. I turned it off and got out.

Drying myself, I went to the mirror and rubbed the steam away. I deactivated my charm and immediately noticed dark bruises around my throat. They weren't part of the charm's pattern, so it hid them, too.

It was a reminder of just how close I had been to disaster. That incubus had been too strong to fight, and if Orion hadn't come along—I shuddered. I'm not sure how long I could have held out. But he was right. I would have eventually succumbed, becoming his plaything until he grew tired of me.

I stared at my reflection, and to my surprise, I could feel my anger rising. *Mom, why did you have to leave me?*

I immediately felt guilty, and my eyes became moist. *It's so hard being alone. It's just not fair.*

I couldn't help but wonder how Mom had done it. She had raised me all by herself. Had gone to work and earned our living. But at the end of the day, she always had a smile for me. *How did she do it?*

I don't know why it came to mind, but I remembered I had a nasty nightmare one night as a child. At my cries, Mom rushed into my room and wrapped her arms around me. She held me until I stopped crying. When she tried to tuck me back in, I balked. "I'm scared," I had said.

She smoothed the hair out of my face and smiled at me. "It's all right, my precious jewel. I will always protect you. Just like your father did us." And for the briefest moment, a tear came to her own eyes. Even at my young age, I could tell she still missed him.

But then she smiled. "I'll show you," she said.

She then lowered her *zouvaiyut.* and shared her love directly with me—something only a succubus will do with those they trust completely. With her barrier down, she fed her feelings to me raw. I was instantly wrapped in her love. And I knew she was right. I was her precious jewel. She would die for me.

And in a way, I guess she had.

I blinked at my reflection, and a chill went down my spine as a new thought took hold. The van, the bad men, the ransacked apartment, the faked shoplifting, and of course, Mom's death. All those bad things.

What had Grandfather said? There was no way a normal human could have murdered her. Then why had she been killed? What could she have possibly had that they wanted?

I heard someone walk past the bathroom door, and I instinctively looked at it. From the emotions of the person passing by, I knew it was Orion. No doubt just making it back. I faintly heard him talking to Rore.

Thinking I should get dressed, I looked at myself in the mirror one last time. The light caught my amulet. It was just a simple design, actually sort of gaudy. But Mom had worn it every day since I could remember. She never took it off. And when I had turned seventeen, she had given it to me, to be killed only three months later.

Grandfather had called the necklace the Morning Star Brilliance and seemed shocked she had not told me about it. But it was just a piece of jewelry. *Wasn't it?*

A loud knock on the door interrupted my thoughts. I jumped, startled.

"Lapis?" Orion called, irritation in his voice.

I held my towel to my chest despite being safely locked behind the door. I felt for my illusion charm. "Yes," I answered.

"When you come out, would you come to my room?" He paused. "We need to talk." He didn't sound happy.

"All right," I answered. I looked in the mirror and touched the charm to activate it.

Only nothing happened.

My heart jumped up into my throat. I touched it again. It gave a vibration but did not activate.

I stared in the mirror in horror. My horns were clearly visible, and my tail waved in agitation.

Orion shifted on the other side of the door, but he did not move away.

"Are you going to come now?" he asked, a hint of anger in his voice.

I had to make him go away. "As soon as I get dressed," I called. "Unlike you, I don't normally parade around naked."

I felt a flash of embarrassment from the other side of the door, but he didn't acknowledge my jibe.

"I'll be waiting." He hesitated like he wanted to say more, but moved away instead.

I couldn't take my eyes off my reflection in the mirror. *You'll likely be waiting for quite a while.* I wondered how long I could stay in the bathroom before they forced me out. With no other choice, I pulled on my clothes.

When I was done, I thought I would give it one last try. I crossed my fingers and touched my charm one more time. *Please, Protector, let it work.*

The charm gave a warning vibration, and slower than normal, the illusion grew around me. I nearly collapsed in relief.

I looked at myself in the mirror, and a normal human girl looked back. One thing was clear—I *had* to get my charm recharged. I could no longer afford to wait. I had to find a succubus to help—

But a new thought interrupted, the realization chilling me to the bone. Tonight's events were even proof. No one in my clan would help me. If I approached them, all they would see was a succubus playing dress-up—an innocent to exploit. Despair settled on my shoulders. If I tried to get their help without something substantial in return, I would fail. And I had nothing to offer.

My only choice was to plead with my grandfather once more. And if that didn't work—

Talk to Terra. Maybe I could work something out, but it would probably cost me my human transformation.

I took a deep breath and opened the door. But first things first. I needed to talk to Orion. Best to get my thrashing over with.

I went down the hall to his room. The door was closed, so I knocked. "It's me."

"Come in," was his terse reply.

I hoped this conversation wouldn't take long.

And there would be no shouting.

When I opened the door, the scent hit me first. It wasn't bad, pleasant actually in a masculine way, and fully Orion. For a moment, it reminded me of being enveloped in his transformed bear arms.

Orion's room was about the same size as Rore's but seemed bigger. Hers was bursting at the seams with stuffed animals, clothes, a desk, and chair, while Orion's was sparse. He had a twin-size bed that seemed too small for his large frame. There were awards on the walls and a shelf in the corner full of books.

Orion himself was standing on a small mat. He wore jeans but was barefoot and had his shirt off. It looked like I had interrupted some kind of exercise. Yoga maybe?

I shut the door behind me and leaned on it. *Be polite, Lapis,* I told myself.

"Thank you for saving me. You know, at the airport. I hope you got away without trouble."

He picked up the T-shirt on his bed and slipped it on. I tried not to watch the flexing of his lean muscles, but my gaze was irresistibly drawn to them. I forced my eyes away and to the awards on the wall.

Three were from taekwondo, but there were two others.

"You're a writer?" I asked in surprise. I stepped closer. "In poetry?" They were for successive years of high school literature achievements.

He shrugged indifferently. "Competition was light those years."

"Wow, I never would have guessed. Perhaps you'll let me read one." I turned and smiled at him.

But only a frown greeted me. "Why did you go to the airport?" he demanded. "Are you doing drugs? I won't stand for someone bringing trouble to my family."

I shook my head emphatically. "I never have and never will. When I was a freshman, I knew a girl that started down that path. It didn't end well."

"Then why?" he asked levelly. "Why did you go willingly into that creep's backroom?"

Defiance crept into my voice. "I needed some information."

"That doesn't match what I saw. You were checking out all the people arriving. Especially the ones alone. And then, when that guy noticed you, you went to him." His expression saddened. "You're not . . . selling yourself, are you? If it's money, I can try to help."

I blinked at him in surprise. I felt my face flush, thinking back over my actions. It *would* have looked like I was trying to pick up a customer.

"No," I shook my head in denial. "I don't do that. I've not . . . I haven't even . . ." I trailed off. *Dated* was what I was about to say. But Orion didn't need to know that.

He looked relieved. "Then why?"

I opened my mouth to respond but was literally saved by the bell—the one on his phone.

He glanced at the device lying at the foot of his bed. A text had popped up. I couldn't help but read along with him. It was from Chaleta.

He glanced guiltily at me before picking it up and responding.

He sighed. "I told her to leave me alone."

"Then ignore it."

"I can't. She says she's alone and depressed." He looked down at his phone. "She has a history of self-harm and is afraid to be alone."

"Where are her parents? Or Zeek, for that matter."

"Her parents are on a cruise. Not sure about Zeek."

He sighed in resignation. "I've got to go see her."

I grabbed his arm. "Don't. She . . ." I wanted to add—*She wants to turn you into her plaything*. But I stopped myself. By clan code, I couldn't interfere. I had already done too much. Even now, I could be taken before the clan elder.

I hastily added, "She might have put that curse on you."

He frowned. "I don't think it was her. She never had the opportunity." He looked back at his phone and sighed reluctantly. "I better go."

This just screamed of a setup. I grabbed his arm. "Take me with you."

He looked at me like I had grown another head. "I don't think so."

"She's not being honest with you. I can help you keep things under control. Be a neutral third party."

He didn't even hesitate. "No."

We glared at each other. He left me no choice but to play my trump card. "I'll tell Rore."

He grimaced. "Don't do that, or at least give me a half-hour head start."

I shook my head. "Either you take me with you, or I'm going to tell this instant."

He shook his head. "I have to do this by myself. It will be a chance to prove the curse is truly broken. Besides, Rore will probably follow me anyway. She always seems to know when I slip out. I'm not sure how she does it. I even turn my phone off."

I saw my opening. "If I come with you, she won't follow."

"And just how are you going to keep my nosey sister out of this?"

"I'll tell Rore that you and I are going out on a date. She'll definitely leave us alone."

He frowned, then realization slowly dawned on him. "She doesn't think we're . . ." he pointed to both of us.

I nodded.

"Damn."

"So, are you taking me?"

He rolled his eyes. "Do I have a choice?"

"Not really."

He just sighed. "Just don't hold me back."

I grinned. "I think you've already seen that's not a problem."

Chapter 16

SLIPPING AWAY from Rore was easier than I thought. I simply strode into her room and announced, "Orion and I are going out." And started changing my clothes.

Rore didn't question me. She sat on her bed watching while wearing a knowing grin. "Okay." Her quickness in agreeing made me a little uncomfortable.

"Don't get any ideas," I quickly added. "We're just going to hang out for a bit."

Rore nodded, a twinkle in her eye. "Whatever you say."

I grabbed the jacket and skateboard before fleeing the room. I wished she'd been just a tiny bit freaked out that Orion and I were together.

About half an hour later, Orion and I arrived at Chaleta's house. He had transformed into an eagle and flew the distance while I had traveled via skateboard. I swear Glitch was getting faster every time I rode him.

Orion rang the doorbell, and there was hardly a pause as the door opened to a brightly smiling Chaleta. But it quickly turned dim when she saw me. Her emotions shifted to disappointment and, surprisingly, a trace of apprehension.

The foyer behind her was dimly lit, its soft light pooling invitingly at our feet. Her snug jeans and daring, off-the-shoulder blouse highlighted her model-perfect figure. She wore minimal makeup, and her hair fell loosely around her shoulders. This girl was not the least bit depressed. On the contrary, she was in full-bore seduction mode.

"Are you all right?" asked Orion, genuine concern in his voice. I expected to sense feelings of attraction from him. He *was* male, after all, and she was beautiful. Not to mention, she had done everything in her power to make herself seductive. But unlike the other night, he didn't react. I wondered if that was connected to the curse he had been wearing.

She pouted. "I thought you were coming by yourself so we could have some alone time." Her eyes flicked to me. I just smiled. Outwardly, she was the pleasant hostess, but inside I had totally pissed her off.

Orion kept his expression neutral. "We were in the middle of a serious discussion when I got your text. Lapis came along for company."

Her mouth widened into a smile, but I couldn't help but notice it didn't reach her eyes. "Well, do come in."

Chaleta led us deeper inside to an intimate gaming room.

The lights had been dimmed, and a video screen took up one entire wall. Various gaming consoles and equipment rested on a shelf underneath it. A plush loveseat sat on the opposite wall, perfect for a couple to sit comfortably together. Next to it was a padded chair, currently occupied by a large stuffed animal. Candles illuminated a small table with a tray of sodas, cookies, and snacks. I eyed the seating arrangement. Only two places. Someone had planned well. I immediately plopped down on the loveseat, leaving Orion to sink down beside me.

Chaleta's eyes were daggers. She was outwardly calm as she moved the stuffed animal to the floor and seated herself in the chair across from us. Her plans for the evening were quickly going down the toilet.

She opened her mouth, but I was quicker. "Where's Zeek?" I asked.

Outwardly, she shrugged with calm indifference. But inside, her level of apprehension skyrocketed. "I don't know," she said. "I don't keep track of him. I haven't seen him this evening."

There was something about her statement that didn't ring true. I wished I had a truth spell.

"So, are you feeling calmer now?" asked Orion. "Your message said you were having a bad time."

She smiled sweetly. "I'm doing much better now. Especially since you're here. This house gets spooky when no one else is here." She looked down. "And our last discussion didn't go so well."

"We can't stay long," Orion explained. "It's late, and I have to get up early." He shifted on the loveseat. "So, what did you want to talk about?"

"It's kind of private." She glanced at me.

I shrugged. "Don't mind me." I pulled out my phone and pulled up a game I had seen. "I won't listen."

She glared at me. "No, I meant . . ."

I didn't know how to play the game, but that wasn't going to stop me. "Yes!" I exclaimed. "Got it!"

Orion furrowed his brow but couldn't resist leaning over to see what I was doing.

Chaleta's level of frustration was rising. She jumped up and went to the table of refreshments. "Orion, you have to try one of my cookies. I made them myself."

She put a couple of chocolate chip cookies on a plate and brought them over. "Here. This is just for you. I put lots of love into them." She smiled sweetly.

Orion shook his head. "Thanks, Chaleta. But I have to be careful what I eat."

She took one and waved it in front of his face. "Take just one bite. They're delicious."

Orion shook his head. "Chaleta, I'd rather not."

"Please. You'll love them."

Her apprehension grew, and my gut told me something wasn't right. I leaned my shoulder against Orion's and peeked at the cookie. "It does look good. Chocolate chip is my favorite," I said.

Then I snatched it out of her hand and took a big bite.

Chaleta's eyes grew round in horror.

"Mmmm," I mumbled as I took another bite. "Yummy." The chocolate chips were super sweet, but they also had a faint metallic taste.

"That was for Orion," she said in disbelief.

I smiled. "He said he didn't want it. I was merely eating his leftovers." I took another bite to emphasize the point. I popped the rest in my mouth.

Her hands curled into fists as her frustration tipped over into anger. Her vampire magic reached out to ensnare me, but I was confident it couldn't touch me. Zeek had tried the same thing the day before. I wanted to laugh, but instead smiled sweetly at her.

But my expression twisted into a frown. I was beginning to feel nauseous, and to my horror, I felt a weakening in my magic. Like something was sucking my store of power out of me.

My eyes went wide in shock. This had never happened before.

Her vampire magic made contact, feeling like a dark snake slithering across my skin. It crawled up my arm, tightened around my neck, and then sank deep into my chest, where it began to enwrap my soul and squeeze my will from me. I found myself adoring her. I wanted to get down on my knees and sing her praises.

I didn't understand. Her magic shouldn't affect me. Then I gasped.

Something was in the cookies.

But there was more to come. My illusion charm began to vibrate, pause, and then vibrate again, frantically warning that the last of its magic was being sucked away.

Chaleta smiled smugly back and poured more magic into me. I rose and raised my arms toward her, heading for a hug. She was the last person in the world I wanted to touch, and especially now that my illusion was about to drop.

"I . . . I'm sorry for . . . for eating the cookie," I said, unable to stop the words.

My illusion charm was going bonkers. Its warnings coming faster and faster, until suddenly—they ceased. My eyes widened in shock. The charm which I had worn like a second skin for most of my life began to fail.

I had to get away.

I panicked. I grabbed what was left of my own magic and hit Chaleta with a wave of absolute disgust. She slapped a hand over her mouth, eyes wide in shock, and fled the room. I could hear retching sounds as she retreated.

Orion looked horrified at the swinging door and then back to me.

I couldn't wait. I bolted from the room.

"Lapis!" Orion called after me.

I took off toward the front door at a dead run. I was outside in a flash, leaping over the two steps to the driveway. I stumbled and fell to my knees.

At that moment, my faithful charm gave one last vibration—and died.

I felt it. It was probably just in my head, but I knew when my constant companion left me. I felt naked and exposed, like I had never been before. Everyone could see I was a succubus. One glance and they would know the truth.

Even Orion.

I scrambled up and ran flat out down the driveway. But I skidded to a stop halfway down. Across the street, people were strolling toward their cars and saying their goodbyes. A party must have broken up, and the guests were leaving. I couldn't go that way—with the well-lit street, I would be clearly visible.

In a panic, I turned left and fled through a gap in the hedges that lined the driveway. The tall hedges did an excellent job of blocking the light from the street, making it harder for even my night vision to see the grounds. I flailed through bushes and low-hanging branches, seeking a way out.

I tripped and fell to my knees. My stomach churned, and I gave up the contents of my stomach, the foul metallic taste of the cookie filling my mouth.

I quickly rose, bounced into a tree, staggered, and resumed my flight. I became confused and lost all sense of direction. I leaped into a tall hedge, hoping it led to the street, and ran headlong into an ornamental iron bar fence. I banged my head so hard I saw stars. I staggered, but my left foot got caught in the bars, and I lost my balance. My ankle flared in pain as I fell hard on my side.

I lay stunned, taking deep gulps of air as I tried to collect my thoughts. My forehead hurt, and my ankle throbbed. *Damn. Damn! DAMN!*

I drew up my leg and tried to rub away some of the pain. Whatever had been in the cookies had stripped away all my magic. I could barely sense any emotions at all. And then I had a horrible thought. What if Orion had eaten that cookie? What would have happened?

Oh, no. I left him behind!

I tried to jump up, but immediately fell, the pain in my ankle excruciating.

"Lapis!" I heard movement through the bushes behind me.

Orion! I was filled with both relief and dread. I couldn't let him see me.

I crawled over to a thick bush, sitting down underneath it, and huddled into the smallest ball I could possibly be. I covered my head with my jacket, leaving only a slit to see through.

Please Protector, don't let him see me. Don't let him see the monster I really am.

When I saw his light through the bushes, I knew it was over. I blinked back my hot tears.

"Lapis?" he asked.

"Please . . ." I croaked, my voice on the verge of sobs. "Don't look at me."

To my shock, the light snapped off.

"Are you all right?" he asked. I sagged in relief when I felt his concern. Although weak, my ability was there. I must have expelled whatever was draining my magic when I threw up. I could feel it gradually recovering.

"No," I sobbed. I kept my head down and covered—my tail tucked under me.

"What's wrong?" He made no move to come closer.

"My . . . my cosmetic charm stopped working. Something in the cookie drained its magic." I blinked at the tears threatening to come, doing my best to hold them back. *Please believe the lie.* "I . . . I have a congenital defect that makes me ugly. I didn't want you to see it. You'll hate me."

There was the barest pause as he digested my words. "Lapis," he said softly. "I could never hate you. Especially for how you appear."

I rambled on. "When my charm broke, I tried to run away. But I twisted my ankle." It sounded dumb even to me.

"No wonder, with you running blindly through the bushes," he said kindly. "I'm surprised you didn't break your neck." He paused. "Which foot?"

"The left."

He came around, light still off, and sat cross-legged at my

feet. Being careful not to look in my direction, he drew my hurt foot into his lap. I resisted, but he was insistent. He carefully removed my shoe and shined his light on it. He took pains to keep the light away from my covered head. I winced at his gentle probing, which was firm, warm, and without the least bit of tickling.

"I don't feel anything broken. I think it's a sprain," he finally said. He then slipped my shoe back on and gently tied it for me. "Let's try standing."

"*No!*" I shook my covered head. "You'll see me." I pulled the jacket tighter over my head. "I'll manage on my own from here."

He sighed. "What happened to your . . . charm?"

"It was already low. But something in the cookie consumed all its magic."

He was silent for a moment. I could feel indignation rising inside him. "She tried to feed that to me."

I nodded. "Yeah."

"I don't appreciate someone drugging me." He paused and then added so softly I could barely hear him. "Nor my friend."

He sighed. "So your charm is just out of magic? Not broken?"

"I'm not sure, but it's been warning me for a while that I was running out."

He thought for a moment.

"Was that why you went to the airport? To get your charm recharged."

I sighed in resignation. "Yes. I came here to find my grandfather, hoping he could help me fix it. The charm is unregistered, so getting it recharged is expensive. I was looking for someone to do it at the airport."

"So you have no way to recharge it?"

I shook my head. "No."

He thought for a moment and then sighed. Then he pulled out his phone and hit dial.

I nearly panicked. "Please don't call the police."

He shook his head. "I'm not." Then he put the phone on speaker, so we both could hear.

"Hey, bro." I was surprised to hear Rore's perky voice. "Why in the world would you be calling me on your date? You must need a *favor*."

"Your deductive reasoning astounds me." He sighed. "The skateboard died on Lapis, and we think it's out of magic. Can you recharge it?"

"That's strange," she answered. "Skiff said it would never need another charge." I could almost hear her shrug. "Oh well, Just put the phone up against it."

Without looking, Orion held the phone over his shoulder.

I took it. "She can do that over the phone?" I asked, unable to contain my surprise.

"Oh, yeah. Not only did Skiff do something to our phones, but my little sister has enough power to run this whole freaking city for a week."

"Two weeks!" came Rore's reply through the speaker.

"Yeah, little miss show-off," he said in typical brotherly disgust.

She giggled.

In the dark, I fumbled the phone against my charm.

"Wow," I heard her muffled voice. "I can feel it from this end. It's totally empty. Well, I'll just give it one of my super-duper special charges."

And then she began to sing. I felt the hairs on the back of my neck stand up. My eyes went up in surprise as her power enveloped me. While Chaleta's magic had felt like a dark snake, Rore's felt like a cool spring breeze, gently caressing my skin and enveloping me like a reassuring hug. One of those breezes touched my charm, and the power flowed. My arm tingled. This was nothing like the other times I'd had it recharged. Those had been almost painful.

After a minute, her singing trailed off, leaving the air feeling empty and hollow without it.

"That should hold you for now," she said. "And Orion, for this little favor, you get to do the dishes tomorrow."

He huffed. "Yes, your majesty."

"You and Lapis don't do anything I wouldn't do!" She giggled and dropped the call.

I handed the phone back to Orion.

He looked embarrassed. "That's my sister."

I activated my charm, and it roared back to life. I could feel its power. But unlike the last charge, the magic had emotions attached to it. Rore's emotions. I'd never felt anything like this. It was almost like a piece of Rore's heart had been placed into it. I guess the other witches had removed all traces of themselves when recharging it. But Rore hadn't bothered. I hope that didn't come back to haunt her.

But for me, it felt like my friend was right with me. It made my lying to Orion seem worse.

"Is it working now?" he asked.

I chuckled. "Oh yeah. Your sister is very talented."

"I know," he said flatly, but I could feel the hidden love and admiration behind the words. Then they shifted to sadness. "If only she would see it and not doubt herself so much."

He stood and held out his hand. "Come on. It's late, and we need to get home."

I hesitated, looking up into his shadowed eyes. "You don't seem bothered that I'm hiding my appearance from you. From your whole family."

He shrugged. "Why should I care? And honestly, I don't think they would care either." He sighed. "Lapis, you have a good heart. That's what makes you beautiful, not your appearance."

I blinked at the sudden welling in my eyes. I definitely did not have a good heart. I lied to people every day—a fake and a coward. But soon, if Terra kept her promise, maybe I wouldn't be anymore.

I slipped my smaller hand into his much larger one. His grip was firm and reassuring as he tugged me to my feet and slipped a steadying arm around my waist.

"What would eating the cookie have done to you?" I asked.

He shrugged. "It's hard to say. I don't carry any charms and only have my natural magic. I guess it would have prevented me from shifting. Maybe she was afraid I was going to change into a rabbit and run away." He helped me take a step. "How's it feel?"

"Hurts."

"Thought so."

He stared at my foot, thinking.

I looked up at him. "Are you going to speak to Chaleta about it?"

He nodded. "There also might be a little yelling involved. It was probably a prank, but it was still stupid." He sighed. "Can you stand here a moment?"

I nodded and balanced myself on one foot. He stepped back into the bushes and returned a moment later with the skateboard.

I shook my head. "I don't think I can ride it now."

"I know," he calmly answered. "But you *are* going to ride." And then he began to undress. I looked away. When he was done, he handed me a small pack. "Will you carry this for me?"

I took it while keeping my head turned. "You know it's impolite to undress in front of a lady."

I could feel his delight in embarrassing me. "It's for a good cause," he said.

I saw a faint flash of blue light, and then I felt something nudging my back. I turned to find a beautiful white stallion standing beside me. He whinnied and pointed with his nose toward his back. He moved closer, and I managed to grab his mane and throw a leg over him. I had never ridden before, and it seemed like I was a hundred feet off the ground. I clung with my knees, afraid I would fall off.

He looked over his shoulder to make sure I was aboard, and then he moved gently forward.

The swaying motion surprised me, and I nearly dropped the board when I grabbed a handful of his mane. He slowly picked his way through the bushes, careful not to go under any low-hanging trees. It didn't take him long to find the driveway and then onto the road.

I clung to him, afraid I might fall off, but he stayed steady underneath me. I could feel his powerful muscles working and the soft clop of his feet as he moved. After a bit, I relaxed and began to move with him. I began to enjoy it.

Sensing I was growing more comfortable, he increased his

pace, moving from a walk to a jog. I easily matched him. "This is great!"

He glanced over his shoulder and increased his speed, moving to a gallop. The wind blew through my hair, his warmth and strength reassuring beneath me. I had never experienced anything like it.

All too soon, he slowed, and we approached his home. He took me directly to his open window, which was high enough that I didn't have to pull myself up. I just slipped right in.

I tested my weight on my ankle, and while it still hurt, it was not quite as bad as before. I looked away from the window just in time because a naked Orion came in right behind me.

I waited for him to dress before turning to face him, but I wasn't exactly sure what to say.

"Thank you for saving me from a cookie tonight," he said, then frowned. "That sounded really weird."

I grinned. "Yes, it did, but you're welcome. And thank you for getting Rore to recharge my charm. That is a load off my mind. You have no idea."

We stared at each other, neither one of us knowing what to say. After a few moments of awkward silence, I turned and hobbled to the door.

"Lapis," he called after me.

I stopped and turned, leaning against the doorframe.

"I . . ." he hesitated. "Your secret is safe with me. I won't tell anyone about your charm."

I smiled. "I know." And I did. I had no doubts he would keep it safe.

His mouth opened to say more, but he didn't.

"See you tomorrow," I said.

"Yeah."

I left and went to Rore's room, where an extremely curious witch instantly attacked me with an insistent demand.

"Spill it! How was your date?"

I couldn't help but smile. "I stole his cookie."

Her eyes went as large as saucers.

Chapter 17

FROM MY ADVENTURES the prior evening, Rore's friendly interrogation, and her healing magic on my ankle, I was exhausted. It was like all my prior struggles caught up with me, and I slept like the dead. I awoke late, finding Rore already up.

After my morning business, I made my way to the kitchen. Rore was sitting at the table, the crumbs of her breakfast indicating she had already eaten. Orion leaned against the counter with his arms crossed. He was frowning as he looked down at the floor, but when I entered, he eyed me, and one edge of his mouth curled up slightly.

"Good morning," he said.

I blinked. Had I detected a note of happiness? His emotions

were their normal swirl with a hint of pleasure. Could it be because of me?

Rore put her phone down and patted the place next to her. "Orion made breakfast this morning," she announced. From the twinkle in her eye, I got the impression this was a rare occurrence.

He turned and punched buttons on the microwave. "It's just an omelet," he said.

Rore grinned knowingly behind his back.

When it beeped, he set my plate in front of me. I was impressed—it was nicely done. My stomach reminded me that I was starving, and I didn't hesitate to dig in.

Orion hovered nearby. He was uncharacteristically nervous.

"It's good," I said. "Thank you for fixing this, but I thought you were a vegetarian."

He nodded. "I am, but not completely vegan. I do eat eggs and drink milk. Just no meat."

I shivered at the thought. I couldn't imagine a world without hamburgers.

"Where's Andromeda?" I asked.

"Work," Rore and Orion said simultaneously. They looked at each other and smiled. I already knew she was a veterinarian. She and two other doctors had a small practice.

Rore sighed. "She usually treats only cats and dogs, but today she was consulting on a parrot from the zoo."

I nodded. "That sounds interesting."

Rore leaned closer. "One time, she treated an anaconda." She shivered.

"Don't like snakes?" I asked.

The siblings exchanged glances, and I realized I'd stumbled into something they didn't want to discuss.

Orion suddenly moved toward the back door. "I'm going to meditate." And like a shot, he left the room.

Puzzled, I turned to Rore. "Is it something I said?"

She shook her head. "It's not you. He's embarrassed about what happened a while back. Although it wasn't his fault." She sighed. "You know, when shifters are young, they don't have complete control of their ability."

I shrugged. "I've heard it's like that for most magicals." I was supposed to be a mundane human, so I didn't mention the problems I had growing up.

She sighed. "When we were younger, Mom took us to her office to see an anaconda that someone had abandoned. They were keeping it until the zoo could take it. Orion knew he wasn't supposed to, but he touched it."

"Did it bite him?"

She looked away. "No. This one was sleeping. Everything went fine. Until we got home." She paused and looked down at her plate. "Orion wanted to watch a program that I didn't. We argued, and . . . he lost his temper."

I shrugged. "All siblings do that."

She gazed at me levelly. "He turned into an anaconda. A big one."

I shrugged again. "So."

"He came after me, but Mom got in his way. He wrapped around her and started squeezing. She had to use her magic to make him stop."

I was puzzled. "Why did he do that?"

"Orion couldn't help it. Being a shifter, he has to touch the animal at least once to transform into one. After he touches it for the first time, all he has to do is think of it, and he'll change." She licked her lips nervously. "But if he touches a new animal, he will transform into it next time, whether he wants to or not. It's why he's so particular about what he eats. He doesn't want to transform into something he's not expecting. Also, the further away from humanoid it is, the less control he has over his instincts. Mammals and most birds are generally all right. But a reptile doesn't think like we do. Orion avoids them. If he transforms into one, he loses all his intelligence and begins to operate on instinct only."

"That's scary."

"It is. But it's normal for shifters." She smiled. "He's a bit of an exception because he can transform into anything. Most shifters are limited to mammals or birds. But so far, there's no animal he can't change into."

"Is that how he was able to transform into an ogre?"

Rore nodded. "But we can't figure out where he touched one. We were so careful."

"True," I said. "They aren't exactly on every street corner."

She shrugged. "Maybe someone was playing a sick joke. Hades, it could have been someone in disguise." She leaned forward conspiratorially. "You know there are illusion charms that can even make a Night-clan look human."

That was hitting a little close to the mark. I tried to keep my face neutral and decided a change in topic might be needed.

I got up and took my plate to the dishwasher. "So, what are you doing today?"

As I was putting the dish in, my necklace slipped out of my shirt, and the amulet dangled free. I didn't think anything of it.

Rore joined me, putting her own plate in. "I might go to the mall later. Do you want to come? You still have that gift certificate Grandmother gave you."

I made a face. Another crowded place flooded with emotions might be more than I could handle right now. "Maybe later."

"Ah, come on, Lapis." She glanced at my neck. "There's a jewelry store going out of business. You could pick up a cool necklace or pendant. They have some nice ones."

I grinned and held up Mom's amulet. "I'm happy with this one, thank you."

And then her eyes did the strangest thing. They slid over my amulet like it wasn't there. She snorted. "Really, Lapis. Every girl could use a little something. Your neck looks bare."

I blinked. I had my amulet right there. I held it closer to her. "I have this, Rore. It's called the Morning Star Brilliance."

At the mention of the name, a slight shiver went through her, and then she looked out the window. "I need to go check on Orion."

She immediately turned to leave. I watched her retreat, wondering at the weirdness of the exchange. I looked down at the amulet. It was like she didn't see it. I blinked at it a moment. No, it was like she was being told to ignore it.

I went outside to where Orion and Rore were talking. I held up the amulet. "This is called the Morning Star Brilliance. What do you think of it?"

They turned away, continuing their conversation, while refusing to look at the necklace. *Why wouldn't they see it?*

I dangled it directly in front of their faces, but they didn't even flinch. "Don't you like my necklace?" I asked.

Simultaneously, they turned away.

"I guess I better go for a run," said Orion. He immediately left through the patio gate.

"I need to get to the mall." Rore went inside, my invitation to go with her forgotten. A moment later, I heard the front door close.

This was so weird.

"They won't see it," I whispered. "It's like it blocks its existence from them." I held it up. Could it possibly be enchanted? Something to make people avoid it?

I wouldn't even know what it was called if—

I gasped.

Grandfather had called it by its name.

My eyes went wide. He not only could see it, but he knew what it was.

I cocked my jaw. I guess another visit to my grandfather was in order.

I needed to ask him why.

Orion insisted on coming with me, saying I shouldn't be alone. I didn't argue. I needed the moral support.

We took the bus into the city, walking the last few blocks to my grandfather's house. On the way over, I pulled out my necklace and waved it in front of a few passersby. Most people avoided it, and a few even turned around, heading in the opposite direction. Orion just calmly walked beside me, not commenting on my odd behavior.

But I did get one reaction. I showed it to a mother and her small child. The mother didn't see it, but the child did. She commented it was pretty, which earned the child a tug on her arm as the mother continued down the street.

I nodded to myself. I guess it was why I could remember my mother wearing it. And perhaps why she gave it to me on my seventeenth birthday. There might even be some type of proximity effect since I was around her so much.

After proving to myself that the effect was real, I tucked the necklace safely into my shirt. I was determined to get some answers. Either I was going crazy, or some potent magic was involved.

Walking up to my grandfather's house, I was filled with apprehension. We paused at the gate, and I took a deep breath to steel myself. I prayed this wasn't a repeat of my last visit.

Orion reached for the gate, but I placed a hand on his arm, stopping him. "Do you mind waiting here?"

I could feel Orion's concern. "I don't mind going in with you."

"I would like to have you with me," I said, my eyes searching his, "but it's best if I go alone. While he might yell at me, I don't think he'll hurt me."

He nodded, clearly uncomfortable. He glanced at the house. "I'll be right here if you need me."

It warmed my heart to feel his determination, and I took strength from it. I could do this.

I went through the gate, its loud squeak marking my entrance. At the door, I knocked and waited, bracing myself for rejection once more. But there was no answer. I knocked louder. Still nothing.

A breeze tugged at my clothes and tousled my hair. With it, an uneasy feeling settled over me. Something wasn't right.

I stepped back and opened my senses. Grandfather had likely shielded himself, so I might not be able to detect him. But I had to try something.

While my tail was not visible, it was still there. It was not as good as my horns, but it was better than nothing. I touched the house with it, seeking any unusual feelings.

Everything had emotions, even down to the smallest bug. It was a constant background noise. When I was a child, Mom and I had played hide-and-seek to practice hiding my emotions. But she always found me. I knew I was doing it correctly. Mom even admitted it to me. Yet, she still found me when there was no physical trail to follow.

One time, determined to win, I hid in the basement of the house we were renting. It was supposed to be out of bounds, but I had sneaked down the rickety stairs and hid by the washing machine. But it only took her a couple of minutes to find me. Of course, I got a lecture about going down there alone, but it frustrated me. What was I doing wrong? So I asked her. *How did you find me?*

I remember her smiling and gently brushing a strand of hair behind my ear. It was like she had been waiting for me to ask the question.

"It's simple, my precious jewel. I simply look for the hole."

I gave her a puzzled look. "The hole?"

She nodded. "When you mask your emotions, you also mask those immediately around you. You can't help it. So I just look for where you're not."

So with my tail on the door, I felt all the emotions coming

from inside. The gentle feelings the door had absorbed over time, the tiny bugs inside, the studs in the frame, the dining room table. It was all a soft drone of noise. I sorted through it, looking at anything that might not fit—a blank spot, no matter how small—

I gasped. There was one in the back.

"Grandfather!" I called and knocked on the door. Unexpectedly, the thick door moved inward. *Was it not latched?* A quick inspection gave the reason. The door had been forced. I pushed against it, and it slowly creaked open. In alarm, I quickly stepped inside.

In the den, I found his chair overturned, with books and knickknacks scattered across the floor—many of the fragile pieces had been shattered. I gasped when I saw splotches of blood. The wood in his chair vibrated with the recent emotions of anger, frustration, and fear. *A struggle?*

"Grandfather!" I called, panic entering my voice. Sadly, I dared not call the police, at least until I figured out what had happened. If this was a Night-clan action, then the same could happen to me. I had to think of the Strewerts.

Sensing the emotional hole, I walked carefully in that direction. I went toward the back of the house, glass crunching under my feet. I passed a small bathroom, and peering inside, I saw it had been ransacked. But I took hope. There were drops of blood on the sink, but there were also some open bandage wrappers from someone tending to themselves. I went further and into one of the house's two bedrooms.

Lying on the bed was my grandfather—his right hand heavily bandaged, and his face was bruised and swollen. He appeared to be sleeping.

I went to his side and touched his arm, carefully putting my fingers on an uninjured section of his skin.

His eyes immediately sprang open. Because I was touching him, I could feel his fear at being startled. But as recognition settled in, he calmed and relaxed back into his pillow. He tried to speak, but his mouth was too dry.

I took the glass of water from the bedside table and held it to his lips so he could take a few sips. He grimaced in pain as he lay back. I adjusted his pillows so he could sit up better.

"What happened?" I asked gently.

He frowned and stared at me. "*You*, is what happened."

I was puzzled. "Me?"

He nodded. "They came looking for the Morning Star Brilliance. When they couldn't find it, they decided to see what I knew. I hoped that if I kicked you out, I might be spared." He looked down at his bandaged hand. "But it didn't work."

"They think I gave it to you?" I asked in disbelief.

"Apparently."

"I don't even know what it is." I pulled it out and held it in front of him. "You can see it, can't you?"

He nodded.

"What is it?"

But he didn't answer and just glared at me.

I was getting irritated. "What did I do to make you hate me? Why are you so pissed off? I'm sorry they followed me here, but I had nowhere else to go."

He snorted. "Why would I hate you? I don't know you. I'm still not even sure you're her child. You could be one of *them* trying to trick me."

I cocked my jaw to the side. "How do I prove it to you? There's got to be a way. Maybe something only I would know."

He considered me for a moment. "Your mother sent me a package about a year ago."

"She what?" I gasped.

He nodded. "I had the same reaction. I was shocked to receive something from her after so long. The message with it said it was dangerous and to hide it in case something happened to her." He held my gaze. "I think I know why she did it now."

"What was it?"

He pulled his hand back. "I'm still not convinced you're my granddaughter. For all I know, you're just a succubus pretending to be her." He considered me a moment before continuing. "You say you're my child's child and that you truly are my granddaughter. If what you say is true, you'll have no trouble finding what your mother sent me."

We stared at each other. Well, if that was the way he wanted to play, so be it.

I pulled out my phone and texted Orion that I was all right and going to be a little longer. Then, after putting my phone away, I shut my eyes and concentrated.

Whatever it was, it would hold the residue of my mother's emotions—like an emotional signature. It was a signature I knew quite well.

To my surprise, I felt not one or two but many radiating her faint presence. The house was filled with them. I looked to the bedroom across the hall—my mother's old room—and saw it also had been ransacked. I doubted what I wanted was in there.

I looked up, almost as if I could see through the ceiling. The house was small, and I doubted it had a second floor, but there might be an attic.

I walked back toward the front of the house. I opened several closed doors until I found a steep flight of wooden stairs leading up. A doll sat on the third step, leaned back into its corner. Mom had loved it at one time—enough to imprint that feeling on it. But I didn't think that was it. Grandfather more than likely had placed it there as a decoy. I looked up into the darkness of the attic, where I detected other signatures. I went up the steps.

The attic was hot and dark. I could barely make out a string hanging down in front of me. I pulled on it, and a tiny bulb illuminated a low, unfinished attic with bare plywood for the floor. It was filled with unused stuff—a decades-old TV, a disassembled bedroom set, and boxes and boxes of just *stuff.* Everything had been opened and strewn about the floor. Someone had been searching in a hurry. Likely the same ones that had ransacked the downstairs. I could feel Mom's presence scattered along with the rest—another doll, an old school project, a children's book. Their signature was of a younger version of my mother, not the more mature woman that had raised me. I wished I had time to go through them, but these were not what I needed to find.

I had to hand it to my grandfather. The old geezer wasn't making this easy. Then I spotted it. A child's play stove lay on its back in the corner. It was bright pink with knobs across the front and had pictures of fake burners glued to the top. I could feel the joy the child version of my mom had poured into it during her play. I frowned. But there was something else about it. A hint of my mother's more mature signature. I went closer.

I bent down and opened the plastic oven door. Nothing appeared inside, but my emotional senses told me otherwise. I put my hand inside and felt a lump that didn't match the smooth plastic I was seeing. I probed further, finding something had been taped to the back and then hidden with an illusion charm. I got my fingers under it and pulled.

The illusion immediately dropped as I pulled out something padded with bubble wrap and bound with duct tape. It felt like a small box of some kind.

I took it back downstairs.

When I walked into the room with it, Grandfather nodded, and his lower lip began to tremble as tears came to his eyes. "It really is you."

I couldn't help but have a few of my own. "Yes, it is."

He held out his arms, and I gave him a hug, which was rightly returned.

"I'm sorry, but I had to be sure."

We separated, and he pointed to it. "Open it. She went to a lot of trouble for this. I hope it's worth it."

I carefully stripped off the wrapping to reveal a polished wooden box slightly smaller than my hand. It had a latch on top. I swallowed as I pressed the latch and slowly opened the box.

Inside, resting on a bed of red velvet, was a highly polished stone of deep violet with a rune carved into it. But what caught my eye was what was with it—a man-sized ring of solid blue.

Was it made from the gemstone called lapis lazuli? My namesake? I couldn't take my eyes off it.

But what was truly surprising were the faint feelings emanating from it. Mom's feelings. Gemstones didn't radiate emotion well, so a lot of feelings must have been poured into it.

I showed it to Grandfather. "Why would she send me this?"

He looked back up at me. "The ring was your father's."

My mouth fell open. "Father's? How did she get it?"

He shrugged. "I'm not sure. Maybe the answer is in the memory stone."

I shook my head. "What?"

He pointed with his chin. "The stone with the rune is a memory stone. She wanted to show you something and you alone."

I licked my suddenly dry lips. "What do you mean?"

"A memory stone is made to hold a person's selected memories, and only the person it's keyed to can receive them. If the stone is tampered with, it cracks, rendering it useless." He looked up at me. "Do you know how to use one?"

I shook my head.

"You hold it in your hand and then think of an image that will unlock it. If the image matches and you're the person its intended for, the jewel will then play the memory. There could be more than one inside, but they will be short."

I nodded and looked down at it.

He leaned forward. "Also, be careful where you release the memory. It will only play once, and while it plays, it will seem that you are that person. It will have your complete attention, and you won't be able to interrupt it."

"You make it sound scary."

"In a way, it is. I've only done it twice. Your grandmother left me one for after she died. And your mother sent one for me with that package. It was a brief message saying the name of the necklace and to make sure only you got it. Apparently, having the memory put directly into my brain somehow bypassed the necklace's protections."

Should I do it now? I was tempted, but the time didn't feel right. I relocked the box and stuffed it into my jacket pocket. I would play it later.

I scanned the bedside table and saw no signs of a meal, not even crackers.

"Have you eaten?" I asked.

He shook his head. "Too sore."

I patted his arm. "I'll fix something. Then I'll come back—"

"No!" he interrupted. "You should leave now. For both our sakes."

I cocked my jaw, having had just about enough of this. "I refuse. You need something to eat." I narrowed my eyes and pursed my lips. "I'll be quick and leave right after."

He struggled to sit up. "I don't want to be beaten up again, and I don't want to see a young girl hurt."

I put a restraining hand on his chest. He winced but laid back down. "I'll make this quick."

Before he could reply, I left the room and found the kitchen. Like the rest of the house, it was a mess, with the cabinets' contents spilled onto the floor. I rooted around and, a few minutes later, carried in a steaming hot bowl of chicken noodle soup and not-too-mashed-up crackers. I helped him sit up.

"Do you need help eating? I don't mind."

"Hell, no. I'm not that feeble."

I gave him the bowl, and he took a tentative first bite, then quickly tore into the rest. While he was eating, I picked up what I could and placed it back on the shelves where it seemed to fit. What was broken, I put in a trash bag and set it by the door.

I paused when I saw a picture of Mom among the wreckage. It was one of her graduating, my grandfather at her side. I looked toward the bedroom. Perhaps there was one last question I needed to ask.

Orion interrupted my thoughts with a text, asking if I was all right and if I would like a burger. Like I was going to turn that down.

When I heard Grandfather scraping the bottom of the bowl, I went back to the bedroom. He looked up guiltily, every one of the crackers gone.

"I guess I was a little more hungry than I thought."

"Want more?"

He shook his head. "I better let this sit first."

Then he considered me, a faraway look in his eye. "You're so much like your mother it's unnerving." He seemed to catch himself. "You better be going now. You've done what you said."

I set the bowl down on his dresser. "Yes, I did. But I have one last question."

He considered me for a moment. "You want to know why your mother and I never talked."

I nodded. "What happened?"

"Your father," he said coldly.

"Wait. You mean you wouldn't talk to her because of who she

fell in love with?" Mother had talked to me many times about how much she loved my father and missed him. I think it was why she never dated.

"And she chose a loser," he spat.

I jumped up, fists clenched. "My father was not a loser."

He snorted. "You never met him, so how could you possibly know? He was a selfish bastard, more interested in playing hero than in taking care of his family."

"He saved our lives!"

"Because he put you in danger in the first place. Him and his other three friends, saying they were going to save the world. Until he attracted the wrong kind of attention and got himself killed." He looked away. "I told her if she married him, then we were through. She said screw you, and I disowned her."

"And you forced her to live a life of near-poverty and spend the rest of her life with no family."

He leaned forward and nearly spat at me. "For our own protection! She brought that down on her head. Not me."

"Well, I hope you're satisfied now. She's dead, and you've alienated your only granddaughter. Now, how does that feel?"

I turned and headed for the door.

"Lapis!" he called after me. "Wait!"

But I didn't want to see him. His stupid pride kept them apart. I had hoped I had at least one family member, but apparently, all that was left was a bitter old man. I stormed out and slammed the door behind me.

I stomped up the sidewalk and out the gate. Orion was leaning against a tree with a white bag in his hand. My phone buzzed, no doubt telling me he was back.

He held up the bag and then frowned as he took in my bearing. I walked up to him and looked up, blinking back angry tears. "I'm done with him."

Orion put his arms around me and pulled me into a hug. I swore I wasn't going to cry, but I did lean into his strength and took comfort in his concern.

Chapter 18

AFTER I HAD composed myself, Orion led me three blocks over to a large park, its entrance lined with ornamental shrubbery and an arch over the top announcing Edgemont Victory Park. There was lots of open grass and a few young trees—nothing like the massive oaks from the park near Orion's house. I quickly realized this must be the part that had been rebuilt after whatever event had destroyed the area.

Orion guided me to a bench, and we ate our hamburger and fries in comfortable silence. Basic comfort food. Exactly what I needed and a welcome relief from the vegetarian diet of the Strewert household. Orion took a bite of his, and my eyes went up in shock.

"Aren't you a vegetarian?"

He grinned around his sandwich. "Shiitake mushroom."

"You're eating a mushroom burger?" I made a face. "I admit they can be tasty on pizza or in spaghetti, but as a replacement for a burger? That goes against the nature of the universe."

He chuckled. "Mushrooms are perfectly nutritious. Good for you too."

"You know what those things are grown on, don't you?"

"Yeah," his eyes sparkled. "Adds flavor."

I shivered and turned back to my own. "I'll stick with the tried and true."

We sat in silence for a bit, taking in the park scenery. In the distance, a group of boys were playing baseball, while a little closer, a couple sat on a blanket, a toddler playing on the grass beside them. Two teen girls holding skates walked close to us, talking animatedly. I could barely catch a snippet of their conversation. "*Did you see last night's episode? Devon finally killed the evil succubus. It was so cool.*" Then they stepped out of earshot. It was the same old nonsense. I knew the show, and it was full of stereotypes—*wrong ones*.

Orion wadded up his paper and held his hand out for mine. I put the last fry in my mouth and gave it to him. He walked them over to a nearby trash container, returning to sit beside me. "Do you want to talk about it?"

I sighed and leaned forward, looking at the ground between my sneakers. "Not really. The old man has let his pride keep him away from his own daughter. I don't understand it." I shook my head. "But there's a bigger problem. He was beaten up yesterday, and they tore up his house searching for something. When they couldn't find it, they applied some *persuasion* to get him to tell them where it was."

He looked alarmed. "Did he call the police?"

I rolled my eyes in his direction. I thought he was kidding, but from his face, I could see he was serious.

I shook my head. "It wouldn't do any good."

And it wouldn't. Once they found out he was an incubus, they would figure out some way to make it come back on him. They'd assume it was a drug deal gone bad, or someone extracting a payment.

Orion nodded. "So, why was your grandfather beaten up?"

I shrugged. "He said they were looking for—something." I nearly said Morning Star Brilliance but stopped. Orion wouldn't be able to hear it. "He doesn't have it, nor has he seen it."

Orion pondered the information.

My eyes shifted to the expanse of grass behind him. In the distance was the beautiful building I had seen from Terra's limo on my first evening in town. The structure was even more majestic by day. But as I looked at it, I thought it seemed out of place on its hill. Alone even. It made me sad to look at it. *A vault*, I wanted to call it. I shook my head. I don't know why I keep thinking it looked like one.

I jerked my eyes away and continued our conversation. "Whatever those people were looking for, it's somehow connected to me. They didn't bother him until I visited." I looked down. "Combine that with the people in the van that tried to kidnap me, and it adds up to me being a liability." I looked at him levelly. "I don't want to see your family hurt because of me." I sighed. "I guess I need to talk to your grandmother about this. She won't get involved with another clan's business, but maybe she knows what's going on."

"Her office is not that far from here."

I shook my head. "Not today. I don't think I can handle any-more."

He nodded.

I glanced at the vault again. Something about it drew my eye. "What is that building over there?" I asked. "It looks out of place." I nodded in that direction. "There's not a walk or any-thing going up to it. Just grass."

Orion turned and looked behind him. "What building?"

I pointed. "Right over there. The big one on that hill."

He shook his head. "I don't see anything. It's just grass."

I pointed again. "It's a squarish building with marble col-umns all around and is about the size of your house."

Orion again looked at where I was pointing. "Lapis, there is nothing there."

I leaped up from the bench and started walking toward it. Frowning, Orion continued to sit for a moment and then fol-lowed me.

He quickly caught up. "There's nothing there."

The building was a little bigger and a little farther than I thought. But as I drew near, I could tell it had perfectly smooth marble columns set against an unbroken marble wall. From the direction I approached—I thought it was the north side—there was no entrance. But what looked like steps were on the left, or east side of the building. I altered course in that direction.

We got within about fifty feet of the structure when Orion stopped. It was like he wanted to follow me but couldn't.

"Orion?" I asked. "What's wrong?" I could feel his distress.

He looked right at me. "This is stupid," he stated. "There's nothing here. Just a bunch of grass." He waved his arms to illustrate the point.

I pointed again to the structure. "You don't see this huge marble building?"

He shook his head and looked worried. "Lapis, maybe the stress today has been too much for you, and you're seeing things. Let's go home and you can rest. I'm sure Mom knows someone to help." I could feel fear and uncertainty radiating from him.

A chill went up my spine. It was eerily similar to the necklace. *What was going on?*

I didn't want to make him any more uncomfortable. "Orion, just stay right there for a moment. Then we'll go back to your house."

He nodded but didn't look comforted.

I approached the structure, finding grand marble steps leading up. It reminded me of a government or academic building. In fact, it could have come straight out of some book on ancient architecture.

I was about six feet away when the grass went from well-maintained to completely unkempt. It was like whoever was running the mower had just stopped—the uncut area making a perfect circle around the building.

I looked up at the entrance. The steps went up to a high porch held up by the columns. The columns were huge, bigger than I could wrap my arms around. At the back of the porch, set into the building's perfect marble walls, was a large brass double door. It was highly polished, without the least trace of tarnish.

There could be only one conclusion. It was magically protected—which would also explain why Orion was not reacting to it. *But why was it letting me in?*

"Lapis?" called Orion. Obviously in distress. "Please come back."

I looked up at the structure. I was filled with a certain reverence. And curiosity.

I stepped inside the circle.

"Lapis?" Orion called in panic. "Where did you go?"

"I'm right here," I called back, but he obviously couldn't hear me.

I took another step inside, and Orion seemed to relax. He looked around, seemingly unconcerned. "I wonder where Lapis went?" He muttered before turning and walking away.

Wow. That was powerful magic. Not only could Orion not see me, but he forgot where I had gone.

Turning back to the vault, I took in its elegant columns, marbled steps, and brass door. I sighed. It had to be here for a reason, and I was going to find out why. So, I started climbing the stairs.

I stopped at the top and looked out across the park. From my slightly higher elevation, I could see the entire area. There were the two girls that had passed, now speeding along on their roller skates. The couple with the small child had finished their picnic—the mother gathering their stuff while the father chased the child. In the distance on the baseball field, someone had hit a home run, and the audience was cheering. And halfway back to the park bench, Orion was slowly walking, head down, seemingly quite puzzled.

None of them were aware of this building. It was hidden in plain sight. *Why?*

I turned and walked through the row of immense columns to stand in front of the brass doors. I could see no lock, latch, or hinges. Just a massive set of doors that fit so closely into the marble doorway that I doubted I could squeeze a credit card between them.

I reached out a hand to touch the surface.

"That's far enough, Lapis."

I jumped at the voice. I whirled to find a solid gray cat sitting behind me. His long tail wrapped elegantly around his feet. The cat had one green eye and one blue.

"Bast!" I cried and sidestepped, both away from the door and away from the cat.

I looked for a place to run.

"Calm yourself, Guardian," he said reassuringly. "I will not harm you. But the *Vault of Silent Whispers* will, which is why I need to speak with you before you hurt yourself."

He calmly regarded me as I tried to slow my pounding heart.

I waved an arm around me and continued to inch away. "What is this place?"

"It is here to protect something critical to this world. So do not touch the door."

I stopped. "Why can't I?"

"I can't tell you."

I frowned. "Can't or won't?" Accusation rang clear in my voice.

He stood and strolled toward me, and I backed up a step in return. He rolled his eyes and sat back down. "I am literally unable to speak of this place. The magic imbued into the vault is extremely powerful. Should I try to break its hold, I might damage it."

"Then can you tell me why no one knows it's here?"

"Sorry."

I ran my hand through my hair in frustration. "Can you at least tell me why I can see it and no one else can?"

He shook his head. "No."

I sighed and walked away, before turning and walking back. "Can you tell me why you're here?"

"I am the Custodian of Secrets. I guard the vault."

"And you don't even know what you're protecting?"

"Oh, I know. But I can neither speak it, write it, nor imply it. I am totally bound by it. Its makers wanted to ensure its safety, so they didn't give me much leeway. Of course, they never imagined things would get this bad."

"You're Aether-Clan. Are you saying this is more powerful than you?"

"No, I'm saying I don't want to hurt it. It's just fulfilling its purpose."

"You're acting like it's alive."

"In a sense, it is." He considered me. "It's not intelligent like we are, but that doesn't mean it won't bite if threatened. That's why I had to come. If you touch the door, you will see how alive it is."

"You're right," I glared at the cat defiantly. "I don't believe you." I strode over and slapped my hand against the door.

There was a loud crack, followed by an immense electric shock, and finally, the sensation of flying.

The next thing I knew, I was looking up at the clouds filling a wonderfully blue sky and wondering how I got there. My whole body was tingling, and the muscles in my arms and legs gave little twinges—not to mention a deep throbbing pain in my arm and head. I was sure every ounce of strength in my body had been drained. I mustered what little I had to roll my head to the side. I was lying on the grass just in front of the building's steps—Bast was sitting on the lowest one.

"Believe me now?" he said.

I couldn't even open my mouth.

"Rest for a moment. You'll be able to move again soon." He seemed to smile. "You're lucky the vault likes you."

I managed to move my jaw. "I'd . . . hate . . . to be its enemy."

Bast started washing his paw. "Needless to say, don't do that again. Next time, it will kill you."

"Right."

I felt the tingling in my body start to subside, and my strength begin to return. I managed to sit up.

I shook my head, trying to clear the fog, and instantly regretted it, since it made the throbbing in my head worse.

"That was not the smartest thing I've ever done," I said rhetorically. A sudden thought occurred. "When I leave, will I forget about this . . ." I waved at it. "Monstrosity?"

A cloud passed in front of the sun, and the light dimmed. I jumped when a miniature bolt of lightning landed in the grass just beyond my hand. I jerked it back.

I quickly stood and faced the vault. I bowed. "Apologies, ancient one. I have been rude. Please forgive me."

The cloud moved out from the sun, and the sky brightened. A temperamental building, I thought, wisely keeping the words to myself.

Bast moved to cleaning his fur. "I suggest you treat the Vault of Silent Whispers with respect. As I mentioned, it might bite. But it also might purr if you stroke it carefully."

I glanced over at the singed spot just two inches from where my hand had been. "I can see your point."

Bast looked up from his grooming. "And to answer your question, no, you won't forget as long as you have a badge, but no one will believe you either."

"A badge?" I asked, puzzled.

He stopped grooming and just looked at me.

I frowned and put my hands on my hips. "This will be very frustrating."

Bast nodded in agreement. "It is very inconvenient at times."

I sighed. "Is there anything at all you can tell me about the vault or these badges?"

"Nothing, I am sorry. If you wish to know about it, you will have to seek the answers yourself."

"Well, in that case, I'm going to go back. This was a total waste of time."

I turned away and started walking toward Orion, who was now sitting on our park bench. But I had a sudden thought. I turned back to Bast, who was still sitting on the bottom step, watching me. He seemed to know I was not really done yet.

I sat down cross-legged in front of him. "Why are you helping me?" I asked. "This is the third time you've warned me about something. Why? And please don't give me that crap about not being able to answer."

I could swear he smiled. "Because I am the caretaker of the vault, and you are its Guardian. Guiding the Guardian is what the Custodian does. And you . . ." he resumed licking his paw, " . . . must fix this broken world."

I closed my eyes and held the bridge of my nose. "What does that even mean?" I huffed in disgust. "I feel like I'm caught in a bad video game."

I rose and stomped away. This was ridiculous!

"Lapis," Bast called after me.

I paused and turned.

"Find the Champion, the Paladin, and the Adept. You don't have long before it begins."

"What?" I asked in frustration. "Find who? And before what begins?"

"The wheels are in motion. No one can stop it now. You must quickly gather your allies. Talk to the gremlins. They are immune to the magic."

I shook my head. "*Bast—*"

Dizziness flashed through my brain, and suddenly, everything was different.

"Who's Bast?" asked Orion.

I blinked up at him, completely disoriented. I was now sitting beside Orion on the bench we had eaten lunch on. *How did I get here?*

Astonished, I looked around. The vault was still in the distance; the couple with the child were still having their picnic. I could hear the voices of the teenage girls holding skates walking past. "*Did you see last night's episode? Devon finally killed the evil succubus. It was so cool.*"

I've been here before.

"Are you done with your wrapper?" Orion asked.

I looked down and realized I was holding the wrapper from my sandwich. I slowly looked at Orion. He had his hand extended, waiting for it. He wiggled his fingers impatiently. I handed it to him. He got up and walked the remains of our meal over to the trash receptacle like he had done before.

What had just happened?

I glanced at the vault, wondering if maybe I had dreamed it.

My phone chimed with an incoming text. I pulled it out and looked at it. It didn't have a number. I felt the hairs on the back of my neck stand up.

Find the others. It read. *Choose your allies now!*

"Lapis," asked Orion. Concern was radiating from him. "You look pale. Are you all right?"

I didn't know how to answer him. I looked back down at the screen, and the message changed before my eyes.

Hurry, Guardian.

Hurry.

Chapter 19

I WAS QUIET AS we rode the bus back to the Strewerts. My brain was on overload, thinking through what I had learned from both Bast and my grandfather. I could tell Orion was discreetly watching me. Several times, he looked like he wanted to say something but didn't. His feelings were a swirl, but they gave me no clue of what he was thinking.

As we walked in, we met Rore waiting by the door. She was dressed to kill, her emotions bubbling with excitement.

Orion went to his room, leaving us to talk.

I gave her the once over. "Going out?"

She smiled. "Yes. It might even be a hot one."

"Are you and Skiff . . .?"

A car horn interrupted me. Rore smoothed down her dress. "Do I look all right?"

I nodded and returned her grin. "You look wonderful."

She leaned close. "Don't wait up for me, if you know what I mean." She paused. "I also made some cookies. Completely veg, so Orion can have some. They're on the table."

In a flash, she was out the door. I looked out after her and was shocked to see that it was not Skiff's old sedan. Instead, it was a sparkling red sports car. I ran to the door hoping to catch her, but she was already in, and Zeek was speeding away.

Her going out with him made me uneasy. I grabbed my phone and hit Rore's number. A moment later, I heard an answering ring from her bedroom. I sighed and shook my head. She'd left it.

I guess she was trying to move on from Skiff. *But with Zeek?* He'd acted like a jerk at the party, and being a vampire only reinforced my low opinion. I shrugged. There was nothing I could do about it. I hoped Rore knew what she was doing. With her powers, I had no doubt she was protected from his influence. But still. *A vampire?* I hoped she didn't get burned.

I glanced toward the table and the chocolate chip cookies. I was normally a chocolate fan, but after Chaleta's cookies, I didn't think I would look at them the same way. But Orion might like one—it might soften the blow of Rore leaving with Zeek. I put two on a plate and took them to his room.

His door was open, so I poked my head in. "Cookies?" I offered. "Rore said she made them."

He looked up from his phone and frowned. "They can't be that good. I love her to death, but she could burn water."

I chuckled. "We each have our gifts."

He smiled at me and took a cookie, shoving the whole thing in his mouth. He absentmindedly chewed as he typed.

I was trying to think of a way to tell him about Rore when he beat me to it. "I'm going over to Skiff's house. He's upset."

I nodded. "I just saw her leave with Zeek."

He shook his head. "I don't understand it. She hates that guy. He's a vampire, of all things."

"I'm sure it's just a phase."

He shoved another cookie in his mouth. "These are pretty good. Which means there is no way she could have made them."

I smiled. "She could be learning."

"Maybe." He looked back down at his phone and then stood. "I'll be back in a little while."

Before he could leave, I put a hand on his arm. "I wanted to thank you for going with me today. It meant a lot. I couldn't have done it without you."

He smiled and gave a slight nod. "Anything for a lady."

I suddenly realized how close we were standing. There was a cookie crumb in the corner of his mouth, and I ached to wipe it away. His lips were so . . .

I caught myself and looked away. "Well, try not to get into trouble. Rore said she would be late."

"And you stay out of trouble. Don't be going through my sock drawer."

I wrinkled up my nose playfully. "I promise. Besides, the good stuff will be in the *underwear* drawer."

He gave me a surprised look and blushed.

I had a sudden thought. Bast had said to talk to the gremlins. Unfortunately, Glitch couldn't talk, but Skiff had Datiel in his laptop, and he could.

I called after Orion. "Hey, can I tag along?"

Orion hesitated. "I guess. I need to keep him occupied, so you might be by yourself."

"That's okay. I could use the time to do a little research, assuming Skiff doesn't mind me borrowing his little gremlin."

He shrugged. "I don't think Skiff would mind."

I suppressed my grin and walked with Orion to the door. If what Bast said was true, maybe a gremlin could finally give me some answers.

I was certainly ready for a few.

We heard the piano playing while still halfway down the block—a fast-tempo piece being played so loud and so fast it was almost unrecognizable. With a look of concern, Orion didn't knock but led us straight inside.

Today Skiff wore Mozart on his T-shirt, and his hair looked more disheveled than it did the last time I was there. He was bent over the piano and his hands were flying across the keys.

"Hey," said Orion, giving Skiff a friendly pat on the shoulder.

But Skiff remained focused on his playing and didn't even acknowledge our presence.

I could feel his anguish and hurt, and I ached to take it away from him. To just make it stop. But I didn't dare do that. He needed to feel those things so he could process what had happened. Instead, I eased in beside him on the bench and pulled him into a gentle sideways hug. "I'm sorry," I whispered.

He stiffened, but then his fingers halted, and his shoulders slumped. He patted my hand. "Thanks, Lapis. I appreciate that." He pulled free and turned to face Orion. "And you too, bro."

He held out his fist, and Orion gently bumped it. "Sorry, man."

He nodded. "I just don't understand it. This whole breaking up thing and now she's dating other people. Her actions are not following what she said."

Orion sat on the other side of the bench. "I don't understand it either."

Skiff slapped himself on the side of the head. "I hate being smart. It's always been so difficult around others. Rore was one of a few that treated me like an equal." He sighed heavily. "But now being a genius has even cost me my girl." He looked down and shook his head.

Orion looked my way. "Would you mind if Skiff and I went for a walk? I bet Skiff will let you use his laptop for your research while we're gone."

I nodded. "Sure."

Skiff stood. "My laptop is in my room." He raised his voice a little. "You hear, Datiel? I said it was okay." He turned back to me. "Thanks."

They left out the front door, and I made my way to Skiff's room. Opening the laptop revealed two cartoon eyes looking back at me. "Hello, Lapis," the gremlin said through the laptop speakers. "What can I help you with?"

I was puzzled. "How did you know my name?"

The cartoon mouth grinned. "I have many ears. And I know more than you would ever believe."

A chill went down my spine. "Such as?"

"Oh, for instance, Skiff likes to search for women in bikinis, and he follows everything on Rore's social media. Orion gets up every day at six and meditates. He actually studies for tests. And the Twilight-clan elder follows everything you do." His grin turned mischievous. "Very interesting, considering you're a succubus."

I gasped. "How . . .?"

"One of my family helped with the charm disguising you. It's pretty sophisticated and an excellent piece of work." He grinned. "But don't worry. Your secret is safe with me." A zipper replaced the cartoon mouth. "Us Night-clan have to stick together." He winked.

I couldn't help but grin. "Thanks."

He took on a more serious expression. "So, what can I help you search for? Would you like me to bring up pictures of *guys* in swim trunks? Like this one?"

A picture of Orion at the beach flashed on the screen for two seconds before the cartoon face returned. He was grinning like the cat that ate the canary. "How about some more like that?"

I could already tell that Datiel differed from my little skateboard friend. While that one extruded exuberance, Datiel was more cynical and wanted to play tricks. I needed to be careful of what I asked.

"Sorry, but that's not what I'm looking for."

His mouth returned to normal. "Then how about women's underwear? Skiff sometimes searches for that."

I felt sorry for Skiff. The gremlin was revealing all his secrets.

I shook my head. "I was recently told that you are immune to the magic that protects The Vault of Silent Whispers. Do you know anything about it? It's in Edgemont Victory Park."

The cartoon face seemed to shrug. "No one knows. You will not find any references on it. I have only heard its name mentioned by other gremlins."

I sighed. I didn't think it would be that simple. "Do you have an aerial picture of where the park is now?"

"Hmmm. Yes, here we go." He put up a high-resolution picture. I mentally traced the landmarks I knew of, and sure enough, there was a square blob where I thought the vault was. I patted my lips in thought. Evidently, whatever magic was going on was not an illusion. It was something more complex—like it was changing how people perceived reality.

"Can you find an aerial picture of this area from about twenty or thirty years ago?"

"Hmmm." He thought for a moment. "There are not many online resources from that time. Ah! Here we go." He brought up a grainy picture thirty-four years in the past. There were houses and buildings stretching across the area, and it appeared to have been densely populated—but that square blob was still right there. Whatever happened years ago had not touched the vault.

"What can you tell me about the disaster that wiped out that area about eighteen years ago?"

Several windows popped up with news articles from that time. I picked an article from a local newspaper and read how a series of storms had devastated the area—practically leveled it. I looked at the date of the article. The year jumped out at me. It was the year before I was born.

I did the math. I was born in January, and this event

happened in June. Mother would have been pregnant with me. I cocked my head to the side at a sudden thought. "When was the summer solstice during the year of the disaster?"

"June 20th."

The same day Father died. There were too many coincidences.

"What information do you have on Grant Midnyte?"

"There is no reference to that name."

I blinked in surprise. "That can't be right. No obituaries?"

"Nope." The cartoon face came back. "Kind of odd, actually. There's no reference to the name at all. Even in other countries. It's like it is forbidden or something."

This was a complete dead end. I decided to try a different tact. "Is there anything on a necklace called Morning Star Brilliance?"

The cartoon face screwed up in thought. "Not much. There are a few references, but they are from over fifty years ago."

He showed me an academic article. It was hard to read and used words half a mile long, but it mentioned a myth that the necklace was one of four badges given to those guarding the Protector's deepest secrets. Surprisingly, it said the necklace was only for shapeshifters. *Then why did Mom have it?* I wondered if maybe the research was wrong or perhaps the necklace ended up with Mom by mistake.

I spent the next hour searching and reading, ending up more confused than when I started. What I learned was that besides my necklace, Morning Star Brilliance, there were three other badges—Eye of Blue Blaze, Evening Star Light, and Hand of the Maker. Admittedly, some pretty weird names and none had pictures.

I paused in thought. Someone must suspect I had one of

these badges and wanted it for themselves. But why didn't they just take it from me? The obvious answer was that they couldn't. Likely, the magic wouldn't let them get close. In a sense, it protected the wearer. I guess I was fortunate that Mom gave it to me.

I grew cold. Mom used to wear this necklace every day. She even wore it in the shower. Which means she gave up that protection when she passed it to me. But why would she do that? And how did she get it in the first place? I didn't think she was one of these protector people.

My eyes went wide. There was only one reason she would have given it up—*to protect me.*

A hand touched my shoulder, and I nearly jumped out of the chair. I whirled to find Orion leaning over me. He stepped back in alarm. "Sorry to startle you." He pointed over his shoulder. "It's getting late. We should go."

I put a hand over my heart and nodded. I turned back to the laptop and began closing out the search windows.

Datiel whispered to me. "Hey, hang on a second."

I paused.

The little face popped up, wearing a mischievous grin. "Hold up your phone."

An odd request, but I fished it out of my pocket and held it facing the screen. He studied it a moment before smiling. "There, that will do nicely."

I frowned. I looked at the screen of my phone and was shocked to see a miniature version of Datiel looking back. It winked. "Our secret, okay?"

I grinned. "No problem. And thanks."

He grinned proudly.

Orion and I went back to his house. We didn't talk as we walked, but I could feel a complex set of emotions radiating from him, centered on concern and frustration. No doubt, he planned to confront Rore about what she was doing to his friend.

When we arrived, we found Rore was back and sitting cross-legged in the middle of her bed and combing her damp hair. She must have just showered. She had a faraway look and was humming. I slowed at the room's entrance, trying to read her emotions. They were a confusing swirl.

Orion went right in. "What's the deal with going out with Zeek? You hate him."

At the mention of Zeek's name, her emotions briefly spiked but quickly returned to their unusual swirl. She gazed up at him with a dreamy gleam in her eye. "He's not so bad. I'm going to see him tomorrow."

"What about Skiff?" he demanded.

She frowned. "We broke up, remember? Besides, he's going away to college, and I'm sure he'll find someone there."

Then it hit me. The spike of emotion had been off the charts. It was love.

Oh no, I groaned to myself, unfortunately recognizing the symptoms. I couldn't imagine how this had happened.

Rore had been tapped.

She belonged to Zeek now.

Chapter 20

I LAY ON MY pallet, staring up at the ceiling. Sleep was nowhere to be found, and I had been lying there for at least an hour. My brain was reeling, with so many pieces floating around—the necklace, Mom giving it to me, the destruction around the vault, and finally, Rore being tapped. It was the last one that was the most troubling.

I heard a gentle snore from where she lay in bed. I felt bad for her and wished I could have prevented it. I had been so focused on Orion and so sure he couldn't touch her. Tapping someone should be impossible for a witch of Rore's strength. Not to mention, illegal. Of course, Night-clan didn't necessarily follow the law—especially if you had clout. I was also afraid this could start a clan war. She was the granddaughter of the Twilight-clan elder, and Terra would not let this slide. She would demand someone be punished.

If someone told her.

Someone like me.

If I said anything, I could bring down my clan on me. Mom had told me what had happened in years past when a Goblin was upset with a vampire tapping his employer and exposed him to the human police. The next day they found the Goblin's body in an alley, and the vampire had vanished—along with his victim.

I rolled to my side, trying to get more comfortable. I was sure this was going to affect my favor with Terra. She'd been concerned about Orion, and I had overcome that, but I hadn't expected this from Rore's end. If Terra found out, my favor was toast.

Still restless, I turned the other way. The amulet shifted under my shirt, making me think of Mom. Why had she given me the necklace? Why would she think I needed protection? And the ring? What was its purpose? Maybe the answers were in the memory stone—some clue that would fit all the pieces together.

I glanced over at the sleeping Rore. But I needed to do it somewhere that was completely private. I would be unresponsive for the time I was in the memory. I wondered if it was like a dream where I might even act out some of the scenes my mind was seeing.

I sighed. Sleep wasn't going to happen, so I might as well do something.

I got up quietly, trying not to make any noise, and pulled the box out of my suitcase. The bathroom was the only place I could think of to play it. Maybe if I sat on the floor, I wouldn't make too much noise.

On bare feet, I silently padded out into the dark hall. A gentle seam of light came from under Orion's door. Its warm glow called to me.

I looked down at the stone in my hand. I couldn't shake the feeling I was about to learn something I would not like. And it scared me. In my eyes, Mom was perfect. She had been my one anchor in life. And I was afraid that if I stepped behind her eyes for even a moment, it might shatter that illusion.

Unexpectedly, I saw a shadow under Orion's door, and then it swung open. He stood just inside, his hair mussed, shirtless, and wearing just gym shorts. I tried hard not to admire his form.

He rubbed one eye. "Are you all right? Do you need something?"

Speech seemed to leave me. "I . . ." I looked toward the bathroom and then back at him. I pointed to my intended destination. "I was . . ."

He nodded. "All right. I thought something was wrong." He stepped back. "Goodnight."

He closed the door. I watched his shadow under it, but his presence did not recede. It was like he knew I wasn't done.

"Orion?" I said, softly.

He opened the door again. "Yes?"

"Can . . . can I talk to you for a moment?"

He stared at me—his eyes locked with mine. I could feel the confusing mix of his emotions, but there was one that came to the fore briefly before fleeting away. While it warmed my heart,

I knew it was deadly. I had no time for his affection—nor did I deserve it.

Orion pulled the door wider.

I walked inside. He pulled the chair out from his desk for me and then sat on his bed, waiting. I took the chair and looked at him, not sure how to proceed.

"What did you want to talk about?" he asked gently.

I stared down at my bare feet. I needed to trust someone—even if it was just a little. I looked back into his eyes.

"Can you help me with something?" I asked hesitantly.

He shrugged. "If it's within my power."

I held out my hand to show him what I held. "Grandfather gave me a memory stone. It's from my mother. I want to play it, but I'm afraid. Could you watch over me while I do it?"

Surprisingly, he seemed pleased at the request. "Yes, I don't mind. What do I need to do?"

I looked down at the stone. "I'm not sure. I've been told to lie down and then activate it, so I guess you just need to keep watch."

He nodded. "I've never done one before, but I understand they can be unnerving—like watching someone else's dream. But once started, it can't be stopped."

I nodded. "That's what I've heard."

He patted beside himself. "Lay down here."

I nodded and reclined on the bed. The covers smelled of Orion, and I breathed in his scent, finding it unexpectedly calming.

He pulled the desk chair up beside the bed. "Do you know how to activate it?"

"I think so. Grandfather said you have to bring the right image into your mind. Then it will start."

He nodded.

I took a deep breath, steeling myself for what was to come. I had a really bad feeling about this.

Orion took my small hand in his—the contact heightened my awareness of his emotions. The poor guy liked me. The warmth I felt saddened me, knowing there was no way I dared return it.

But at the same time, it strengthened me. I returned the squeeze, and he smiled reassuringly. I took a deep breath and let it out slowly. *I guess I was as ready as I would ever be.*

Closing my eyes, I thought of my mother. I held the image in my mind of our last breakfast together. Only nothing happened. I tried other images of my mother, but still, nothing happened.

I frowned. If it wasn't her image, what could it be? It had to be something common between us. Then it came to me—I was thinking of the wrong person. Mom wouldn't have set it to herself. She would have set it to her most precious thing.

Me.

I refocused and thought of a photo I had seen of myself as a newborn. I was only hours old, with my mom holding me and smiling.

With a loud click, the memory stone unlocked. I felt my body relax as my consciousness faded and a new one crept in.

My mother.

She glanced up from the memory stone she held in her hand and into the eyes of her mirrored reflection. I recognized our small apartment's bathroom.

The memory was perfect. On a certain level, I was aware it was not me, yet on another, I was her in every aspect.

Mom wore a simple button-up blouse and jeans. Her illusion charm was deactivated, so I could see her beautifully majestic horns. She was wearing the necklace, so this must have been before my birthday. But the memory went further. I could feel the difference in our bodies. I could feel her breathing and the difference in the way her larger bust moved in her shirt. Also, the balance of her head felt different, which I realized came from the larger horns she carried. But strangest of all, I could feel her emotions. She was totally open. I could feel the warmth of her love, her concern, and a trace of fear.

"Hello, Lapis," she said to the mirror. "Feels weird greeting you like this, but the accursed protection magic prevents me from writing anything down or even making a video. Instead, I thought I would try leaving you some memories. I hope this works."

I felt her grasp the stone tighter as sadness rose inside her. "The memory of making this will likely fade after I give you the necklace. I've kept it longer than I should have, knowing this would happen." Her eyes grew teary. "I did not want to lose the memories of my one true love, but I can wait no longer."

She looked down and drew a ragged breath. After a pause to collect herself, she looked back into the mirror. "So, I am giving you the necklace. I feel that your fate is larger than mine. Grant sure thought so. And if that is true, you will need every bit of protection you can get. I have seen the enemy circling. It's like they can smell me, know that I am there, yet can't quite find me. It's the magic of the amulet. Once I give the necklace to you, my baby, the blinders will be lifted, and I will become their prey."

She took a deep breath. "You may doubt that these memories are real, but they did happen. The magic protecting the Vault of Silent Whispers is strong and permeates the entire world. All of us are affected, and it warps our perception of reality to suit its needs. The storage in the stone is not sufficient to retell my life, but I've included the important pieces."

She smiled. I could see a tear in her eye. "Remember Lapis, you will always be my precious jewel."

The scene abruptly changed.

Mom was on a wooden deck looking out over someone's backyard. It was night, and the light from the windows splashed across the meticulously maintained landscape. Behind her, inside a huge house, a party was in full swing, with loud dance music playing and drunken laughter over top of that. She didn't like it. The people were becoming obnoxious, and the throbbing base was giving her a headache.

I could feel she was younger, just a few years older than my own age. She was in her human disguise and was wearing a light summer dress. As she looked over the well-maintained yard, she was contemplating leaving. Her friends had insisted she come, but parties really weren't her thing. They were loud and held too many emotions. She much preferred a quiet evening with her cat. Her loyal friends had all drifted off to conversations with young guys, or a young girl in one case, and left her to fend for herself. Not that she minded. She was used to it. They were often puzzled by her lack of interest in any of the young men they introduced. They were all nice, well maybe except for that one, but they were all human. And she knew what the humans would think of her if they knew what really lay under her disguise. She sighed. She thought it was about time to pack it in.

Someone walked up to the rail next to her and leaned on it. Her eyes went up in surprise, and Mother gave him a suspicious sidewise glance. She could feel no emotions from him. Blocked, possibly. Whoever it was must be hiding their identity. Just like she was.

A young man leaned on the rail. He wore a sports jacket over a T-shirt and a nice pair of jeans. He was nothing spectacular, but she found him handsome.

He sighed. "A little noisy inside."

"It is," she said without looking at him. Mom took a sip of her soda. She offered nothing more, and they stood in silence for a few minutes. The singing of crickets was audible over the sound of the thumping music.

The lack of emotion from the newcomer intrigued her. Only a few would consider blocking emotions and most of them were within Night-clan. Emotions could be quite powerful if used the right way. Maybe he was a witch wearing a protection charm, or perhaps a wizard with a general-purpose blocking agent. Wouldn't it be funny if he was a vampire and thought she was easy prey? Wouldn't he be disappointed.

As she considered the possibilities, she couldn't help but wonder—if she couldn't feel his emotions, then perhaps he couldn't feel hers either. She didn't think he was dangerous, but she should probably go back inside just in case.

She sighed. Besides, she'd done her duty. Her friends

couldn't complain. It was a little early yet, by their standards, but she was ready to go home.

"What's a nice girl like you doing in a place like this?" he asked unexpectedly.

She couldn't help but smile. *Did he actually ask that?* So corny. She looked up to see him smiling at her.

She couldn't help but smile in return. "What makes you think I'm a nice girl?"

He turned to face her, his elbow leaning on the rail and his smile never faltering. He had a pleasant smile—perfect white teeth. He looked human, but as she knew well, looks could be deceiving.

"I'm an excellent judge of character," he said. "You're definitely a nice girl." He held out his hand. She couldn't help but notice the solid blue ring he wore. "I'm Grant Steel, by the way."

"Eiheth Midnyte." She took his hand, and the two shared a smile.

He gazed at her for a moment. "I think I'm in love with you," he stated.

Confident bastard, isn't he? Yet, for some reason, she didn't doubt his confession. He seemed so earnest.

She couldn't help but smile. "Is that so? Will you be proposing tonight, then?"

He took her hand and kissed it. His eyes never left hers. "I think we should date first. Maybe dinner tomorrow night?" His eyes sparkled in the lights coming from the house.

He was just so brazenly confident. Best to let him down easy. She couldn't let some spark of emotion lead her astray.

"I . . ." But she paused. She truly liked his smile, and she had been spending a lot of time with just her cat. Her head came up, and she returned his confident gaze. "Tomorrow evening. Seven. My apartment."

He grinned broadly and kissed her hand again. "Gladly."

The memory suddenly changed.

Mom was in a small living room. It took me a moment to recognize it was a less cluttered version of Grandfather's house. I sensed some time had passed since the last memory—the view out the window showed brown leaves falling from the partially bare trees.

Mom sat on the sofa across from her father, while Grant sat next to her, holding her hand, their fingers intertwined. They were not wearing their disguises, and my suspicion was confirmed that he was of my race—an incubus. His horns were quite handsome. Only today, there was no confident smile. It had been replaced by a frown.

"I forbid it!" shouted Grandfather. "You absolutely cannot marry him."

Mom shook her head sadly. "But Dad, I love him. And he loves me. We'll make it work. We want to be wed at the winter solstice—"

"No!" Grandfather spat. "His family are the Steels. They've been partnered up with Aether-clan for generations. That clan is evil. Being aligned with them can only bring sorrow. I will not have it. It's only a matter of time before ruin will come to us all. Your mother must be rolling in her grave at the thought."

"Mr. Midnyte . . ." started Grant.

"Leave!" Grandfather shouted. "Leave now!" He pointed to the door. "Or I will throw you out."

The two incubi glared at each other, but Grant finally rose. "Please don't do this, Mr. Midnyte. I don't want it to be like this."

Grandfather said nothing and pointed to the door.

Mom stood with him. "Dad, please. Give us your blessing. I am going to marry him."

Grandfather's eyes narrowed. "You do, and you will never be welcome here again. You will be dead to me."

Mom stared back at him coldly—her anger hot. "Your daughter? You would do that to your very own daughter?"

"If you go with him," he spat, "I have none."

A tear came to Mother's eye. "So be it."

She turned. She took Grant's hand and stepped toward the door.

The memory changed again.

Mom, in a white gown, walked down the aisle of a magnificent hall. Her horns were on full display, and she was proudly wearing her pink ribownna—the ones I had seen her with many times over the years. Her excitement and happiness were off the charts as she and her second, a friend named Constellation, walked stately past friends and relatives. Mom had been afraid that Constellation would have turned down her request since she was a witch and might be uncomfortable at a Night-clan function. But her friend had gladly accepted.

As she neared the front, she sadly noted an empty spot in the second row. Her father, my grandfather, was not present. She sighed and turned back to the front, determined not to let it ruin their day.

A moment later, Grant and his second walked down the aisle and took his place beside her. He wore a black tux and was grinning so broadly it looked like his face would split. You could tell from his expression that he was just as happy as Mom. They held hands and turned to face an older person clothed in a hooded black robe. He held a golden staff, a symbol of his office.

The older person raised his staff. "I am here this evening, as one of the Night-clan elders, to hear a petition. Who brings forth this plea?"

"I do," Grant spoke loud and clear. "I petition the clan to allow a marriage. I wish to take Eiheth Midnyte as my wife. In proof of my vow to forever be hers, I give up my family name to join with her for all eternity. To have and to hold as my forever lifemate. The Protector as my witness."

The elder turned to my mother. "And what say you?"

She responded, smiling in joy. "I also petition the clan to allow this marriage. So we may start a new family that will grow and prosper. For this honor, I will accept his oath and return my own. He will henceforth go as Grant Midnyte, my husband, and forever my lifemate. The Protector as our witness."

"Your petition is heard and accepted," intoned the elder. "You may seal your pact."

Mom leaned forward and kissed my father. When she leaned back and looked into his eyes, I knew he was truly her lifemate.

And again, I was off to another memory. Only this one was stronger than the others, and it took me deeper into its clutches. My own consciousness was almost overwhelmed. I felt I was treading water, trapped in the depth of its emotion and horror.

All around me, the world was on fire.

Flames danced large as Mom struggled through the debris. The flames were searing, and the air was filled with dark, choking smoke. Mom coughed, praying this wasn't hurting her baby.

Baby!

Mom tripped and lunged forward, but suddenly a muscular arm encircled her. His familiar touch brought comfort, and the brush of his emotions calmed Mom's fears.

She turned to look into Grant's face. It was smudged with soot, and his hair was plastered to his head with sweat. Yet, his horns stood tall and proud—an incubus in his prime. He was gorgeous even to my eyes. But his shirt was ripped and pants torn—I could see blood leaking from them.

"I've got to get you out of here," he said, his voice rough from the smoke. "Over there." He pointed.

He led her behind a partially standing wall.

Up ahead, she saw an opening—a path to safety. She tugged on his hand. "We can get out that way."

But he resisted, unmoving. "You go ahead. I'll catch up."

She wheeled to look at him. "No!" She grasped his tattered shirt in her fists. I could feel the terror welling up inside her. The fear of losing someone so very close. Her lifemate. "Come with me. You've done all you can. You can't stop him. He's too far gone."

In the distance, Mom could feel it—something huge and filled with deep, dark fury. It struck fear into Mom's heart—

And it was headed their way.

"I have to try," my father said. "Unless I do, he'll destroy the entire city trying to find the vault. Maybe even you." He stroked her hair. "Besides, he's my partner. I can't abandon him."

"I'll go with you. Perhaps—"

"You can't," he cut her off sharply. "You have to take care of our child."

"No!" she yelled. She shook her head violently. "Both Erica and Constellation are dead! They murdered them and turned Brondson into a raging monster. The only reason I'm even aware of what's really happening is because of this." She held up the necklace from around her neck—the one I was so accustomed to seeing her wear. "Constellation got it off Brondson and gave it to me before she was killed." She gripped his shirt tighter. "I will not lose you too. Not to some Aether mission that has nothing to do with us." Her voice caught. Tears were in her eyes as she gazed up at him—begging. "Please don't go." She put a hand on her abdomen. "Don't leave us."

He brushed her hair out of her eyes and seemed to drink in her appearance. And she knew. He was taking one last look and was trying to burn the image into his mind.

"Please don't . . ." she begged. Her bottom lip quivered.

"I have to." He touched the necklace around her neck. "This isn't enough." He raised his hand and pulled off his blue ring. He put it in her hand and closed her fingers over it. "Keep this for the baby. In case something goes wrong, make sure our daughter gets it. She will need its power."

"What about you?" she croaked. "You'll forget everything."

"The residual effect will last for a while, so that will not be a problem." He sighed and kissed her closed hand. "If I can't stop him, it won't matter. Then he may come after you." He gripped her shoulders. "You need to get as far away as you can."

She gazed into his eyes. Mom shook her head but could not find the words her heart needed to say.

He pulled her into a fierce hug and kissed her. There was no barrier between them—their raw love was immense. I didn't know my mom could feel such emotion.

He smiled down at her. "Take care of our daughter." He smoothed her hair one last time. "I know she'll be as beautiful as her mother."

"How can you possibly know our baby's a girl?"

He gave her cheek a gentle caress. "I just do." He grew serious. "Now go!"

He urged her along the clear path while he turned to run in the opposite direction. Mother moved forward but looked back. "Protector, please keep him safe," she whispered. I felt a tear run down her cheek. "I will watch over our child. I swear."

As the memory drew away, I was thoroughly confused. Where was the smoke, the flames? Where was my baby? *Where was my husband?*

In frustration, I beat against something that was firm but yielding. I had to go to him. I had to save him.

As the memories retreated and I became aware of myself, I stilled and was racked with deep sobs at the sense of loss. Mom, oh, Mom. I missed you so much. You protected me before I was even born! And my father. He died to protect both of us.

I gradually realized two strong arms held me, while someone stroked my hair and murmured reassurances.

As I gradually figured out where I was, my tears slowed. All the memories had been so vivid. I was in Orion's room, on his bed, and he was holding me. Despite myself, I snuggled in deeper into his reassuring embrace. From the contact, I could feel his deepest emotions.

They were so beautiful. Too beautiful for someone like me. I could easily get lost in them. Lay beside him all night. But that was something I couldn't afford to do right now.

I pulled back and looked up at him. His face matched the concern he was radiating. "Are you all right?" he asked softly. "You were thrashing around, and I didn't want you to hurt yourself."

I nodded. I expected him to ask what I had learned, but he kept silent, respecting my privacy. He rolled out of bed and returned with a bottle of water from his desk. He offered it to me.

My mouth was dry—I could almost taste the soot from the memory. I took it from him. "How long was I under?"

He shrugged. "About thirty minutes. I wasn't really watching."

I scrubbed my hands across my face and glanced out the dark window. It had to be early morning now, but it felt like an entire year had passed. Weariness settled over my body. The memory had taken a lot out of me, both in strength and magic.

The memories Mom left had filled in several pieces, but not all of them. My parents were somehow involved with the disaster that happened years ago, which was connected to the vault. Plus, Father had died protecting us from something big. But what?

I got up and bowed formally to Orion. "I can't thank you enough for watching over me."

He shook his head. "You don't need to be so formal. You would have done the same for me." But he then stood erect and bowed in return. "Your thanks is graciously accepted." As he rose, he smiled. "Maybe I should thank you instead. It's not every day I get to cuddle with a beautiful young lady."

I blinked at him. Was he flirting with me? *Me! Of all people.*

I became flustered. "I . . . I better get to bed." I turned and fled the room, closing the door softly behind me, my heart hammering in my chest. I didn't dare be around him right now.

I lay down, listening to Rore's gentle snores and thinking of all I had just learned.

My mother had been protecting me, and she had been disowned for marrying Father. The vault had a magic that made people forget, and others had died protecting it many years ago.

Rore turned in her sleep, facing away from me. She mumbled something and settled back into her slow breathing. I sighed. I had to find some way to help her with Zeek. I didn't know how I would do it, but I owed her a lot. Without her, I would never have been introduced to her grandmother and given a chance at a favor.

I smiled at the memory. I had been afraid of Terra at first. In fact, things hadn't looked too good. But by the time we passed the vault, things had settled down—

My eyes went wide. I gasped and sat up.

We had been driving along, and Terra's whole attitude had suddenly changed. She had been completely indifferent to me—until I had asked what the building was.

She was surprised I could see it.

Terra knew the vault existed.

Chapter 21

THERE WAS NO traffic as I made my way downtown. Morning rush hour was still hours away. Fortunately, my little Gremlin-powered skateboard was eating up the distance.

Despite the hour, the air was sticky with unspent humidity, and from the distant flashes and low rumbles, a thunderstorm was nearby. I hoped I made it before it rained.

My destination was Terra's building. I had to talk to her. *She knew.* She could not only see the vault, but more importantly—

She had recognized my necklace.

She had known all along, and it was likely why she made me the offer. Not to protect Orion—that was only an excuse. But to keep me close. I had to get to the bottom of this.

The thunderstorm was looming quite close when I reached Terra's building. A few splatters of rain fell as I made my way around back to the parking garage. It was nearly empty, but I recognized Terra's limo in her parking spot. I hurried to the elevator but suddenly froze.

The elevator door was open, and the magi-sig reader hung partially off the wall, swinging from a single wire. I gasped. Someone had forced their way inside.

I stepped into the elevator and pushed the button for the top floor. The elevator lurched upward, but the door didn't close, and I could see each floor as we passed.

When I reached the top floor, I found the beautiful entrance foyer completely wrecked. Graffiti was sprayed on the walls, but even to me, it looked staged.

This was a Night-clan operation. I could feel the traces of emotion.

Then I saw him. Behind an overturned desk, two feet were sticking out. Werewolf feet. I ran around the desk and saw a large wolf lying unmoving in a pool of blood. Mac. And I knew without checking that he was dead. There were no feelings. Just background emotions. They'd shot him before he had a chance to defend himself.

Oh, Protector.

I turned and ran into Terra's apartment, but after a panicked search, I didn't see her. I ran the other way into her office. It had been ransacked with broken glass and papers everywhere—

And Terra lying on the floor.

She was in pink silk pajamas and only one slipper on her foot. Her left arm and several fingers lay at odd angles, while her face was a mass of cuts and bruises. Thankfully, her chest moved, but her breathing was irregular and came in gasps.

I knelt beside her and whipped out my phone. But before I could hit enter, she whispered, "Not yet." She reached out with her good hand but dropped it almost instantly.

I shuffled closer. "You need help."

Her eyes were bright as she looked at me. "You've got to stop them," she croaked. "They'll destroy everything."

"Let me call. I can't do healing magic, and you're hurt bad."

She grabbed my arm, her grip unexpectedly strong. "Get the badge. Now."

I looked at her with my phone in one hand, my thumb hovering over the emergency button.

"Please," she begged. The lightning flashed outside, and thunder shook the building.

I lowered my phone and stood. The display case had been turned over, and the glass broken. All the dragon bones were gone, but one piece of jewelry was lying on the floor where it had fallen—the bracelet. I remembered from my research that there were four badges of the Protector, and one of them was a bracelet. It was called the *Hand of the Maker*. Before, I would have been puzzled as to why it hadn't been taken, but now I understood. The vault's magic protected it.

I scooped it up and knelt back beside Terra.

"I have it," I said softly. "Now let me call."

"No," she said firmly. Then, with a painful grimace, she reached up and took out that ugly green earring, nearly ripping it from her ear. She held it out to me.

"Take . . ."

I held out my hand, and she dropped it into my palm. As I looked at it, I made the connection. This was another one of the badges—*Evening Star Light.*

She swallowed and took a deep breath, grimacing in pain. Taking my hand in hers, she curled my fingers over the badges. "I give these . . . to you. They are for the Paladin and the Adept."

I looked down at our joined hands. "I don't understand."

"For . . ." Her breath caught. "Your . . . allies."

It was as if she had exhausted every ounce of strength she had left. Her head relaxed to the floor.

I hit the emergency button on my phone. "*What is the nature of your emergency?*"

"There's been a break-in at the Twilight-clan headquarters. We have injured. One person is dead." I gave the address, and in the distance, I heard sirens.

"Guardian . . ." Terra whispered faintly.

The sky flashed brilliant white, and the thunder was so loud it rattled the windows. Outside, the rain began to pour, pounding the windows in its fury.

I bent closer. The words were so soft, I almost couldn't hear them over the rain.

"Please save us."

I awoke gradually the next morning. The kind of awakening where consciousness slowly seeps in—the house silent, a bird chirping outside, the sound of a car moving down the street. Then, with the blankets wrapped comfortably around you, you pray to the Protector to please be allowed to lie there for just five more minutes. Yet, you know, that isn't going to happen. There are things that have to be done.

I opened my eyes to see gentle sunlight streaming in from Rore's window—the rainbow still hanging from the curtain rod. It felt so good and so comforting. I tried to burn it into my memory and store it away for some future time because—

I had to leave.

The events of the prior evening wouldn't stay away. I had waited by Terra until I heard the EMTs coming up the elevator. Then I had slipped down a staircase and out. I had arrived back at the Strewert's just before dawn—tired and wet. The house was empty, and the family was gone—no doubt having been called to the hospital. In a way, I was glad because I didn't have to explain anything. I was too exhausted to do more than get undressed and fall to my pallet.

Now, in the bright light of morning, it all became crystal clear. I couldn't stay any longer. The amulet might protect me, but it would do nothing for those I cared about.

Last night, Terra had been tortured. I didn't know how much she told them, but it couldn't be good. If they could take down a powerful witch, the elder of Twilight-clan, then I didn't stand a chance. Even if Terra survived, my chances of living to collect any favor were nil.

And on top of that, I had now become a liability. The desire for the necklace and other badges would make them come after me. Or those I cared about. Grandfather was right. I couldn't stay close to those I cared for.

I had to leave.

With a sad sigh, I sat up. Rore's unmade bed was empty, and

the same feeling permeated the house. I couldn't believe they had trusted me. But then again, that's the way they were. I would forever be grateful to them.

I dressed and packed my clothes into my small suitcase. I borrowed a plastic sandwich bag from the kitchen to store my new jewelry pieces—the three badges. I paused and examined them—a ring, a bracelet, and an earring. Terra had said they were for my allies. But all I saw was trouble. I thought about leaving them, but it might draw unwanted attention. With a sigh, I stuffed them into my bag. I felt sad for Terra. I was not the person she thought I was. I was no Guardian. I was just a succubus trying to survive in a world gone crazy.

I folded up all the blankets of my pallet. I almost wished someone would come back and try to talk me out of it. But I also knew it wasn't going to happen.

I took a single sheet of paper and wrote a note that simply said *thanks* and then signed it. I left it in the center of Rore's bed. I thought about leaving my phone but decided to take it with me. I would have to get rid of it at some point so they couldn't track me. But the advantages of having it were greater than not. But I did turn it off.

When I was done, I made sure I hung Orion's leather jacket back where it was supposed to be and propped the skateboard back in its corner. The sadness the little gremlin projected almost made me cry.

I took one last look around the room. I eyed Rore's dresser drawer. I knew she kept her money in an envelope there. She was saving for a present for Skiff. Would that even happen now that she'd connected with Zeek? I knew I had failed my friend, but it was just one more in a long list. I hoped things with Zeek didn't go badly.

I went to the dresser and pulled open the drawer. I looked down at the envelope. It was just a classic white letter envelope, but she had drawn hearts on it. So like Rore. I didn't know the actual amount, but from what I had seen, it was likely enough to buy me a ticket to the west coast. I stared at it for several minutes. It fit right in with what I was. Succubi were the lowest scum. Do anything for money—lie, cheat, steal, even sell their bodies. Some said it was in our nature. It was the main reason I kept my appearance hidden.

I reached for it but stopped with my fingers just above it. I would definitely be in character. Society shunned me. I could easily rationalize it.

I shook my head and pulled my hand back. Once I crossed that bridge, there was no going back. I might be a succubus, but I was not a thief, prostitute, or liar. I was me.

I slid the drawer shut. I would not betray my friend's trust.

I turned, and my eyes locked with Orion's standing in the doorway. I had been so focused on the envelope that I didn't notice him enter. He looked at me with sad eyes.

"I didn't take anything," I said guiltily. "You can check."

"I know," he said softly. "I knew you wouldn't."

He just stared at me with those sad eyes. His emotions were a complex mix of relief, fear, and sadness. A lot of sadness.

"How's Terra?" I asked.

He nodded. "She's going to live. The doctors said they got to her just in time. Even a few minutes longer, and we would have lost her." He sighed. "She'll have a long recovery, but we'll still have her grouchy self around." He looked down. "Mac didn't make it, though. The attackers killed him to get to her. They've been friends for a long time."

He looked at me sadly, and I nodded.

"Do they know who did it?" I asked.

He shook his head. "The police say it was a protest over her clan policies, and it's consistent with the graffiti on the walls. They think she was just in the wrong place." He sighed. "Good thing they called 911 before leaving."

Thank the Protector the police didn't suspect me.

Orion looked off into the distance. "The timing of the call was a little weird, but at least they called." He trailed off. I followed his eyes to the jacket I had worn hanging on the peg. It was still wet. His eyes then traveled to my sneakers, which were also still damp, and then up to my eyes.

"Were you involved with last night?"

"No!" I denied venomously. "The memory last night . . . I . . . I just wanted to talk to her."

He considered me for a moment. "It was you. Wasn't it?" He shifted, pulling himself erect. "You're the one that called."

I opened my mouth to deny it. To tell the lie. But I couldn't. Not to Orion.

I sighed in resignation. "Yes."

"You saved my grandmother's life."

"I hope so."

He stared at me for a moment. I was waiting for the accusation. *Why didn't you wait for them? Why didn't you help? Why . . . ?*

But instead, he came closer and gently clasped my shoulder. "Thank you."

I looked into his eyes, and his gratitude was real. True, I had called, but I left her lying on the floor. I abandoned her. And he was thanking me? I didn't deserve it.

I looked down to hide my trembling lip. "I have to leave." I picked up my suitcase. "I've stayed too long. I have bad people looking for me."

He nodded. I wasn't sure he completely understood just how bad it was. "Are you going to your grandfather's?"

I shook my head. "He doesn't want me." I suddenly felt the need to explain. To let him know it wasn't him or Rore or anything related to their perfect life. "Remember when I told you he'd been beaten up?" I looked down. "They were looking for me."

He didn't respond, but I felt his emotions ramp toward anxiety, and his determination increased. "I can protect you."

I frowned and took half a step forward. I was so close I could feel his breath. "You might be able to. But what about Rore? What about your mother or, for that matter, your recovering grandmother?" I searched his eyes. "It's too much, Orion. I don't want anyone else to be hurt on my account. That's why I have to go."

We stared into each other's eyes, and he finally nodded. "Where are you going?"

I shrugged. "The bus station. I think I'll try the west coast." I gave him a weak smile. "Maybe I can be a movie star."

He opened his mouth to say something but instead closed it. He held up a finger for me to wait and then turned away.

He went into his room. I heard stuff shuffling around, and then he returned. He took my hand and shoved several banknotes into it.

My eyes went wide. "I can't take this."

He closed my fingers around it as he held my hand. We gazed at each other. "Please. Maybe it will help."

"But . . ."

He put a finger over my lips. "Take it." He stared into my eyes. "Please."

I sighed and nodded, stuffing the money into my pants pocket. It was enough to buy that ticket and perhaps a meal or two. It definitely would help.

He took my bag. "I'll walk with you to the bus station."

"No, you don't—"

He put his finger over my lips again. "I really want to," he said softly, his eyes moving to mine. I could feel the emotion inside of him. I could feel his acceptance. It was all so dangerous.

I stepped back. "I have to go."

He nodded sadly and stood aside for me to pass.

We left the house and walked in the direction of the bus stop. I was planning to take that one downtown and from there to the bus station.

We only got three blocks before a flashy sports car pulled to the curb ahead of us. Orion and I both froze.

A smiling Zeek got out. He was dressed in an expensive sports shirt and slacks with his sunglasses pushed stylishly on top of his head. He could be posing for some fashion magazine.

A chill when up my spine.

But unlike before, I couldn't feel his emotions. He was shielded. Which meant he probably knew what I was.

Orion immediately stepped in front of me, his anger rising. But Zeek stopped and held up his hands.

"Wait," he yelled. "Before you turn into some obnoxious beast and kick my butt, I'm not here to fight. I just want to talk. Then if you want me to, I'll leave."

"So talk." Orion growled.

Zeek nodded. "As you probably know, Lapis has some rather unsavory people looking for her. I've come up with a way to make them all stop." He gazed at me levelly. "We want to make you an offer."

I wasn't going there. "Not interested."

"Are you sure?" The vampire cocked one eyebrow. "Especially after all the violence we've been having since you came to town. Why just last night, I heard the Twilight-clan elder was assaulted." He grinned. "Such a shame."

My hands curled into fists. "You didn't . . ."

Zeek looked insulted. "Do you honestly think I would stoop to something so low, considering what I am?" He grinned.

I wasn't sure if he was lying or bragging.

He continued. "I've already met with Rore and explained everything. She thinks it's a great idea."

I gritted my teeth. "Of course she would."

A brief smirk touched his lips.

Orion frowned. "When did you meet with Rore? She's at the hospital with mom."

Zeek looked pained. "*Was* at the hospital." He grinned. "She's with us now."

Orion sucked in a breath.

I put a hand on Orion's shoulder and glared at Zeek. "What do you want?"

He grew serious. "Come with me and talk. We mean you no

harm, and you will be free to go at any time. But Lapis, I think you will find our offer too good to resist." He glanced above my head to where my horns would be. "If you know what I mean."

Yeah, he knew. I frowned. "How do I know you're telling the truth and not trying to suck us into one of your schemes?"

Zeek rolled his eyes. He pulled out his phone and sent a quick text. A moment later, Orion's phone rang, and I recognized it as Rore's ringtone.

Orion answered, holding it up for a video call. I tried to keep an eye on Zeek as I glanced over at the screen. Rore smiled back.

"Are you all right?" Orion asked.

"Of course," came the cheery response. "They've been very nice and are bringing me bagels. They just need something from Lapis and are offering to pay for it! Seemed like a good deal to me."

"Are you being forced?" he asked her.

"Heaven's, no," she grinned back. "I'll show you." She then panned the camera around her, showing she was in a big, empty building. *Warehouse, maybe?*

I couldn't put my finger on it, but something was off with Rore. She was bubbly and bright as always—but it wasn't quite her.

Rore continued. "Zeek will bring both of you here, and then we can talk this out." She looked off-camera, and her face lit up. "Breakfast arrived. I have to go. Tootles!" The connection ended.

Orion and I exchanged a glance. This had trap written all over it.

I crossed my arms. "I'm not going."

Zeek sighed dramatically. "Please come talk with us, Lapis. We *must* maintain appearances."

My eyes narrowed. *The bastard.* He was blackmailing me. He was going to reveal my secret. I glanced at Orion. *Did I care?* I was leaving and would likely never see him again.

But as I took in his features, I could see the concern written on his face. And from inside him, I could feel just a touch of something much deeper. I sighed heavily.

Unfortunately, I did care.

A lot.

With Orion and I squeezed in the back, Zeek drove us to a bleak industrial park about twenty minutes away. The single-story buildings along the street had seen better days, with many having long-faded "For Sale" signs and high uncut grass.

He whipped us into the parking lot of a large, unmarked building with sickly pink siding and a row of grimy windows just below the roofline. I wasn't impressed. The vampire immediately hopped out, while Orion and I shared a nervous glance. We held each other's eyes for a heartbeat before reluctantly getting out.

Inside, the building was empty and strangely cold—the slightest shoe scrape echoed eerily and set me on edge. The interior's concrete floors were bare save for bits of cardboard, loose paper, and dirt. A few glaring lights hung from the ceiling, supplementing the scant illumination the grimy windows provided. It looked like some gangster hideout straight out of a crime movie.

Rore sat in the middle of the building on a hard metal chair, wearing simple jean shorts and a T-shirt. Her bright red hair stood out brightly against the gray backdrop, providing the room's only color.

She looked up from the game on her phone, giving us a beaming smile. But strangely, she didn't move out of the chair. I couldn't help but notice how her eyes followed Zeek like someone reuniting with their long-lost love.

"Hello, Zeek," she said brightly. "I've missed you."

The vampire didn't even look her way. He went to a plump man in the far corner, reclining in a much more comfortable chair, boots propped up on an old metal desk. The seated man was dressed in a black suit and a bowler-style hat, with round, darkly tinted glasses perched on the end of his long nose. I think he was trying for a British goth look but wasn't pulling it off. His narrowed eyes and arrogant smirk made me instantly dislike him. Not surprisingly, I couldn't feel his emotions.

He rose to meet Zeek, and the two leaned close for a short whispered exchange. Their eyes never left us.

Orion and I trotted over to Rore. I tried to keep the concern off my face, but her emotions felt all wrong. Love and longing were much too bright, and any hint of discomfort or apprehension was completely absent. I had never seen this mix before.

"Rore," I asked. "Are you all right?"

"Of course." She smiled brightly. "There's no wifi here, which sucks, but I've been playing a game on my phone. Zeek said it was all right."

Orion took her hand. "Come on, sis. Let's get out of here."

She shook her head. I saw her other hand grip the seat as if she was afraid he might jerk her up. "I can't, bro. Zeek said I need to sit here until we talk."

Orion and I exchanged a glance. He turned to Zeek. "What have you done to her?" he demanded.

The vampire gave an exaggerated shrug. He started strolling in our direction with the man in black following. "I haven't done anything. She has just found her one true love." He smirked and pointed to his chest. "Me."

I wanted to smack that smirk off his face. I knew exactly what he had done. Her very will was his to command. She would gladly slit her own throat if he asked. I wondered how long he'd been working on her. Surely, before my appearance. It might even explain her breakup with Skiff. Either that, or he was a much older and more powerful vampire than he appeared. I grew cold. Or maybe she'd eaten a cookie that had drained her power.

I took a deep breath and examined her emotions more closely. I noticed a pattern to her oddness. Like an extra emotion that didn't belong—a black smudge on her beautiful landscape. And it was disrupting the others. It had to be Zeek's tap. I thought I could take it, and I ached to try, but I wasn't sure what it might do to me. If my magic couldn't process it, then I would also fall under its control. Even if I succeeded, it would bring down the wrath of Night-clan. One didn't interfere with the prey of another.

I fought down my frustration and turned to Zeek. "All right. You said you wanted to talk, so talk. What is this bargain you're so excited about?"

Grinning broadly, he held up a single finger. "First, let me introduce my assistant, Ernest Llewelyn. Without him, this discussion would not be possible."

Still holding our gaze, Zeek held out a hand in Ernest's direction. The man reached behind his back and pulled out a thin metal band with a diameter just larger than my spread hand. Its smooth surface was a deep black, so deep it seemed to devour any light nearby. It was like nothing I'd seen before, and I had no idea what its use was. But one thing I did know—it throbbed with powerful magic. It made my stomach queasy.

Zeek took it with no apparent problem and placed it on his head as if it were a crown. He gave us a self-satisfied smile as the band adjusted itself to fit snugly around his head. The way it flowed gave me the creeps.

"Now we can talk," he said. "Morning Star Brilliance is heavily protected and without this Aether-built neutralizer, I wouldn't be able to see or talk about it. Ernest here figured out a spell to charge it because it's magic drain is quite high."

I glanced at Rore and Orion. They were watching our exchange but didn't notice Zeek's new headband. I could only assume the device was filtering their reality, just like my necklace. I frowned. Then why was Ernest grinning? He was following the conversation just fine. Maybe he had one of the rings under his hat, or then again, perhaps he was just that powerful. My eyes went wide as realization struck. I gasped. "*Sorcerer.*"

I fought the urge to take a step back. Sorcerers were bad news. They didn't have the limitations of witches. If they needed more power, they just took it. Curses were their specialty—a type of charm that was a parasite of magic, leaching it out of the person it was applied to, whether they wanted it or not. Even among Night-clan, sorcerers were feared.

Ernest gave a slight bow at the recognition. "Indeed. The

best in all of Night-clan. Hard to believe a weakling like you and I are from the same clan."

With the conversation now shifted away from the necklace, Orion was once again following the discussion. And quick to protect me. "She's not Night-clan," he protested. "She's a human. That's Dawn-clan."

Zeek went to stand behind Rore. He gently massaged her shoulders. Her eyes closed in pleasure—I thought she was going to melt.

The vampire nodded thoughtfully. "Oh really? Is that what she told you?"

Orion frowned. "Just look at her. She couldn't be anything else. She's completely human."

Zeek leaned down and whispered into Rore's ear, but loud enough that we could all hear.

"She's been lying to you, dear. She's not *human*." He looked at Ernest. "Isn't that right?"

Ernest chuckled and snapped his fingers.

I felt a flash of magic. It momentarily engulfed me, searing me with its power. I gasped at the intense pain, but it quickly fell away.

Then, to my utter horror—

My illusion dropped.

Chapter 22

ORION SUCKED IN a breath. His eyes immediately went to my horns and then my tail. When his gaze came back to mine, his expression hardened. "You're a succubus," he said, dumfounded. He searched my eyes. "Why . . .?"

My heart sank. "It . . . it wasn't against you," I stammered. "I've been doing this for most of my life. It's what my kind does."

While Rore might be under Zeek's control, there was nothing wrong with her reasoning—or her indignation. She frowned deeply. "What your kind does? Lie? I thought we were friends?"

"We are—"

She cut me off. "We *were*," she stated flatly. She folded her arms. "I bet you've been changing my emotions. That's why I liked you the first time I saw you. You were *making* me." She glanced at her brother. "Orion must have been affected, too. No wonder he's been ga-ga over you. You made him love you."

I shook my head in denial. "No, I didn't. It doesn't work like that."

"Cut it out, Rore." Orion frowned at his sister. "She hasn't been manipulating our emotions." Then he turned my way and glanced at my horns, suddenly unsure. "Have you?"

I opened my mouth, but no words came out.

Rore cocked her head to the side with an ugly smile. I could feel her off-balance mix of emotions swirling. They almost made me sick.

She glanced at her brother and then at me. "All right, Lapis, tell me you haven't manipulated Orion. Tell me you've *never* changed his emotions." She held out her hand. It glowed a gentle blue. *A truth spell.* "Take it Lapis. Tell us the truth."

I heard Ernest snicker behind me.

I gave a strangled sob. "It was just a little. His anger . . ."

She jerked her hand back. "See Orion. She's a succubus through and through. Feelings are like ice cream to her. She can't stay away. They're thieves too. I wonder if we should check her bag for the family silverware. I bet she didn't take the TV because she couldn't make it fit."

Orion's face slid to anger, his emotions a confusing whirl of hurt, fear, and anger. "You influenced me?" he accused. "Without me even knowing?"

Their words were like a dagger to my heart. "It wasn't like

that. I changed them just enough to help you control your anger."

Orion was shocked. "And here I thought you were a good influence on me," he spat. "But it turns out you *are* the influence."

"But . . ." I protested weakly. "I did it to help. Terra knew."

Rore's eyes grew large. "It was you. You're the only one from Night-clan that could have gotten close to her."

Orion's anger turned hot, and his glare was piercing. "Did you hurt my grandmother?"

"No!" I shook my head. "Terra was good to me. I wouldn't hurt her!"

Rore rolled her eyes. "Like I'd believe that." She glared at me. "You disgust me. I think you should leave before I do something we'll both regret."

I stared at her in disbelief. *This couldn't be happening.*

Zeek grinned. "I believe I have a solution to this little problem. I propose a trade."

Ernest produced a thickly stuffed manilla envelope and placed it in Zeek's hand. He held it up. "This contains a plane ticket to San Francisco and enough money to last six months, maybe more if you stretch it. There are also directions to the Goodmere Research Center. They are doing research in turning magicals into mundanes." He smiled cruelly. "Isn't that what you wanted? To be human?" He waved the envelope back and forth. "I've also included the name of a succubus that will help you while you get settled."

As Zeek waved the envelope back and forth, my eyes couldn't help but track it. *Being human.* He knew the one thing I would give anything for. It was too good to be true.

I glared at him. "The Night-clan elder will not let me leave."

Zeek seemed surprised. "Oh, but he would. Especially since my father has been exiled to Europe, leaving me to manage things in his absence."

I gasped. "You can't be."

He smirked. "That's right. I'm the elder now. Father screwed up eighteen years ago, and I pushed him out. So you see, I have complete authority to do whatever I want."

I wasn't sure what to say.

He grinned. "I tell you what Lapis. I'll sweeten the deal. In addition to making you human, I will promise to release Rore and stop harassing Orion. I'll even leave the Twilight-clan elder and your grandfather alone." Zeek was practically beaming. "Sounds like a bargain, doesn't it?" His eyes narrowed. "All I want in return is that gaudy bit of jewelry around your neck."

I stepped back and put a protective hand over it. "But my Mom gave this to me."

"So." He shrugged. "Look what happened to her. She knew the elder in Philly was looking for it. That's why she gave it to you Lapis. Not to protect you, but to take the heat off herself."

I gritted my teeth at the comment, but my eyes were drawn to the envelope. "How do I know you're not lying?"

He considered me a moment and then nodded. "I'll just have to give you proof." He stepped over to Rore and held out his hand. "Dear, would you help me out?"

She smiled adoringly at him. She took it, and their joined hands glowed blue.

He faced me. "If you make the exchange, I promise to do everything I just said. No further harassment of Terra or your grandfather. Rore and Orion are released. And I give you the tickets."

Their hands pulsed green.

I glanced at Orion. "And you won't harm them?"

"Of course not." He stroked Rore's cheek as their joined hands pulsed green. "How could I possibly hurt this young lady? She loves me."

I hesitated. "And I'll really be made human."

He nodded. "Everything's arranged."

Their hands glowed green one more time.

I hesitated. I looked at Rore, Orion, and then the envelope.

Zeek held it out to me. "Take the deal, Lapis. They don't want you around anymore. You're a succubus. There is no way you could be friends with them. They despise you for what you are." He patted Rore's shoulder. "Isn't that right dearest?"

She glared at me. "You lied to us. Leaving would be best."

Orion frowned at his sister's proclamation. I could feel the mix of emotions coming off him—anger, hurt, uncertainty. But most prominent was concern. He looked at the floor. "Lapis, I don't understand this offer he's making. It might be best, I just don't know." He looked up and gazed into my eyes. "But please, don't do anything that might get you hurt."

Sadness enveloped me. The fool still cared. I'm not sure he got it. He couldn't trust me. I'd lied to him. It's just what my kind did. He was better off without me.

I sighed heavily. I knew what I had to do.

I reached into my shirt collar and unfastened the necklace. It felt strange not to have it around my neck. I gazed down at the necklace one last time.

"I'm sorry, Mom," I whispered. Then I gave it a kiss.

I blinked tears as I held it out to him. "I accept."

Zeek slowly reached out but surprisingly didn't take it. He cupped the jewel in his hand and smiled smugly, confident of his victory. "Thank you, Lapis. You've just put the fate of the world into my hands. Maybe now we can get rid of our Aether chains and claim our rightful place. We will finally be free." His smile turned mocking. "Under me, of course." He chuckled. "But then, you'll not remember. Ernest has a special curse just for you. Everything you knew about the vault will disappear. You won't even remember the pair behind me. I can't let you have a reason for coming back." He took a deep breath. "And so we must part. Thank you so much, *Guardian,* for giving up your heritage for two youths that don't even like you."

I blinked at him in sadness. *But at least they would be safe.*

He looked away, but then looked back. "By the way, about that promise. You really have spent too much time pretending to be a human."

What?

I followed his gaze to Rore, whose emotions were boiling rapidly in their confusion. With tears in her eyes, she raised her hand. It started glowing blue, then switched to green, alternating between the colors.

She lied. There was no truth spell. It had been an illusion.

As there was no promise.

Zeek pulled away the necklace.

Before it even registered, Ernest hit me with a curse. The wave of magic washed over me, making me writhe in agony as it probed into my mind, digging deep for what it wanted. As it pulled back, I felt my precious memories drip away.

It left me feeling deserted and alone. No one loved me, no one cared.

I stood there, staring at the man in front of me. I blinked at him in confusion. I couldn't recall his name.

The world felt different, but I wasn't sure why. My brain was fuzzy—like a dream where I knew the answer, but it was just out of reach.

The man in front of me was playboy handsome and fashionably dressed, but there was something about him I didn't like—probably because he was a vampire.

"What did you do to her?" yelled a young man I also didn't recognize. He was kind of cute but upset about something. Angry even. Maybe I could talk to him. I think I'd like him.

A man dressed in a black suit, dark glasses, and hat snapped his fingers. Glowing red magical bands appeared, binding the young man's arms and hands. He couldn't move.

The playboy guy spoke to the fellow in black. "Take her to the airport." He grinned at me. "She's harmless now. While I'm tempted to keep her for our brothel, we better get her as far away as we can. That stupid cat might try something." He sighed. "She's useless now, at least to us. But I'm sure the Night-clan elder in San Fran will find a use for her. She's just another dumb succubus now."

Why am I useless? And I don't think I'm dumb. I glanced around the unfamiliar room. He wanted something from me a moment ago. Did I give it to him?

Mom had given me something important. What was it? It was for my last birthday. Was it a mobile phone? I had been wanting one of the new models. I frowned. *No, that's not right. It was . . . something important.*

The playboy guy shoved the envelope into my hands. "This is yours. You've earned it." He chuckled.

I looked at it, not completely understanding. There was a plane ticket and money inside—I knew that. But how did I earn it? I shrugged. It didn't matter. I was going to San Fran, and I was going to be human.

I looked over at the two young people across from me. They were familiar for some reason. *What were their names?*

"Do I know you?" I asked them. It seemed to be taking forever for my brain to process information.

Concern flashed across the young man's face, quickly followed by anger. I could feel it radiating from him. The skin on his arms began to turn rough, and I could see the beginning of scales forming. He looked at it in horror and immediately damped down on the emotion, forcing his skin to return to normal.

Why was he changing? Was he a shifter?

The young woman looked like she was going to cry. "I had to do it Lapis. Zeek said it was for the best. He said I had to."

I guess she meant the playboy. Zeek turned to me and smiled. "These people are of no concern to you now. They found out you were a succubus and despised you for it."

I nodded. That's right. They had been angry because I had changed their emotions. It was because I had to protect myself.

No, that didn't feel right. It was something else.

Something important.

Zeek pointed to the door. "You can leave now. Enjoy your trip."

I activated my illusion charm, then waved at the two young people. "I'm sorry I made you angry. I was only trying to help."

The young woman in the chair seemed horrified. The swirl of her emotions was thick. I casually noted that a vampire had tapped her. Zeek, most likely. I felt sorry for her, but there was nothing I could do. I was just a useless dumb succubus.

The young man looked so sad. I could feel the emotion rolling off him. "Lapis," the young man called. "Don't go."

I was confused. "You don't like me. Why do you want me to stay?"

He stared at me for a moment. I felt warmth and longing. *For me? Why was he going to miss me?*

I smiled. My heart warmed, although I had no idea why. "I wish I could stay, but I have to go. I have a new home now."

The man in black pulled me toward the door, then paused. He grinned hopefully. "Can I drive your car?"

Zeek gave him a look that would have killed a lesser person. "No," he said flatly.

The man in black huffed in disappointment. "I'll have to get my keys." He went to a backpack along the wall and rooted through it. I stood, unsure of what I should do.

Zeek turned back to the young man and woman. "Now, for you two, I have something exciting planned."

"You said you'd let us leave!" the girl said, confused. "I've sat here all day for you. I even said the things about Lapis you told me to. I thought you loved me."

"I do." He smiled. "And you've been a tremendous help. You see, I need something big and bad to take down a certain *building*. A building in the park that no one can see. My fool father tried it a decade and a half ago. He had a good plan but didn't know about the Protector's Knights. While his destruction got rid of the knights, he did not accomplish his primary objective. He left this all for me." He nodded. "So I'm stealing his plan with a few modifications. And you both have a very important role."

"I won't help you!" the young man growled.

Zeek nodded like he was dealing with a small child. "I know. But you will. Your role is very simple. All you have to do is transform into something big, strong, and impervious to magic." He grinned. "A dragon would do nicely."

The young man snorted. "I can't. Dragons are extinct. I would need to touch one to do that."

Zeek grinned. "Or eat one. How were the chocolate chip cookies? Taste good?"

The young man was confused. "Cookies? The only ones I've had recently were the ones my sister made."

Zeek nodded.

He looked at the young woman. "Where did you get the cookies from, my dearest?"

The young woman buried her face in her hands. "No!" she wailed.

Zeek frowned, his voice taking on a more serious note. "Rore, where did the cookies come from?"

The young woman looked up in heartbreak. "You gave them to me. You said they were special."

Zeek turned back to the young man. "They were flavored with powdered dragon bone. All I have to do is ramp up your anger, and you'll have no control."

The young man looked determined. "I will not transform. Thanks to Lapis, I have my anger under control."

Zeek sighed dramatically. "Yes, she forced a bit of improvisation on me. Originally, Chaleta was going to tap you, and along with Ernest's curse, you would have been completely under our control. It worked perfectly when we tested it with an ogre." Zeek rolled his eyes in my direction. "But then a certain succubus interfered, forcing us to use Plan B and getting your sister involved."

"I will not help you," spat the young man.

"Oh, really. Then perhaps I might need to give you some inspiration."

His eyes glanced at Rore.

The man in black finally found his keys and pulled me outside. We got in a simple black sedan and headed for the airport.

I felt sorry for the young people back at the warehouse. While they both seemed nice, they were none of my concern. I couldn't get between another Night-clan and their prey. That would be very bad for me. No, I was going to my new home.

But why did I feel like I was forgetting something . . .

Something important.

It was mid-afternoon when the man in black dropped me off at the airport. He just pointed, and I got out carrying my little suitcase. He was silent as the door slammed shut, and without looking back, he drove away.

Unlike my earlier visit, the airport was packed with people. I hoped the freaky shopkeeper wasn't there. I doubted he would try something with it as crowded as it was. I smiled. That had been a close call. I was glad that the security guard had heard me shouting and investigated. He'd been cute for a human. If he hadn't come along, I might not have gotten away. The guard reminded me of that young man back at the warehouse.

I slowed. No, that didn't feel right. It had been something else that saved me.

Something important.

I shrugged. I got away, and that was what was important.

I stepped toward the sliding entry doors but stopped when I saw a gray cat sitting beside the entrance. Strangely, he had one green and one blue eye. I liked cats, so I squatted in front of him and spoke softly. "Hello, Mr. Cat. You traveling too?"

I stroked his fur, and he just sat there impassively, just looking up into my face. The cat seemed familiar, but for the life of me, I couldn't remember where I had seen a gray cat recently. Strangely, I could feel powerful emotions pouring off him—sadness and defeat. Strange feelings for an animal.

"Don't feel sad, Mr. Cat. I'm sure your owner is close by. I'd offer you some food, but I don't have any."

I gave him one final pat and stepped inside.

I was surprised when my phone rang. I pulled it out and saw it was someone named Skiff. I wondered how that had gotten there. It must have been left over from the previous owner.

"Hello," I answered.

A young man replied. "Lapis, have you seen Rore or Orion? I can't reach them."

I shook my head. "Sorry, but I think you have the wrong number."

I started to disconnect, but he caught me. "This *is* Lapis, isn't it?"

"Yes, but I don't know a Rore or Orion. Sorry."

I disconnected and deleted the contact from my phone. I hated scammers.

I made my way to airport security. After waiting in line for what felt like hours, my turn finally came. I set my phone and suitcase on the conveyor belt, then stepped through the metal detector. I made it through without a beep, but the agent checking my luggage called me over.

"Open your bag, miss. There is a magically shielded object inside. We need to make sure it's not contraband."

That was odd. I couldn't imagine what it could be. I opened it up, and he searched through it, pulling out a plastic sandwich bag with costume jewelry inside—an earring, a bracelet, and a ring. I certainly didn't remember packing them. Could someone else have done it?

The agent sat the jewelry off to one side and ran his detector over the rest of the suitcase. Satisfied, he closed it and said I was good to go.

I pointed to the clear plastic bag. "What about those?"

He didn't even glance at them. "Hurry along, miss. We're busy today." And he was off to someone else.

I thought that odd. He wanted them out and then just walked away. People were waiting behind me, so I stuffed the jewelry in my pocket.

When I finally made it to my gate, I realized I had a couple of hours to pass before my flight, so I ate a burger and then just sat back, watching people. It was relaxing to sample their emotions as they went back and forth.

As the last of the sun was going behind the horizon, I saw my plane pull up to the gate and the passengers disembark. The flight crew were the last ones off.

I realized it wouldn't be long now. I'd never been on a plane before, so I was looking forward to it. I couldn't help but wonder what San Fran would be like. Maybe I could get into acting. I snorted. Not likely. I was just a useless, dumb succubus.

"Would you look at that?" I heard someone say.

I glanced over at the video screens scattered around the waiting area. One of the local news services was talking about some strange solstice ritual being conducted at the park. A girl, in a flowing white robe, hands tied to a post behind her, stood in a grassy area near the top of a hill. There was a close-up, and I was surprised to see it was the red-headed girl from the warehouse.

I smiled. Now that was cute. Dressing up like that for solstice. It must be some publicity stunt.

But then I frowned. From her expression, she seemed to be in pain. The announcer was saying the girl was in distress, but a strong magical barrier was keeping the responders away. An expert had been summoned to see if they could get through it. There was another close-up of a tall, skinny young man in a black T-shirt. He was beating against the barrier and shouting at it. He wasn't the handsome young man in the warehouse, but he did look familiar. Police finally grabbed him and dragged him back.

I looked away. There was nothing I could do about it. I blinked and put a hand to my cheek, surprised to find it wet. *Why was I crying?* I couldn't help them. I was just a dumb, useless succubus.

Motion caught my eyes, and I glanced over to the side. The cat from before sat watching me intently. Strange that a cat, of all things, would be inside the building. I went searching for someone to tell, but when I pointed a janitor in his direction, the cat was gone.

When I got back, I found my flight had been called. People began moving toward it, so there was no time to look for the cat. I glanced back to where the little animal had been. He had seemed so sad—like his whole world was ending. I felt sorry for him, and I hoped he found his guardian.

I gathered my suitcase and glanced at the video screens again. The young girl was still tied to the post, but now her head was slumped against her chest. I hoped they got to her soon.

I pulled out my ticket. The sandwich bag with the jewelry was pulled out with it and fell to the floor. Like an escaping creature, the blue ring popped out and rolled away. With a sigh, I stepped out of line to chase it and finally caught it in the middle of the aisle. I huffed at it, thinking I probably should leave it behind. I again wondered where I had gotten it.

Gripping the ring tightly to prevent yet another escape, I scooped up my belongings and dashed to my gate, where I claimed the last place in line. With too many things in my hands, I juggled them around so I could present my ticket, but I dropped the ring again. *Dammit!*

I set my case down and picked up the ring. I held it up—its blueness called to me, but my mind whirled in confusion. I seemed to remember it belonging to someone I had never met. Yet that person had wanted to protect me—even though I hadn't yet been born.

"Miss," said the agent. "Your flight." He indicated the jetway.

Oh, right, the dumb succubus was going to miss her flight.

But the ring wouldn't let me. My eyes went wide as I felt residual emotions coming from it. Ones I recognized. They were from Mom. She had held this ring. Spent many a night just holding it, imbuing it with her feelings.

The ring was made of lapis lazuli. My namesake.

Her precious jewel.

Then I realized it was Mom's final message to me. It was buried in my very name. The ring of lapis lazuli had to be mine, and she had intended for me to wear it. Because it symbolized what I was.

A precious jewel.

And I needed it to do something.

Something important.

I slipped the ring on my finger.

It immediately blazed in a bright blue light. I was instantly enveloped in powerful magic. It flowed over me, my skin flared a hot white, and I almost heard the curse crackling as the ring burned away the evil magic.

It was like a veil had been lifted from my eyes. Orion! Rore! Skiff! I looked up at the monitor and saw Rore was in trouble.

The impact of what Zeek had said suddenly hit home. He was going to make Orion so angry he would transform into the deadliest thing possible—a dragon. With its magical resistance, he would be unstoppable.

And he would destroy the vault trying to get to Rore. If the vault didn't kill him first.

"Miss?" asked the agent. "Your ticket."

My eyes traveled to the jet outside. It was getting ready to depart.

"*Miss?*" the agent said in irritation. "Final boarding." The jet was going to take me where I could be changed into a human. My lifelong dream.

It suddenly didn't seem quite so important. I couldn't abandon my friends. *Even if they didn't like me.*

I pulled my ticket back. "Sorry, I've changed my mind."

I turned away from the gate, grabbed my suitcase, and ran up the concourse.

I prayed I wasn't too late.

Chapter 23

WHEN I GOT to the terminal's exit, a certain gray cat was waiting for me. The rushing people didn't seem to notice him, and even though he sat right in front of the door, the traffic just flowed around him like a river around a boulder.

"Took you long enough," he said.

I would have punched him if he'd been a person. "What do you mean, took me long enough?"

"To put on your true badge. It is your heritage."

"You mean the necklace wasn't the one?"

Bast lifted his front paw and began to wash it. "No. After the death of the previous knights, the chain of succession was broken. The necklace belongs to another."

I looked at the ring and thought back to my mother's memories of her future husband while he leaned against the deck's railing. His hands had been clearly visible, and the unusual blue ring had drawn my mother's eye. I wondered how she had been able to see it. Like the necklace, wouldn't the protections have prevented it? Something else to ask about.

"The *Eye of Blue Blaze*," I said in awe. "This ring was my father's."

"Like I said. Took the Guardian long enough to assume her post."

"Then who does the necklace belong to?"

The cat looked up in irritation. "You should know by now that I can't tell you. They are protected."

I growled in frustration. "I haven't got time for this."

I stepped toward the door, ready to rejoin the flow of people.

"Wait," Bast said calmly. "Surely you're not planning on walking the whole way."

I wheeled on him in exasperation. "I was going to hire a ride. Unless you have a car hidden behind you."

He stood and trotted toward the door, which smoothly opened for him. The crowd parted around him without noticing he was there.

I followed him outside. Bast looked to his left and sat down on the curb. "He's running late."

"Who?" I asked in confusion.

He said nothing, just continued looking down the street.

I was completely outdone with the cat. "I don't like your attempt at being the cool, silent type. It's pissing me off. By the way, why don't you just wave your magical . . . *tail* and fix everything. Aren't you an all-powerful Aether?"

He looked up at me in irritation. "My power is more limited than you think. We must move carefully, lest we cause more harm than good. Besides, I am bound to not directly interfere." He looked back down the street. "Ah, here he comes." Bast seemed to smile. "Every knight has their steed."

Then I felt it. I turned in its direction—the intense joy could only be one thing. I looked down the entranceway and saw a small blur approaching, weaving through the cars like they were standing still. It slowed and came to a stop right in front of me.

My skateboard.

Glitch!

He was raring to go.

I turned, and my bag was missing. "What happened to it?"

"I've sent it ahead. It will be waiting for you when you need it."

I looked over at Bast. "Couldn't you just magic me straight there too?"

His tail waved in irritation. "I could. But then you would die." He didn't elaborate.

I frowned. "Another one of those, *it's restricted* things?"

"No. The gaps between the worlds are cold and airless. A suitcase full of clothes would not be affected. However, you would arrive a freeze-dried carcass."

"Oh," I said, taken aback. "Maybe I won't go that way."

He said nothing and started licking his paw.

But I wasn't going to back down. "When this is over, you and I are going to have a little talk."

Bast gave one deep nod. "Of course. Now that you've accepted your role, there are some things you need to know. But now, see to your allies. They need your guidance." And I could almost see him smile. "God speed. Night Hope Guardian."

Then he turned away and pranced off into the crowd.

I frowned. *That cat.* And contrary to what he might think, I was only going to help my friends. I hadn't accepted any role.

Had I?

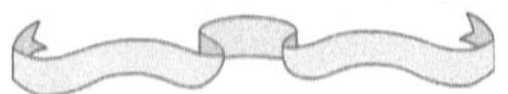

Night had fallen by the time I reached the park. But the darkness was pushed back by the festive lights and booths scattered throughout the area. I scooped up my board and darted through the milling people, headed in Rore's direction.

It had been a tough decision. I desperately wanted to go to Orion first but decided I needed to prioritize Rore—she appeared to be in the worst trouble. Orion hadn't made an appearance yet, so I had to assume he was holding out for now. I was terrified I was making the wrong choice.

Up ahead, I could see a mile of police tape encircling the area where Rore was being held. A crowd was packed against it, watching with interest. I was surprised the bystanders didn't have more concern for what was happening. There was even a hot dog vendor and a cotton candy stand close by. And I was pretty sure I knew why.

Overshadowing it all like some stolid soldier was the vault itself. It was likely responsible for the unusual behavior of the crowd. Rore knelt a few feet outside the ring of uncut grass, carefully positioned in that transition area when people began avoiding the vault. The police tape had been laid out in an odd semicircle, which stayed out of range of the vault, yet cordoned off Rore and her shield. I couldn't see her well from where I stood, but she seemed to be in pain. I ached to go to her side. But there was no way I was getting through that shield without help. And I bet a certain genius knew how to do it.

I stopped just outside the crowd's edge and looked around. I was sure he was there. I closed my eyes and felt through the throng of people, searching for just the right mix of emotions. It was kind of like picking out a single instrument in a symphony. But I found him—

I went to the left. Sure enough, off to one side, the police had set up a command center. They had erected an open-sided tent with tables, chairs, and a couple of laptops. Sitting handcuffed to a chair was Skiff.

Everyone was on their phone and so busy they paid little attention to me as I walked up to him.

"Lapis!" he exclaimed. He tried to jump up but, because he was handcuffed, was promptly jerked back down. "I thought you had left town!"

I gave a sad smile. "I almost did." I brightened. "But I won't abandon my friends."

Skiff shook his head. "We've got to save Rore. I'm not sure what's going on with her, but it's like she's under some compulsion."

I was reluctant to tell him about her being tapped. "Whatever it is, we need to get through the barrier to save her."

Abruptly, a middle-aged police officer took me by the arm. "I'm sorry, miss. You need to leave. You're interfering with police operations."

I looked at him. I was tired of this. I put my hand over his and ramped up his love to the max, dialing in a lot of concern. "Your wife needs you," I whispered.

His eyes went wide. He turned and took off toward the parking lot. "I've got to get home to my wife. She needs me."

Skiff watched the exchange with interest. He gave me a half smile. "I think I just figured you out. I always thought something was different about you. The gremlins act strange when you're around, and you have a certain way with people. There is only one race that can do that."

I shouldn't have been surprised. He was a genius.

I sighed. "Will you keep it to yourself?"

"As long as you're going to help me get my girl."

I grinned. "Deal. Now let's go tackle that barrier." I looked around. "Maybe I can find the one who has a key to your handcuffs."

"No problem." He stood up, and the handcuffs fell off. He smiled proudly. "When you're friends with gremlins, things break."

The furthest away of the laptops gave a loud pop and emitted a puff of smoke. All the police huddled around the broken device, suddenly too busy to notice us leaving.

The perks of having gremlin friends.

We made our way to the police line surrounding the barrier. Uniformed officers were stationed along the inside perimeter to keep the people away. I sighed. Getting closer was going to be a problem.

I looked up at the vault. The shadows of the surrounding lights played across it, giving it menacing shadows. Bast had said the vault had some level of intelligence, and it had responded when I praised it. Maybe there was a way. But I would need Skiff's help. Bast had told me to choose my allies. Well, guess what?

I turned to the young man. "Do you trust me?"

He frowned. "Why are you asking that? Of course, I do."

I smiled sheepishly. "Please don't think I'm crazy, but I have to do this."

I fumbled in my pocket and pulled out the bracelet. *Hand of the Maker* was its name. I couldn't think of anyone more qualified for something of that name. I took a deep breath to say something, but didn't have a clue what it should be. *Here, take this* didn't seem appropriate.

I grabbed Skiff's hand. He looked at me curiously but didn't try to stop me. "Would . . ." and the words just came. My voice got deeper and picked up an authority I didn't have. "I request you, Stancliff Albert Daemynson, become the Shadow Adept Knight. Will you aid the Guardian in fulfilling her role as a Protector of Secrets?"

Skiff looked at me wide-eyed. "I-I will."

"For your role, I give you this badge, Hand of the Maker. Use it well." I slid the bracelet onto his wrist. It gave a burst of blue light and seemed to resize itself to fit him perfectly.

I smiled. That wasn't so bad. But his eyes went large, and he sucked a breath. His gaze traveled up as he took in the vault's majesty. "Holy sh—"

I slapped a hand over his mouth. "Not now. I know it's overwhelming, but I'll tell you about it after we free Rore."

He nodded numbly, staring up at the vault. I turned and faced the shadowed building. I took a deep breath, preparing for my gamble. "Vault of Silent Whispers," I called. "This Guardian requests your help. Please push these people away. They are innocents, but they are a barrier to saving one of my allies. Please help us."

I don't know if I was expecting lightning, a beam of light, or a gong, but I had expected something. Anything. But the building sat sulking in shadow. I sighed sadly. It wasn't working. I'd have to figure out some other way to get the police to let me—

I paused. A gentle breeze caressed my cheek and ruffled my hair before going still. I raised my head. For three heartbeats, the night went completely silent—not a sound was made—the world held its breath.

Then the noise returned. As one, the police, the reporters, the vendors, and the entire crowd—all turned and just walked away. It wasn't like something bad had happened. They were still laughing, talking, and protecting, but they had just decided to do it elsewhere. The realization chilled me to the bone—the most profound moment of my life. The power of the vault humbled me.

I was supposed to be the Guardian of that kind of power?

Skiff looked around in amazement. "What did you do?"

I shook my head and pulled him forward. "I don't know. But watch what you say. Please don't piss it off."

We stepped closer to Rore's barrier. Through it, I could see her on her knees, weakly swaying back and forth, barely staying upright. She was sickly pale, and her ordinarily bushy hair was slick with sweat. Her hands were bound behind her, while a steel collar was around her throat and chained to a stake in the ground.

The shield itself was completely spherical and shimmered with a pale pink glow. Even from a couple of feet away, I could feel its power.

I turned to Skiff. "So, how do we get through?"

He shook his head. "We can't. That's a level-four magic sphere. It would take level-five magic to get through it."

"But where is it coming from? Maybe you could have a gremlin break it."

"First, even the strongest gremlins are only level two magic. For my work, their advantage is they don't have a corporal body." He sighed. "Second, the shield's magic isn't coming from a device."

"Then where is it coming from?" I asked in confusion.

He pointed. "Her. That's Rore's barrier. She's an extremely powerful witch."

"Level-four? Rore? You've got to be kidding."

He shook his head. "I've known her since we were kids. She's always been powerful. It's one of the reasons she has no friends. They're afraid of her."

"She's doing this to herself?"

Sadness radiated from him. "Yeah, but even she can't maintain this level of a barrier for long. It's draining her magic. It's like she can't stop. If it keeps going . . ." He swallowed. "She'll die." He seemed to get a grip on himself. "This is so out of character for her. I don't understand why she would do this."

I frowned. One never interfered with another clan member's prey—especially vampires. And Rore fell into that category. To do so would bring down their wrath and likely get me severely punished, if not killed.

I glanced at Rore. She collapsed to her side. She was burning out.

"I know what it is," I stated flatly, coming to a decision. "Zeek's a vampire and he tapped her."

He stared at me in shock. He didn't argue because he knew I was right. It fit all the facts. I sadly watched him deflate like a balloon. "There's no way to help her," he whispered.

I looked at Rore through the barrier. *Level-four.* Heavy artillery couldn't get through it.

I touched it and immediately jerked my hand back. I shook my stinging hand—it was like sticking a finger in an outlet. But for that barest moment, I had felt her.

I had a sudden thought. I looked up at the barrier. This was a projection of Rore's mind. *Could I use that?* But I would need help.

I held out my hand to Skiff. "We're going to try something."

His face was pained as he watched Rore. "Anything."

I took a deep breath. "Talk to her."

Confused, he shook his head. "She can't hear me."

I turned to the barrier. "The words are not what I'm after."

I again slapped my hand against the barrier. Painful tingles shot from my fingers, up my arm, and down my body. My instincts were to jerk away, but I held firm, willing myself to maintain contact.

Inside the glowing sphere, Rore's head rolled. I could see a trickle of blood leaking from her nose.

Skiff started hesitantly, his voice a whisper. "Rore, please drop the barrier." Then louder. "I want to be together with you again."

I seized on the emotion pouring out of him and channeled it into the barrier. I didn't dare change it. This was something you just couldn't fake. All I did was amplify it. *Level-four? Well, hades, I'm going for five.*

I got nothing back but pain. I gritted my teeth and ramped it up some more.

Then I felt it—a whisper at the fringes of my comprehension. It was a swirl of off-balance emotions which felt revolting. I sucked a breath and tried something new. The exchange went two ways, so while I fed her Skiff's, I started pulling on Rore's feelings of doubt, anger, and hopelessness. All I got were mere drops, but I felt an ember begin to grow and expand. Her head sluggishly rose, and she looked our way—but her eyes quickly went to Skiff.

I felt the barrier weakening, and I thought we might be able to win. If I could just balance her—

I was caught off guard as her emotions began to slide back. I saw Rore's gaze shift to a new person standing off to the side. *Zeek.* He stood watching us with a smirk on his face. The barrier's weakening slowed and reversed, gradually increasing in strength. I was going to lose her.

I was maxed out and on the verge of having everything collapse. My own magic wasn't infinite, and I could feel myself tiring. As I stared at Rore through the barrier, I could feel his compulsion and the artificial emotions he was causing. The off-balance swirl was sickening. Zeek was killing her, and he didn't even care.

And it really pissed me off.

It's strange how the mind works under pressure. I flashed back to a little grade-school girl crying in a mud puddle while her tormentor laughed. The gloating from Zeek was oddly similar. I couldn't help it as my anger, hot and rich, enveloped me.

I hated bullies.

My head purposely rose, and I turned my glare on Zeek. Without even thinking, I reached inside myself and pulled on every ounce of magic within me. To my surprise, my father's ring answered the call, glowing a bright blue and feeding me power. I grabbed the evil emotions Rore had been emitting and then sucked more through the barrier itself. All of them. Every last one of Rore's disgusting feelings. I even grabbed that revolting blot on her soul, suddenly recognizing it as Zeek's tap. Then I changed them all into a hot mass of fear, disgust, and loathing.

Locking eyes with Zeek, I expelled them straight at him. My aim was true.

Zeek's eyes went large, and his hands flew to his throat. He staggered and fell, before climbing to his feet and fleeing as fast as he could, running a zig-zag course into the night.

With Zeek's tap gone, Rore gasped as she was flooded with Skiff's feelings. The barrier instantly dropped. Skiff shot forward and pulled at her bonds. Thanks to his gremlins, they crumbled at his touch.

I knelt beside them. Rore lay in Skiff's arms, looking up at him in adoration. "I felt you," she said in awe. "I never knew how much you cared. And I hurt you so badly. I'm so sorry."

He stroked a sweaty strand of hair out of her eyes. "It's not important right now. We're together. That's all that matters."

I smiled. She was going to be all right.

I went to stand, but a sudden hand shot out to grasp mine. Rore gazed at me intently.

"You helped me. Even after all the horrible things I said and did."

I wasn't sure how to respond, so I kept it simple. "It's what friends do."

A tear rolled down her cheek. "I didn't mean them. Zeek told me what to say." She squeezed my arm. "I'm so sorry. Please don't hate me."

I gave her a warm smile. "I don't hate you. And Zeek won't bother you again."

She sighed sadly. "I didn't figure out what he was doing until it was too late. By then, I was so far gone nothing mattered. All I wanted was to please him." She looked at Skiff. "I'm tainted now. Once you're tapped, you can never go back. He'll have control over me forever."

"No, he won't," I stated.

She looked puzzled. "But how . . ."

I grinned. "You have a succubus for a friend."

"You . . . You fixed it?"

I nodded. I didn't mention that I had violated one of my clan's laws to do it, and my father's ring had provided the power to blast it away.

She jerked me into a hug. "My friend. I can't thank you enough."

I smiled, pleased that she was going to be all right.

Then I felt it.

A burst of emotion so strong and so loud they would have noticed it on the other side of the globe. I turned to look toward the west, in the direction of the warehouses.

In the distance, I saw a violent eruption of fire and smoke. It was followed seconds later by the boom of the explosion and a roar that chilled me to the bone. A sound like thunder combined with tortured steel reached something primal inside of me. The hairs on the back of my neck stood up.

Oh no.

The orange glow of a huge fire lit the sky. A streak of flame shot upward and arched through the night. It was then I saw a monstrous shadow moving. I had no doubt it was coming this way.

He hadn't been able to resist.

It was Orion.

Chapter 24

I SIMPLY STOOD and stared. It was too much for my mind to comprehend. Columns of fire would streak from a huge shadow, and wherever the column touched, an explosion would erupt with flames leaping for the sky. It felt like something from a bad monster movie. Only the thunderous blasts reaching my ears a few seconds later confirmed that these were real. Unfortunately, he was heading this way.

They likely tormented him until he had transformed into the fiercest beast he could. They had already given him the template.

A dragon.

Its hide was immune to magic and so tough no explosives

could penetrate it. If that wasn't bad enough, its skin was as hot as lava—anything touching it would instantly ignite. And with its reptilian brain, Orion couldn't control it.

This is bad.

I glanced at the vault just behind us. They intended for Rore to draw Orion to this spot, and in his present state, he wouldn't be able to tell friend from foe.

Rore gasped, knowing exactly what it was. "That's Orion. And I did it to him. I gave him Zeek's cookies." Her hand flew to her mouth. "I've sentenced him to death."

I gripped her shoulder. "You didn't know."

"You don't understand," she looked up at me sadly. "He'll only be able to maintain that form for a short time. The magic that drives it comes from him." She looked up at me pleadingly. "He'll die of magic depletion."

A blue-uniformed policeman stopped nearby with a megaphone. "We have an emergency. Weather radar indicates an F5 tornado is coming this way. We have to evacuate the area."

Tornado?

Then it hit me. The amulet. It must be on Orion and protecting him. *The bastards.* Orion was going to lay waste to the area, and the people wouldn't even know what they were fighting. It eerily resembled the news articles from eighteen years ago.

I looked down at the ring on my finger. This must be what happened all those years ago. My father had tried and failed. How could I succeed where he hadn't?

Choose your allies.

To stop something that big, I needed help. And I knew just where to get it. I dug in my pocket, and the plastic bag was still there with Terra's earring.

"Rore!" I wheeled to her. Her pallor was already improving. "Will you help me save Orion?"

She looked at me with tears in her eyes. "Of course."

I took Rore's hand. Placing the earring in her palm, I closed her fingers over it. It had been Terra's, so I thought it appropriate. The voice of the badge engaged more rapidly this time, and the words of authority spilled out. "I request you take the role of the Twilight Shield Paladin. Will you aid the Guardian in fulfilling her role as a Protector of Secrets?"

Rore blinked at me in surprise but managed to get out her confirmation. "I-I will."

"For your role, I give you, Aurorah Constance Strewert, this badge, *Evening Star Light.* Use it well." Blue light leaked through her closed fingers. When she opened her hand, the earring had changed. It still had a single emerald, but its setting had transformed to a more modern style that perfectly fit Rore.

She stared at her palm and then turned to look at me. But after only a second delay, her eyes went wide at the vault behind us. "What is that?"

"I asked the same thing." Skiff patted Rore's shoulder.

"I'll explain later," I said. "Right now, I need to get to Orion."

Skiff shook his head. "You . . . you can't be serious. If what we learned in history class is correct, you won't even get close. You'll be burned to a crisp."

"I don't know what else to do! If we don't stop him, he'll either destroy the vault, or it will destroy him. And if I delay him, the dragon form will consume all his magic. Either way, people will get hurt." I glanced in his direction. "And he dies."

"You can do it," Rore said quietly. "If anyone can, you can."

She sat up and stripped off the white robe to reveal shorts and a T-shirt underneath. "Do you have your phone?"

I touched mine in my back pocket. "Yes."

"Go to him. Call me when you get close." She smiled brightly. "I have an idea." She turned to Skiff. "And you're going to help me."

He frowned back playfully. "I think I'm in trouble."

She smiled. "You have no idea."

I looked away, slightly embarrassed at the emotional bond between the couple. It was much stronger than it had been. In my attempt to reach through her barrier, I might have accidentally strengthened it. I wondered if it was permanent.

Rore hit dial on her phone and waved for me to go.

The sound of an explosion rocked the area. In the direction of the warehouses, a fireball rolled skyward.

Orion was getting closer.

I had Glitch stop a block away from the advancing Orion to size things up. I was totally unprepared for just how big and how destructive he was.

The dragon had to be bigger than a large house—easily three or four stories. Legends had said it was the magical equivalent of a dinosaur. But I could sense that the comparison was incorrect. This was not even in the same class, but a completely different species—one that didn't belong to this world.

He had four legs, two wings, a tail, and a long sinuous neck. The hind legs were huge and powerful, carrying most of his weight. But the front legs weren't tiny, appearing to be joined to the wings in a complex dual shoulder joint. The wings had to be vestigial since they didn't look sturdy enough to support flight. But they did regularly rise and fall with every few lumbering steps. His enormous head had three sharp horns—two just behind his eyes and a single tall one just over his nostrils.

People were fleeing his path, but fortunately, he didn't seem interested in them. Instead, he was focused on the vault and headed right for it.

I got as close as I dared, but the heat radiating from his skin was too hot. He could make things burst into flame simply by walking close. Most of the damage he was causing was just by brushing up against them. The magic being consumed in that form must be tremendous. We had to get Orion to change back soon, or he would die.

I closed my eyes and focused. I could feel his emotions roiling inside him. There were several mixed in, but mainly a deep, dark, and ugly anger. His balance was all out of whack, which had to be what drove his current transformation. Getting that anger under control had to be the answer to changing him back. Unfortunately, his anger was as big as he was.

I tried to reach into his emotions but was immediately repelled—the backlash so strong I became instantly nauseous and threw up what little I had in my stomach. I steadied myself against a wall and wiped my mouth. I wasn't about to try that again. His dragon hide must be protecting him.

I had an inspiration. I ran in front of him and waved my arms, trying to attract his attention. Maybe I could get him to recognize me. But he walked right past. I got so mad at him I threw a loose brick at him, but he didn't even notice.

He kept walking, his eyes fixed in the direction of the vault.

My phone buzzed, and I held it up to my ear.

"How's it going?" Rore asked immediately. It was hard to tell over the sound of the destruction, but it sounded like she was in a car.

"Not good. I can't get within ten feet of him, and when I tried to touch his emotions, I got a violent kickback."

"I was afraid of that," she said.

Skiff jumped in. "His hide has an active magical shield that not only prevents anything from getting in but will actively attack anything that tries to. It's similar to what Rore was doing with her shield, just on a larger scale." He paused. "I think you're going to have to touch it."

I looked up at the enormous dragon as it slowly, but steadily, drew away from me. He passed close to a car, and its paint began to turn black, peel, and then burst into flames. Touching him was going to be extremely difficult.

"And just how am I supposed to do that? He's as hot as lava."

There was a pause and then Rore spoke. "I'm going to shield you."

"You can't do that!" I shouted. "You just got back on your feet—"

"Lapis," Rore interrupted. She waited until I stopped talking. "I called Mom," she said matter-of-factly.

I blinked, not understanding. "So?"

"She healed me."

The ramifications sank in. "She gave you her magic, didn't she?"

"That's right. She has one of Skiff's special phones, and she healed me right through it. Gave me a recharge, too."

"I'm not going to risk hurting you again."

"Lapis, let me do this," she said pleadingly. "I don't want to lose either of you."

Skiff jumped in. "Datiel's got it all calculated out. I'm going to help Rore adjust her shield to absorb the heat around you and transfer it here."

I couldn't help but chuckle. "And what the hades are you going to do with it?"

"Dump it in the river."

"What?"

"The river is the largest body of water around. It's up right now, so its flow will absorb a huge amount of heat. Datiel has been taking measurements, and we think it will work."

I looked up in disbelief. "On his back? How in the Protector's name am I going to do that?"

"Datiel says that Orion will be passing an office building in about five minutes. You have to get up on the roof."

I looked toward the dragon and saw the building. It was at least six floors high, and he was going to pass within twenty feet of it. "The jump will be too far."

"Do you still have Glitch?" Skiff asked.

"Yes."

"Then take him with you. I've got a plan."

"There is no way I can make that jump."

There was a pause. "Dammit, Lapis." There was anger in his voice. "You chose me for this protector thing. Now let me do my job. If you do what I say, you will be on Orion's back. But you can't argue with me. Just do it."

I hated when people were right.

I started running toward the building entrance. Glitch

jumped out of my arms and like a bullet, raced ahead. When I caught up with it, the front doors had been bashed in and a path of destruction led up the stairs. *A skateboard could do that?* Something else to ask Skiff about.

I ran up the stairs and reached the top floor to find the skateboard sitting underneath a metal ladder leading up to a door overhead. I could see a heavy latch and a padlock, so I was doubtful I could proceed further. Through the windows in the stairwell, I could see that Orion was almost at the building.

Tucking the skateboard under my arm, I scurried up the ladder and pulled on the padlock. Something snapped inside and it sprang open. Of course, a gremlin must have done something to it.

The roof was flat, with the occasional pipe sticking up and an industrial AC unit off to the side. A short wall of about three feet high encircled the building's perimeter. I ran to the edge and saw Orion approaching. He would be beside the building in only a handful of seconds.

I pulled out my phone, and it immediately dialed. No doubt Datiel anticipating my need.

Skiff answered and started talking immediately. "You need to ride the skateboard toward the edge. It will accelerate very rapidly and will throw you over to Orion."

"It's too far!" I shouted.

"Do you trust me? I've got this calculated out. Datiel is already explaining to Glitch what needs to be done." He paused. "This is the only way."

I sighed. I picked up my skateboard and hugged it to my chest. "Glitch, will this work?"

There was a burst of joy and, surprisingly, confidence.

"You won't have time to stop. Will you be all right?"

The little gremlin went quiet for a moment. He turned sad, but quickly switched to a burst of admiration. I wasn't sure how to interpret that, so I asked a different question. "Will we ride together again?"

The response was instant joy. Although I didn't think he could feel it, I squeezed him tightly against me.

I kept the line open and jogged over to the opposite side, where I put Glitch down and pointed him to where Orion was going to pass. I steeled myself and stepped aboard.

"Are you on the board?" asked Skiff.

"Yes."

"Squat down on it and prepare for a rapid acceleration. *Really* rapid. Glitch will cover the distance in three seconds. As soon as you feel it move, begin your leap upwards."

I gauged the distance to Orion. It was much farther than I was expecting. And even from where I stood, I could feel his heat. This was impossible!

"Are you ready?" came Skiff's question.

"No, I'm going to get killed."

"I'll make you a deal. If you die, you have my permission to kill me."

I couldn't help but chuckle. "You have a deal."

"Leave the connection open. Rore's going to be doing her stuff now."

Rore's beautiful voice started singing. Maybe it was her magic, but that girl had a voice. A green glow grew around me, and I felt a gentle pressure all across my skin. I couldn't describe it other than it was cool and felt like protective arms wrapping around me. With it, there were faint emotions—Rore's concern, her fears, and her caring. Surprisingly, I could feel traces of Skiff too. He must be holding her hand.

Skiff's voice came through clearly, projecting confidence. I decided not to mention that I could feel his apprehension through the connection. "When you're ready, just tell him to go."

My heart was beating in my throat. But I had to smile at the warm embrace around me. She was protecting me with her very soul. What more could one ask for?

I could see Orion's dragon head over the top of the wall as he lumbered past. I wiped the sweat off my forehead and rubbed it on my jeans. I took one last deep breath and shoved my phone in my pocket.

Wait . . . Wait . . . One second more . . .

"GO!" I shouted.

The skateboard launched forward. It accelerated so rapidly I was sure some magic was holding me in place. Just before the edge, I leaped.

The skateboard crashed hard against the wall and splintered into pieces. "*Glitch!*" I screamed.

But I was already moving. The forward momentum carried me over the edge, and I sailed across the gap. I saw nothing but air between me and the concrete below. I was airborne for only a handful of seconds, but it was enough to know I never wanted to do that again.

Orion's back was about ten feet below me and was broad enough to be an easy target. As I arched toward it, I thought I just might make it.

Something huge and green suddenly blocked my path. My brain had time to register that it was Orion's wing. I hadn't taken its rise and fall into my timing. I tried to twist, but it was too late.

I crashed hard.

Chapter 25

I CAUGHT THE leading edge of his wing in my chest and felt something snap. I tried to cry out at the sharp pain, but couldn't—the impact had knocked the wind out of my lungs. My momentum pushed me forward, flipping me onto my back, where I began to slide feet first down the slick membrane toward the lower edge. Dazed and gasping for breath, I instinctively rolled and clawed for purchase at the impervious skin, but couldn't stop my slide.

The membrane had a scaley texture, but other than supporting branches of cartilage, it was completely smooth. The wing had been rising when I impacted, which added to my rapid descent. But just as I was about to slide off the edge, the wing reached the apex of its path and reversed, driving downward. I became nearly weightless. The shift in direction was all I needed to grab the bony ridge of the edge and flip myself over onto it, so that on its next upward swing, I was pressed into it enough to find a more stable position.

I settled into a branching of the wing's cartilage and put a hand over my throbbing ribs. Gradually, I could breathe again, but it felt like my lungs were on fire. I was pretty sure I had broken something.

Ignoring my pain, I used the web of cartilage to ease my way closer to Orion's body. The wings abruptly stopped their steady movement and then snapped violently downward. I grabbed what little purchase I could as my lower body became airborne for several long heartbeats.

The wing paused and then extended upward. At the same time, I felt the dragon stop walking. His long, sinuous neck turned in my direction. He must not like me on his wings.

With Rore's magical barrier protecting me, the wings hadn't seemed that hot. But as the head drew near, it felt like an open oven. Orion eyed me suspiciously while I held still, hoping he would leave me alone. But he bared wickedly sharp teeth and then roared in rage at my presence. My organs shook, and I could smell the stinking sulfur on his breath. In frustration, he shook his wing again, but when I stubbornly held on, he snarled and brought his large head closer.

I wasn't sure what to do. If I let go, I would fall and be crushed against the concrete below, but if I stayed, he would bite me in half.

Which meant I was going to have to try something. I

clenched my teeth at the pain and moved to a crouch as his head came closer. When he was almost to me, I leaped up, bounced off the wing, and used it as a springboard to sail up and grab the single horn over his mouth. I swung up and over, straddling his snout.

Orion froze. I grinned as the shock of the maneuver worked its way through his reptilian brain. As I expected, he started whipping his head violently, nearly throwing me off. But I hugged the horn tightly and, with my knees, maintained a firm grip on his snout.

He paused when I refused to fall off. He shifted weight and tried to swipe at me with his front claw. But he moved slowly, giving me plenty of time to dodge to the opposite side. After several attempts, he reared his head in frustration, gave one last shake, and decided to ignore me. He looked back toward the vault and resumed his journey. Since he could see it, the amulet was likely on him somewhere. But there was no chance I could find it on his enormous body.

From my perch on his head, the vault was clearly visible. We had cleared the last of the office buildings, and it was only open grass separating us. There were only minutes left before we reached it. As I feared, I could see dark clouds gathering over us, illuminated by the occasional flash of lightning. I cursed, remembering the little bolt that had knocked me on my butt. The abnormal clouds had to be the vault getting ready to protect itself and likely the reason eighteen years ago the area had been destroyed for blocks surrounding it.

The pain in my chest was growing worse, and it was becoming more difficult to breathe. I had the sudden urge to cough, and when I did, the hand covering my mouth came away speckled with blood. I stared at it, realizing I may have punctured a lung.

I heard my name through my phone's open connection. "Lapis!" Skiff cried. "You've got to hurry. Rore can't handle much more."

"I'm doing the best I can!" I yelled back.

A lightning bolt landed in front of us, blowing a large hole in the ground.

Knowing I had no time to spare, I steeled myself and opened my awareness. The backlash was intense. It was like I was walking through hot coals while getting electrocuted. I jerked back and nearly passed out. My head throbbed, and I was starting to wheeze.

This was not going to work—I couldn't get through his magical protections. I looked up at the approaching vault. Another blinding bolt struck in front of us, more intense than the last. From its closeness, I knew there would be no more warnings.

My head drooped as I grew weaker. I was tired, hot, and every breath was agony. I couldn't think, and it all felt so hopeless.

I looked down at my hand holding on to the dragon's horn, the ring clearly visible. I shouldn't feel so bad—my father hadn't been able to stop his friend either. Those evil people had set this up well. It was impossible to beat. A futile mission. I was going to fail too—just like he did. Orion and I were going to die. And I never got to tell him that he was a pretty nice guy. I felt a tear leak down my cheek.

I could feel my vision narrowing, the gray creeping toward me. I was losing consciousness.

My head dipped forward and one of my horns came to rest on his. "I'm sorry, Orion," I whispered. "I wasn't good enough."

And then I felt him. I felt his anger. His loneliness. His longing. I realized his horns were not covered in scales—I could reach him!

I coughed and winced at the pain. I closed my eyes and concentrated. I pulled on his anger, his fear, and his hurt. I pulled and pulled, drawing it into myself. And when I couldn't handle any more, I fed it back to him, changed to peace and calm. His steps slowed and then stopped.

He gave a mighty roar and seemed confused. But to my disappointment, the anger continued to bubble inside him. And it began to undo what I had done. He started walking toward the vault again.

"Lapis!" I heard Skiff say. I guess my phone was still on. "Get clear! Rore has to drop the barrier."

I could feel the surrounding air tingle, like an electric charge was building. My hair stood up. I could only assume the vault was about to unleash its final defense.

I gasped for a breath, and once more, I pulled on Orion's anger. Again, I changed it—only I knew it wouldn't be enough. So I did the only thing left. Something I had promised I would never do.

I dropped my *zouvaiyut*.

His emotions came to me raw. They were painful. They scorched me more than his skin ever could. But I took them. Took them all. And this time when I changed them, I fed them back raw. My own feelings went with them, mixing in my deepest emotions.

I remembered the delight of being with him at the pizza

parlor. How cool he was as he rescued me from my kidnappers. How frustrated I was as we argued at the party. And how he cared enough to hold me as I experienced my mother's memories.

"Please, Orion," I whispered. "If you have any feelings at all for me, let your anger go. Please change back."

Then, as I barely held onto consciousness—

I kissed him. Right on top of his scorching, scaly head.

There was no way he could have felt it. I'm not even sure why I did it. But Orion's huge, lumbering body stopped. Inside him, I felt something answer me. I felt him connect with me. And for just a moment, I felt him return my feelings.

I was losing it and wasn't sure I could keep my seat any longer. I coughed again, and more blood came up. I slumped forward, every last bit of energy taken from me.

I sensed Orion turn away from the vault, and the clouds overhead began to dissipate.

I smiled. His anger was gone.

I blacked out for a moment, but the next thing I knew, I felt arms around me. A young man's arms, and I could sense from his feelings surrounding me that Orion had made it.

As the blackness sucked me back down, I had one last weird thought.

I'd kissed a dragon.

Chapter 26

I AWOKE SLOWLY. I could hear beeping in the background and the muffled sounds of people walking. There was something foul in my mouth and down my throat.

Plus, someone was snoring.

I tried to open my eyes, but my lids refused to cooperate. I managed to get one open, but focusing was beyond me. My head was turned slightly to the side, and I could make out someone asleep in the chair beside me. I dully noted the person was too old to be Orion before my lids drifted closed again. Exhausted from the effort, I drifted back to sleep.

Later, I awoke again. I had no idea how long I had been out, but it must have been several hours. I opened my eyes to bright sunlight streaming through the window. The sounds of movement I'd heard before came from an open door and people walking past. The infernal beeping was still there, but this time, I recognized an antiseptic smell. *Hospital?*

I groaned and tried to move but was rewarded with a sharp pain in my chest and arms. I wisely decided to just lie there. Thankfully, the foul taste in my mouth was gone, but I was painfully thirsty.

I turned my head to see someone standing over me. I recognized them, but my groggy brain refused to give me a name. He was too wrinkled to be an angel of mercy. Rather, the old man looked like he'd recently visited hades. He wore his human disguise, but his clothes looked like he had slept in them.

Grandfather smiled down at me. "You're back."

I pried my dry lips apart and tried to wet them with a sandpaper tongue. "Water," I croaked.

He brought a cup with a straw to my lips. "Take sips," he cautioned.

I leaned up, wincing at my chest, and took a sip. It tasted sweeter than anything I'd ever had. I took another before he pulled it away.

"The nurse said to take it slow. So let's see how that does before we try more."

I nodded weakly. "Where?"

"St. Majesty's Hospital. You gave us quite the scare. You got caught up in the storm, and the building you were sheltering in collapsed and caught fire. The EMTs got you out."

I heard the beep of the heart monitor quicken. "This is a Twilight-clan hospital."

Grandfather nodded. "I know. But the Twilight elder insisted you'd get better care here. She said you were her employee and plans to cover everything."

I settled back. So Terra had survived. With that thought, memory flooded back—the vault, Rore's power, the dragon. I heard the beeping of the monitor speed up again. "What about Orion?"

"You mean the young man that found you? He's fine. He wanted to visit. Actually, a couple of them did. But I asked that they wait until you were stronger."

My battered brain was like a train getting started—moving gradually but gaining momentum. Grandfather still wore bruises from the beating he took. One that I had inadvertently caused. Now that I had the ring, he would have no memory of what those brutes were hoping to find. But it begged a question.

"Why are you here?" I asked. "I thought you hated me."

He smiled sadly and shook his head. "I may be a prideful old fool, but I don't hate you." He gently took my hand and gave it a soft squeeze. "When the call came that you were in the hospital, I was in a panic. It was then that I realized just what a fool I was. You're all I've got." He looked down. "I never had the chance to make things right with your mother. My pride kept me from seeing my daughter again. Kept me from knowing my grandchild." His gaze held mine. "I would like to fix that. If you'll let me."

I considered him for a moment. Then I opened my arms, and he leaned in for a very gentle hug. It hurt, but it was worth it.

Grandfather stood. He was blinking at his suddenly wet eyes and turned away in embarrassment. "When you're out, you can live with me. That is, if you want. I'm sure we'll butt heads, but you're welcome if you'd like. At least until you get your feet under you."

I smiled. "I would like that."

The nurse came in and was shortly joined by the doctor. Grandfather went outside while they examined me. My physician rattled off a whole litany of injuries—broken ribs, a punctured lung, magic depletion, ruptured eardrums, along with second and third-degree burns. Thankfully, I had an excellent healer, and they were able to stabilize me. A few more treatments, and I should be good as new. However, the doctor advised me to stay out of collapsing buildings in the future. He thought it was funny. Me? I think I'd also broken my funny bone.

Though limited, the interactions tired me out, and I slept again to awake in my dimly lit room. I felt much better. No doubt because of their healings, which were likely the reason for my long periods of sleep.

I smiled at the gentle snoring coming from the chair beside me. Grandfather should have gone home. But yet, I was glad he was with me. I had someone now. I wasn't alone.

I looked up at the dimly lit ceiling and reviewed the events of the last few days. It was sad that the vault was influencing everyone—altering their memories to protect itself. They wouldn't know it was a dragon that had caused all the destruction. Nor that we had stopped it. I couldn't help but smile at the thought. They also did not know I had kissed a dragon. Made history, and no one even knew.

My smile faltered. No. One person did. *Orion.* He must be furious with me now. Sure, I got him turned back into a person, but I had seriously manipulated his emotions, as well as my own. So seriously that I may have inadvertently bonded myself to him, and he to me. From the ache in my heart, I was pretty sure I had.

I shut my eyes and leaned back into my pillow. It would be best if we stayed separated. The bond would fade over time. He might miss me for a while, as I would him, but Orion could go on to find himself a true lifemate. While I knew it was the best course, I took no comfort in it. I already missed him.

I looked at my hand and saw I still wore the blue ring. I dared not take it off, lest I forget. But I suspected there was more to it than that. Much more. For now, I was going to keep it and learn what it meant. With that thought, I drifted back to sleep.

I stayed in the hospital for two more nights, and they released me on the third. Grandfather stayed right by my side. It gave us a chance to talk. I realized he was a grouchy old incubus, with strong opinions and a quick temper, but I came to understand he deeply regretted the way it turned out with Mom. It had left a deep scar. My heart broke for both of them because she loved him too. Only their pride kept them apart.

During my stay, I asked for no visitors. It was a coward's thing to do, but I couldn't face my old friends' disappointment in me. Especially Orion.

So I moved in with my grandfather. He gave me Mom's old room—not that there was much choice, since it was only a two-bedroom house.

While he had declared he had been angry with Mom, the room had been left untouched—the walls having the same pink color and the bed covered with the same pink spread. There were even two faded rock band posters from twenty years ago. I couldn't believe Mom had actually been into them.

But the room had something else in it that was less material. Houses gradually absorb emotions over time, and if you open your senses, you can feel them. I cried the first night. I could feel my mom in the room's walls and furnishings. They were from a younger version of her, but they were gently reassuring. After my first good cry, I wasn't sad anymore. I had finally come home.

Grandfather took me to get my charm recharged, which discharged while on Orion's back. It was completely empty. The middle-aged witch was filled with disgust as she did it, having no love for my kind but needing the money. When she was done, it felt dirty—like her loathing contaminated it. It was nothing like what Rore had done, like a hug on a pleasant spring day. I would have to get used to the charm's new feelings, but it made me realize how much I missed her. How I missed the gentle arguments she and Skiff would have. Her bubbly personality.

And Orion.

I sent one last text to Terra explaining what I was doing. I felt I owed it to her. I had learned that Terra had barely survived her brush with death and from what I gathered from the news, was already back at work. I was sad, though. She would likely have no memory of what had transpired since her badge had passed to Rore. The elder probably wondered what she had seen in this poor succubus, and I seriously doubted she would even respond. However, I was surprised that she answered only a few minutes later, asking me to please stay in contact.

I received several texts and calls from the gang of three. But I ignored them. On my second day home, the trio came to visit. But I had grandfather turn them away and return the phone Terra had bought for me. I hated to give up my connection to Datiel—the gremlin seemed to like me for some reason, but I felt it was necessary.

And of course, Glitch. I mourned the loss of my little friend. I didn't think he would have died from the skateboard's destruction, since he had no body, but I would likely never encounter him again.

Grandfather watched after me during those first few days. We talked a lot. One day, he even took me to get donuts and introduced me to his friends at the donut shop. They were just as old and grouchy as he was, but in a friendly way. They were a good crowd and made me laugh. It was fun for a while, but their banter made me miss my friends—an emptiness that just wouldn't go away.

It was the day of the second Solstice festival that Grandfather approached me. It was a redo of the one Orion had messed up, or the "weather event" as they thought of it. The city's elders decided we needed another, so they called this one Solstice Day Two. There had been a big marketing campaign about it on the local news, and it promised to be bigger than the previous one. They were even going to have live bands.

Grandfather knocked on my door and entered. I was plopped down on my bed with a book continuing to research the vault and the badges. I had just come back from a trip to the city library. I had come up empty, but I had checked out two books which I thought might be related—one about a coverup of the previous park disaster, and the other about the connection between cats and aliens. I was getting desperate. It was much harder to look things up without fast internet and my gremlin friend, but I was trying.

"Lapis," he said, leaning on the door frame. "Do you plan to rot in this room? I've seen mushrooms with a better social life."

I should have been insulted. But I had come to realize it was just his way of showing concern.

"No," I said. "I'm going to get a job. I've already applied to a couple of fast-food places nearby. I can't have you paying for all my expenses."

"I'd rather you apply at the university."

I sighed. *This again.* "You know I can't afford it. Maybe after working for a year, I can save up enough to start."

He frowned. "We'll see."

I knew the subject wasn't done yet. We'd talked about it before, but neither one of us had the money, and loans were out of the question. No one would give money to a succubus. We were viewed as too risky.

The college thing was a common argument of late. But he wasn't pursuing it today, so he must have something else on his mind.

"You know the Solstice Day Two festival is tonight," he said brightly.

I nodded, and he continued, "I never got the chance to take my granddaughter to a festival. Would you want to go with me?" He looked down sheepishly. "That is, if you're not too embarrassed to be seen with an old man."

I set the book aside and threw my arms around him in a fierce hug. "I would never be ashamed of you. I would love it."

He pulled back. "Really?" He seemed genuinely surprised. "You'd like to go?"

I gave him a mock frown. "Will you dance with me?" It was a tradition with the younger set that an unattached female could ask any unattached male to dance, and if she was the first, then she got him for the entire evening.

He was practically beaming. "I would love to, but only if some young fellow hasn't snagged you first."

I hugged him again. "I doubt that will happen."

"I'm not so sure. A young lady as beautiful as you can have any male she wants."

I rolled my eyes. "Grandfather."

He grinned. "Walk over about eight?"

I grinned mischievously. "Think you can walk that far, old man."

He looked at me in mock disbelief. "I am *not* an old man." He grinned. "I'm just youth challenged." And with that, he made a hasty retreat.

I chuckled and went back to my book.

I actually got into the connection between cats and aliens. I thought the author was crazy, but he was very entertaining. He fully believed that cats built the pyramids. The proof was that the height of the pyramids was a multiple of the average domestic cat tail length. I wasn't convinced. But when he called out a particular cat that had risen to god status, I began to see the author in a new light. The cat's name was Bast.

I frowned. It couldn't be. He couldn't be that old.

I suddenly noticed how much time had passed. I glanced at my new phone and saw I was going to have to hurry to make it on time. I slammed my book and hurriedly went about getting ready.

I wanted to look nice for my grandfather, so I decided on a sundress for this evening. Shortly after coming to live with him, he took one look at my wardrobe and off to the store we went. I'm not a dress kind of person, but he insisted I needed at least one for special occasions. I happened to think tonight was special.

But when I looked at myself in the mirror, I felt something was missing. The horns completely messed with fixing my hair. It was a common succubus problem. There were things I could do, but I had never been satisfied with them. Scanning over my limited selection of accessories, my eyes settled on my last birthday present. The *ribownna*. They were one of the few things that were strictly from succubus culture. I glanced into the eyes of my reflection. *Did I dare?*

I couldn't help but think of something Terra had told me once. "*As long as you hide, society will never change. You should be proud of what you are.*"

And I was. I had saved my friends. I had prevented the vault's destruction. I had—

Kissed a dragon.

When I stepped into the den, Grandfather gasped and put a hand over his heart. "You look wonderful." I could see his eyes dancing over the ribbons I wore wrapped around my horns. "You're the spitting image of your mother." His eyes began to tear up, and he blinked them away. "I was such a fool." Then one corner of his mouth curled up. "I hope your mother is looking down on us with a smile."

I pulled him into a hug. "Me too."

He looked up at my horns. "It's a shame to hide your ribownna under your illusion charm."

I gazed into my grandfather's eyes. "I'm not going to use it. I'm tired of hiding. If they don't like me, then that's their problem."

He looked at me for a moment, then reached into his shirt and deactivated his own illusion. He stood up straight, displaying his older yet still majestic horns. He held out his arm, and I gladly took it. Without another word, yet smiling broadly, we walked arm and arm over to the park.

It was only a few blocks, but it was packed with people everywhere. A few smiled at us, but others just stared. I didn't care. This was a piece of cake.

Or cotton candy.

I pointed to a truck selling the confection and tugged on his arm. "You said you were going to buy me one."

He brightened. "I did indeed." He reached for his wallet and frowned. He sighed. "I left my money at home. Let me run to get it. I'll be right back."

"I'll go with you," I volunteered. "If I'm not careful, all the grannies will start hitting on you." I looked up proudly at his horns and smiled.

He shook his head. "No, you stay. I'll be right back." And with no time to argue, he left. As he was turning away, I couldn't miss the smile on his face. *Was he up to something?*

So I waited. There were lots of emotions floating around, creating a cacophony of noise. I basked in the gentle buffeting of their feelings. To think I had wanted to cut out this part of me. It was unthinkable now. It would have been like removing my eyes.

A gentle summer breeze ruffled my hair and plucked at my dress. With it, I felt a gentle brush of feeling. Very faint. Fingers gliding over silk. It was impossible to describe. It was like a feeling of a feeling.

I sucked a deep breath, and a chill ran through me.

My body turned by its own accord until I faced the direction the sensation came from.

Orion.

He was here.

I couldn't help it. My feet started moving in the direction of the feeling. I didn't have to go far before I saw him. He had his back to me, so he didn't notice my approach. He was dressed in jeans and a simple dress shirt. But it was his feelings that I drank in. He was annoyed. Disappointment ran through him. He didn't want to be there. And underneath it all, faint and hiding in the background, was an aching loneliness.

I started to step forward but paused, my shoulders sagging. Chaleta was already there. She was dressed model perfect in designer jeans and a sleeveless black top that highlighted her dainty shoulders. Her makeup was perfect, and she had turned her smile up to radiance level. Any normal male would have been mesmerized. But Orion just seemed annoyed.

Rore and Skiff were on either side of him like they needed to protect him.

Chaleta ignored the other two, having eyes only for Orion. "Well, hello. What a surprise meeting you here."

Rore, never one to back down, huffed and stepped in front of her brother. "Hello, Chaleta. Having fun at the festival? You haven't seen Zeek, have you? I have a couple of fists that are aching to rearrange his face."

Skiff's hands were curled up tight, and I was pretty sure he would land those punches before Rore could even move.

Chaleta glanced over at the pair with a scowl. "Oh, grow up. Zeek isn't here. He had something traumatic happen during the storm, and I understand he's gone to the west coast to visit some relatives." She smiled evilly and leaned forward. "But confidentially, I also hear he's having emotional problems."

She turned back to Orion with a seductive smile. She stepped in close and put a hand on his chest. "Why don't we dance a little? It'll be just like old times."

He stared at her for a moment. I could feel his emotions churning. The old me would have turned away, saying I was not good enough, just another dumb succubus. I smiled. But the new me—

Had kissed a dragon.

I stepped forward.

At that moment, Orion looked up and noticed me. His eyes went wide, and his jaw dropped. His surprise and longing flowed into me.

Chaleta used a finger to turn his head back toward her. "Orion, I was talking to you. Now, dance with me." She smiled seductively. "You know you want to. Besides, I'm the first one to ask you. By tradition, you have to."

I stepped up behind her and grabbed her shoulder, turning her to face me. She gasped.

"Chaleta, give it a break," I said, looking up into Orion's eyes. "You know he doesn't want to."

Rore's burst of joy as she spied me almost knocked me over.

She shoved Chaleta out of the way and wrapped her arms around me. "Lapis!"

Skiff came right behind her and hugged both of us. "You're here!"

I blinked rapidly, quickly controlling my own emotions. "Yes, I'm back."

Chaleta smirked in that self-assured way she had. She glanced at my horns. "I thought you might be a low-life. Why don't you go hide under a rock, like the rest of your kind."

Her attitude hardened my resolve. I slowly turned to face her. "I'm not going anywhere until I speak with Orion."

She snorted. "Like he would have anything to do with a *succubus*. Besides, you're too late. I've already asked him to dance." She grabbed his arm and tugged him toward the dance area. "Come on Orion. You're mine tonight."

I grabbed Chaleta's arm and spun her to face me. I channeled all my succubus fury and brought it to the surface. I didn't release it, but she saw it bubbling hot in the cauldrons of my eyes. "You didn't ask him," I stated. "You commanded. You don't command the one you care for. You ask. Politely. Because having them is a privilege, not a right."

I turned my back to her and gazed into Orion's eyes. "Orion, would you please dance with me this evening? I would really like to have your company."

He smiled and held out his hand. "Yes, my lady," he said firmly, taking my hand. "I would love your company." And at the touch, I could feel his delight at having me with him.

Chaleta frowned. I could feel the waves of righteous anger coming from her.

Rore bounced up and down in excitement. "Chaleta, I think you've been outmaneuvered."

Chaleta huffed. I felt her dark magic gathering. "How can you possibly . . .?"

I wheeled on her and poked her in the chest. "Listen, little Miss Vampire. Don't you dare try to use your hocus pocus on my friends. If you do, you will face my wrath."

She glared at me, and I just glared right back. Her haughtiness immediately returned. She dismissed us with a flick of her wrist. "You can have the low-life shifter. I was only doing him a favor anyway."

She turned on her heel and stalked off into the crowd.

I faced Orion. His beautiful brown eyes bored into me, and I could sense his relief, his joy—and his anger. "Don't you ever do that again," he growled.

My smile faltered. "I'm sorry. I thought she was bothering you."

He shook his head. "Not that. I mean disappearing. I've missed you. I didn't know . . . I-I wasn't sure . . ." He searched my eyes. "Can we dance?"

Just then, the band struck up, and music filled the air. It was a slower number, and the crowd cheered around us. Rore gave me a knowing smile and then dragged Skiff away into the other dancers.

Orion led me to a clear space and took me in his arms. It was a slow song, and we swayed to the music.

We danced in silence for a moment, but I had to ask. "You really missed me?"

Then the idiot did the stupidest thing.

He kissed me.

His lips were so soft and firm at the same time. The flood of his emotions was overpowering. His love. His joy. And a few other emotions I wasn't sure I was old enough to enjoy yet. It took my breath away.

"Does that answer your question?"

I leaned my head against his chest. "It does. Quite nicely."

I glanced over at Rore, who was watching us with a huge grin. She gave me a thumbs up.

Orion was an excellent dancer. "When we stop," he said, "I'll give you your necklace back. In all the confusion, I ended up with it."

I shook my head. "Keep it. We'll talk more about it later, but I think it actually belonged to your father."

He stopped dancing. "How do you know that?"

I urged him to resume dancing. "I've got a lot I need to tell you." I pulled him in closer. "But later."

So Orion and I danced. I felt safe and content in his arms. It was true the evil people were still out there. We had thwarted their plans this time, but I knew they would try again. I also had no clue who these knights were and how my little band of friends fit in with them, nor a clue as to what the vault was protecting. But I would not worry about it tonight. I had a home, good friends, and a boyfriend. What more could one ask for?

I glanced over and immediately stiffened. A dancing couple moved aside to reveal a gray cat sitting in the middle of the dance area. His tail was curled up around his paws in the classic sitting cat pose. People were all around him, but none would venture too close.

He was smiling at me.

He rose, stretched in that way only cats can do, and trotted off into the crowd.

I had the feeling I would see Bast again.

Acknowledgments

As always with my books, many people went into making *Midnyte's Dragon Kiss,* and I am grateful to each and every one of them.

Allison did a fantastic job as my copyeditor. I'm convinced she has some superpower to see things no one else can. Her suggestions definitely made this a better work. Special thanks go out to Callista and Kasey for being sounding boards in some of the original thinking for the novel and helping to focus the book's intended audience. Also I want to thank my beta readers, Jill, George, and Christopher. Their input and corrections were invaluable, and their questions made me pause and think. Special thanks to Joan and Stephanie for not only their advice but their encouragement. And finally, thanks to Daniel for his drawing on which the novel's main character is based. If I hadn't seen the picture, I wouldn't have realized—*that character has a story.*

Once again, my wife deserves major kudos for putting up with me during the creation process. Her tastes in literature run very different from mine, so she was reluctant to offer advice. But when I talked to her about a particularly difficult passage, she would simply nod and give me cookies. It must have worked.

Other Books by Jessie D. Eaker

The Coren Hart Chronicles
Thief of Curses
Queen of Curses
Assassin of Curses

A Study of Curses (A series companion)

Unlikely Survivor Series
Monday After the Apocalypse

Vault of Silent Whispers Series
Midnyte's Dragon Kiss

About The Author

Jessie Eaker lives in central Virginia with his wife, son, their cats, and (her) parakeets. Originally a native of North Carolina, he's lived in Virginia so long, he's lost his southern accent (much to his wife's disappointment). When not writing, he watches anime, reads, and works on his ever-growing list of things to fix around the house.

Check out jessieeaker.com for his latest works and updates.